DOGS AND GODDESSES

Also from St. Martin's Paperbacks

THE UNFORTUNATE MISS FORTUNES

by

JENNIFER CRUSIE

EILEEN DREYER

ANNE STUART

DOGS AND GODDESSES

JENNIFER CRUSIE,

ANNE STUART, AND

LANI DIANE RICH

CALUMET CITY PUBLIC LIBRARY

St. Martin's Paperbacks

NOTE: If you purchased this book without a cover you should be aware that this book is stolen property. It was reported as "unsold and destroyed" to the publisher, and neither the author nor the publisher has received any payment for this "stripped book."

This is a work of fiction. All of the characters, organizations, and events portrayed in this novel are either products of the author's imagination or are used fictitiously.

DOGS AND GODDESSES

Copyright © 2009 by Jennifer Crusie Smith, Anne Stuart, and Lani Diane Rich.

Cover design by Mara Lubell of Works Progress Design

All rights reserved.

For information address St. Martin's Press, 175 Fifth Avenue, New York, NY 10010.

ISBN: 0-312-94437-3
EAN: 978-0-312-94437-7

Printed in the United States of America

St. Martin's Paperbacks edition / January 2009

St. Martin's Paperbacks are published by St. Martin's Press, 175 Fifth Avenue, New York, NY 10010.

10 9 8 7 6 5 4 3 2 1

This book is for

Bailey, Bernie, Bowser, Leo, Lucy, Max,

Milton, Rags, Veronica, and Wolfie

ACKNOWLEDGMENTS

We would like to thank our beta readers, Eileen Cook, Heidi Cullinan, Sally Fifield, Samantha Graves, and Lynda Ward, for reading some really flawed first drafts;

Mara Lubell, for the D&G coffeehouse logo and type design;

Charlie Verral, for being the fabulous godfather/host to another collaboration;

Amy Berkower and Jodi Reamer, Jane Dystel and Miriam Goderich, and Stephanie Kip Rostan, Monika Verma, and Elizabeth Fisher, for having the patience of saints;

Jen Enderlin, for making everything we did better;

and Alesia Holliday, for grace and Google.

AUTHORS' NOTE

Although we did extensive research for this book, we also created the history of Kamesh to fit our story. Nothing in this novel should be taken as historical fact. Kamesh never existed. Nobody worshiped Kammani Gula. As far as we know, there were no dying and resurrected kings in ancient Turkey. We made it up. It's fiction, we can do that.

ONE

Abby Richmond's ancient two-toned station wagon shuddered to a stop in front of the dust-covered windows of the Temple Street Coffeehouse, and the Newfoundland beside her sat up and barked.

"Bowser, I think we're in trouble," Abby said, peering through her windshield at the old building. "It doesn't look like much of an inheritance."

Bowser tried to lumber to his feet, but even in a full-sized station wagon there wasn't enough room for a full-sized Newfie, so he settled back down again, looking up at her with his dark, gentle eyes.

"Yeah, I know; you need a patch of grass and something to eat," Abby said. "The lawyer said there's a place to park in the alley around back. Let's reconnoiter."

Bowser replied with the low raspy sound that meant agreement. Bowser tended to be a very agreeable dog. Abby pulled back out into the sparse traffic on Temple Street, managing to just miss clipping a Lexus, and drove around the corner in search of the elusive alleyway that belonged to the building. She pulled in and parked, then let Bowser out.

There was a small, brick-walled courtyard in back, and Bowser rushed toward the thick green grass with a muffled yelp of gratitude as Abby wandered over to the stone bench. The only piece of litter was a yellow flyer, and she picked it up and shoved it in her pocket before she sat down. The smell of honeysuckle was in the air, and the June sun was bright overhead. She'd always thought of Ohio as flat and brown compared to the lush ripeness of landscaped Southern California, but this courtyard was an oasis of greenery.

She looked up at the back of the three-story building she'd inherited. It looked in decent enough shape, and her mother, the Real Estate Goddess of Escondido, would doubtless be able to sell it quickly and profitably. If Abby decided to let her.

"What do you think, Bowser?" she said. "Do I hand this over to my mother . . . ?" Her cell phone rang, the booming strains of the "Ride of the Valkyries." "Speak of the devil." She flipped open her cell phone with a sigh of resignation. "Yes, Mom."

"Have you reached that godforsaken town yet?" Amanda Richmond demanded.

"I'm here."

"I suppose it's as bleak and scrubby as it always was."

"It's actually very pretty around here," Abby said. "How long has it been since you've been here?"

"Thirty years, and I'm never coming back. Does the building look like it's worth anything? I've got connections in the Ohio real estate market, and the sooner we move on it, the better."

Abby looked up at the building. The back was painted lavender, the bricked courtyard was lush and overgrown, and a wide set of stairs led up to the French doors. The roof looked solid, the windows a little dusty. All in all, it looked like home.

"I haven't decided yet. I may want to stay here for a while."

"What?" her mother shrieked. "Don't be ridiculous—you're a California girl. You don't belong in the flatlands."

"It's actually quite hilly," Abby pointed out. "And I'm not sure where I belong."

Her mother's silence was evocative of her disapproval, but Amanda Richmond hadn't become the Real Estate Goddess of Escondido without learning how to play her clients. And her daughter. "Someone's been trying to get in touch with you," she said abruptly. "Some moldy old professor. Apparently my mother promised him cookies, or something equally ridiculous. I didn't want to give him your cell phone number, but he was quite insistent. She was probably sleeping with him."

"Don't be ridiculous!" Abby said. "That's my grandmother you're talking about!"

"That's my mother I'm talking about," Amanda said, her voice tart. "And you hadn't seen her in more than fifteen years. Neither had I, for that matter, but I doubt she'd have changed her spots before she died. What are you going to do about the building?"

"Live here," Abby said, defiant.

Another moment of angry silence. "Very well. Professor Mackenzie will be looking for you. Be prepared to deal."

Only her mother could slam down a cell phone, Abby thought, pushing up from the bench. Bowser ambled over to her, his plumy tail swishing back and forth. "Amanda's flipped, Bowser," she said.

Bowser, of course, said nothing.

"Let's go check out my inheritance."

The first floor of the building was like a railroad flat—two long and narrow rooms. The French doors opened up into a kitchen, with a wide island in the middle, a series of commercial ovens and a storeroom on one side, semi-enclosed stairs on the other. The front room was dusty, chairs piled haphazardly around the room, the afternoon light filtering through the fly-specked storefront windows, but even with the musty, closed-up scent, she could still find the faint trace of cinnamon and coffee on the air.

"I guess I shouldn't have been so quick to annoy my mother," Abby said, looking around her before heading back into the kitchen. That part of the building was at least relatively dust-free, and she tried to imagine her grandmother moving around the room, an apron tied around her waist. Maybe something like *Chocolat* with Johnny Depp lurking around the corner.

Except she could barely remember what Granny B looked like.

According to the lawyers, two of the three apartments upstairs were empty; she ought to grab her duffel bag and find out where she was sleeping. She turned to the stairs at the back, then let out a shriek.

Someone stood there, silhouetted against the bright sunlight, and as Bowser made an encouraging woof, she wondered whether it was the ghost of Granny B. Then he moved into the room, and he most definitely was a far cry from a little old lady. He was tall, lean, and much too good-looking to be showing up at her back door.

"I assume you're Abby Richmond?" the man said in a cranky voice.

Damn, he was pretty. In a disagreeable, uptight sort of way. He was wearing a suit—Abby hated men in suits. He was in his late twenties, maybe early thirties, with dark blond hair pushed back from a too-clever face. He wore wire-rimmed glasses, and he was looking at her like she'd shot his dog. Except he wasn't the type to have a dog.

"Who's asking?" she replied, mildly enough.

"Professor Christopher Mackenzie," he said. "I've been trying to track you down for days."

"You have? I just arrived here a few minutes ago."

"I know. Your mother told me I'd find you here."

Abby managed a tight smile. "How helpful of her. What can I do for you, Professor?"

"Your grandmother contracted to make cookies for a reception I'm holding tomorrow for the math department. I'd like to know whether you're going to fulfill that contract or if I need to make other arrangements."

Abby glanced around her. "I think you'll be making other arrangements," she said. "I just arrived, and I don't bake."

"Fine. In which case you can return my deposit."

"You didn't give me any money."

"You're your grandmother's heir. Your mother assured me you'd either return the deposit or fulfill Bea's obligations."

"My mother knows I don't have a red cent to my name."

"Then you'd better learn to bake."

Why are the gorgeous ones always assholes? Abby thought with a sigh. "What do you need and when?"

He didn't look particularly pleased that he'd gotten his way. "Six dozen cookies for tomorrow evening."

She'd made Christmas cookies in the past, hadn't she? Burned half of them, but she could be more careful. "Where should I deliver them?"

"I'll pick them up. And don't even think of skipping town."

Abby made a derisive noise. "I'm not going on the lam over a few cookies, Professor."

"Your mother said you were unreliable."

"My mother . . . ," Abby began heatedly, and Bowser moved closer, leaning against her leg. "My mother," she said in a calmer voice, "doesn't know anything about me. You'll get your cookies, Professor."

She waited until he closed the French doors behind him and disappeared down the wide back steps. "What an asshole," she said under her breath. She followed him, determined to lock the back door before she had any more unwanted visitors, and her eye caught the yellow sheet of paper on the floor.

She picked it up.

BE A GODDESS TO YOUR DOG!

The Kammani Gula Dog Obedience Course

This two-week immersion course will teach you
to communicate with your dog
while commanding complete obedience.
Learn the ways of the goddess Kammani Gula,
whose sacred animal was the dog,
under the tutelage of Noah Wortham,
anointed Kammani Gula instructor.

"Well, one thing's clear, Bowser," she said, crumpling up the paper. "We don't need no stinkin' classes."

Bowser gave a small bark of assent, and Abby rubbed his massive head. "Let's go shopping, baby. It's Slim-Fast for me and ground round for you."

She opened the back door, and a sheet of yellow paper came swirling in on a breeze in the otherwise still afternoon, smacking her in the face like flypaper. She pulled it away and stared at it. Another dog-training flyer.

"Persistent, aren't they?" she said to Bowser. "What do you say, pal? You think we ought to go to this dog-training class so I can learn to be a goddess? Maybe see if anyone there happened to know Granny B? We can always go shopping afterward."

Bowser arfed, agreeable as ever.

"Okay," she said. "Dogs and goddesses it is."

And they headed back out into the afternoon sun.

Daisy Harris watched as seventeen pounds of Jack Russell terror leapt into the air, snapped at either a hallucination or a wish, and landed with a circus performer's *Ta-da!* flourish on the manicured grass of the Summerville College campus.

"That's not normal," she said.

Bailey looked up at her, panting, as if to say, *Want me to do it again?*

"*No,*" Daisy said.

He'd been a lot cuter when he was living with her mother.

Bailey darted forward, dragging her a good three feet and seriously aggravating her tiny person's complex. She dug in her heels and pulled back, but then he decided to run back to her, taking away the opposing force she was straining against. Daisy landed on the grass with a thunk just as Bailey charged her, licking her face over and over again with sloppy, stinky dog tongue.

"Stop . . . just—*agh*!" she sputtered, pushing at him. " 'No' means 'no,' Bailey!"

Bailey hopped back, panting, then jumped up in the air again, did a half twirl, and landed at Daisy's feet.

"Peg taught you that, didn't she?" Daisy asked, then heard a crackle under her and looked to see a piece of bright yellow paper, some kind of flyer—

"Daisy!"

Her mother's voice trilled from behind her, and Bailey barked and strained against the leash, a little bundle of excitement and mayhem. Daisy pushed up off the grass just as her mother approached, a tiny, platinum blond Jackie O, right down to the scoop neckline and the pillbox hat.

"Oh, no," Peg said, reaching her hands out toward the rear of Daisy's khaki capris. "Your pants."

"Hands off my ass, Peg," Daisy said, shooing her mother away.

"Hi, Bailey!" Peg knelt over Bailey, and Daisy felt a flood of relief run through her. It was over. Two days of incessant barking and chewed-up shoes and her things knocked out of place and picking up poop with little plastic Baggies . . . over. It was almost too good to be true.

"Okay, then. See ya," Daisy said, then turned to walk away.

"Wait; wait." Peg straightened and grabbed Daisy's arm. Daisy sighed; she should have known it wouldn't be that easy. Christians in ancient Rome had escaped lions with less trouble than Daisy had escaping her mother.

"This is just a test visitation to see if the allergies are gone," Peg said. "It's going to take me a few minutes to . . ." She eyed Daisy. "To know for sure."

"No, I've handed over custody. I'm done. I don't know how you suddenly get allergies to a dog you've had for three years and I don't care, but—"

"Are you implying that I lied to get free dogsitting out of you?" Peg's eyes went wide with innocence and just a touch of indignation.

"Are you implying there isn't precedent for that suspicion?" Daisy said.

Peg's eyes went back to normal and she shrugged. "Fair enough."

How did I come from this woman? "Look, you said two days. You said the doctor had some kind of shots for you and . . ."

"Well, the doctor—"

"*You said two days.*" Daisy tried to control her breathing as the panic sharpened. "It's not that Bailey isn't . . ." She stared down at the tiny dog that had torn up her life for the past forty-eight hours. ". . . kinda cute, kinda, but I don't have room in my life for your dog. I have a CD rack to re-alphabetize thanks to him, and some couch pillows that will never be the same, and—"

"I thought you two would have fun," Peg said. "I thought you'd enjoy having a roommate for a while."

"He's not a roommate," Daisy said. "He's a dog. Roommates don't shed or, ideally, poop in your bathtub. Which reminds me: have you ever thought about obedience—"

"Let's discuss it some more." Peg grabbed Daisy's elbow. "We can sit down . . ." Peg scanned the campus, then pointed to the huge, stone-step temple where Summerville College housed the history department. "There."

She pulled on Daisy's arm, but Daisy resisted. A lifetime in Summerville, four years attending college there, and another ten working in the humanities department, and Daisy had managed to never set foot in that temple. It was about half the size of a city block at the base, and clicked upward in diminishing squares for three formidable stories, looking like a tremendous, ugly stone wedding cake. It was a notable claim to fame for Summerville College to have a genuine Mesopotamian ziggurat in the center of campus, sure, but the thing wasn't exactly welcoming.

"Let's just sit down on the grass," Daisy said. "I'm already stained."

"Don't be silly," Peg said, pulling on Daisy with a force that belied her miniature stature.

Bailey barked and danced at their heels as they walked. Peg didn't seem to mind her leash arm being yanked around from side to side; just watching it drove Daisy crazy.

"You know," Daisy said, "you really should think about training—"

"Tell me," Peg said, looping her arm through Daisy's. "What's new? Anything?"

"New?" Daisy sighed. "Let's see. Scratches in my wood floors, those are new. My inability to sleep through the night because Bailey barks at the door, that's new. Oh, and let me tell you about the newly violated ficus plant at the office—"

Peg stopped walking, shooting a horrified look at Daisy. "Barking at the door? Why didn't you let him sleep on the bed with you?"

Daisy stopped walking about fifteen feet from the temple steps and turned on her mother. "Sleep with me? Are you insane?"

Peg shook her head. "No. It's nice. He crawls down under the sheets and keeps your toes warm."

Ugh, Daisy thought. "Look, I'm not a dog person, okay? I mean, Bailey's . . ." She shot a look at him as he panted happily up at her, and felt an odd sense of guilt. ". . . fine, for a dog, but I don't like animals. I like a clean apartment and clothes without dog hair on them and—"

Just then, something flew at her, smacking her gently in the side of the face. She grabbed at it and pulled it back—another yellow flyer. She glanced around, looking for a student with an armful who needed a serious talking to, but there was no one. Daisy glanced at the paper and started reading:

BE A GODDESS TO YOUR DOG!

The Kammani Gula Dog Obedience Course

" 'Be a Goddess to Your Dog!'?" she said. "Now I've seen everything. Although it wouldn't be a bad idea for you and—"

"Be a what?" Peg snatched the flyer away from Daisy and read it, her eyes widening, and then . . .

. . . she sneezed.

"Oh, no," Daisy said, backing away. "You go train that dog and be a goddess; I have CDs to alphabetize."

"Ah-*chooo*!" This one hit so loudly that Daisy could hear it echoing off the stone of the temple.

"Ah, crap," Daisy said.

Peg reached into her tiny purse, withdrew one of her classic monogrammed handkerchiefs, and blew her nose so loudly that Bailey barked twice and hopped up in the air, ostensibly to check on her.

"Oh, no." Peg held out her leash hand to Daisy.

" 'Oh, no,' is right," Daisy said. "As in 'no.' No way, no how, no—"

"The doctor said that if my allergies didn't go away from the shots, he knew a great specialist in . . ." Peg hesitated, tapping her foot and glancing around; then she smiled and snapped her fingers. "New York! That's right. Manhattan. The Garment District, actually. Isn't that funny?" Peg grabbed Daisy's hand and shoved the leash and the flyer into it. "I'll be back in a week or so."

"A *week*?" Daisy tried to shove the leash back into her mother's hand, but Peg moved freakishly fast.

"Or so!" Peg called back, scurrying across the campus. Daisy tried to run after her, but Bailey was pulling toward the step temple.

"But . . . no . . . I can't . . . ," Daisy said, and then felt a crunch of paper under her feet. She looked down: another yellow flyer. She bent over to pick it up and Bailey yanked on the leash, but she yanked back.

"Knock it off," she said, then pulled up the flyer, uncrinkling them both, her eyes trailing over the text, catching on *teach you to communicate with your dog while commanding complete obedience. . . .*

"Complete obedience." Daisy showed him the flyer. "See that?"

Bailey barked, hopped up in the air, and landed with an ungracious splat that didn't seem to bother him in the least. Daisy glanced at the details on the paper. The class was starting in half an hour. She could do that. She scanned for the location. . . .

"Crap."

The history department.

Daisy looked up at the step temple while Bailey darted around her, barking, yanking her arm almost out of its socket. She wasn't going to make it through the next week—*or so*—of dogsitting if something didn't change. Maybe going into the creepy building and learning to be a goddess would help.

She looked at Bailey, who hopped in the air again, landed, turned around twice, lifted his leg to a patch of grass even though he'd long ago run out of urine, and barked twice at nothing.

"Certainly can't make things any worse," she said, put the flyer in her back pocket, and started for the building.

In her office on the ground floor of the step temple converted into a history building, Professor Shar Summer looked at the pink metallic appliance on the desk in front of her and thought, *My life has hit bottom.* She was forty-eight years old, her grandmother was running her life from beyond the grave, and her lover of two years had just given her a Taser instead of a commitment.

A cold nose pressed against her leg under her desk, and she reached down and patted her best friend, her black-and-gray long-haired dachshund, Wolfie.

"Now you don't have to be afraid anymore," Ray said as he checked his watch. "Problem solved."

I didn't say I was afraid; I said I didn't like living alone. "Thank you."

"I got the pink one," Ray said, evidently sensing his gift had missed on a few points.

"Perfect." Shar put the lid on the Taser box, trying to be fair. Maybe if she were more passionate about Ray, he'd be more passionate about her. She tried to imagine Ray passionate about anything—finding the Ark of the Covenant, rescuing a kidnapped bride, defeating a mummy—but it didn't work. Too much tweed. Of course she couldn't picture herself doing any of those things, either.

She shoved the box to one side of her desk with the rest of the stuff she didn't want: the green department newsletter, the yellow flyer she'd found on the floor, miscellaneous notes from her students explaining why they couldn't turn their work in on time, the list of places she'd tried to find citations for her damn grandmother's damn book—

"Are you okay?" Ray said.

No. I can't find anything on this stinking Mesopotamian goddess my grandmother wrote about, I'm sleeping with a man who gives me a Taser instead of moving in with me, and I can't remember when I really cared about anything except my dog. Shar rubbed her forehead. "I'm fine. I just have to find some sources for this goddess and then the book will be done, and once that's out of the way . . ."

"I don't see why you're bothering with it at all." Ray checked his watch again.

"I told you, my mother promised her mother she'd finish her book, and I promised my mother I'd finish the citations. It's like a family curse. Most of the sources were easy to find but this Kammani—"

"Your grandmother and your mother are dead," Ray said, shooting his shirt cuff over his watch. "Listen—"

"I don't think that relieves me of the promise," Shar said. "You don't go back on your word just because somebody *dies.*"

"You do if they don't have a publisher," Ray said. "Carpe diem, Shar."

You couldn't carpe your diem with both hands, Shar thought, and tilted her chair back to stare at the ceiling. If this were a movie, she'd stand up and say, *It's over between us, Ray,* and then she'd meet somebody fabulous; he'd walk right through her office door and say, *I've been looking for an intelligent, mature woman with an advanced degree in Assyriology. Let me take you away from all—*

"Professor Summer?"

Shar let her chair fall forward, back into reality. One of her grad students—pretty, procrastinating Leesa—stood in the doorway with a hi-I'm-here-to-ask-for-something smile and then came in and put some papers on the already-buried desk. "Here's the outline you asked for, but I don't have the chapters. I was wondering—"

"No, you can't have an extension," Shar said, annoyed with her for screwing up her movie hero fantasy. "I told you your topic was too broad. Narrow it down to what you've already done—"

"What's your topic?" Ray asked, leaning against the wall, all professorial.

"Passion and Joy in Mesopotamian Culture," Leesa said.

"Maybe narrow it down to one Mesopotamian culture and one idea?" Ray said. "The concept of joy in Sumerian poetry?"

"That's what Professor Summer said," Leesa said. "But I didn't want to restrain myself."

"Restrict," Shar said, and then realized that Leesa probably didn't want to restrain herself, either, but before she could say, *Never mind,* a beefy brown-haired undergraduate stopped in the doorway and scowled at her.

"Professor Summer, you screwed up my test. I put Hera for Mesopotamian mother goddess and you marked it wrong."

Doug Essen. Wonderful. Shar said, "Hera is not Mesopotamian. She's Greek."

"Well, Greece is right there, isn't it?" Doug said belligerently. "She coulda gone next door, had a little nookie with some hot Mesopotamian god, been a mother goddess that way, right?"

This is my life, Shar thought. *This is what I've spent forty-eight years to achieve.* She looked at Doug and suddenly he looked a lot like Ray. And Leesa. Like one more damn pothole in her dusty road of life.

"Yes, Doug," she said through her teeth. "She could have walked seven hundred miles north, hung a right at the Euphrates, and had a gang bang with the entire pantheon of ancient Middle Eastern deities. *But she still would have been Greek.*"

"That's not fair," Doug said, sounding about three. "You have to give me another chance."

Ray and Leesa had stopped talking to watch; definitely time to get rid of Doug. "Okay. You write me a paper with footnotes that show research proving that Hera was a Mesopotamian Mother Goddess and I'll give you credit for that essay question." *And good luck with that, since Hera was* Greek.

"A paper," Doug said, looking suspicious. "Where am I gonna find out that stuff?"

"I'd start with the library," Shar said. "Books, not DVDs, so Disney's *Hercules* is out. If it's colorful and it's moving and it has catchy songs, you may not footnote it."

Doug looked at her with suspicion, but she kept her face blank, so he scowled at her and went off to pay somebody to write a research paper for him.

"Jeez," Leesa said, watching him go. "So about my extension—"

"No," Shar said.

Leesa stopped. "Uh, okay, look, I'll talk to you later. I'll, uh, call." She backed out of the door, clutching her sliding books, and as she waved good-bye to Ray and disappeared, a yellow flyer fluttered down to the floor.

Ray picked it up and put it on Shar's desk. "That wasn't like you."

"That was exactly like me." Shar shoved herself back from her overflowing desk. "The real me, not the good sport. I'm tired of the book; I'm tired of this job—" *I'm tired of you. . . .*

"What are you talking about?" Ray said. "Do you feel all right?"

"I'm great." Shar put her head on her desk.

"You're not tired of your job; you love it. Don't do anything dumb like quitting. You've only got five years to go to retirement. And they'll go fast. The first twenty-five years went fast, right?"

She lifted her head and stared at him, appalled, but he wasn't the problem. She was. She straightened in her chair and faced the truth: she had to change. It wasn't too late, she could still set herself free—okay, her hair had gone gray and she was pushing fifty, but she could find joy and passion; she was *not* trapped. She could do anything she wanted; she could even decide to not look for Kammani Gula anymore. That thought gave her a sudden, giddy sense of freedom. *The hell with my grandmother and the hell with Kammani Gula. Nobody has ever heard of her; Grandma probably made her up. I'm going to just* delete *her—*

"Don't get perimenopausal on me," Ray said.

Shar glared at him and then realized that if she could delete Kammani Gula, she could delete Ray, too. "I think we should see other people."

Ray stared at her. "I just got you a Taser."

"You can have it back."

"It's pink."

"I—"

A yellow paper blew through the window and splatted on her desk. "What the hell?" She picked up the flyer and read it for the first time. " 'Be a Goddess to Your Dog! The Kammani Gula Dog Obedience Course' . . . Oh, *hell.*"

"Shar, are you listening to me?"

Kammani Gula. Right there. She looked up at Ray with her heart sinking. "Somebody else besides my grandmother knew about Kammani Gula."

"Who cares?" Ray said, looking mad. "Are you serious about breaking up with me? Because I have to tell you, it'll be a lot easier for me to find somebody else than it will be for you."

"Damn it," Shar said, staring at the flyer, feeling the weight settle over her again.

"Exactly," Ray said. "I know you're feeling down, but don't—"

"I was going to delete her, but now here's somebody else using her name. She must have been real." She looked at the flyer again. The dog class was in the auditorium, right across the hall, and it started in five minutes. She had no excuse for not checking it out. "I have to go to this damn class so I can find out where Kammani Gula came from. *Damn it.*"

"I was talking about you ending our relationship," Ray said stiffly. "But since you've made a foolish decision based on a spur-of-the-moment hormonal surge, I'm going to my six o'clock class. We'll talk about this tomorrow."

"Oh, good," Shar said miserably, but he was already out the door.

Wolfie pressed his nose against her leg again.

"We're going to a dog obedience class," Shar told him, pushing back her chair so she could look into his soft brown eyes. "We'll find out who this Kammani Gula was, I'll make some notes, and then we'll go home and eat popcorn and watch a movie. That's our evening. Can you stand it?"

Wolfie barked once and it sounded like approval, so Shar let it ride.

She stacked the papers on her desk, put the box with the Taser in her purse, and found Wolfie's leash to take him across the hall to the auditorium, trying not to feel defeated. It was a *good* thing that she was keeping her promise to her grandmother. And as for Ray . . .

"We can change our lives slowly," she told Wolfie as she hooked his leash on his collar. "Forget popcorn; we'll have *pretzels* tonight."

Wolfie barked again, and she was pretty sure this time she heard contempt in his voice.

That's fair, she thought, and dragged him across the hall.

TWO

Aside from the stone walls and the harsh echo of Bailey's toenails scratching against the floor, the inside of the step temple wasn't as creepy as Daisy had expected. Even though it was June, the few students who stayed for summer classes gave it some life, and the recessed lighting that had been carved into the ceiling made the hallway seem a lot like all the other academic hallways on campus—slathered with the slightly intimidating air of academia but otherwise normal.

"Old auditorium, old auditorium," Daisy mumbled as they descended the stairwell to the ground floor, Bailey straining on the leash the whole way. "Where is the old auditorium?"

"Are you on your way to the obedience class?"

Bailey gave two sharp barks and Daisy looked up to see a tall man with dark hair looking down at her. For a moment, she felt stunned. He wasn't an undergrad, that was for sure; the smile lines around his eyes crinkled a bit deep for that. But, taking in his worn black T-shirt and sun-bleached blue jeans, he didn't seem a professor type, either.

"Um . . . yeah," she said. "How'd you know?"

Bailey barked again, and the guy met her eyes with a deadpan expression. "I possess a rare intuitive gift."

"Right," Daisy said, tightening her hold on Bailey's leash. "Duh."

If I'd known you were here, I would have come into this building sooner.

"Follow me." He led her deeper into the belly of the building, finally pushing open one of a pair of heavy wooden doors and holding it for Daisy and Bailey. "Class is going to start in just a minute. You guys have a seat."

"Okay." Daisy watched him as he led the way into what looked to be a large old-style auditorium, the kind that had rows of folding chairs. The windowless room had a square dais set up on shallow stone steps with a big—*stone block? sacrificial altar?*—podium in the center. Behind the podium hung a heavy black curtain, which obscured what Daisy figured was the other half of the room (the cute guy disappeared behind it, so *something* else was back there) and in front of it were seven folding chairs organized in a half circle. Five of them were filled, and Daisy chose the empty seat in the middle, between a skinny brunette and her huge black bear of a dog, and a gray-haired professor type with her black-and-gray wiener dog. Bailey hopped and barked and strained while the black bear stood still and the wiener dog whined and skirted under his mistress's chair.

"Sorry," Daisy said, reaching out to grab Bailey's harness. "He's not my dog." She turned her eyes on Bailey. "Bailey, *stop*."

Bailey jumped up and licked her face and she shouted, "Ugh!" and swiped at her mouth. The room went quiet and Daisy heard a mutter of disgust come from the right end of the semicircle; a wraith of a girl with straight black hair and bug eyes glared at Daisy while the creepy black Chihuahua in her lap breathed a *heh-heh-heh*–sounding growl. Daisy recoiled a bit, then felt a hand on her shoulder and turned to see a smiling teenage girl offering her a stick of gum; at the girl's feet stood a foxhound that kept his cool even as Bailey skittered around him, barking like a maniac.

"Hi, I'm Gen; this is Ziggy," the girl said as Daisy took the gum. "It's so gross when they French you, isn't it?"

"Oh my god, *totally,*" a voice said from behind Gen. Daisy leaned forward to see another teenage girl with a round face smooching at her fat, ancient poodle, who was wearing what appeared to be a tiara and a pearl necklace. "Isn't it, Baby? Yes, it is. It's so *gross.*" She smiled at Daisy. "Hi, I'm Bun."

"Thanks." Daisy tucked the gum in her pocket as Gen moved back to take her seat at the left end of the circle, followed by Bun and Baby. Bailey yipped in mourning as Ziggy retreated with Gen; then, recognizing the limits of his leash, he darted under the professor's seat and did something to which the wiener dog objected mightily.

"I'm so sorry," Daisy said, pulling Bailey back on the leash. "He's not my—"

"You are welcome to this place." A husky female voice came from behind the altar—*no, podium, podium*—and Daisy looked up to see a big-busted, wasp-waisted, dark-haired woman in a long, tight linen wrap dress emerge from the curtain and look down on them. She was extraordinarily beautiful in a piercing-dark-eyes, stern-full-lips, jaw-like-a-commando kind of way.

She could make a fortune as a dominatrix, Daisy thought as the woman said, "I am *Kammani.*"

She said this as though announcing that she was Madonna or the Pope, obviously expecting a reaction, but only the bug-eyed girl lowered her head in reverence. The teenagers giggled, the skinny brunette and her huge dog seemed unimpressed, and the professor sighed and shifted in her seat as if exasperated.

Kammani's eyes trailed over the seats, finally locking on the empty one between the professor and Bug-Eyes. She took in a deep breath, and did not look happy. Daisy wondered if she and Bailey could make a break for it and maybe find a nice, sane obedience class at the Y, but she didn't want to do it while Kammani was watching. Although Daisy didn't really believe that the woman could shoot death lasers with her eyes, she kinda believed the woman could shoot death lasers with her eyes. She tightened her hold on Bailey's leash and he yipped and scrambled his toenails on the floor, trying to rush Kammani.

"Noah Wortham, my attendant, will assist"—her eyes locked on Bailey—"those who need assistance." Her eyes trailed the room again, from woman to woman, and then she disappeared behind the heavy drapes as Noah emerged and walked over to the teenagers, who giggled louder. Daisy leaned toward the professor.

"Times like this, I'm glad I'm not a virgin," Daisy said, and the professor smiled.

"Why?" the skinny brunette said, her eyes wide.

"Oh, because of the sacrifice," Daisy said, grinning.

"*What?*" the brunette said, and her dog moved closer to her protectively.

"Oh, nothing," Daisy said. "Dumb joke." Bailey jumped four feet in the air as Noah walked over to them, and Daisy shifted her focus to the cute trainer.

"Why does he do that?" she asked. "That's not normal, right?"

"It's normal." Noah smiled at Daisy as he handed the brunette a dog cookie. "Hi, I'm Noah."

The brunette took the cookie. "I'm Abby. This is Bowser." She gave Bowser the cookie and he inhaled it.

"Hey, Bowser." Noah shifted over and gave Daisy a cookie. "Hi."

Daisy felt her face spread into a goofy smile. "Hi."

Bailey scrambled his front paws over Noah's knees, and Noah knelt down and petted him. "Hey, guy."

"His name is Bailey. I'm Daisy."

Noah looked up, his eyes locking on hers, and Daisy

as grateful for the poor lighting as she felt herself flush. riminy. It was like high school all over again, only this ne with dogs. Bailey leapt up and slobbered all over oah's face and Daisy grabbed his harness and pulled him ack, shoving the cookie at him to keep him off the cute ainer.

"I'm sorry," she said. "He's not my dog."

"It's okay," Noah said, wiping at his face. "Jack Rus-ells are enthusiastic like that."

"Enthusiastic, huh?" Daisy said. "That's some diplo-atic phrasing."

"Let me show you something." Noah motioned for her kneel on the floor.

Daisy glanced at the brunette, who had a wry expres-on that told Daisy she saw right through the whole ing; then she looked at the professor, who was observ-g them with detached interest.

"Okay." Daisy knelt down next to Noah as he put one and on the tip of Bailey's ear, rubbing it between his umb and forefinger. Bailey sat down and panted quietly though good behavior was something with which he ad a passing acquaintance.

"Big faker," Daisy muttered to Bailey.

"Sorry?"

"Nothing," Daisy said. "It's just that he's impossible o matter what I do, but you rub his ear for half a second nd suddenly he's calm."

"It's a pressure point." Noah took Daisy's hand, and aisy put a concerted effort into ignoring the tingles she elt at his touch. He guided her fingers to Bailey's ear, eeping hold of them there, his touch gentle and yet oddly owerful. "Just put your thumb and forefinger on opposite des and rub gently right . . . there."

Noah kept his hand on Daisy's, helping her find the ressure point. Bailey panted happily, his focus flickering from her to Noah and back again. As their fingers move in time together, the lighting seemed to change, to g brighter. The stone floor and walls seemed to shift to less oppressive gray, and the heavy drapes seemed les black and more a deep, shimmering midnight blue.

"Weird," Daisy said, her eyes on Noah.

"Yeah," Noah said, his voice quiet.

Then he stood, and Daisy looked up to see Kamma standing behind him with a tray of drinks, staring down Daisy in disapproval. Kammani's presence in the roo was huge, and Daisy felt like a little girl being reprimande by the teacher. Slowly, she shifted back up to her seat a Noah moved on to offer a dog cookie to the professor.

"I'm Noah," he said.

"I'm Shar," Daisy heard the professor say. "And this i Wolfie. Can you tell me—"

"You will drink," Kammani said, handing Abby a Dixi cup. She almost smiled at Abby—not quite, but there wa approval in her eyes as she watched Abby take a sip—b when she turned to Daisy, her eyes were dark again.

"You will drink," Kammani said again, her voic sharper than it had been with Abby.

"Why?" Daisy sniffed at the cup. "What's in it?"

Kammani stared down at Daisy; she seemed the typ of woman who was not accustomed to being questione Daisy squared her shoulders, looked Kammani in the ey and spoke slow and loud.

"What. Is. In. It?"

Light flashed in Kammani's eyes, but Daisy didn back down. This woman had interrupted her flirting; sh was not going to get away with intimidation tactics, too.

"It's a tonic," Kammani said. "Very delicious. Drink i and you will know."

"It's really good," Abby said.

Fixed under Kammani's gaze, Daisy raised her cup.

What's the worst that can happen? she thought, and drank.

After half an hour of be-the-alpha-dog lecture from the very attractive Noah, Shar got tired of waiting for an opening to ask about Kammani Gula again. So when Noah called two little dogs into the circle, she slipped out of her chair and stole through the curtain in back of the altar to find Kammani, Wolfie padding behind her on the stone floor. The area behind the curtain was as large as the space in front but dark as all hell, and Shar was moving cautiously toward the back wall, her hand out in front of her to keep from running into anything, when Kammani spoke from behind her, making Shar start and Wolfie yelp.

"You have left the others."

"Yes." Shar turned, seeing the woman's hourglass shape dimly in the gloom. "Could you tell me where you found the name Kammani Gula—"

"*I* am Kammani Gula," the woman said, a thrill in her voice, and Shar squinted to see if she was kidding. "You have not drunk your tonic." She gestured to the gap Shar had left in the curtains, and Shar saw the full cup of punch she'd stashed under her chair.

"I'm not thirsty. Look, I think it's very creative"—*weird as hell*—"that you took the name of a goddess as your own, but what I need is your *source,* the place where you found her name."

She stopped as Kammani moved to the gap in the curtains to frown out at the teenagers who were making kissing noises at two new dogs. She raised her hand, and the dogs came daintily across the floor and into the darkness to her, leaving Noah dogless.

He walked over to Daisy and said something, and Daisy handed him Bailey's leash.

I'm sorry I'm going to miss that, Shar thought, and turned her attention back to Kammani. "Okay. So what I need to know—" She stopped again, distracted as she saw the dogs up close: even in the dim light, they looked like tiny tan giraffes with fluffy white pom-pom crowns and little grinning faces, one taller and more slender, the other one shorter with sharper, deeper, smarter eyes. "My god, those are Mesopotamian Temple Dogs. I thought they were extinct."

"Bikka and Umma," Kammani said. "They are at my side always, to serve me."

Bikka and Umma smiled up at Shar, their bizarre little doggy faces alight with intelligence. Well, Umma's was. Bikka's bore a striking resemblance to Paris Hilton.

Wolfie grumbled.

"Right," Shar said. "About Kammani Gula. I'm familiar with Gula, the Goddess of Healing whose sacred animal was the dog . . ." She looked down at the Temple Dogs again. ". . . but I can't find anything about Kammani Gula except for the first chapter of my grandmother's book. Could you give me your sources for her?"

"Your grandmother is writing a book on the goddess?" Kammani tilted her head, more human now in her curiosity.

"Was," Shar said. "A book on Mesopotamian goddesses. After she died, my mother finished writing it, and I promised my mother I'd complete the citations—"

Kammani faded back into the darkness as Umma took a dainty step closer to Wolfie and Wolfie pressed close to Shar's leg.

"Hello?" Shar squinted after Kammani, annoyed that she was being ignored again, and then Kammani returned, holding another cup of punch.

"This tonic is a recipe from my family," she said. "You

will drink my family's tonic, and I will show you Kammani Gula for your family's book."

"I don't think . . ."

"*Drink,*" Kammani said in a voice that had some thunder in it.

Shar took the tonic. Holding wasn't drinking, but maybe Kammani wouldn't notice.

Kammani nodded once. "I will show you Kammani Gula and then you will return to Abby and Daisy."

"Who?" Shar said.

"Bring your cup." Kammani went to the altar again and came back with a flashlight.

Shar followed her to the center of the wall, and Kammani clicked the flashlight on.

A huge naked goddess sprang into sharp relief, towering over them.

Wolfie barked, and Shar said, "*Oh,*" and almost spilled her tonic.

"Kammani Gula and her priestesses," Kammani said, gesturing to other figures down the length of the wall. "She inspires great passion in those who follow her. Can you not feel it?"

"No." Shar took a couple steps back to see the stone goddess better, Wolfie still pressing close. "I don't do passion. I do research."

Kammani Gula was a large-eyed, full-breasted, tiny-waisted, winged woman standing on two Mesopotamian Temple Dogs, a whip in her left hand and a knife in her right.

"She's . . . lovely . . . ," Shar said. *And armed.*

Wolfie whined.

"But I need a *source* for her—," Shar began.

"The inscription is here." Kammani pointed her flashlight at the cuneiform carved into the wall next to the figure, and Shar leaned closer to translate.

Kammani Gula, Goddess of Love, Goddess of Life, Goddess of Healing.

Damn. Okay, so it was a source. But it was a source on a stone wall backstage in a college auditorium in Ohio and it hadn't been authenticated or even *noticed* until now and that was going to raise some questions.

Shar smiled tightly at Kammani. "You know, I've been in this auditorium many times, and I've never seen this bas-relief. This part behind the curtain is always dark and full of boxes, but still, you'd think somebody would have seen this and mentioned it to somebody. My grandfather brought this temple back from Turkey and had it rebuilt as the history building, and even *he* never mentioned it. So I'm skeptical—"

"Your grandfather moved this temple," Kammani said, her voice sounding odd.

Shar nodded. "It's the only step temple in Ohio. We're very proud. But I think I would have—"

"You know nothing, then?" Kammani sounded upset. She tightened her grip on the flashlight, and the beam jerked onto the next figure.

Shar sucked in her breath.

The figure next to the goddess was male.

He was tall, looming over her on the wall, and his forehead was broad, crossed with commalike stone curls, and his eyes—

Kammani moved the light back to the goddess. "You can see—"

"Give me that." Shar took the flashlight from Kammani and focused it on the man again, letting it play over him as she took in the hooded eyes, the square jaw, the broad shoulders, the slim hips, the massive calves . . .

She drank some tonic.

The taste flooded her mouth and filled her senses, biting and sweet, honey and cinnamon and something like the night sky, anise maybe, warm and rich and satisfying. She sipped again, inhaling the scent, and the heat of it went into her bones as she looked at the man.

He looked powerful. Forceful. Certain. *Skilled* . . .

She felt herself flush, and Wolfie whined at her feet and pressed closer.

"Who is he?"

"Samu-la-el. God of the Summer, King of Kamesh, Defender of the North, Slayer of Demons." Kammani recited the titles as if she were saying, *Plumber of Sinks, Mower of Grass.* She took the light from Shar and moved it back to the huge goddess on the wall beside him. "Kammani Gula is the great goddess, mother of all things, and those who follow her . . ."

Shar listened with one ear, knowing Kammani Gula was important, but . . .

Slayer of Demons.

She took another drink and felt the heat flood her again, and then she saw the knife in the goddess's hand and realized what it meant.

"Oh, hell. She *sacrificed* him." *Bitch.*

"For the good of the people," Kammani said, sounding annoyed at the interruption. "A good king dies for his people, and then his goddess raises him again. *He serves his goddess.*"

Kammani glared at her for a moment and then went back to praising the goddess, and Shar sipped her tonic, trying to concentrate. She had to be practical: the guy on the wall had been dead for several thousand years, and she had her grandmother's book to finish, and—

Slayer of Demons.

She ripped the flashlight out of Kammani's grasp and put the light back on the god.

Samu-la-el. He was beautiful and that bitch Kammani Gula had killed him. Shar stared up into the hooded eyes, empty sockets now because the clay and stone imbedded for eyeballs were long gone, but still piercing, staring down at her, transfixing her. This was a guy who kicked demon ass and took invader names. In cuneiform, of course, but still—

God, he was amazing. She stared at him, her head swimming, feeling breathless, dizzy—

"Daisy and Abby are waiting for you," Kammani said, sounding annoyed. "You should be with them."

Get off my ass; you're not my grandmother. Shar drained her cup, letting the richness of the drink flood her, and then she put the cup on the floor and reached out to touch the cuneiform that spelled the god-king's name. *Samu-la-el.* Not the kind of guy who'd give a woman a Taser. She let her fingers slip to trace the line of his side as it tapered to a flat belly, slim hips—

Wolfie barked, and she jerked her fingers away and turned to say something to distract Kammani from the fact that she'd been feeling up a stone god, but Kammani's gaze was through the curtain and across the room where the two teenagers were feeding one of the Temple Dogs something orange. Kammani yanked the flashlight out of Shar's hand and turned it off. "You will join Abby and Daisy," she said, and walked off through the slit in the curtains toward the teenagers, leaving Shar in the dark.

She couldn't see the relief anymore, but he was there. She put her fingers on the wall again, reaching up this time to feel the comma curls across his forehead, wondering who had smoothed them and comforted him after battle, who had put her head on that broad chest and sighed, who had wrapped her arms around him, risen to those hips, cried out in the night—

Wolfie barked, and Shar dropped her hand.

He's dead, he's dead, and you are too old and too practical for hot dreams of cold heroes.

She turned her back on him and looked down at Wolfie, who was trying to avoid the little Temple Dog Umma's polite but insistent gaze. "Come on, baby," Shar said, "we're finished here," and led him and Umma through the curtain to the circle where she sat down, dizzy with tonic and a little depressed.

Slayer of Demons, she thought, and closed her eyes.

Abby shifted uncomfortably in her chair, and Bowser moved a little closer. "I shouldn't really be here," she whispered to the tiny blonde next to her. "Bowser's a perfect gentleman."

"Heh. Wanna trade?" the blonde whispered back as the professor picked up her punch cup from under her chair, looking depressed. "So, why'd you come if Bowser's so well behaved?"

Abby shrugged. "Instinct, I guess. I just arrived in town and I kept running into flyers and I thought it might be a sign."

"From who? Kammani? 'Cause I can tell you right now she's a fruitcake, extra fruit." The blonde hauled her hyper Jack Russell back toward her.

"No, from my grandmother. I just inherited her coffeehouse, and I . . ."

"Oh my god," the blonde said, taking a good look at Abby. "You're Bea's granddaughter?"

The trainer glanced their way and grinned goodnaturedly, but Kammani, who was just a little too much like Abby's mother for Abby's comfort, glowered. "Did you know my grandmother?" Abby whispered, only slightly chastened.

"Oh, hell, yes. Bea was the best." She held out her hand. "I'm Daisy. I live on the third floor. You're my new landlady."

A moment later Kammani was looming over them,

looking pissed. "You are not obedient," she said in the tone that Abby's mother used when a client was being difficult.

"Just making friends," Daisy said with a grin.

Kammani's eyes narrowed, and to Abby's surprise she didn't object. "Good. The three of you shall be friends."

"Three of us?" Abby asked, confused.

Kammani looked over at the middle-aged professor sitting beside them, holding the cup she'd taken from beneath her chair and looking at Kammani with clear dislike. "The two of you and Sharrat."

"Shar. Sharrat was my grandmother," the older woman snapped.

Kammani seemed to control herself with an effort. "The three of you shall be friends," she said again, and glided away before anyone could do more than stare at her.

"So," Daisy said, leaning toward Shar. "What's the verdict on this one? I'm leaning toward spooky with a side of nuts."

Shar rolled her eyes. "She's just upset because somebody dropped a house on her sister."

Abby leaned forward and said, "*Beetlejuice!*" delighted to find another fan.

Daisy looked confused. "Not *The Wizard of Oz*?"

Shar shook her head. "Nope, sorry, *Beetlejuice*. A cinematic masterpiece. You'll have to come over and watch it—"

Her voice broke off and she looked surprised at what she'd just said, but Abby thought, *That would be fun. Movie night with the girls*. She lifted her cup. "I'll be there. As the undead one would say, 'Let's turn on the juice and see what shakes loose.' " She looked in her cup. "Except I'm out of juice."

"I haven't touched this yet," Shar said, holding out her cup. "I'll share."

"Me, too, please," Daisy said, holding out her cup.

Shar said, "Absolutely," and divided her cup among the three of them. "Because We Shall Be Friends."

Daisy giggled. "Hell, I can always do with some friends. And Abby's new in town—she needs friends, too." She knocked her paper cup against Shar's with an ineffective thunk. "All for one and one for all." She tapped Abby's as well, and they all drank the remnants.

"You will take tonic with you," Kammani said, suddenly before them again.

Abby inhaled her drink in surprise and coughed as Shar started and Daisy said, "*Crap,* you scared me."

Kammani presented glazed ceramic bottles to them as if she were handing out treasure.

"About that source—," Shar said as she took hers.

"All will be explained when you return on Tuesday," Kammani said, and moved toward the back of the room again.

Abby squinted at her ceramic glazed bottle. "This tonic is really good." She took another slug of the sweet, spicy liquid. For tonic like this she could manage to come back, maybe long enough to find out what was in it.

"I don't want to come back," Shar said, sounding more like a rebellious child than a dignified, gray-haired professor.

Which reminded Abby of Christopher Mackenzie, who was nowhere near gray-haired and far too dignified himself, and if she was going to have to go buy ingredients for his cookies, she'd better get a move on.

"We'll all come together," Abby said. "We won't let the scary lady get you."

Shar shook her head. "It's not the scary part; it's the waste of time. I have work to do."

"Who doesn't?" Daisy said, and her dog yanked at her leash, practically hauling her out of the chair.

She was small and strong, Abby thought, but not much of a match for a spastic dog like Bailey. She straightened as Noah came around the circle with handouts.

"Here's the class list with phone numbers." He handed one to Abby while he smiled at Daisy.

"Thanks." Abby rose, and as she did, she caught sight of Kammani in the shadows at the back of the room.

She was watching them.

"I'm telling you, Kammani's nuts," Daisy said as Noah moved on, passing out the class lists. She nodded at the thin, dark-haired girl at the end of the circle. "There's another one in the last chair there. She's been staring at me all evening."

"Mortuary Mina," Shar said, and when Abby and Daisy both looked at her, surprised, she added, "Grad student in the history department. Writes all her papers on disasters. If somebody died horribly in history, Mina's your woman."

"Good to know," Daisy said, and then her dog jerked her away. She met Abby's eyes. "See you back at the coffeehouse?"

Abby nodded. "Where's the nearest grocery store? I need to make cookies."

Bowser woofed beside her, and damned if it didn't sound like he said the word "cookies." He'd always had a sweet tooth.

"Kroger's out on Route Fifty-two," Daisy said absently. "You're going to bake?"

"There's a butthole professor who seems to think I inherited my grandmother's obligations as well as the old building, and I'm not interested in fighting him. You want a ride?"

Daisy glanced toward Noah, who was scratching the tiaraed head of one of the dogs. "It's a nice night. I think I'll walk," she said, trying to sound innocent.

Shar leaned closer and said, "A professor? I know most of them. Do you need help?"

"I don't think Professor Mackenzie is likely to be reasonable."

"Oh, Christopher." Shar nodded. "He's a good man, but he has a tendency to tunnel vision." She stopped and looked back at the curtain. "I guess we all do." She turned back to Abby. "Let me know if you need me to run interference. You've got my number."

Abby looked at her, startled. "That's very nice of you. . . ."

"Well," Shar said, "you know. Friends. Or else." She stood up and put down her empty cup. "It was lovely meeting you both," she said, and then she let her dachshund pull her to the door, a drab, quiet, totally nice woman with not much life left in her, and Abby wondered if she was going to end up just like her. Dried up and old before her time.

The teenagers shrieked with laughter and the sour-looking dark-haired girl—Mortuary Mina—took her black Chihuahua and slipped behind the curtain, shadowing Kammani, and one of the little Temple Dogs looked after Wolfie and then padded gracefully back to the altar. Abby looked down at Bowser. "Let's blow this Popsicle stand. We got cookies to make."

"Cookies," Bowser barked, and Abby jumped, startled.

"What did you say?" The moment the words were out of her mouth she realized how absurd that was. She shook her head, as if to clear the cobwebs that had surely set up shop. "Never mind; I'm imagining things. Let's go."

Bowser woofed in agreement, a totally doglike sound, and Abby felt some of the tension drain away. It had been an extremely long day, and she'd been nuts to come here without taking time to settle in. They walked out the auditorium doors, across the hall, and out of the building onto the quadrangle. Her car was parked nearby, and it wasn't until she climbed into the driver's seat and Bowser had stretched out beside her that she let out her breath.

"This is a very weird place, Bowse," she said absently, rubbing his massive head.

He looked up at her out of his dark, wise eyes. "You're telling me," he growled.

And Abby let out a scream.

"Bailey, *heel!*"

Daisy jerked on the leash as Bailey dragged her to the grassy patch behind the step temple. She leaned back and dug in her heels, trying to balance her purse, the ceramic bottle, Bailey, and her sanity.

"Heel! Heel! *Heel!*" Something snapped under her left foot. "What the— *Heel*!"

Bailey stopped straining against the leash and danced back to her. Daisy dumped her bottle and purse on the ground and sat, then pulled off her left sandal. The heel had broken clean off. Bailey sniffed at it and then licked Daisy's hand.

"Don't kiss up now, dog." She held the broken heel to her sandal, checking for a way to fix it just to get home, because walking on one heel while being attached to Bailey was a suicide mission. She picked up the ceramic bottle and pulled out the cork. Maybe she could substitute it for the heel . . . no. Too short.

"This is what you get when you buy cheap shoes." She took a breath, catching the sharp scent of the temple tonic wafting up from the open bottle. She glanced at it, focusing on the pretty carnelian flower embossed on the side, the rich orange-red coloring almost swirling under the glossy surface. She lifted the bottle and took a generous swig. Damn, that stuff was good, sharp and exotic like an umbrella drink on a beach. It made her feel . . . not drunk. Relaxed. Calm. Happy, as if her life was better than she remembered it being. She took another drink, then looked at Bailey, who was doing his signature *Let's go! Let's go!* shuffle-dance two-step.

She recorked the bottle and turned her attention back to the sandal. "I'm telling you, these classes better work, or I'm going to throw myself in the river."

"River!" Bailey barked.

Daisy's grip tightened on the sandals in her hands, and she slowly turned to look at Bailey. Either she was crazy or she'd just heard words in his barks.

"Did you just . . . ? No. You didn't." She tried to relax her shoulder muscles. "Because that's impossible."

"Possible!" Bailey barked again.

Daisy froze, feeling a little dizzy, then looked at Bailey.

"M-m-maybe . . . there's a . . . throat c-c-condition in dogs . . . ," she stammered, gripping her sandals as though they were her firmest link to reality. "It's a condition. Sure. Because there's no way I'm really hearing a dog ta—"

"Dog!" Bailey barked.

"Holy crap!" Daisy screamed, and shot up.

Bailey hopped straight up in the air. "Crap! Crap! Crap!"

She felt a snap in her hand and looked down to see she'd snapped the toe off the good sandal. "*Crap.*"

"Everything okay?" Daisy twirled to see Noah walking toward them. "I heard a scream." Noah's eyes locked on Daisy and he smiled as he recognized her. "Hey there. You okay?"

"Yep." Daisy looked down at Bailey. "Saw a spider. A terrifying, but likely imaginary, spider. I think it's gone now." She tightened her hold on Bailey's leash, then knelt down to pick up her purse and—her whole body relaxed as she saw it—the ceramic bottle.

Right. She wasn't crazy. She was sauced. *Thank god.*

"Everything's okay." She straightened up. "I think maybe I drank too much."

"Too much!" Bailey yipped.

Daisy turned the bottle in her hands, searching for some kind of labeling. "This has got to be . . . what? Seventy, eighty proof?"

"I don't think there's any alcohol in that," Noah said.

"No?" She glanced down at Bailey. "Yes, there is." She raised her head and her breath caught as she looked in Noah's sharp blue eyes, all warm and . . .

Whoa. Daisy wasn't sure if the sudden whoosh she felt was from the guy or the bottle, but either way, it was time to go home.

"Well, it was nice meeting—," Daisy started, but then Bailey jumped straight up into the air, twirled, and landed.

"Ta-da!" he barked.

"—you," she finished, then jerked on Bailey's leash. "*Stop that.*"

"Stop what?" Noah said.

"Not you. Him. He keeps—" She stopped herself before she could say, *talking,* and then Bailey leapt into the air again, and she said, "—doing that."

"The jumping?"

"And . . . other stuff. He might be making me literally insane. Can dogs do that?"

"Jack Russells are challenging dogs, but you can handle it." Noah gave her an encouraging smile.

"I'm beginning to doubt that," she said; then a flash of hope shot through her. "Hey, but if I come back for Tuesday's class, can you fix him? Because I have to tell you . . ." She looked at Bailey, daring him to speak again. ". . . I'm not sure anything we picked up tonight has been all that helpful."

"Training takes time. You'll get it."

Daisy noticed the crinkles around Noah's eyes deepening as he smiled down at her, and felt a flutter of excitement, and then Bailey barked, "I want a cookie!" and she decided striking up a flirtation during a mental breakdown wasn't the best timing.

"Well, I'd better get him home," she said. "It's been hours since he's humped my couch pillows. I wait any longer, he's gonna get the shakes."

"Wait." Noah motioned down at her feet, then met her eyes again. "I can't let you just walk off barefoot. Where are you going?"

"I'm on Temple Street, right over the coffeehouse."

"Then you're right on my way." He nodded in the direction of town. "If you don't mind taking the scenic route through the park, we can get to Temple Street without touching pavement."

"Park!" Bailey said. "Park! Park!"

"*Okay,*" Daisy said to Bailey, then smiled up at Noah. "Let's go." She gave him the bottle to hold for her, held on to Bailey's leash with one hand, and tucked the other in the crook of Noah's arm.

"Thank you," she said. "It's nice of you to be so concerned about my feet."

"Well, it's not just that," he said. "I hate to see a couch pillow get lonely."

Daisy laughed, and Bailey hopped up and twirled. "I like him."

"Me, too," Daisy said.

They made their way across the rolling green of campus, the grass tickling Daisy's feet, keeping them cool, making her feel powerful and connected to the earth. *I need to walk barefoot more often,* she thought. As they walked, Noah showed her how to get Bailey to heel, and it almost worked. Then he told her a joke she'd already heard, but it was so funny when he told it that she had to stop to catch her breath. She didn't get her first *Uh-oh* until they were almost through the park, when he mentioned that Bug-Eyes from class was his cousin Mina.

"You're related to her?" she asked. "By blood?"

"That's usually how it's done."

"No, I mean—" She shot him an exasperated look. "You know what I mean. She's just . . . no offense, but she seems—"

"Insane?" Noah nodded. "She is. My father got out of the family with his sanity mostly intact, although he's doing this comb-over thing that has me concerned." He nudged her with his elbow. "I just threw my family's crazy closet wide open for you. I usually don't let women meet Mina until never. Now it's your turn. Fair's fair."

"Well," she said, "my mother believes there's no outfit in the world that can't be made better by a pillbox hat. No one's seen the top of her head since 1982."

Noah stopped walking and looked down at Daisy. Daisy stopped walking and looked up at him. Bailey leapt in the air and barked, "Hat!"

"That's the best you've got?" Noah said. "Hats?"

"Well, it starts with the hats, revs up with her total lack of boundaries, and ends with her pretending to have allergies so she can dump her dog on me and go shopping in New York under the guise of seeing a specialist. It's a whole gestalt of crazy."

He hesitated, then nodded and started walking again. "All right, I'll give you a pass. Plus bonus points for coining 'gestalt of crazy.' Can I use that?"

"In what?"

He lowered his eyes. "I write songs."

"You're a musician?" Daisy had a vision of Noah surrounded by braless teenagers and empty beer bottles in a smoky room while his bandmates cooked heroin with spoons and Bic lighters. *Uh-oh.*

"I wouldn't call myself a musician," Noah said. "I write songs. Play when I can. The rest of the time, it's odd jobs to pay the rent."

"Oh." Relief. "Like dog training?"

"Like whatever. Dog training is the flavor of the week." He shrugged. "I'm good with dogs, and my aunt Miriam—Dad's sister, Mina's mom, the source of all batshit—asked me to help out her old college roommate with the class, so I figured, why not? I'm not one to turn down a job that pays."

"Don't you want . . . I don't know. Something more stable?"

"Not really."

Daisy went quiet as the *Uh-oh*s flew fast and furious around her. No goals, no real job, family tree full of nuts. Great. Well, she didn't have to marry him.

She could just sleep with him.

"So," he said, "what do you do for a living?"

"I write Web code for the humanities department. It's pretty boring."

He eyed her sideways. "But stable."

She gently squeezed his arm. "Is that a dig?"

"No. I'm just saying everyone makes choices."

They moved closer to cut through a line of buckeye trees, and then they were at Temple Street, almost home. Despite the fact that she saw Temple umpteen times a day, Daisy found herself suddenly awed by its colorful strip of storefronts and bars, its streetlights just starting to break into the haze of dusk. How could she have lived there so long, and never noticed how pretty it was?

Because you've never had Kammani's temple tonic before . . .

"So, hey," she said, "back to Kammani, I have to ask: is she full-on nuts or just suffering from delusions of goddess?"

Noah stopped short at the sidewalk and handed her the bottle, then turned his back to her and lowered down a bit. "Hop on."

Bailey jumped up in the air. "Hop on, hop on, hop on!"

"What are you doing?" she asked.

Noah glanced over his shoulder at her. "Piggyback. Let's go."

She laughed, then noticed he didn't laugh with her. "You're serious?"

Noah straightened. "This is a bar street in a college town. The sidewalk is made of broken beer bottles. You're going piggyback."

"I can't."

"Why not?"

"Because . . ." She flushed and looked down the street. "It's childish. And embarrassing."

"Half the fun in life is doing things that are childish and embarrassing."

"But—"

He put his hand on her shoulder, and the warmth shot through her so strongly that she almost felt dizzy just from his touch. He lowered his head and spoke quietly, his eyes on hers.

"Trust me, okay?"

She looked up at him, and before she even understood why, she heard herself say, "Okay."

THREE

Daisy saw Noah's smile widen and her heart quickened and Bailey flew up in the air and barked, "Yay!!!"

She handed the leash to Noah, then took the bottle and her purse in one hand as she grabbed on to his shoulder with the other and crawled onto his back. She tightened her legs around his hips and he straightened, bouncing her into place and . . .

"Hoo boy," she said as the sensations shot through her.

"You okay?" he asked over his shoulder.

"Yeah," she squeaked, then cleared her throat. "I'm fine."

Noah started down the street and with each movement, each breath, a fresh wave of pure want shot through her. The energy pooled within her, tightening in her abdomen, and everything around her seemed to pop and crackle. They crossed the street just as a warm summer wind shot down the street, taking a handful of colorful flyers from the hands of a woman who chased after them, cursing. The colors dancing on the air made Daisy feel woozy, and she closed her eyes, but then the wind on her face made her feel a little too warm in certain places, so she opened her eyes again and tightened her grip on Noah, and—

Oh. Wow.

They passed a parked car, and Bailey must have jumped against it or something, because a loud, rhythmic alarm went off, bursts of sound matching the pacing of her heart, her breath, her desire. The heat rode up her legs, her core, to her face, and she took in a deep breath of air just as Noah bounced her again on his hips to get a better hold of her.

"Oh, hey," Daisy said, gripping the cool bottle, anchoring herself to it and to Noah, holding on to what control she had left.

And then, finally, Noah stopped in front of the coffeehouse. He settled her down gently on the sidewalk, and the warm cement shot another wave of sensation through her body. She looked again at the bottle in her hand; what the hell was in that stuff?

"Well," Noah said. "I'll see you Tuesday at class?"

Daisy looked up, feeling bereft. *Tuesday? Five whole days?*

"Actually," she said quickly, "hell of a coincidence with you being a musician and all, Abby's having an open mike night here tomorrow night."

"Yeah?" Noah looked at the coffeehouse door, where the giant CLOSED sign sat in the dusty window. "It's not . . . closed?"

"No. Well, yes. But no." God, but she was a bad liar. "Abby needs to bring in a little extra cash, so she's having an open mike night, like Bea used to have. Except instead of poets, Abby wants music." Daisy smiled up at him, hoping her face wasn't as flushed as it felt. "I'd love to hear you play."

"Then I'll be there." He waved good-bye to Bailey, and a moment later he'd disappeared around the corner. Daisy leaned against the cool glass of the old storefront.

"Daisy happy!" Bailey yipped, hopping into the air. "Happy, happy, happy!"

Daisy looked down and felt a rush of affection for the little furball. She knelt down and rubbed his head.

"Daisy happy." She stood up, corked the bottle, and

pulled open the stairwell door. "Come on. You go say hi to my couch pillow while I drum up the nerve to tell Abby I've booked her an open mike tomorrow."

"Yay!" Bailey barked, darting up the steps, and Daisy followed, laughing.

Kammani stood at the back of the temple flanked by Bikka and Umma, watching the last of the Three leave while the teenagers, Bun and Gen, gathered their things and giggled at their dogs, a fat poodle mix in a tiara and a resigned foxhound in a bandanna. *Twits,* Kammani thought, and wondered what twits were. There were words in the air in this world, crackling as they came and went, annoying her with their strangeness and inexplicability. This world was not like her old world; it was wrong, ignorant, lacking in respect, starting with the people who had called her back and then not greeted her—

"Ohmigod, I think we lost the Cheetos," Bun said, looking around the floor.

"Ohmigod, I think we *ate* the Cheetos," Gen said, and they collapsed into laughter again.

Kammani thought, *I should smite you into grease spots.*

"They're young," Umma barked.

"Yes," Kammani said. "But they will learn. And then—"

Someone moved in the darkness behind the altar.

"Careful," Umma growled.

The dark-haired girl with the little black dog in her arms came out of the curtains and bent her head. "I bow before thee, O Goddess. I am Mina Wortham. My mother has sent me because I am your Chosen, the youngest woman of age in our family. I will do your bidding."

"Your mother?" Kammani said.

"Miriam Wortham," the girl said, and Kammani thought of the lone, fervent little woman who had greeted her when she'd awakened, who had bowed low and brought clothes and food and money and a machine that played flat disks. "So you can see the world you will rule, my goddess." Mina looked like Miriam, eyes bulging with devotion, thin chest heaving with passion, a dark raw nerve. Her little black dog breathed heavily, too, making a *Heh heh heh* sound as he smiled, his eyelids half-closed.

Kammani walked up the three shallow steps to the altar to look down on Mina Wortham. "You say you are chosen. Tell me how you will serve me."

"My name is *Death*," the girl said almost hissing the word. "I will serve you by *bringing an end* to any who oppose you."

Kammani closed her eyes. *Seven priestesses and this is the one who remembers*. "You are not Death. You are the human manifestation of the abstract principle of the cessation of life." Mina frowned, and Kammani tried again. "You are not a goddess; you are a priestess charged with helping the dying among my people to find Ereshkigal's kingdom in the Netherworld."

The girl blinked.

Kammani spoke slower. "You are Mina Wortham, *a priestess only*. You will serve me, forsaking all others, staying virgin and aloof, giving your life to me. And you will kill no one." *Unless I tell you to.*

Mina bowed. "I am untouched by man, and I am your priestess, your servant, your slave, my goddess."

Kammani nodded. "Welcome, Mina, descendant of Munawirtum. You are the seventh of my priestesses—"

"And the most powerful," Mina said, tasting the words.

"No," Kammani said, wondering if Mina knew what happened to people who interrupted a goddess.

"And I will stand by your left hand, and I will smite your enemies," Mina went on, her voice rising.

If this had been the old world, Mina would have been a scorch mark on the stone by now, or at least a small furred creature with a collar.

But she needed Mina, needed Mina's family of devout worshipers, women who had not forgotten over centuries . . .

Bun and Gen were at the big double doors now, leaving a welter of papers and bags behind them, whispering and giggling as they looked back at Mina, no idea that they were in the presence of Divinity.

They've forgotten me, Kammani thought with a chill. *Only Mina's family remembers, and their numbers are not large enough to give me the power I need—*

"Shall I smite them?" Mina said.

"No, Mina. You may not smite anyone," Kammani said, and Mina looked rebellious as Bun and Gen escaped, unscathed.

"You say I am not the most powerful," Mina said, coming closer. "Why? I am the most faithful."

"There are others who come before you." Kammani looked back at the three chairs in the middle of the semicircle.

Mina stiffened, following Kammani's gaze to the center chair. "Daisy? She's *nothing.*"

"On the contrary, she is very important." Kammani watched as Mina's eyes narrowed.

"She can't be important; she's not even five foot tall," Mina said. "She can't even control her *dog.*"

"She is one of the Three." Kammani stared out over the temple, remembering their presence, feeling the power and passion they were repressing within themselves. Once she'd brought them back to her, released all that power in them, once they were open to her again—

"The Three?" Mina's eyes grew greedy.

Kammani walked down the shallow steps, tired of the girl's neediness, leaving Mina to seethe behind her.

Bun's and Gen's chairs were covered with papers and Kammani picked one up. A magazine. Miriam had brought some of those, too, but not like these. *InStyle,* she read on the first cover, savoring the new word. *People. Star.* Pictures of women falling out of their clothing, men with jutting jaws and empty eyes, babies in jewels. *Celebribaby.* Another word from the air. She shook her head and went back up the steps to the altar.

"*The Three?*" Mina said, spitting the words. "The three who sat in the middle? *They* have power? That little shrimp Daisy? Old Professor Summer with her gray hair? That skinny weakling with the big dog? *They're* the most powerful?"

"They will be," Kammani said. "When they follow me."

"What about *me*?"

"You?" Kammani turned to her. "You are my seventh priestess and your birthright is to serve me."

"Yes, my goddess," Mina said, but her eyes slid left.

"Begin now." Kammani dropped the magazines on the altar. "Discover all you can about the Three. Then come here tomorrow and tell me."

"Yes, my goddess." Mina straightened, sticking out her chin over her little dog, who *heh-heh*-ed. "I will serve you; I will be the most powerful; I will smite your enemies; I will—"

"You will bring what I require and do nothing else," Kammani said.

Mina set her jaw, as if biting back words. "Yes, my goddess. My mother said to tell you that she'll bring your breakfast tomorrow at eight if that is suitable. Waffles and strawberries."

Kammani nodded, and Mina left, and Kammani sat

down on the step below the altar, alone in her temple, and thought about her priestesses.

Nin-kagina, Belessunu, Abi-simti, Humusi, Sharrat, Iltani, Munawirtum.

But now they were Gen, Bun, Abby, Daisy, Shar, Vera, and Mina. . . .

They were not like their ancestors; they'd need training—Vera had not even come when summoned—but they would be hers again. The Three were steady and sane, and they would give her the power she needed, they and Samu-la-el. She would raise him tonight in the sacred room at the top of her temple, and he would stand at her side—

"Biscuit, biscuit, biscuit," Bikka said, wriggling under Bun's chair for some kind of bag that crackled when she pawed at it.

Umma looked back over the deserted temple to where the Three had sat as Bikka crunched something.

"Wolfie," Umma said.

Kammani looked at her sharply, but the little dog said nothing else, so she went up the steps to the altar and picked up the biscuit box there. She gave Umma one while she thought about the work of her evening. She had to check the cask of the still-fermenting elixir, evoke the spirit and the body of her four-thousand-year-dead consort, and learn more about this new world that made women weak and dogs mute.

But afterward, when all is ready, I will rule this new world as I ruled the old one and they will all follow my bidding.

She picked up the papers from the altar. The lettering on the top one said: *BABY CAMISOLE'S FIRST BLING!* over a picture of a baby draped in sparkling stones.

Because on their own, they're idiots, she thought, and put all the magazines in a stack to read later.

Bowser didn't speak again, and Abby managed to calm herself down long enough to go shopping. By the time she made it back to the Temple Street Coffeehouse, she'd almost sideswiped a Lexus, crushed a shopping cart at the mammoth Kroger, and only barely resisted the temptation to call her mother in hysterics. The memory of just how unhelpful Amanda Richmond could be in a crisis was enough to bring her to her senses.

She pulled up into the alleyway behind Granny B's lavender building. Bowser lifted his head, tilting it slightly in that quizzical look that only dogs could perfect.

"Home," Abby said, and slid out of the car.

It took her three trips into the back kitchen of the coffeehouse to unload all the stuff she'd bought. Butter, cream, honey, cinnamon, licorice, enough flour and sugar to consume what little money she had left, along with a six-pack of Diet Coke. Bowser trotted beside her, his mouth full of the soup bone she'd brought him, and while it occasionally sounded as if he was mumbling at her, she ignored it, taking another swig from the ceramic bottle Kami had given her.

Fortunately someone, presumably Daisy, had kept the kitchen clean and dust-free, and the baking pans and bowls were easy enough to find. It didn't keep Abby from muttering imprecations about the professor beneath her breath, and eventually Bowser dropped the bone to look up at her.

"Liked him," he growled.

"You're man's best friend," she replied, cranky. "Who says you're any judge of character?"

Bowser just looked at her, then picked up the bone again.

"Blabbermouth," Abby said beneath her breath, pulling on one of the aprons she'd found hanging on the door to the storeroom. It was lavender as well, decorated with sparkly dragonflies and bejeweled organza ribbons, with *Bea* spelled out in rhinestones across the top. Clearly dear old Granny B was a far cry from the sweet little old lady Abby had fantasized about. And a far cry from her buttoned-up, uptight, real estate–obsessed mother.

She found a stack of notebooks under the wide center island, a treasure trove of recipes and memories, and she squinted at the handwriting, feeling a headache coming on. She took another swig of the tonic, and the curlicues of old-fashioned script suddenly sorted themselves out and became legible. She twisted her long hair back into a bun, pulled out the mixing bowls, and set to work.

She had her first tray of cookies in the oven and was elbow-deep in her second batch of cookie dough when Daisy walked in, a bemused expression on her face, her chaotic dog by her side.

"I saw the light on and I thought I'd check," Daisy said. "I take it you found the grocery store."

"I did. And it turns out baking isn't that hard. You just have to relax."

Daisy leaned forward, peering at the dough. "Looks good. Smells good, too. I think you're a natural."

"Maybe," Abby said.

In fact, it had been surprisingly easy. She glanced over at Bowser, who'd abandoned his bone to have a low, inaudible conversation with Bailey. Abby shook her head. "Weird," she muttered under her breath.

She turned to Daisy, about to say something, then thought better of it. If she asked her if she could hear her dog talking, Daisy might run screaming out of the place, and Abby needed the rent. Not to mention the friend. No, the talking dog was nothing more than her imagination and too much stress. She'd been driving for days, talking to no one but Bowser. It was no wonder he was talking back.

CALUMET CITY PUBLIC LIBRARY

"Have you thought about what you're going to do with this place?" Daisy asked.

"I don't know." Abby picked up a shamrock-shaped cookie cutter, then shook her head and dumped it back in. "I'm leaving things kind of open."

"Well, what do you think of Summerville?"

"I like it." Abby pulled out a gingerbread man–shaped cutter and tossed it back. "Even if there are certain obnoxious professors who think they can tell someone what to do." She rejected a plain circle, a paw shape, and a baby bootie. She picked out a heart, shrugged, and kept it, returning the basket back to the shelf.

"Um, okay," Daisy said, "but I was thinking—"

Abby cut a heart. "And now he expects me to just drop everything and bake him cookies. All I wanted was some answers about my grandmother, and he just—" She perked up suddenly and sniffed the air. "Just a minute." She walked over to the wall oven and pulled out the pan of cookies, warm and buttery, with sun shapes embossed in the tops. *Absolutely perfect*, she thought, beaming down at them.

"Did I miss the timer going off?" Daisy asked.

"No," Abby said. "I didn't set one."

"So, you just . . . know when they're done?"

Abby nodded, staring down at the cookies. "Seems that way."

"You're definitely a natural, then."

Daisy was moving around, looking far too nervous, and Abby wanted to plant her hands on Daisy's tiny shoulders and hold her still for a moment.

"What's up?" Abby asked in her most patient voice.

"Well . . . I really need you to open the coffeehouse tomorrow night."

Abby picked up the heart-shaped cutter and went back to work. "Why?"

"Well, Bea used to have these open mike nights, and

they were so fun. People would flock in and do poetry readings, although I was thinking that maybe we'd just do music at this one—"

Abby stopped cutting. "Granny B used to have open mike nights?"

"Yeah. She loved poetry and music, all kinds of music. And colors. Anything bright and anti-establishment. She was so . . ." Daisy trailed off. "You didn't know her well, did you?"

"No," Abby said simply, trying to ignore the ache inside her. "But . . . I feel a strange sort of connection to her, as if . . ." She looked down at the cookies. "I haven't seen her since I was a little girl. Is it weird that I miss her?"

"No. She was great. She had this laugh . . . hell, you could hear it for miles. And she had this way of inspiring people. Artists, poets, the lovelorn." Daisy had a distant look in her eyes. "So, about this open mike. . . ."

"I'm not so sure it's a good idea," Abby said.

Daisy leaned over the counter, her expression plaintive, her focus unshakeable. "Look, you've already got a start with the cookies, and if they taste as good as they smell, they'll sell like mad. The front room won't take long to clean—all we have to do is dust and then drag in a few extra tables and chairs, get the coffee machine cleaned and running, and we're golden. I'll oversee all that. I can clean; I can wait tables; I am an excellent coffee pourer. I used to help Bea when things were busy, I know the register and everything."

"Okay."

Daisy snapped her fingers. "Oh, and I bet Shar would help. And maybe those two little giggly girls can help me wait tables if we're desperate. Not Mina, though; she's the Grim Reaper in a miniskirt." She blinked, seeming to finally process what she'd heard. "What did you say?"

"I said okay," Abby said. "Granny B would have done it, right?"

"Are you kidding? Bea would have held a circus in here if it would get me laid. She always thought it was sad that she got more action than I did. I wasn't too crazy about it, either, but Bea—"

"Wait." Abby laughed. "All this is to get you laid?"

"No." Daisy put her hands over her eyes. "Yes. Kind of." She pulled her hands down. "It's Noah. From class. He's completely wrong for me, but he gave me this piggyback ride and I almost had . . . fun. It's been so long since I've had fun, Abby."

"I know the feeling," Abby said, glancing down at her ridiculous apron. At least Granny B had been enjoying herself—more than her two descendents put together.

"Tell me about it," Daisy said. "Bea would have loved me getting together with a musician; that was just her style. It was horrible that she died, but at least she went boinking."

Abby straightened. "My mother said . . . She had a heart attack, I thought."

"Um." Daisy hesitated, then shrugged. "Yeah. She just had it while she was straddling Mr. Casey. From Casey's Hardware, down the street?"

"Good God." No wonder her mother hadn't wanted her anywhere near Bea. The Real Estate Goddess of Escondido never lifted her skirts for anyone less than a millionaire. Abby wiped her hands on her apron, then picked up her heart cutter. "You know what? We're going to do this."

"Really?"

"Yup." Abby cut out another cookie, then admired it. "I mean, if Granny B would have gotten you laid, then it's my obligation to see it through."

Daisy's face lit up. "Oh, that's great! I have to tell you,

though, I don't usually get like this over a man. I think I might be a little bit drunk."

Abby laughed. "Well, I don't usually bake. Or fight with math professors. I think it's just been one of those days."

"It's been a good day," Daisy said. "I'm gonna go get Bailey and print out some flyers to put around town. You need any help baking?"

Abby shook her head. "I've got this under control. I'm actually having fun. I might try some new recipes, see what I like. But tomorrow, if you could help me clean—"

"Oh, absolutely! I'll take a half day. They owe me the time, trust me."

Somebody knocked on the front door to the coffee-house.

"You want me to get that?" Daisy asked.

Abby shook her head. "I'll take care of it. You go on to bed."

She switched the light on as she walked through the deserted shop, brushing the flour off her hands. Bowser had abandoned his bone and was sticking by her side. She was perfectly safe. Whoever was silhouetted in the glass door, making such a fuss, wouldn't have a chance against a behemoth such as Bowser—

She slowed as she recognized who it was.

"Good," Bowser growled.

"I don't think so," Abby said, and opened the door to Professor Christopher Mackenzie.

FOUR

Professor Mackenzie had shed his jacket and tie. His white shirt was open at the collar, the sleeves rolled up, and his hair was rumpled as if he'd been shoving his hand through it in exasperation.

"What are you doing here?" Abby said, ignoring the odd, tight, fluttery feeling in the pit of her stomach when she looked at him.

He had the grace to look slightly uncomfortable. "I wanted to make sure you were actually going to bake cookies for the reception. And there were several dietary restrictions I neglected to mention."

She crossed her arms over the apron, and she could feel the sparkle and bows. She was Granny B's granddaughter; she wasn't going to let herself be intimidated by a stranger, no matter how good-looking. "You're a control freak, aren't you, Professor?" she said mildly. "Don't you have more important things to do than chase around after cookies? Life would be a lot simpler if you'd just ordered them from a bakery and didn't worry about the tiny bit of money you'd given Granny B."

"Two hundred dollars," he said.

"Two hundred?" she echoed. "They must have been some cookies."

"Your grandmother's prowess was legendary."

She'd already heard a great deal about her grandmother's legendary prowess. "I never really knew Granny B. . . ."

"And I'm not about to enlighten you," he said, looking uncomfortable. "In fact, if you had a cell phone I could have simply called and given you my instructions."

"I have a cell phone. I just don't give the number out to strangers. And it's a little late for instructions, don't you think? You should have thought of that sooner."

"I did. I came back earlier and you'd gone out."

"I went to the dog class."

"You did?" He looked surprised, and for a moment, quite human. "Your dog doesn't look like he needs much training."

Bowser had moved past her to brush up against the professor's long legs. Mackenzie was wearing jeans now, which should have made him more human. Unfortunately, it also made him more attractive, in a snarly kind of way, especially since he was also absently stroking Bowser's head and Bowser was looking blissful.

Traitor, Abby thought.

"I don't like people touching my dog," she said.

"Mind your own beeswax," Bowser said.

"Beeswax?" Abby echoed, astonished.

"What about beeswax?" Mackenzie looked confused as he rubbed Bowser's ears, and the sight of those long fingers was making Abby feel uncomfortably warm. "Your dog came to me. It wasn't my idea."

"That's true," Bowser rumbled.

Okay, this crazy night was getting even crazier. She needed to get Mackenzie the hell out of there before she became even more unhinged and jumped his bones. Because as annoying as he was, there was something about him that seemed to call to her. "Come here, Bowser!" she said firmly.

Bowser gave her a long-suffering look and shuffled back to her side. "Like him."

"Did you hear that?" she demanded.

"Hear what?" Mackenzie said, staring at her as if she'd grown a second head. "Don't tell me you're hearing voices?"

She certainly wasn't going to tell him her dog was talking to her. "Of course not. Don't be ridiculous—why would you think something like that? I'm fine." She looked up at him. Big mistake. His eyes darkened behind the gold-rimmed glasses, and for a moment she was lost. There was something unfamiliar in the back of his eyes, what she might almost have thought was . . . attraction. But he'd made it very clear he found her to be nothing more than an annoyance. Still, why had he shown up here with such a feeble excuse?

"Your cookies will be ready by tomorrow night. If you have special dietary requirements, let me know," she said in her most reasonable voice. "I'm opening the coffee-house for tomorrow night, and I can switch out the cookies if there's a problem."

He looked away, glancing around the barren front room. "Tomorrow? You think you have time for that as well as my cookies? You have delusions of grandeur, Miss Richmond."

"I've never known anyone to be so obsessed with cookies," she said. "Just let me worry about how I'm going to accomplish all that. Now go away and let me bake."

He'd opened his mouth to respond when suddenly Bowser knocked against her, unbalancing her so that she stumbled against the professor. He put out his hands to catch her, and for a moment they were too close, close enough for her to feel his body heat—the sensation was disturbing, erotic—and it seemed as if his fingers caressed her arms as they'd caressed Bowser's head.

Then sanity returned, and she yanked herself away, stumbling a little bit. "Sorry. I'm not usually so clumsy."

He didn't move, staring down at her. She was a tall woman, but he was well over six feet of lean muscle, muscle she'd felt when her Newfoundland had shoved her into his arms.

"I'll be here to pick up the food at six-thirty tomorrow," he said abruptly.

For a moment she said nothing. She could still feel his hands on her arms, feel the warmth of his body. For some idiotic reason, she wanted to move back, to rest against him, to have him draw her closer.

Yup, she was insane.

And he didn't seem to be going anywhere. Much as she wanted to believe that the dark expression in his eyes signified instant attraction, she knew better. Something was bothering the uptight professor, and she had no idea what it was.

"Are you sure you're not hearing voices?" he said.

"The only voice I'm hearing is yours and I can do without it," she said, doing her best to sound reasonable. She didn't want to touch him again, but he wasn't moving, so she gave him a little shove toward the door, trying to ignore that heat that raced up her fingers to infuse her entire body. "Tomorrow, Professor," she said, giving one last shove out into the street, and then closed the door behind him and locked it.

"He likes you," Bowser said, trotting along beside her back to the kitchen.

She stopped inside the brightly lit kitchen and gave her dog a stern look. "Listen, I don't mind hallucinating, I don't even mind you tripping me up and sending me into his arms, but since you're in my imagination, you might as well say things that are reasonable. He thinks I'm crazy, he hates me, and I hate him."

"I wouldn't count on it," Bowser said.

"My imagination," Abby muttered under her breath, heading back for the cookie dough.

And Bowser said nothing at all.

Shar walked down Temple Street with Wolfie pulling on his leash as if demons were after him while she tried to concentrate on important things, like her grandmother's book. It wasn't working, not just because of the mind-blowing stone god or the fact that she'd just invited two complete strangers to watch movies at her house—*Sure, come on over, I live in the top two stories of the step temple, you're going to love it*—but because Temple Street, the street she'd walked down every day of her life, was suddenly alive with color: the brilliant yellow front of the boutique on the corner, its windows filled with red and orange gauze skirts; Bea's coffeehouse, with its peeling lavender storefront and hand-lettered CLOSED sign on the door; Casey's Hardware Store with its placards of blue and silver paint in the window—*My god, those blues*—the acid green facade of Lionel's Bar, and even the plain corner market throbbing white behind its baskets of glowing red apples and cool green peppers that seemed to deepen in color as she went by.

Those blues, those blues. She backtracked to Casey's window, pulling a resistant Wolfie with her. The strips of paint were beautiful, glowing, ultramarine and lapis, sea and sky. Her mother had left the kitchen half-painted when she'd died. Maybe . . .

"Come *on*," Wolfie barked, and absorbed by the color, Shar said absentmindedly, "Just a minute," and went inside.

Behind the counter, Mr. Casey, who'd been selling paint there since she'd been three, said, "Hello, Shar."

"I want paint," Shar said.

"Stone gray or sand beige?" he said.

"Blue," Shar said. "Blue like the night sky and—"

Mr. Casey pointed toward the paint samples on the wall, and Shar went over and began to pull out strips, the colors so bright they made her heart pound, midnight blues and amber yellows and peppery reds, while Wolfie kept pulling toward the door, growling low in his throat. By the time she was finished, her credit card had a hole in it, Mr. Casey was looking very cheerful, and she was the owner of eighteen gallons of paint to be delivered the next day.

Wolfie yanked her out the door.

She let him drag her home, still dazed by all those colors, and by the street where she lived, by houses she'd seen a million times suddenly fresh and new, and by the streaky sunset glowing down on her as it sank behind her house, sitting squarely at the end of the street. She slowed as she saw her home, staring at it as if for the first time, the top two layers her grandfather had taken from the step temple and moved down the street looking like a stone wedding cake, powerful and brooding now in the dusk. It had been home for her entire life, but now she saw it as a temple, the way it must have been thousands of years ago, and she wondered if a god-king had walked there once, spoken there once, slept there once—

Wolfie barked and jerked on his leash.

She shook her head to get rid of the god, went up the walk, and opened the front door. Wolfie ran inside ahead of her, more frantic than usual, growling and whining as he began to circle through the four square rooms on the first floor, two on each side of the big stone staircase. He ran through the wide arch into the living room on the right, then through the dining room behind it and then left into the kitchen and finally out through her mother's old bedroom and back into the hall to drop, panting, at her feet, still tense.

"Good job, Wolf, you're fierce." Shar patted him and then dropped her keys and bag on the hall table beside the phone where her answering machine had a glowing "3" on it. She sighed and pushed "play" and heard: "This is Doug Essen. I'm gonna drop that paper off at your office tomorrow—"

"It doesn't matter; Hera is still Greek," Shar said, and erased his message, feeling annoyed by his whiny baritone. The hell with undergrads who didn't study.

"Professor Summer, this is Leesa," a light voice said after the next beep. "Calling back, just like I said. The thing is, I need an extension on my extension because things have come up. You know. Life. So if that's okay, just leave me a message. Thanks."

"I don't know Life. I gave that up for research," Shar said, and erased her message, trying not to think about how not much had ever come up in her life. If that god-king had shown up during her master's work, she'd have missed her deadlines, though; she was pretty sure of that.

"Shar, this is Ray," Ray said after the next beep. "I've been thinking about what you said today—"

"Well, that's a first," Shar said, and erased his message.

"Listen to me," Wolfie whined. "Listen to me; this is bad."

"What?" Shar said absentmindedly, and then it registered—*her dog was talking to her*—and she looked down at him, stunned. *"What?"* She took a step back. "What the hell? Are you *talking* to me?"

He barked at her. It could have been, "Yep!" but it was probably just a bark.

"Wolfie?" She waited for him to say something else, but he ran into the half-painted kitchen—part stone gray, part sand beige, all boring—and began to lap up water, so she followed him in and poured herself another glass of tonic as she thought about her life: complaining students, annoying significant other, talking dog . . .

She took a drink. Her dog wasn't talking. The drink

was talking; that was what was talking. *I just have to get a grip,* she told herself, and said to Wolfie, "So how about a movie? I'm thinking something with violence tonight."

She went into the living room and sorted through the DVDs on the shelf, stopping at *Gladiator*: *A HERO WILL RISE,* the cover said, and she thought of the god on the wall.

"Maybe this one," she said to Wolfie as he came waddling out of the kitchen, and Wolfie whined, "That place, that place, it was wrong," and she dropped the DVD.

"*Wolfie?*" she said, and he panted up at her, silent again. "Okay, you have to stop doing that. You're really freaking me out."

Wolfie sighed and sat down to scratch his ear.

She sipped her drink again. It didn't taste like alcohol, but it was definitely potent. That had to be the answer: Wolfie was *not* talking to her; she was drunk.

Well, that was pathetic. Drunk and alone and watching movies and hallucinating that her dog was talking to her. If there was ever a sign that a change was needed . . .

"I have to get a new life," she told Wolfie. "So we're going back to that class on Tuesday so I can see Abby and Daisy again." *And that stone god—*

Wolfie barked, "No, it's bad there!"

Shar put her glass down with a clunk and stared at him. "Okay, just for the record, I know it's the drink talking. But why are you so upset about the auditorium? You were even getting hit on by a cute dog."

Wolfie barked, "There's nothing good there."

"Not true." She closed her eyes and remembered the strength in hooded eyes, broad shoulders, flat stomach, massive stone calves. A guy with calves like that wouldn't leave a message on an answering machine; he'd show up at the door. And there wouldn't be any damn Taser if she asked for help, either: he'd *tear apart* anything that worried her; he'd *die* for—

"Hey!" Wolfie barked.

"Do you mind?" she said to him. "I'm fantasizing here."

She looked back into the dining room where she'd spread her grandmother's research out on the table. Reams of Mesopotamian goddess research. Shar took another drink and surveyed it all. Her grandmother's work. But not hers.

"The hell with you, Sharrat," she said and then hunched a little, almost expecting a thunderbolt to hit her. Her dog was talking to her; thunderbolts from the dead would not be out of the question, especially if the dead was Grandma Sharrat.

Wolfie barked, clear as day, "It's wrong there."

So she was projecting her fears onto her dog. Except she wasn't afraid of the auditorium or Kammani or the god-king—her mind stalled there for a moment—so maybe Wolfie really was talking to her. She took another drink. Oh, well. She'd had much less interesting conversations with infinitely less interesting people. "Let's forget the movie and make it an early night."

She patted his silky head and then went through the living room, picking up her bag on the way, and then up the worn stone steps into the smaller top-floor room that had been her bedroom all her life. She put the bottle and the glass on the nightstand and took Ray's Taser box out of her bag and put it on the nightstand, too—*maybe he'll drop by and I can Taser him by accident and then tell him it's his own fault for giving me such an insensitive gift*—and then she went into the bathroom and changed into her gray flannel pajamas. When she came back, Wolfie was standing beside the bed.

"Up," he barked.

"You bet." She picked up his furry, squirmy little black-and-gray body and put him on the bed, and he nosed under the duvet. Then she got into bed, trying not to knock his teeth out with her knee. "You're a sweet baby, Wolfie."

Wolfie crawled back out from under the duvet, his big shiny brown eyes staring at her over his long black nose, his soft little upper lip quivering over his massive overbite. "Don't drink that."

He lunged for the glass, and she caught it before it fell over. "Hey, watch it." She drained the glass as she caressed his smooth little head, thinking, *Why can't men be this wonderful?* Not the overbite, but the steady, uncomplicated, loyal love and devotion?

Wolfie put his paws on her chest and touched her nose with his. "Don't drink. It's bad."

"It's gone." She turned her glass upside down, drowsy now. "See?" His brown eyes were so anxious and his little face was so tense that she stroked his head and added sleepily, "It's okay, Wolf. I won't drink any more."

Wolfie relaxed and licked her cheek. "Good girl. Sweet baby. Love you forever."

"Love you forever, too." Shar turned out the light and snuggled down under the covers, her head spinning as Wolfie burrowed under the duvet to curl up beside her. She slipped into sleep, images racing by in fast forward: pale, thin Abby gathering up huge, sweet Bowser in her arms; organized Daisy spinning with frantic Bailey; fierce little Wolfie, pacing back and forth on the bed like a black-and-gray lion, muttering, "Bad, bad"; Kammani, raising her arms at the altar, Bikka and Umma dancing by her side . . .

"Wake up!" Wolfie barked.

" 's okay," she murmured to him in her dreams.

"No, *it's bad.*"

She tossed her head and was back in her bedroom again, but now the half-forgotten patterns painted on her ceiling and walls glowed, the big symbol carved into the wall opposite the bed hummed, and the room began to shake.

Wolfie whined.

"Shhhh," she told him, "it's a dream." She reached for the flashlight next to the bed and found the Taser box instead. *Why don't they make Tasers with flashlights?* she thought through the fog and rumble of the dream as she fumbled the box open. Then you could see who you were disabling. And maybe a bottle opener—

A blinding light whooshed up in front of her and she screamed.

A man was standing at the foot of her bed, huge and translucent, glowing silver as he stretched out his arms.

"*Run,*" Wolfie yelped, shooting out from under the covers and hitting the floor with a splat, but Shar caught her breath, looking at the man, broad and bare-chested, his eyes closed, towering above her bed as Wolfie howled, "*Get out; get out!*" from the hall.

The man opened his eyes and his form grew less transparent as he spoke in an ancient language, and Shar thought, *Oh, hell, more damn Mesopotamia,* and lunged forward and Tasered him, sending silver sparks everywhere.

FIVE

The man collapsed, and Shar looked over the foot of the bed at his glowing, unconscious body, now almost solid and covering a lot of her floor.

"Sorry," she said to him, "but I spend all my waking hours on Mesopotamia; I'm not going to dream about it, too."

"Get out!" Wolfie yelped.

"It's okay, honey," she called out. "I got him."

The man looked very real lying there almost naked as the glow around him faded. He looked good, too, broad and well-muscled. Strong. Lots of stamina.

"I've been looking for an interesting man with a little age on him," she said to his beautiful, unconscious face. "But thousands of years? No." She looked around for her significant other. "Wolfie?"

Wolfie slunk back in. "I peed."

"It's okay, honey; it's only a dream."

"On the rug." He pawed at the gray rag rug by her bed.

"It's a dream rug." She picked up the rug and went around the end of the bed, stepping over the man to get to the door that led out onto the wide deck, dropped the rug out there, and then came back and looked at the man again.

Hooded eyes, strong nose, thick curly black hair that crossed his forehead like little commas . . . She reached down to smooth the curls and then realized who he was.

"I'm dreaming about the bas-relief," she told Wolfie, whose tail was lashing now as he stood back from the god, growling. "I'm having erotic dreams about a stone wall hanging."

"No, you're not."

"You're right. This hardly qualifies as erotic. Maybe I shouldn't have Tasered him. It might have gotten interesting."

That was just bluff and she knew it—she wasn't a woman who would sleep with a guy who just showed up in her bedroom, even in a dream—so she picked Wolfie up and put him on the bed and climbed in beside him. "Tomorrow when we wake up, we'll paint the kitchen."

"No, he's *here;* we should go." Wolfie went down to the foot of the bed to look at the god on the floor.

"Leave him alone, Wolfie," she said, settling back, "he's just a dream," and as she drifted off, she heard Wolfie growling at the god.

It sounded like, "Bite you, bite you."

"No biting," she said, and then she fell asleep.

Someone was licking Abby's feet, and it tickled. Normally she didn't like to be to be tickled, but she'd been up till 3:00 A.M. going through the wondrous contents of Granny B's boxes. She'd managed a last-minute shower and fallen into bed stark naked, ending up blessed with the most amazingly erotic dreams of her entire life, and the thought of someone licking her was perfectly acceptable.

"Wakey, wakey," a familiar/unfamiliar voice said from the end of her air bed. She sat bolt upright, half-expecting to be staring into Christopher Mackenzie's deep blue eyes.

Instead she saw Bowser, his tongue hanging out, looking expectant.

She moaned, flopping back on the leaking air mattress.

It was just after six in the morning, she was exhausted, and if she had to spend another day hallucinating while trying to bake enough goodies to feed hungry mathematicians—and, she hoped, a room full of paying customers—she couldn't afford to stay in bed. She looked at Bowser. "You're not going to be talking to me today, are you?"

He didn't say anything. Of course he didn't; it had all been her imagination. She sat up again, yanking the loose sheet around her body, and rolled out of bed. She reached for her jeans, then hesitated. She needed to do a load of laundry, and Granny B's colorful clothes looked like they'd be about her size. She pulled out a turquoise skirt and a chartreuse tank top and dressed quickly, not bothering with underwear, and went to the window overlooking the narrow street. It was going to be a lovely day, with the nighttime mist just beginning to burn off in the early sun. Not a soul was moving around, except some insane jock running. . . .

Bowser had pushed his nose against the window, leaving a big wet slobber smudge. "He's back," he woofed.

Abby didn't know what annoyed her more, the fact that Bowser was still talking to her or that he was right. "Who says he's back? He's just going to run right by. . . ."

Christopher Mackenzie had paused outside the front door of the coffeehouse beneath her.

"Go away," she said under her breath.

"Me?" Bowser said, clearly offended.

"I wasn't talking to you. And I'm not going to talk to you—you're a figment of my imagination."

Bowser pushed his nose against the window again.

"He hasn't even—" The doorbell interrupted her. She threw Bowser an annoyed glance, wondering if she dared dive back into bed and ignore her unwanted visitor.

"Coward," Bowser said.

"Dogs should be seen and not heard."

She pushed open the window and leaned out. "What do you want? It was six-thirty tonight, not this morning."

Christopher . . . Professor Mackenzie looked up at her, and she suddenly remembered she wasn't wearing a bra. She smashed a restraining arm against her boobs and tried to look nonchalant.

"Come down," he said. "I'm not going to hold a conversation at the top of my lungs."

"I'm not going to hold a conversation at all. Go away." She shivered in the cool morning air.

"I have to talk to you."

"Can't it wait till later?"

"You're awake; I'm here. Why wait?"

"Ah, logic," she said. "I'll be right down."

She didn't hurry, half-hoping he would have given up by the time she made her way down the back stairs to the kitchen and through the front coffeehouse, but he was still looming over the glass door, the rising sun behind him looking like a halo.

Ha.

She unlocked the front door, then pushed it open a crack to look up at him. "Yes?" she said in her frostiest voice.

He looked uncomfortable. Well, not physically—he was dressed in an artfully torn T-shirt with the logo almost unreadable, and a pair of gym shorts that had seen better days. His hair was rumpled, his glasses were off, and he was the picture of glowing, sweating health.

"I wanted to apologize."

Oh, shit. It was so much easier to ignore how gorgeous he was when he was acting like an asshole. "For what?"

"For making such a big fuss over the cookies. You're right: I should have just ordered some from elsewhere. I was rude."

She just stared at him through the partially open door.

Bowser was behind her, trying to push past her to greet his new-found buddy, but Abby refused to move. "No problem."

"I don't suppose you have something to drink? I forgot my water."

Bowser pushed past her, shoving the door all the way open.

"Sure," she said, defeated, stepping back. "Follow me."

She didn't want him inside her kitchen, but telling him to stay put would have been rude and a waste of time. Bowser would probably clamp his big jaws around the professor's wrist and drag him in.

He stopped just inside the kitchen door, frozen in place as he looked at her. "You're wearing Bea's clothing," he said, his voice flat.

"How would you know?"

"I used to stop here every morning on my run and she'd feed me cookies." He looked around him at the counters. "Those smell amazing."

Cakes and cookies were piled everywhere in neat white boxes, tied with amber-colored ribbon. He was right—the scent of cinnamon and sugar and lemon and fresh-baked bread was almost orgasmic. She hadn't even noticed when she'd dashed through to get the door, but now, back in the kitchen, with the professor's tall presence, her senses were suddenly overwhelmed, by the scent, the sight, the feel of warmth and heat and sweetness. Granny B's bright, colorful clothes seemed to float against her skin like a subtle caress, and she looked at him, at Christopher, and wanted to rip off the remnants of his T-shirt.

He was looking equally dazed, but she had no doubt it was from the food. She turned her back on him, trying to control the sudden hunger that had surged through her, and opened the refrigerator. "You can have tap water," she said, trying to keep her voice from trembling. She wasn't going to offer him her precious stash of Diet Coke.

"The tap water in this part of Ohio tastes like industrial waste," he said, his voice rough. She gave him a look. "It'll be fine," he added hastily.

She watched him swallow, followed the long line of his throat, and she wanted to put her teeth against his neck, wanted to lick the sweat from him. She was out of her freaking mind. She took a step away, only to come up against Bowser, who was watching them both.

Christopher drained the glass, set it down on the counter, and looked at her like she was a cornered rabbit and he was a hungry fox. And then he shook his head, as if he was trying to clear it. "Maybe I should be going," he said.

Abby was way past thinking. Her nipples were tight, her stomach was knotting, and considering that she wasn't wearing any underwear, it wouldn't take her any time at all to push him on the floor and climb on top of him. What the hell was happening to her?

"Told you," Bowser said.

"What?" She turned to stare at her dog.

"I said I should probably be going," Christopher said.

Her skin was on fire, he was standing way too close, and if he was going to go, then he should just leave, not stand there talking about it while her hormones seemed ready to burst into flames. Bowser was beside her, leaning against her, practically herding her in Christopher's direction. And it would be so easy to go.

Abby swallowed. "You probably should. Look, don't worry about the damned cookies. They'll be ready on time. I have my grandmother's reputation to live up to."

He looked at her without moving, and she had the uneasy feeling that he was surveying her, sizing her up in comparison to Granny B, and she wasn't coming out any too well.

"I don't know if you can," he said. "Bea had a certain . . . air about her. She lived life to the fullest, and she wasn't afraid of anything. That was one of the things I admired about her."

"I'm not afraid of anything," Abby said, taking a small step backward.

He said nothing.

She was pretty damned sure the surge of desire was only going in one direction. Maybe Granny B's lusty spirit was haunting the clothes she'd grabbed. He looked as uncomfortable as she was. Why didn't he just leave? If he were the slightest bit sensitive, he'd know what kind of effect he was having on her, irrational as it was. Fortunately, Christopher Mackenzie seemed the epitome of insensitivity.

She needed to get rid of him. Long enough for her to take a cold shower and put all this insanity in perspective. Get out of these clothes and into something more sensible. "Don't let me keep you from your classes," she said, wondering if she could shoo him out the door without getting any closer.

"I don't teach today."

"Lucky you," she said. "I've got baking."

"I should at least sample what you've got."

She turned so he couldn't see the color flood her face. "No."

"**Give him a cookie, Abby,**" Bowser said.

"No cookies," she said.

"Another glass of water?" Christopher said.

"Hell, no," she said flatly. "I have work to do, even if you don't."

She tried to skirt past him to open the door, but Bowser got in the way, and she tripped. Christopher caught her, pulling her up tight against him, and a wave of hot longing swept over her, like nothing she'd ever felt before. She froze, staring up at him, and he was just as startled. And then his head moved down toward hers, and she closed her eyes, waiting for him to kiss her, waiting for the feel of his mouth, the taste, the desire sweeping through her—

Someone knocked on the front door of the coffeehouse, and he released her so abruptly, she almost fell as the door opened, its little bell jingling a warning. She looked past him, blinking, as a woman in a sensible gray cardigan walked in, saying, "Yoo-hoo!"

"What?" Abby said, wanting her dead right there in front of the cookie case.

"Whatever you're baking smells wonderful!" the woman said. "The aroma is all over the street. Whatever it is, I want some."

"We're not open," Abby said, not meeting Christopher's eyes. "Come back tonight at seven."

"Oh, please." The woman's plain, simple face was pleading. "Just one or two of whatever that is. Or a dozen. Whatever—"

Abby grabbed one of the boxes and shoved it in her hands. "Come back and pay for it tonight."

"Oh." The woman put her nose close to the box and sniffed. "Oh, yes, this is it." She smiled up at Abby and then saw Christopher. "Christopher! What a surprise! Did you come for the cookies, too? I didn't think you were interested in anything but math."

"Hello, Lucille," Christopher said.

Abby took Lucille by the arm and guided her firmly to the front door. "Seven o'clock tonight," she said. "It'll be ten dollars."

"And worth every penny," Lucille said, and Abby shoved her outside. "What are these called, any—"

Abby shut the door in her face and went back to Christopher.

"Did you think I was going to kiss you?" he said.

"Of course not!"

"Why did you close your eyes?"

"So I didn't have to look at you?" she suggested.

He stared at her for a long, thoughtful moment. "I'll see you at six-thirty."

He was gone before she could think of anything to say, and she heard the front door close behind him, the small bells jingling.

"I like him," Bowser said.

Abby picked up Christopher's glass and headed for the sink, and then on a strange impulse she put the glass to her own mouth, where his mouth had been.

"See you," Bowser grumbled.

Abby ignored him. Life was hard enough to begin with, further complicated by the unwelcome presence of the first man she'd ever seriously lusted after. She didn't need talking dogs to make life harder.

Bowser retreated to his cushion by the stairs in dignified silence, but his reproving glance said all that needed to be said. She pulled one of the boxes of cookies toward her, slicing through the amber ribbon with a knife. They lay in plump, perfect little rows, honey-butter cookies with suns stamped on them, and she picked one up and tossed it to the drowsing Newfoundland, who must have sensed it flying through the air. He caught it neatly, and Abby grabbed one for herself, letting her tongue savor the rich pastry. And then she took another. And another.

By 7:00 A.M., the first box was empty and Abby was back to cooking. The smells were delightful; the taste of the cookies was orgasmic.

And yet all she could think of was Christopher Mackenzie in his ratty, sexy T-shirt, with the troubled eyes and gorgeous mouth. And how close he'd come to kissing her.

Daisy pushed through the heavy wooden door of the humanities building, hung a right, and headed down the hallway toward her office, clicking on her favorite pen as she planned out her day. First order of business: get coffee. *Click.* Second order of business: get Lucille to let her take a half day. *Click.* Third, she'd get her highest priority work done and be off to the coffeehouse to help Abby get ready for the open mike.

And fourth, she would see Noah again. *Click click click.*

She felt herself flush at the thought of him, the memory of his quick humor and the feel of his body between her thighs as she rode . . .

Hoo boy, she thought, and clicked her pen again to bring herself back to business. A warm breeze blew through the hallway; some kid must have propped the emergency exit door open again. Oh, well, not her problem. She reached Suite 108, slid inside, and tried to tiptoe past Vera, the department secretary. Her success rate at getting past Vera in the morning was pathetically low, but a girl had to try. . . .

"Good morning, Daisy!" Vera said, her soft voice too sweet to ignore, so Daisy stopped and turned to face her.

"Morning, Vera. I'm just on my way to get some coffee, so—"

"Oh, we'll go with you! We were just going to get some juice!" Vera stood up and glanced down at her ancient Doberman-beagle mix, Squash, who stared back up at her with big, bored eyes. "Weren't we, girl?"

Squash lifted her head, yawned, and said, "You're the boss."

Daisy froze.

"Daisy?"

Daisy blinked and focused on Vera, who smiled brightly,

her eyes turned to beaming little slits under the pressure from her chipmunk cheeks.

"Huh?" Daisy said.

"Want to come to the kitchen with us?"

"Um." Daisy clicked her pen, staring at Squash. "Um." Her heart beat frantically in her chest as she watched the dog, who looked back at her but said nothing.

"Is something wrong?" Vera asked, her smile dimming a bit. "Are you not feeling well? Because I have some vitamins—"

"I'm fine." Daisy struggled to swallow and clicked the pen again, gaining comfort from the gesture. *Click. Normal. Click. Safe. Click, click.* "I actually need to talk to Lucille about some—"

The breeze blew through the office again, and Vera sighed. "Oh, dear. Someone must have left the window in the kitchen open again." She shook her head and started toward the kitchen.

Daisy leaned against Vera's desk, watching as Squash ambled on after Vera. Had she really just heard . . . ? *No.* That was impossible. She couldn't still be drunk; it had been twelve hours since . . .

But I could be crazy. Crazy doesn't wear off.

"Good morning, Daisy!"

Daisy started as Lucille, the humanities department chair, headed toward her, her sensible gray pumps clunk-clunking on the gray Berber carpeting popular with universities and mental institutions worldwide.

Mental institutions, Daisy thought, swallowing hard. *Oh, god.* "Hey, Lucille." She took a deep breath. "You know what? I think I'm gonna need the day—"

"No Bailey today, huh?" Lucille said, brushing what looked like cookie crumbs off her signature gray cardigan. "Such a cute dog."

Right. Lucille hadn't thought so when Bailey had tinkled his cuteness all over the ficus. "My landlady's taking care of him. Speaking of which, I need to duck out early today, personal reasons, so maybe we should prioritize my tasks. . . ." She grabbed a small yellow pad from Vera's desk and clicked her pen, feeling slightly comforted by the gesture. Work. Work would save her. No dogs talked to her when she was writing web code. She could work right up until the moment she had to go help Abby, and then she'd run back to the coffeehouse and work there. Everything was going to be just fine. She clicked the pen twice more.

Lucille frowned at her. "Are you okay? You look a little pale. Is everything—?" Lucille's eyes caught on something over Daisy's shoulder, and Daisy turned to look; Frederick St. Thomas, the new adjunct with thick glasses and an unnatural affection for elbow patches, was headed straight for them.

"Oh, hello, Frederick," Lucille said, her voice a touch higher than usual. "I didn't know you were teaching today."

"I'm not," Frederick said. "I've lost my lesson plans."

"Oh." Lucille smiled at Frederick, the flush in her cheeks deepening. "I'm sorry, I haven't seen them."

Daisy cleared her throat. "So, Lucille, my priorities? There's got to be something you need me to do. Something important and, uh, absorbing?" She clicked her pen and wrote a "1" at the top of the sheet, and as she did, the breeze blew again.

Daisy glanced through the open kitchen door. Squash rested under the table while Vera sipped her juice, both looking as innocuous as ever. Daisy relaxed. What was she so freaked out about? This whole thing was ridiculous. The dog had yawned, not talked. She watched Squash as she tried to convince herself everything was normal. *Click, click, click . . .*

"Oh, here it is!" Frederick said, touching Lucille's shoulder as he reached past her to grab a stapled printout off Vera's desk. "I must have left it here yesterday."

Lucille flushed deeper and traced her fingers over her collarbone, her eyes widening as she watched Frederick. She was acting really strange, but Daisy had her own insanity to deal with.

"I'm going to get some coffee. I'll be right back." As a punctuation on her resolve, Daisy clicked her pen.

And again the breeze blew.

Lucille moved closer to Frederick, as if she hadn't even heard Daisy. "Actually, I'm glad you're here, Frederick. I've been meaning to talk to you about . . . something. I have some amazing cookies I picked up this morning, too; you should have some. They're in my office."

Daisy stared down at the pen in her hand, then looked up as Lucille led Frederick into her office and closed the door.

Something weird was—

No. *Nothing* weird was going on. It was imagination, lack of sleep, and, in Lucille's case, possibly a hot flash. Everything could be rationalized and explained, she was sure of it . . . and she was going to start with the dog. She took a deep breath and headed into the kitchen. Time to put this thing to bed.

"Hello, Daisy! Are you going to join us after all?" Vera stirred her orange juice with a stir stick and tapped it one, two, three times on the edge of her glass before putting it gently on the table. "I have to tell you, I've just started this new powder multivitamin supplement and I feel ten years younger! You should try it." She smiled up at Daisy. "Happy body, happy mind, happy Daisy, right?"

"Hmmm." Daisy took a sip of her coffee and leaned back against the counter, trying to figure out how she might casually prove that Squash hadn't talked to her. She glanced down at the dog. "So, Squash, how are you doing today?"

The dog raised her head, but before she could speak, Vera jumped in.

"Oh, she's doing fine; thank you so much for asking. She had a little tummy trouble last night, though." Vera leaned away from the table and angled her head down at Squash, taking on the smoochy tone people get when talking to very small children. "Didn't you, sweetheart? Diarrhea all gone now, baby?" Vera raised her head and resumed her normal speech for Daisy. "Poor pumpkin, she was just squirting like a water balloon all last night. We even had to miss our obedience class, and I was so looking forward—"

"Obedience class?" Daisy asked, her shoulder muscles tensing. "You were going to go to that? The one in the creepy step temple?"

"You mean the history department?" Vera nodded. "How did you know about— Oh, did you take Bailey?"

"Um. Yeah." *Obedience class. Talking dogs.* In Daisy's mind, loose ends started to weave together, but she couldn't quite figure out what they were weaving into.

"You have to tell me all about it." Vera leaned forward. "Was it wonderful? I bet it was wonderful. The Kammani Gula method, it just sounds fascinating. Tell me, did they give you any dog vitamins there?"

"They gave us tonic. You would have loved it." Daisy looked down at the dog again. "So, we'll see you there next time, Squash?"

Squash lifted her head, her eyes more intelligent than Vera's had ever been. Daisy looked back, feeling confident the dog would *not* speak again, because dogs couldn't talk. A few moments of solid silence from Squash were all Daisy needed, and then she could get back to—

"Looks that way," Squash barked.

"Oh, come *on*." Daisy stamped her foot.

"Oh, look at those adorable shoes!" Vera said, pointing down at Daisy's polka-dotted Keds.

"Huh?" Daisy looked down. "Oh. Yeah, I know they don't go with my suit, but I've been having shoe troubles lately." She looked back at Squash.

"Left one's coming loose," Squash barked.

Daisy looked down. The dog was right. Damn it. "Could you *stop that,* please?"

"Squash, stop that barking," Vera said. "You're making Daisy nervous. Look at her; she's pale as a sheet." Vera looked up at Daisy. "She'd never hurt a soul, Daisy; she's just the gentlest thing. I wish I knew what's gotten into her this morning."

"Me, too." Daisy placed her coffee on the table and knelt down, watching Squash as she forced her shaking hands to pull the pink ribbon laces tight.

Squash met her eye.

"You can't talk," Daisy whispered.

"What's that?" Vera asked.

Daisy straightened up slowly, her eyes on the dog, and heard the telltale one, two, three tap of a stir stick. She looked and just caught Vera pulling her hand back from Daisy's mug.

"Oh, hell, Vera," Daisy said, grabbing her cup and sniffing it, almost grateful for the distraction. "We've discussed this. Come on."

Vera blinked innocence. "What?"

"You know exactly what," Daisy said. "No dropping fiber supplements in my drinks. We shook on it." She eyed Squash, waiting for the dog to say something, but Squash just rested her head on her paws and sighed.

"I did not put a fiber supplement in your drink," Vera said.

"Then what? That vitamin powder stuff?" she said.

Vera shook her head. "I did not put the vitamin powder stuff in your drink."

Daisy sighed heavily. "I'm not going to guess all day. What'd you put in here?"

"Kava kava," Squash said.

"What the hell is kava kava?" Daisy asked, sniffing her coffee again.

Vera shot up from her seat. "It's a natural herb, for tension, Daisy, and you carry it all in your shoulders. It's in your aura. It's all crackling red right around here—" Vera wiggled her fingers near Daisy's right ear, and Daisy thought, *Back off!* and tensed her hand around her pen, clicking it. Then a strong wind blew around them in a quick mini-cyclone, sending a pile of napkins on the table flying all over the floor before dying down as quickly as it had started.

"Oh, dear," Vera said, chasing after the napkins. "That's the second time that happened just today. I wonder what's going on?"

Daisy glanced at the window.

It was shut.

Daisy tucked the pen in her jacket pocket, careful not to accidentally click it again. "Um . . . must be a faulty . . . ventilation . . . system."

"That's not i-it," Squash singsonged from under the table.

"You"—Daisy pointed a warning finger at Squash—"stay out of it."

Vera straightened and looked at Daisy, disappointment on her face. "Please don't take out your anger with me on my dog. I'm the one who violated your trust by putting kava kava in your coffee. Squash is an innocent."

"Sorry." Daisy put her mug down in the sink and turned to the two of them, her arms crossed over her middle. She couldn't deny that she was hearing the dog, but at least if she wasn't the only one . . .

"Vera, does Squash ever . . . talk . . . to you?"

Vera seemed both surprised and pleased by the question. "Well, sure. She talks to me all the time."

Daisy couldn't decide if that was comforting or not. "Okay. So . . . if Squash said something right now, would you be able to tell me what she said?"

"Absolutely."

"All right, then." Daisy glanced down at Squash. "Speak, Squash."

The old dog's eyes lit up, and she barked, "I'd kill for a Snausage."

Vera beamed with pride, turned to Daisy, and said, "She says you're a very forgiving person."

Daisy swallowed and leaned back against the counter. "I think I'm going to throw up."

"Oh!" Vera snapped her fingers and pivoted to her bag. "I have just the—"

But before she could finish, Daisy was out of the kitchen. *I'm not drunk.* Walking through the office. *I'm not crazy.* Grabbing her purse. *Okay, maybe I'm a little crazy.* Going to see Lucille—

Lucille's door was closed, and Daisy rapped on it twice. "Lucille?"

There was a shuffle inside, and then Lucille and Frederick came out, both flushed.

Oh, that is not helping, Daisy thought.

"Well, I'm just going to—," Frederick said.

"Yes, of course," Lucille said, patting her mussed hair as she watched Frederick walk away.

"My personal day needs to start now," Daisy said, trying to keep the wobble out of her voice.

"Fine, fine," Lucille said, and retreated back into her office, a smile on her face.

Daisy decided not to look that particular gift horse in the mouth and pushed out of the front door of her office, hurrying down the hallway to the exit. When she got outside, the sunlight hit her square in the face, and she took a few uneasy steps as her eyes adjusted.

"Hey!" something barked at her feet, and Daisy looked down to see a little pug trailing behind her owner, a goth chick with blue streaks in her hair.

"Watch your step!" the pug barked.

"Stop that barking, Petunia," the goth girl said, and shot a smile at Daisy. "Sorry. She gets excited sometimes."

"It's okay," Daisy said, her knees wobbling a bit as she moved in the direction of home. Home and Abby. Maybe Abby would give her a cookie. . . .

She stopped where she was. *Abby.* Abby had drunk the temple tonic. And so had Shar. If they were having hallucinations, too, then Daisy wasn't crazy, she was drugged, and drugged beat crazy by a country mile. Daisy started toward the coffeehouse where she hoped Abby would be waiting for her with a plate of warm cookies. Then they would call Shar and they'd all share their weird delusions and laugh at themselves for getting so freaked out over something that was really no more than a bad acid trip.

Because that's all this was.

She was almost sure of it.

Shar woke up late as the sun beamed into her bedroom. Everything looked *more* somehow—the carved symbol on the wall across from her bed looked deeper, the gray stone warmer, the ancient painted patterns on the ceiling and walls sharper, and as she sat up, for the first time she felt the slide of her soft, worn Egyptian cotton sheets under her body, really felt them, and thought, *Lovely*. She got dressed, telling a still-fretful Wolfie, "See? Everything is fine," and went downstairs with him padding behind her, thinking about those bright skirts in the window of the boutique. *I'm tired of gray and brown,* she thought as she walked into the dining room, heading for the archway into the kitchen. *I need—*

The god-king was sitting at her table eating a muffin and reading her grandmother's research.

Wolfie snarled, "*Die, you bastard!*" and launched himself at the intruder, and Shar screamed, "*No!*" and grabbed for him as he sank his teeth into the god's ankle.

SIX

"Sit," the god said, and took another bite out of his muffin.

Wolfie sat on command, his teeth still in the god, and Shar fell to her knees beside him, shielding him from above. *"Don't hurt him!"*

"I would not hurt him. He is protecting you." The god nodded at Wolfie, who was still snarling, chewing on his ankle. "Good dog." Then he smiled at her.

Shar looked up into deep, dark hooded eyes, hundreds, thousands of years old, staring down at her, fixing her in place, seeing into her very soul, and thought, *Oh my god.* He'd looked good last night Tasered on her bedroom floor, but in the morning, in the sunlight, he was divine.

"Sharrat," he said, and she realized her mouth was open.

She shut it and looked down at Wolfie, sitting and snarling, his teeth still buried in the ankle. "Wolfie, let go!"

Wolfie let go. "Lemme bite him; lemme bite him again."

"You're not allowed to bite," she said, and then stopped when she saw there wasn't a mark on the god's, no, the *man's* ankle; he wasn't a god, that was ridiculous, he was beautiful, but he was *not* a god. She looked up at him. "You're not bleeding. *How is that possible?*"

"I'm a god." He took another bite out of the muffin he was holding.

He even ate muffins like a god.

Shar realized she was hyperventilating. *Be calm; be sensible.* She took a slow, deep, calming breath and looked at him again. He looked like the bas-relief, massive body, jutting jaw, and those eyes, but he was wearing jeans and a red flannel shirt and sitting in her kitchen in the sun, eating a muffin and reading her grandmother's manuscript, which he had spread out in front of him on the table like the morning paper. She knew he was only a man, but he *looked* like a god. Like a thunderbolt disguised as a lumberjack.

Okay, he's real, he's beautiful, he's in my kitchen, but he is not *a god.* There was an explanation; there was always an explanation if you took your time and looked hard enough. Usually in a footnote. But in the meantime, he was a complete stranger who was sitting at her dining room table, and she had to get him out of her house. After all, he could be insane. There was a lot of that going around.

"You have to leave," she said, trying to sound calm and forceful. When he looked at her blankly, she thought, *Right, like that was going to work,* and stood up, her knees unsteady, and went over to the phone to dial 911. A strange man in her kitchen, you bet your ass she was dialing—

The phone shook in her hand as she picked it up, and Wolfie growled, "Lemme bite him, lemme, lemme," and that was the last straw.

"You are *not talking;* you're a *dog,*" Shar said, her voice cracking, and when Wolfie shrank back, she added hastily, "Nothing personal, baby, you know I love you, but you're—" She stopped, suddenly understanding.

"Oh," she said, filled with relief as she put the phone down. "I'm still asleep and this is still the dream. Of course." She looked into the god's dark eyes, refusing to flinch at the hot power there. She could kick god ass in a dream; *anybody* could kick god ass in a dream. It was her *freaking dream.* "Hi, I'm Shar. And you are?"

"SAMU-LA-EL," he said, with the echo of thunder in his voice, and she stared at him unafraid now and saw again that he was beautiful in the sunlight, his dark hair crisp and curled, his skin bronzed and healthy, and his body straight and proud. . . .

I am damn *good at dreaming,* Shar thought. "So, Samu, what are you doing here? Got a message for me? Because the symbolism of this is escaping me." *Aside from the* huge *wish fulfillment.*

"I AM SAMU-LA-EL—"

"We did that part."

"—RETURNED FOR THE SACRIFICE."

"Yeah, I saw your stone poster in the auditorium last night." Shar pulled out a chair and sat down at the table. "So you came back to die for the crops? Here's some good news: we don't do that anymore." She leaned closer to him. "The whole sacrifice thing? Outlawed. So—"

"OUTLAWED?" he said, and Shar pulled back, her heart pounding. *Dream, it's a dream.* She watched him, his hands planted flat on the table before him. Even his forearms were gorgeous. He could probably lift—

The god shook his head, said, "No," and picked up his muffin again. "These are very good."

"Look," Shar said, breathing again. "I don't believe you're a god."

"He's a god," Wolfie said.

She looked down at him. "I don't believe you're talking to me."

"He's talking to you," Samu said.

"Like I'm going to let the two of you vouch for each other," Shar said, and then realized she was asking for credentials in a dream. She glared at Samu. He wasn't that damn beautiful. "What are you doing in my dream? What do you want? And where did you get that awful shirt?"

"Kammani called me and I rose." Samu took a bite of muffin and then looked at her kindly. "This is not a dream."

"Kammani," Shar said. Great. She had two wingnuts in her REM cycle. "Okay, for the sake of argument, let's say Kammani called you. Shouldn't you be . . . elsewhere? Like Mesopotamia?"

"Hungry," Wolfie said, and Samu fed the last of his muffin to him.

"I do not know what Mesopotamia is. I am here because I rose in the room of the sun, as always. The room in the temple that holds my heart."

Shar froze. "Tell me that's a metaphor."

Somebody knocked on her front door as Samu said, "I am whole again now."

Shar held on to the table. "I've been sleeping *with your heart in my bedroom???" What the hell kind of dream is this???*

The knocking got louder.

"My heart is always with my people, Sharrat."

He smiled at her, and she lost track of time and space for a moment as her world swung around and then clicked into place.

The knocking picked up speed.

"Let me get that," Shar said, pushing herself out of her chair. *This is a dream, a dream, just a dream.*

But god, what a god.

She heard her front door open and Ray call, "Shar?"

"Oh, *hell.*" Shar headed for the living room. Samu started to say something, and she said over her shoulder as she headed for the dining room, "You stay here while I get rid of him. That man does not belong in my dreams."

She went through the dining room and into the living room and found Ray unplugging her small flat-screen TV.

"Hey," Shar said. "What are you doing?"

"There you are." Ray picked up the TV as he gave her one of his goofy grins. "Sorry to barge in, I thought you weren't home."

"I'm home," Shar said. "What are you doing with my TV?"

"I left a message on your machine that I'd be picking it up," Ray said. "After all, I bought it and you broke up with me. The only things you ever watch on it are those dumb movies—" He looked beyond her and straightened. "Who's that?"

Shar didn't bother to turn around. "That's Samu—just put the TV back, Ray."

"Sam who?" Ray looked at her like a wounded puppy. "You're dating someone else already?"

"Dumb ass," Wolfie growled, coming to sit at her feet.

"Why is that dog growling at me?" Ray said.

Wolfie sneered up at him. "Bite him."

"No biting," Shar said.

"He bites?" Ray said. "You never told me he bites."

"Do as Sharrat says or I will smite you, son of a dog," Samu said to Ray.

"Excuse me?" Wolfie said.

Shar looked at the god. "Look, it's 'Shar,' okay? Sharrat was my grandmother, I'm *Shar*."

Ray stepped closer. "Smite me? I'd like to see you try."

"So would I," Shar said. "I'm bitter about that Taser."

Ray looked at her, stunned. "You said you were afraid to be alone in the house, I got you a Taser. What's wrong with you? You're a sensible woman. Why are you acting like this?"

"I'm not acting," Shar said. "This is the real me. In a dream, of course, but it feels real."

"What dream?" Ray said.

"Go," Samu said to Ray.

Ray scowled at Samu. "Who do you think you are?"

"He thinks he's a god," Shar said. "Hence the smiting. Put my TV down first."

"Shar, you know it's not yours," Ray said, keeping an eye on Samu. "I just kept it here because my apartment is small and your place . . ." He looked around the ex-temple. "Isn't. Come on, Shar." He smiled at her, keeping an eye on Sam.

The thing was, if she hadn't been dreaming, she'd probably have let him have it. He had paid for it. She could buy another one. The sensible thing to do would be to avoid an emotional conflict and let it go.

My ass *I'm going to let it go. That's my TV.*

"Shall I Smite him, Shar?" Samu said.

"Give me a minute here," Shar said to him, and then turned back to Ray. "Ray, put the TV down or Samu smites."

"I'm not afraid of Sam," Ray said.

"Dumb ass," Wolfie growled.

"Take the TV, Sam," Shar said, and Sam stepped forward, a mountain in motion, and took the TV from Ray with one hand.

Love it, Shar thought. *Lovin' the god.*

"Hey." Ray grabbed for it.

Sam pointed a finger at him and a small burn mark appeared between Ray's eyes.

Ray screamed, and Wolfie barked, "Do it again," and Shar took the TV and put it on the table so it wouldn't get broken. This was her best dream *ever*.

The doorbell rang and Ray backed up to answer it, angrily rubbing his forehead.

Mr. Casey said, "Morning, Shar," and began to bring in her paint. Eighteen gallons of it.

"What the hell did you do to me?" Ray said to Sam.

Shar waited for Mr. Casey to turn into Winston

Churchill or the Michelin Man, but the sun shone through the open door and Mr. Casey was just Mr. Casey, smiling and waving his thanks for a massive paint purchase and then leaving, and Ray was looking very real and really mad, and she thought, *This doesn't feel like a dream.*

She looked down at Wolfie. "Not a dream?"

"Nope."

"Oh, hell," Shar said, and faced reality.

It was bent.

"I want to know what's going on here," Ray said as Shar sat down hard on her couch.

"So do I," Shar said, looking at Sam with new eyes. *Hell, he's a god.* "Leave, Ray."

"The TV—"

"Go," Samu said, and it sounded like thunder, and Ray turned and went.

"We need to talk," Shar said to Sam.

"Let us speak over muffins," Sam said, and walked back into the dining room.

"Oh, let's," Shar said, and followed him. He kept going into the kitchen, and she followed him to sit down at her table.

She put her head in her hands and said to Wolfie, "There's a god in my kitchen."

"I like him," Wolfie said.

"Last night you didn't," Shar said bitterly.

Sam came back with the bag of muffins, and Wolfie sniffed his pant leg. "No, he's good," he said, and sat down next to Sam.

Sam picked up his muffin again.

"So . . . ," Shar said, regrouping. "Uh . . . You're a god." She looked at him warily. Had she said anything that might annoy him? "What are you doing here?"

"I must find Kammani," Sam said.

"Kammani," Shar said, and thought of the maniacal glitter in that woman's eyes, the massive sense of entitlement, the sweeping assumption that everyone would do as she said. If she was a goddess, that explained a lot.

Of course she wasn't a goddess. Probably. Except Sam had burned a hole in Ray's forehead . . .

"Do you know where Kammani dwells?" Sam said.

"Let me think for a minute," Shar said, trying to hold on to her sanity.

So something had happened last night in the auditorium that was not about dog obedience, they'd all been tricked somehow, and they'd all swallowed tonic, and then her dog had talked to her, and then a god had risen in her bedroom, and now he wanted to go to the woman who'd started the whole mess. . . .

"My head hurts," Shar said.

"You drank too much," Wolfie said, and waddled over to his water dish.

Okay, on the off chance that Sam and Kammani really were gods—there was a small explosion in Shar's brain at the thought—then their meeting would probably advance whatever plan Kammani had, so getting them together would be a very bad idea. She watched Samu as he started on another muffin. He looked sane. Maybe if she talked to him, explained that the world had changed—

He looked up and met her eyes, and her brain stalled out at all the power and confidence there. He was a god. This was not a man who would listen to reason, this was a god who did what he wanted, and anyone would let him because he was tall and dark and beautiful, and because he could burn a hole in your forehead with his finger, and because when he looked at you, it was as if he'd known you forever. . . .

She was in big trouble, no, *the world* was in big trouble, unless she figured out how to get rid of him, send him someplace else, someplace he'd like, someplace he'd fit in. . . .

"I think Kammani's in LA." Shar got up and headed for one of the bookcases in the dining room. "Let me find you my road atlas. I'm sure you'll be very popular as a hitchhiker."

"LA?"

"Hollywood." Shar pulled her road atlas out, found the pages that said *California,* tore them out, came back into the kitchen, and handed them over, trying not to look at him. There was so much of him, and it had been on her side back there in the living room, fighting for her TV, and—

He took the pages and she backed away.

"Just go out the front door and turn left and keep going until you hit the highway. A big wide road. There will be cars. Like chariots without horses. You just stick out your thumb and tell them you're heading for California." She crooked her thumb to demonstrate. "Somebody will pick you up." She took him in again in all his massive glory. "A lot of people will pick you up."

"LA is where Kammani is?" Sam said, looking at the map.

"Yes." Shar took a deep breath and then added without thinking, "You're done here."

He met her eyes, and she lost her breath again.

"If you say it, it is so. Thank you, Shar."

"You're welcome," she said faintly.

He put down his muffin, stood up, and moved through the living room, and she followed him to the front door, slowing when he stopped in the doorway, blotting out the daylight with his bulk. "MAY THE SUN SHINE ON YOU," he said, and walked out, letting the light back into the house.

"You, too!" Shar called after him, and then put her hand on the door frame to steady herself as the air in the room settled down again now that he was gone. "Okay, that was upsetting."

"I liked him," Wolfie barked, sitting with his tail wrapped around him, thumping.

"Good to know you'll sell out for a muffin." Shar looked out the door and felt bereft, which was stupid, going all breathless over a god like some divine groupie, but there had been that feeling for a moment. . . . "Anyway, he's gone, and it's a damn good thing, too."

"No," Wolfie said, but he trotted back to the kitchen calmly and Shar heard him crunch dog kibble from his bowl. Whatever danger he'd been so upset about, he was over it now.

My dog talks to me, and a god rose in my bedroom.

She shook her head. Whatever was happening, it had to be bad. Wolfie talking, that was different and strange and upsetting, but it wasn't going to lead to blood on the sun and lions whelping in the streets. Kammani behind the black curtain, though, standing in front of that altar . . .

"That was a sacrificial altar on that podium," Shar said to Wolfie. "That's an ancient horned altar in the auditorium." Before she'd realized Kammani might have been worshiped four thousand years ago, but that was just an academic fact. Now . . .

"Don't go back there," Wolfie said. "She's bad."

"That's what I'm afraid of," Shar told him, and dialed Daisy's number.

Abby was sitting on the steps that led down into the courtyard, a mug of temple tonic in one hand, when Daisy found her.

Daisy sank down on the step, looking slightly frantic. Then her eyes narrowed. "Were you crying?"

Abby sniffled. "Not really. I was looking through Granny B's stuff and I guess I started feeling . . . I don't know. Just sad that I never knew her."

Daisy reached into her compact purse and pulled out a

travel pack of Kleenex and handed it to Abby. Then she pulled out a pen, which was odd, since she didn't have any paper. Instead, she just flipped it over in her hand, examining it as she spoke.

"Why didn't you know Bea?" she asked. "She was extremely cool."

Abby sighed. "My mother and she didn't get along. My mother's the Real Estate Goddess of Escondido, and she's a very focused, practical kind of woman."

Daisy's eyes narrowed. "And there's something wrong with focused and practical?"

"It doesn't make for a particularly warm and cozy mother. I only met Granny B once, when she came to visit, but she and Amanda had some huge battle about me, and Amanda kicked her out of the house. I never saw her again. I didn't think she cared about me."

"Oh, Bea was one of the most caring people I've ever known." Daisy paused for a moment, then looked at Abby. "So, if you didn't think she cared, why are you sad you didn't know her?"

Abby tilted her face toward the late morning sun, letting it warm her. "I found things. All sorts of things. Pictures of me at Girl Scout camp. Newspaper clippings of when I won ribbons at the local horse show, the program for my high school graduation. And photos of just about every stage in my life. I don't know where she got all the stuff—I can't imagine my mother sending it." She swallowed, not wanting to cry again. "I just feel funny, knowing she was so far away and she still really cared about me. And that my mother wouldn't let me get near her, and now it's too late. I only know it had something to do with something that happened long ago. When I asked my mother, she just muttered something about 'ancient history' and she refused to say anything more."

"Sorry, sweetie," Daisy said, sounding slightly distracted.

Abby shoved her hair back from her face and looked at her. "Are you all right?"

"Me? Great. Hey, has anything odd been happening around you? Anything you can't quite explain?"

"Apart from the fact that Bowser suddenly seems to have developed the ability to speak?"

Bowser was standing in the courtyard, still and regal, and Bailey darted around his legs like a demented dervish.

"What?"

Abby looked at Daisy. "You're looking a little pale."

"Of course I'm . . . Your dog talks? And you didn't say anything until now?"

Abby shrugged. "You didn't ask."

"Fair enough," Daisy said. "How much of the tonic did you drink?"

"Why?"

"Because I drank the whole thing and I've been hearing it, too."

"You can hear Bowser talk?"

"I can hear all the dogs talk. I bet you can, too." Daisy whistled and Bailey stopped whirling and perked up his ears. "Bailey. Say something to Abby."

"Abby pretty!"

"Awww," Abby said, feeling warmed, but then she looked at Daisy. "Oh. Hey. I drank the whole thing, too."

Bowser, seeming to sense the worry in Abby's voice, immediately lifted his head and started toward her, ever vigilant, but she managed a shaky smile. "That's all right, baby. Go play with Bailey."

She heard the low rumble of conversation, but she was just as glad she was too far to hear any more. Bowser was very kind-hearted, but having Bailey leap all over him was beneath his serene dignity, and she didn't want to hear about it.

She looked at Daisy, who was staring at the ballpoint pen in her hand.

"What the hell is going on?" Abby asked.

"Your guess is as good as mine." She put her thumb on the clicky part of the pen but didn't click it. "Has anything else weird been happening with you?"

"As far as I can tell, the rest of life is entirely normal. Except . . ."

"Except?" Daisy prodded as she tucked her pen back in her purse. "What else has been happening?"

"The cookies I've been making. They're good. Better than that, they're amazing. You eat one and suddenly everything seems to fall into place." Abby remembered the look on Christopher Mackenzie's face and could feel her own flushing. "Or not. All I know is they go great with temple tonic."

"I'm thinking maybe we need to lay off the temple tonic," Daisy said.

"Do you think that's it? Bowser never seemed interested in the English language in the past. And there's some connection between Granny B and that dog class. I was searching through her boxes and found all sorts of interesting stuff. Reproduction bowls and pitchers that look like they belong to Kammani, and notebook after notebook full of recipes for some kind of punch. Do you suppose Granny B was trying to make temple tonic? And why? Kammani said she'd just arrived in town, so Granny B couldn't have known her, and yet her name was on all sorts of Granny B's papers and books."

Daisy stood up, restless. "Bea wouldn't do anything to hurt anyone. I know that. But it's weird that she knew about Kammani."

Abby looked down at the brightly colored skirt that somehow felt so right against her skin. Her hands were in her lap, devoid of jewelry, strong and capable and still slightly dusted with flour. "I wish I were like her."

"You're like her," Daisy said. "That skirt looks great on—" Her voice cut off as the muffled sound of "Istanbul (Not Constantinople)" emerged from her pocket. "Hold on a sec." She pulled out her cell phone, small and black and unadorned. A moment later she snapped it shut and rose. "That was Shar. She wants us to meet her at the temple to find out what the hell is going on."

"What temple?"

"Where the class was. I think she's right. We need to find a reasonable, rational explanation for all this." She looked at Abby, her eyes a little wild. "There's a reasonable, rational explanation."

Daisy looked very determined, so Abby just nodded. "Sure."

"Okay," Daisy said. "I'm gonna run upstairs and change and then I'm on my way. You coming?"

Abby rose as well. "Just let me get the cookies."

"Well, hey there," Daisy said as she and Bailey met Shar and Wolfie in the dank corridor outside the history department auditorium. The dogs wagged tails and sniffed each other, but Shar seemed distracted as she handed Daisy a flashlight and said, "Where's Abby?"

"She went to her car to get something. We checked and Kammani's on the roof, sunbathing with Mina, if you can believe it. You'd think Mina would burst into flames." Daisy glanced at the heavy wooden double doors that led inside. "You know, I heard the top two layers of this place are someplace else. Somebody's actually using it for a house. Can you imagine living in something so creepy?"

"Yes," Shar said, and pushed through the doors.

"Shouldn't we wait for— Okay."

Wolfie and Bailey followed Shar inside. Daisy slid in behind them, switching on her flashlight and peering into the darkness of the temple. The place was a pit.

Shar headed straight for the back wall, pushing her way through the curtain, so Daisy followed her and looked at the wall in the light of Shar's flashlight. It was carved with a bunch of stone figures and had weird etchings that looked like impressions made from chicken feet.

"What exactly are you looking for?" Daisy asked.

"Explanations." Shar moved in for a closer inspection.

"In the . . . wall?"

"I want to know what this damn wall means. I want to know what Kammani is doing with the dog class. I want to know why she gave us that tonic and what happened when we drank it. Has anything strange been happening to you?"

"Well." Daisy looked down at Bailey. "Abby and I can hear dogs talk."

"Right. Besides that." Shar frowned at the wall. "You know, this bas-relief has to be authentic. It would be too expensive to fake. Plus, I just met—"

"We can hear dogs *talk*," Daisy said again, louder, in case Shar hadn't heard. "Abby and I. You know, with words. In their barking. Words."

"I know." Shar tilted her head at the relief. "That was one of the reasons why I called you."

"*One* of the reasons?" Daisy took a deep breath, then motioned toward the wall. "What is this stuff, anyway?"

Shar pulled out her iPhone, stepped back from the wall, and snapped the first of the carvings, holding her flashlight in one hand and her phone in the other. "This is a bas-relief of the goddess Kammani Gula and her priestesses." She took a step to the right and snapped a picture of the second carving.

"Uh-huh." Daisy waited for Shar to go on, but instead she stepped to the right again and snapped another picture. "Does it say anything about talking dogs on there?"

"No." Shar took another picture. "I think they just took that for granted."

Right. Well, that was going nowhere, but Shar seemed invested, so Daisy said, "You go ahead and read the ancient wallpaper. I'm gonna find me a nice, modern invoice or something."

Shar stopped and frowned at her, looking puzzled. "An invoice for what?"

"For something illegal." Daisy walked toward the altar, shining her flashlight on the floor so she didn't trip. "Something wrong. Something from the drug dealer that sold Kammani that tonic."

"It's not drugs." Shar moved down the wall to snap another picture.

"Not drugs!" Bailey barked.

"Oh, here!" Daisy said, reaching for a slip of white paper on the floor.

"What?" Shar asked, turning to look.

"Crap. Nothing. Dunkin' Donuts receipt."

Shar was still. "And you thought it might be a receipt from a drug dealer?"

"What?" Daisy crumpled the receipt and threw it in the corner. "Drug dealers need to keep books, too."

Shar turned back to her wall. Daisy went to the center of the room and up the three shallow steps to the dais and the podium there. It was scooped out in the center, its corners sticking up, a pile of tabloids resting in the middle. *Not a podium.*

"What is this big stone . . . thing?" she called back to Shar.

"It's a horned altar."

"Of course." Daisy began to rifle through the tabloids, finding some celebrity mags, most with pictures of the latest celebribaby. *Poor Camisole,* Daisy thought. *What kind of mom names a baby after underwear?*

"Do you think maybe there's something in the ink that can be boiled down and used to make hallucinogens?" Daisy asked.

"No," Shar said.

"Yeah, that's a stretch." Daisy tossed the papers aside and found a small, beat-up laptop with black crystals glued in a skull shape on its lid. *Yes.* Daisy reached for it.

"I'm here." Abby slipped into the room, Bowser lumbering beside her like a bodyguard. She looked around and said, "I think they filmed *The Mummy* here," and then she pulled open her mammoth quilted bag and retrieved a Ziploc full of cookies. "I brought cookies."

Daisy fiddled with the release on the laptop. "Kammani can afford drugs, but she can't afford a decent computer?"

"Kammani has drugs?" Abby asked.

Daisy nodded. "I think she put hallucinogens in the tonic."

Shar spoke from the back wall, around the *zip-click* of the camera in her phone. "I don't think so. Hi, Abby." Shar took a picture of the last figure on the wall and then joined them at the altar.

Abby looked at Daisy, her eyes wide. "You think Kammani put drugs in the tonic?"

"It's a theory. I mean, dogs are talking." Daisy set the laptop down and took a cookie from the bag Abby offered her and bit into it. The flavors popped in her mouth in little sugary explosions—honey and butter and a touch of something exotic. "Oh my *god,* Abby. These are amazing."

Shar took a cookie, too. "So, has anything else interesting happened to you? Since last night? Maybe this morning?"

"No." Abby sounded wary. "Is it gonna?"

Shar sighed. "A god rose in my bedroom last night."

"Huh," Abby said. "All I got was yelled at by a math professor."

"That wasn't a euphemism," Shar said. "A god appeared out of nowhere in an explosion of light at the foot of my bed last night. Look."

She walked back to the wall and put the flashlight on a male figure next to the central goddess, and Abby followed her.

"Oooh," she said. "Who's he?"

"He's on the wall?" Daisy picked up the laptop, still fiddling with the release, and went to look, too.

"He's Samu-la-el." Shar stared at the relief. "He rose and told me he was looking for Kammani, so I sent him to LA so he couldn't find her. The point is, either Sam and Kammani are the best con artists working this side of the Euphrates, or she's really the goddess Kammani and he's really the ancient god-king Samu-la-el."

"They're real," Wolfie said from Shar's feet, and Bailey leapt up and barked, "Real!"

"So I think we better find out what they want." Shar bit into her cookie, still staring at the god.

"Yes!" Daisy said as she popped open the laptop.

"What's that?" Shar asked.

"Kammani's laptop," Daisy said, hitting the power button. "All her diabolical plans are in the recent documents file." Daisy looked at Abby. "No one ever remembers to clear out the recent documents file."

Abby bit into a cookie, and Shar angled the laptop to look at the skull and crossbones on the back.

"That's Mina's computer. She used to bring it to class."

"Well, it's here. Maybe Kammani stole it or Mina's a minion. Let's face it, she's the type." Daisy walked back to the altar and set the laptop down; it booted up to a password lock. "Crap. What do you think her password would be?"

Shar shrugged and turned back to her wall. "I don't know. GrimReaper666?"

Daisy tried it. "Nope."

"Don't worry about it." Shar took another picture of her precious wall. "The answers aren't in there."

Daisy huffed. "Look, computers are real. Goddesses are not. So, my working theory is . . . con artists."

"Sam burned a hole in somebody's forehead this morning," Shar said. "With his finger. I don't think he's a con artist."

"There's a laptop on an altar. Gods don't need technology." Daisy tapped her fingers against the stone and stared at the stupid password lock. "I'm sticking with con artists."

"Can we argue back at my place?" Abby said. "My dough is rising. Kind of like Shar's god. Also, I want out of here."

Daisy typed into the computer. *Death. Rigor mortis. Decomposition.* Nothing. "Damn it. Oooh—'damned.'" She hit the keys again; no joy. "I hate this girl."

"You have to see this." Shar moved to the beginning of the bas-relief and pointed at the first two figures. "Does this remind you of anybody?"

Daisy left the laptop and walked over, squinting at the two round, brainless-looking faces. "Looks like Gen and Bun 1.0."

Abby looked over her shoulder. "Does it say 'Ohmigod' next to them in those hieroglyph things?"

"No," Shar said. "It says 'fertility' and 'birth.' "

"So it looks like Gen and Bun, big deal—" Daisy broke off as Shar moved down the line, putting her flashlight beam on the next-larger figure, one with Abby's round eyes and generous smile.

Daisy moved in closer. "That's you, Abby."

"Abi-simti," Shar said.

"Abigail," Abby said. "But I don't go by that."

Shar moved to the fourth figure, putting the light on the face with its almond-shaped eyes and pointed chin. "Humusi. Look familiar?"

Daisy stopped chewing. This one looked a lot like her mother. And *she* looked a lot like her mother. "Oh, now that's just not playing fair," she said, and felt a chill, then looked past the central goddess and the god-king. "Who's that on the other side of Sam whosis?"

Shar moved down the wall and put the light on the next figure. "Sharrat." Her eyes locked on her stone doppelgänger. "The same name as my grandmother, so it must be a family name. I think these women are our ancestors. Four-thousand-years-ago ancestors."

Daisy's eyes caught on the last two figures. "Who are these?"

Shar moved the flashlight beam and read, " 'Iltani' and 'Munawirtum.' "

"The one on the end that looks like a bug-eyed vampire has to be Mina," Abby said. "Who's the other one?"

Daisy sighed, taking in the squinty eyes and chipmunk cheeks. "That's Vera. I work with her. She missed the class last night because her dog was sick. Don't ask." She looked at the line of faces staring at them from thousands of years ago and stepped closer to Shar, and Abby moved in as well, until the three of them were close together in the dark temple, and Daisy felt a little better.

"Okay, this is fascinating," Abby said. "Sort of. But we need to get back to the coffee shop, since I have to open up in about six hours."

Oh, yeah. The coffee shop. Open mike night. Noah.

"One sec," Daisy said, heading back to the altar. "What was Mina's stone name?"

"Munawirtum," Shar said.

Daisy typed it in; the screen flickered and opened up to the desktop. "Oh my god, guys, I—" She twirled around, the beam of her flashlight landing on the wall while Shar snapped a few last pictures, and Daisy went quiet as her ancient likeness stared back at her with hollowed, stone eyes. A powerful wash of déjà vu hit her like a hard wind, and she felt a familiarity so strong and primal that she knew she'd never be able to understand it entirely.

But it was real.

"What's that, Daisy?" Shar asked.

"Huh? Nothing." Daisy turned back to the laptop and shut it down. "Let's get out of here."

"Right behind you," Shar said, hooking Wolfie's leash to his collar.

"Hate it here," Wolfie said, and strained for the door.

Daisy grabbed Bailey's leash and then, unable to stop herself, looked behind her at the wall again. There they were—Abby, Daisy, and Shar—etched in stone thousands of years before their births.

"Why couldn't it be drugs?" Daisy muttered, and followed Abby out the door.

Kammani sat on the roof of the temple—now two stories shorter than it had been four thousand years ago; somebody was going to pay for that—in the lawn chair that Mina had brought for her, watching an assortment of college students sunbathing on blankets on the stone surface. They should have been worshiping her, but they didn't even notice she was there. They were going to pay for that, too. In fact, that alone was cause for extermination, but she needed more worshipers than she had to get enough power to blow that many people off a roof, and those who'd called her to return still hadn't shown up to greet her. She was going to have to make new converts if she was ever going to rule again. Maybe these sunbathers. Better to spare them until she knew if she needed them.

Needed them. Goddesses didn't need things; this world was all wrong. Even her priestesses Bun and Gen, practically bouncing out of their bikinis, were more interested in keeping a water dish full for Baby in her tiara and Ziggy in his camouflage bandanna than they were in providing for Kammani.

"Sun worshipers," Mina said scornfully from Kammani's feet, where she was spreading lotion on Bikka.

Kammani drew back. "Worshipers?"

Mina looked up. "It's an expression. The people laying out here, they're not really worshiping the sun. They have no understanding of true worship. *I* understand." She let go of Bikka, now gleaming and smelling of coconuts, to try to coax Umma out from under Kammani's chair.

"What are you doing?" Kammani said, feeling her temper rise. The *dogs* were getting more attention than she was.

"Sunscreen." Mina patted the stone with her hand, and Umma ignored her. "They're hairless; they'll burn out here in the sun." She looked up at Kammani. "So might you, my goddess." She held up the bottle. "It would be my honor to—"

"I am the Goddess of the Light," Kammani snapped. "I do not burn." *Touch me and die.*

"Maybe," Mina said, looking sulky. "Things changed

SEVEN

"They're worthless," Mina said, almost snarling. "Dull. *Ignorant.*"

Kammani narrowed her eyes. "What did you find out?"

Mina took a deep breath. "Abby's mother took her away when she was three and she never returned until this week." Mina lifted her chin. "She was not *faithful.*" She brightened. "Since Abby didn't grow up near the temple, maybe she doesn't have any power. And she's the last of her line. Maybe her power will come to—"

"She has power," Kammani said, remembering all that juicy, untapped virginal energy. "And Daisy?"

Mina looked sulky. "Daisy works here at the college building websites. She brought her mother's dog to the class last night. Her neighbor said her mother went to New York to see a specialist for allergies to dogs."

Kammani frowned. "Her mother is not allergic to dogs."

"She's not worthy," Mina said. "Something is wrong with the bloodline. It's *weak. I*—"

"Daisy is not allergic. Where does she live?"

"In an apartment over Abby's grandmother's coffeehouse."

Kammani nodded. "Good. The power of the Three draws them together—"

"It was the cheap rent," Mina said.

A scorch mark on the stone, Kammani thought. "Does Sharrat live far from the temple?"

"She lives *in* the temple, the top part of it," Mina said.

Kammani sat straighter. "She lives *where*?"

Mina sighed. "When her grandfather brought the temple back, he put the first three levels here at the college and rebuilt the top two levels down the street as a house because his wife wanted to live in the temple and he wouldn't sleep in a place where people were sacrificed." She sniffed. "He didn't understand, and she was weak and *allowed* him—"

Kammani silenced her with a glare. "Shar lives in the top two levels of the temple?"

"Yes. The top layer is her bedroom. Your symbol is on the wall there. They had an open house once and my mother made me go." She looked up at Kammani. "Is that important?"

"*Yes,*" Kammani said, wishing she could smite somebody. It explained where the rest of her damn temple was and why Samu-la-el had not come to her in the altar room. He probably rose in the top of the temple as usual, saw Sharrat, and stayed to try his luck.

"I have your symbol painted on *my* bedroom wall," Mina said. "*I* painted it on there. Professor Summer does not know you, but *I* have waited for you since my birth."

Kammani felt . . . she searched for the word . . . sad. No, lost. No, hopeless . . . No, that wasn't it, either.

She sighed. Mina was hers and Bun and Gen would follow at her command, but it wasn't enough. Samu-la-el had risen to Sharrat, not her, and no one was flocking to her worship except the Worthams, a sizable family, but not numbering in the thousands, not in the numbers that had called her name to raise her. She needed those thousands—

Mina grabbed Umma and dragged her out from under Kammani's chair.

Umma barked, "Unhand me, insane one!" and struggled until Bikka barked, "It's good."

"*I* am your most faithful priestess," Mina said, glopping lotion on Umma.

Kammani thought again of the Three. If she had them with her . . ."None of the Three have families, children?"

"No." Mina massaged the lotion carefully into Umma's skin. "They're all only-children and they're all the last of their lines." She smiled over the dog's little head. "The Wortham line has many descendents. We are strong."

How fortunate, Kammani thought. *Many Minas.*

She had to have the Three. "What do they want? What are their hearts' dreams?"

Mina rolled her eyes. "To run a coffee shop, make websites, and teach history. They don't have dreams." The contempt was thick in her voice. "They're just . . . there." She let go of Umma, who crawled back under Kammani's chair, redolent of coconut now, too. "But I—"

"Professor Summer wants to finish her grandmother's book," Gen said from beside them, and Kammani started, surprised Gen had been listening. "It's all she talks about when she's not in class. 'This damn book,' she says." Gen patted her little fox hound. "How hard can it be to finish a book?"

"You never even finished your paper for her class," Bun said, giggling.

"That's different," Gen said, giggling, too. "I was thinking about *other things.*"

"*Guys,*" Bun said, and punched her.

"Yeah, well, I don't think Professor Summer is thinking about *guys,*" Gen said, and they both collapsed laughing.

"Why not?" Kammani said.

Bun and Gen giggled harder.

"She's old," Mina said, drawing Kammani's attention back to her. "She's almost *fifty*. The days she can serve you are numbered, but I am—"

"I am over four thousand years old," Kammani told her.

"But you are the goddess," Mina said, bowing her head. "You are eternally young."

"I am eternal," Kammani said. "Young has nothing to do with it."

Mina sat back. "So what's our plan? Because I—"

"Plan?" Kammani frowned at her. "My priestesses will return to the temple in four days and recognize their destinies, and then we will draw together the people of this world who called me to them."

"Right," Mina said. "How will the people come?"

"They called me," Kammani said, annoyed. "I am their goddess. They must come. They are born to serve me."

"Yeah, that changed," Mina said. "People don't live to serve anymore. They have free will."

Kammani frowned. "What?"

"Free will changed everything," Mina said. "People make choices now and most of them put themselves first. They are not worthy."

Free will. That made no sense. Mortals were born to serve the gods. Kammani looked around at the sun worshipers and began to feel . . . unsure. It was a new feeling for her, closely akin to the other new feeling she couldn't name. *This damn world.* "The temple. They'll come to the temple."

"How will they know?" Mina lifted her chin again, the gleam back in her eye. "If they wanted to serve you, how would they know you're here? You're going to have to reach them. You can't send out three hundred million flyers. I can—"

"How many?" Kammani said, shocked.

"Three hundred million just in this country." Mina leaned forward. "That's why television is the way to go. You can't just announce that you're the goddess and start bossing people around. But don't worry; I have a plan."

Kammani nodded, trying to process the immensity of the number as Mina leaned in even closer, avid now.

"You need something to get people's attention. Like 'Thin Thighs in Thirty Days,' or 'Make a Million Dollars at Home in Your Spare Time,' or 'Get Younger-Looking Skin.' I've been researching for the things that people are most interested in, and they'll come to hear about those things, and then when they're in, you can tell them that they must follow you."

Kammani looked at her, truly angry now. "But *they called me*. I am their goddess. *They shouldn't need to be told*."

"People don't want another religion," Mina said, with obvious patience. "And they sure as hell don't want to serve. They want to be thin; they want to be rich; they want to be young. Give them one of those, and they'll worship you forever. I can show you how to bring them in, I have researched on the Internet and found a way. I will be—"

"Is this a diet thing?" Bun said, sounding alert for the first time, and Kammani pulled back from Mina again. "Because I might come to that."

"No, you won't," Gen said. "You don't go anywhere that doesn't have French fries."

Bun giggled.

"But I will be there, so you must be present to serve me," Kammani said to them, and both girls looked at her, nodded politely, rolled their eyes at each other, and stretched out in the sun again.

Two grease spots on the stone, Kammani thought, and restrained herself with difficulty. If she kept blasting priestesses, she'd end up doing everything for herself. That would be a nightmare. But this damn free will.

Whose blasphemous idea was that? She looked down at Gen and Bun as they lay in the sun, peaceful and mindless. "YOU WILL COME TO ME WHEN I CALL YOU AND YOU WILL OBEY AND SERVE ME."

Bun looked up at Kammani, blinking as if she was unsure about what was happening. "Okay."

Gen didn't say anything—she looked as if she was trying to puzzle something out, but she didn't object.

"We don't *need them,*" Mina snapped.

"Yes, we do," Kammani said, looking at Bun, who smiled back, dumb as sand but now obedient, plus cheerful and sane, a huge improvement over Mina.

"*Not them,*" Mina hissed to Kammani. "*I* can—"

"You will come to me Tuesday at the next class," Kammani said to Bun and Gen, and then she noticed Baby panting heavily under her tiara. "Take your dogs out of the sun now."

"Yes." Bun stood up, her healthy round body practically bursting with youth and fertility. "We'll come when you call."

"We're really good at posters and stuff like that," Gen said, still looking confused but game. "We'll be your right-hand women."

"*No.*" Mina's face twisted as the girls folded their blanket to go. "*I* serve at your right hand," she said under her breath to Kammani.

"You are but one of seven," Kammani said, thinking, *And not for long if you don't stop overreaching.*

Mina drew back, stung.

"Come on, Baby." Bun walked toward the stone stairs, and the fat old poodle sighed and waddled across the roof after her. "See you tomorrow, Mina," she called back. "You can help with the posters."

Mina reached out her hand and closed it into a fist, and Baby collapsed.

Bun screamed, "*Baby!*" and Mina said, "Maybe if you concentrated on *taking care of your dog* instead of interfering—"

"*Stay,*" Kammani said to Mina, and then stood and went to the old poodle. She put her hand on Baby's chest and whispered, "RISE," in her ear and felt the little heart lurch to life again.

Baby rolled over and shook herself and then looked up at Kammani, indignant. "What the hell was that for?" she barked, a rasp in her voice as if she'd been smoking cigarettes for seventy years.

"It was a mistake," Kammani said. "Rest tonight. You will be well by morning."

"I thought she was *dead,*" Bun said, scooping Baby up in her arms.

"Just resting." Kammani watched Baby try to rub her tiara off on Bun's chest. "Take the tiara off, it's stressful for her, and keep her cool, and give her much quiet tonight."

Bun snatched the tiara from Baby's head, and Baby looked up at Kammani gratefully.

"You should have *told* me you didn't like the tiara," Bun said to Baby. "Poor Baby!"

"It's okay," Baby rasped. "You're a good girl."

"Much better without it," Kammani said, warming to Bun, who was cradling Baby and cooing to her now, clearly concerned for her dog. "She will be fine."

"Ohmigod, *thank you,*" Bun said.

"Yes," Gen said, slower, looking at Mina. "Thank you."

Kammani turned to Mina.

Mina lifted her chin, defiant.

You stupid little girl, Kammani thought.

Bun carried Baby down the steps, followed by Gen, gently tugging on her little foxhound, who said, "I'm coming, I'm *coming,*" as Gen kept an eye on Mina.

"You disobeyed me," Kammani said to Mina, putting

enough chill in her voice to drop the temperature ten degrees.

Several sunbathers shivered and began to pick up their things.

"I am Death; it is my nature to end things," Mina said, but her voice was less sure now. Probably because she'd just realized she couldn't move.

"I am Life," Kammani said, drawing closer. "And it is time you learned to respect me."

Beyond them the sunbathers had stopped moving, frozen under the same spell but unaware.

Kammani walked around Mina, and the girl's eyes darted, trying to follow her.

"I am the Goddess of All," Kammani said. "All things come from me."

"All things end with me," Mina whispered back.

"You think this is true?" Kammani stopped in front of the girl who was now completely immobilized, only her eyes alive. "Then end *me*, Munawirtum. If you are Death, END ME NOW."

She met Mina's eyes, saw the girl try, saw the death behind the irises, but it was only a cold wind, sufficient to collapse an ancient dog, freeze a houseplant. "EVEN AT THE HEIGHT OF YOUR POWER YOU COULD NOT HARM ME, MUNAWIRTUM. YOU *SERVE ME*. IF YOU DO NOT, I WILL END YOU." She met Mina's eyes and then drew a long, slow breath, drawing the air from Mina's lungs, watching Mina's eyes widen in panic as she began to suffocate. Kammani waited until she felt Mina's grasp on life loosen and then exhaled into her, releasing her body at the same time, and Mina fell to her hands and knees, sucking in air, her body arching and heaving as her fingernails scratched at the stone floor.

Mort skittered away, making frantic little panting sounds.

Kammani watched Mina. Her old priestesses would never have disobeyed her. Those were the good days, when she'd had all seven around her and none of them had been fruitcakes.

Fruitcakes? She shook her head. This world and its words.

Mina gagged, still trying to get enough oxygen to her brain.

"GET UP."

Mina climbed to her feet, her shoulders still heaving.

"WHO ARE YOU?"

Mina drew a long shuddering breath and wiped the back of her hand across her eyes. "I am . . . Mina Wortham."

Kammani nodded. "IF YOU DISOBEY ME AGAIN, I WILL SHOW YOU NO MERCY."

Mina nodded, her chest heaving.

"IF YOU OBEY ME, I WILL INCREASE YOUR POWER."

The gleam came back in Mina's eyes, dark and greedy.

Kammani walked over to Mina, and Umma came with her, pressing close as she made her voice gentle this time.

"Remember this, Mina. You serve *me.* You have no free will, you have no will at all, you are my handmaiden, my servant, my slave, and my desires are your only desires. If you cannot curb yourself, if you think of yourself before me again, I will end you and choose another from your family."

Mina looked up, anger in her eyes, and Kammani tried again.

"I AM THE GODDESS OF ALL THINGS, I BRING THIS WORLD LIFE AND I BRING THIS WORLD DEATH, AND ALL THINGS ARE AS I WISH THEM. DO YOU UNDERSTAND?"

Mina nodded.

She'd nod if I said, I bring this world a Dunkin' Donut and a Slurpee, Kammani thought, and then wondered what the hell a Dunkin' Donut and a Slurpee were.

Mina shuddered in front of her, and Kammani took pity on her.

"Mina, go home and make your plan for drawing my people to the temple. You may tell me about it tomorrow. Do not kill anything on the way."

Mina scooped up Mort and tottered for the stairs as Kammani released the rest of the students on the roof from sleep.

Mina looked back at the last minute. "I will not fail you, O Goddess, for I am your handmaiden, Death."

Several of the sunbathers looked up at that, saw it was Mina, shook their heads, and went back to basking.

When Mina was gone, Kammani looked at Umma. "My handmaiden Death is a slow learner."

"Crazy," Umma said.

Kammani nodded. "But the Worthams are the only ones who believe. Until we find the thousands who called me, it is their belief alone that makes me whole. . . ." Memories of millennia sleeping fitfully under the sand rose up before her. Never again. Even if it meant keeping Mina close, *never again*.

Bikka picked her way through the sunbathing bodies to join them, her little white muzzle dusted with orange.

"Cheetos," she said, and Kammani frowned at her.

Umma sighed and lay down on the warm stone, and Kammani settled back into her lawn chair to consider her return to power.

I need the Three, she thought, and realized that she'd never needed anything before. Wanted, yes, taken, yes, but needed . . .

She picked up her lemonade, feeling that strange new feeling again.

"I hate this world," she told Umma, and comforted herself with planning its domination.

At quarter after six, Shar surveyed the coffee-house and thought, *Kammani's probably going to eat our brains, but at least this place looks good.* The coffee shop was bigger inside than it looked from its shabby little lavender storefront, the front room going back a good thirty feet from the windows. The pastry shelves and counters were a mismatch of old wooden display cases and the linoleum was peeling up as fast as the old wallpaper was peeling down, but the big windows across the front of the store flooded the place with light now that Daisy was polishing them, and the tin ceiling was high and . . .

"I like this place," Wolfie barked.

Bailey leapt up and barked, "This place!" and Abby came out of the kitchen to see what was going on.

"I'm trying to think of a rational explanation for Kammani showing up and the dogs talking," Shar said as she bent to clean the dust off another chair seat. "So I'm thinking fraud or delusion or demonic possession. . . ." *But the bas-relief is real. And I saw Sam smite—*

The street door opened and a man came in.

Daisy zipped across the floor to stop him. "We're closed," she said, blocking him. "We open at seven."

"Something in here smells really good," he said. "Like butter cookies, only—"

"We're *closed*." Daisy shoved him out the door and locked it, and as she turned away, Shar saw a woman in a gray cardigan and tweed skirt stop to talk to the windbreaker guy, and then some guy in a jacket with elbow patches came to stand behind her, and she turned and blushed and smiled, and then a boy in a baseball cap lined up behind him, looking impatient.

"What is it with these people?" Daisy said. "What do they want?"

"I don't care." Shar put down the dust cloth she'd been using to clean the chair seats. "I want to know what Kammani wants and how she's making all of this happen. A nice, sane, non-supernatural explanation . . ." She picked up a cookie from the counter and bit into it, starving. Another bite of cookie, buttery and light and heavenly, and thought of Sam, tall and broad and bronzed and dark-eyed—

I shouldn't have sent Sam away. I want him back.

She took another bite of cookie and chewed faster, thinking of those crisp curls across his forehead, remembering the hint of equally crisp chest hair from his open collar, her imagination dropping lower. . . .

I want Sam.

Shar started to take another bite of cookie before she'd swallowed the last one and then stopped.

"What's wrong?" Daisy said. "You're not wiping chairs."

"I was all right before I ate this damn cookie." Shar put the last bite on the counter, got her laptop out of her bag, and opened it to bring up iPhoto and the pictures of the bas-relief.

"What cookie?" Daisy said, coming over. "There's a cookie in your computer?"

"I was reading the inscriptions back in the temple, and next to Abby's ancestor it said 'hunger.' "

"Dig it," Daisy said to Abby. "You're the priestess of hunger."

"Me?" Abby said, her eyes narrowed.

"Your last ancestor was." Shar absentmindedly picked up the last of her cookie. "And whenever I'm with you, I'm hungry. For something." She popped the cookie in her mouth and chewed, and Sam rose up her in mind, shirtless this time.

She glared at Abby. "Do not give me any more of those cookies."

"Okay," Abby said.

"Where's my ancestor?" Daisy said, looking closer at the computer screen.

"Right there," Shar said, trying to figure out the markings. "Yours said 'great action, chaos,' something like that."

Daisy grabbed another cookie. "Oh, that's not disturbing at all. What's yours?"

Shar pulled up the Sharrat photo. " 'Ending, finishing—' "

"What? Like death?" Daisy said, shocked.

"No, that's Mina." Shar pulled the pictures out of iPhoto and resized them to line up all seven of them on the screen. "I think each priestess represented basic attributes of human existence. Like the two teenagers, Bun and Gen. The first one's ancestor was Fertility, so she probably took care of people who wanted children. The other one—"

"Bun," Abby said. "Gen is the taller one and Bun is the rounder one."

"Bun's ancestress was Birth, so pregnant women who prayed to Kammani would go to her. Then there's our three, Hunger and Chaos and Finishing, whatever that meant, and the next one, Iltani, is Life, so sick people would go to her."

"Vera," Daisy muttered. "Hawking vitamins since the dawn of time."

"And the dying, god help them, went through Mina's predecessor."

"Always go to the expert," Abby said, and took a cookie.

Shar nodded. "I think this is why Kammani called us all to the dog obedience class; she wants priestesses again—"

Somebody knocked on the door, and Abby looked up, frowning at the line outside, which had grown considerably since Shar had last looked. Abby picked up the plate of cookies and headed for the door.

"So we just say no," Daisy said.

Shar looked at her, exasperated. "I don't think it's going to be that easy. She's already changing us. Can you tell me that nothing weird has happened in your life in the last twenty-four hours?"

"Aside from the talking dogs?" Daisy asked. "Does a magic clicky pen count?"

Shar raised her eyebrows. "A what?"

"Hang on," Daisy said, and went to get her purse.

At the door, Abby was passing out cookies to the crowd, saying, "*One,* you get one, and you go away and tell everybody in town how good they are, and then you come back when we open in an hour and buy a lot more. Go away now."

Daisy came back with a red pen that said: *Summerville College—Magic Happens Here* and clicked it.

Nothing happened.

Daisy clicked it a few more times.

Abby came in from the outside and put the empty plate on the counter. "What is she doing?"

"Clicking her magic pen," Shar said.

"Why does that sound dirty?" Abby asked.

"The clicky-pen thing might have been my imagination." Daisy sat down at the table by the counter, got out her notepad, and clicked her pen again. "Let's focus on the facts. What does Kammani want from us? You said we're Hunger, Chaos, and Finishing." She wrote that down and then looked at it, tilting her head. "You know, that could also be Lust, Sex, and Orgasm. So we're . . . what? Ancient sex counselors? Abby in charge of lust, helping people with foreplay, and me sex, doing the mechanics, and you . . ." She grinned at Shar. "You'd be telling people how to come."

"That can't be right." Shar sat down beside her.

"There's a pattern." Daisy pointed at Abby behind the counter. "Abby just started baking and people are clawing at the door because they're hungry for her work. I met Noah, things got chaotic and he gave me a piggyback ride, and . . ." Her voice trailed off and they watched her for a moment as she clicked her pen. "Never mind." She leaned over the table to Shar. "So tell me about this god that rose in your bedroom, Shar. Did he . . . finish you?"

"No," Shar said. "I've never had an orgasm."

"Well, that sucks," Daisy said.

Shar shook her head. "I think it's got something to do with this whole Kammani thing. Abby's underweight, not eating, you're trying to control Bailey, control chaos, and I don't . . . finish. That can't be a coincidence."

"So you've *never*? Ever tried a—" Daisy held up her pen and clicked it fast, several times. A small breeze blew through the room.

"Yes." Shar pulled Daisy's hand down. "The ones with four D batteries and the ones that plug in and the ones from Japan with the rabbit ears. No joy. Ever tried chaos?"

Daisy drew back. "Are we talking euphemistically? Because, yes, I've had sex. Everyone's had sex."

"I haven't," Abby said.

Daisy turned to her, stunned, and Abby said, "I've just never wanted to," but Shar's eye was caught by movement outside the window. The woman in the frumpy gray sweater and the man in the sport coat with leather patches were staring intently at each other, cookies in hands; a man in a business suit was pulling at his tie as if it was strangling him; and a boy in a football jersey was standing too close to the boy in the baseball cap, glaring down at him.

"*Never?*" Daisy said, and clicked her pen again, and Elbow-Patches Guy grabbed Gray Cardigan and planted a kiss on her just as the businessman tugged his tie open and the football jersey boy pushed the kid in the baseball cap.

"*Daisy, stop that,*" Shar said, standing up.

Daisy looked around, clicking her pen. "What?"

The boy in the baseball cap hit the kid in the football jersey as the businessman ripped off his tie and Elbow Patches plastered Gray Cardigan up against the window.

"*Give me that pen!*" Shar grabbed for it, but it was too late; chaos erupted outside, sweeping down the line, people tearing clothes off as if they'd been dying to do it for years, people bursting into song, people breaking into arguments, people sweeping other people into lip-locks as the wind whipped around them—

"What the hell?" Daisy said as Wolfie came running out of the back room.

"What?" he barked.

"Kammani." Shar watched as the people in line acted on their desires. "She's reawakened some genetic memory in the two of you, and now Abby and her cookies make people realize what they want, what they're hungry for, and you and your pen make them act to get it."

"I didn't do that," Abby said. "I have no clicky pen."

"You have *cookies,*" Shar said as Wolfie barked on. "And now I have to finish this. Except I don't know *how.*"

"No, it's okay; you don't have to. Look." Abby pointed out the window.

"What?" Shar said, and then she saw the two boys who'd been fighting, bruised and bleeding but no longer swinging, looking up into the face of the god who held them apart by their necks, his black hair like little commas across his furrowed forehead, his hooded eyes dark with displeasure.

Oh, Shar thought.

He spoke and the rest of the crowd melted back into line.

I bet he's using his god voice, Shar thought as Wolfie barked, "Sam's here!"

Sam looked through the store window and saw Shar, all that power looking right into her, and her heart stopped, and she thought, *That's a god,* and gave up pretending she didn't believe and, much worse, that she didn't care.

Sam dropped the boys and headed for the door, and Shar remembered that she'd eaten Abby's cookies. Several of them. She looked at Daisy. "You click that pen, I'll break your arm."

Daisy put the pen in her back pocket.

Sam came in, scooping up Wolfie, and Shar told herself that he was just a god, nothing to get excited about, as her heart pounded and her breath went.

"Thanks a lot for breaking up that fight," Abby said to him. "Want a cookie?"

"*No,*" Shar said, and turned to Sam. "This is Daisy and Abby. They're my friends." She turned to Daisy and Abby. "This is Sam. He's a god."

Abby looked at her. "Your luck's about to change, Shar."

"Oh, *funny,*" Shar said as Sam put an ecstatic Wolfie back on the floor. "So. You're back."

"Kammani is here, in this town," he said to her sternly. He looked great stern.

"Yes, she is," Shar said. "But until I know what you're up to, I'm not helping you find her." *So there.*

He looked down at her, exasperated, and for the first time, he looked human. "If Kammani is here, she was called back by the people."

"I sincerely doubt that," Shar said.

"It is not your place to decide. She has called me to

lead them, and she called you, all of you, her priestesses, to serve her. We must obey."

"Serve her?" Daisy said. "Back up there, god guy. I don't serve anybody."

"You have no choice," Sam said, looking sterner by the moment. "You are called."

Shar looked at Daisy and Abby. Daisy looked back, shaking her head, and Abby's eyes were narrow with anger.

"I'm not a dog," Daisy said. "Nobody *calls* me, okay?"

"Well, I'm not answering," Abby said, and stalked back into the kitchen.

"Now you've upset Abby," Daisy said. "*Called*. Please. Haven't you heard of free will?"

"No," Shar said. "He hasn't. It wasn't something the Mesopotamians went in for."

"Mesopotamians?" Sam said.

"We need to talk," Shar said, and dragged him off to a table in the corner.

Abby stomped around the kitchen, thoroughly annoyed. Just her luck. She'd found out she was descended from a Mesopotamian priestess and instead of it being cool, she was supposed to wait on Kammani, who didn't strike her as the epitome of benevolence. Really, she wasn't in the mood to serve anyone at all, unless it meant wonderful food.

She looked at the tray of cookies. If eating them showed you your heart's desire, then it was worth testing. She'd been resisting them since breakfast, but she picked one up and popped it in her mouth. Waiting for her handsome prince to arrive.

Shar and Sam were still talking—their low voices carried to the back—and Abby grabbed her iPod, turning it on as loud as it could go. Right then her heart's desire was a little Otis Redding. She'd spent her life trying to avoid serving anyone—she wasn't about to start now.

It was Otis singing "Try a Little Tenderness," and there was no way she could stand still with that. She ate another cookie, and then she began to move, sliding and shuffling and wiggling her hips in the most deliciously naughty way, doing a 360 spin like James Brown, only to come smack up against Christopher Mackenzie, who was looking at her as if she'd lost her mind.

Not that she wanted to choose him over Otis, but she yanked the earphones out and stared at him. Clearly the magic cookies didn't work—they were supposed to bring her what she really wanted. "Aren't you a little early?"

"I was in the neighborhood," he said abruptly. He looked uneasy, probably because he'd caught her dancing around like a maniac. "Do you know there's practically a riot outside your door?"

"I know," she said evenly. "It's being taken care of." She jerked her head toward the pile of boxes on the counter. "There they are." *Now go,* she thought.

Before she could stop him he pulled the amber ribbon off one box, took a honey cookie, and popped it in his mouth. And then he closed his eyes as a look of pure, sensual pleasure washed over his face.

He opened his eyes and took another cookie.

"Hey, I only baked eight dozen," she protested. "Don't you think you ought to leave some for your guests?"

"I'll need more," he said abruptly. "At least another two dozen, just to be on the safe side."

"I don't have another two dozen—I've got a line of people outside, remember? Besides, you don't need cookies."

"I need cookies," he said, his voice low and oddly sensual.

She stared at him, fascinated. He looked the same, though a little more rumpled, but for some reason she wanted to jump his bones. Maybe it was the cookies after all. Because right now, if she had to choose between world peace and Christopher Mackenzie, world peace would lose.

This was crazy. All right, she accepted the fact that she had a ridiculous case of the hots for him. The question was, did it work the same way with him?

Nothing like trying a little scientific experiment. She grabbed a fresh cookie off the parchment sheet and popped it into her mouth, letting the rich flavor dance across her tongue, and suddenly she was feeling very wicked. Hungry. Wanting. Lustful. And Christopher Mackenzie was standing right there, waiting.

Hell, she was a priestess to an ancient goddess. She ought to have some privileges. "Don't you think you've had enough cookies, Christopher?" she said in a low, seductive voice.

He flushed. He looked like a little boy who'd been caught with his hand in the cookie jar. Almost literally. "I need more," he said, stubborn.

She was almost touching him. She reached up and pushed the wire-rimmed glasses off his face, so she could look into his clear blue eyes. "Why?" she whispered.

"You have a crumb on your mouth," he said, trying to sound cold, but there was just the faintest tremor in his voice.

Maybe the cookies worked on whoever was closest. Because she could *feel* the heat, the longing in his body, even as she could see his clockwork mind trying to refuse it.

"You can have it if you want." She expected he would touch her lips, take the crumb away, and the thought was deliciously enticing.

"Yes," he said. And took it with his mouth.

He didn't kiss like a math professor. He kissed her like

she was a dark chocolate and he was a sugar junkie. His mouth caught hers, his tongue stealing the lingering crumb. He tasted of honey cookies, and so did she, and the taste exploded in their mouths so that she was trembling, clinging to his arms to hold herself upright. A moment later he'd picked her up and planted her on the wooden counter, moving between her legs, kissing her with such force that she wanted to lie back on the butcher-block counter and pull him over her, wrap her legs around him, make him as crazy as he was making her. . . .

"We got any more honey cookies . . . ? Oh, hey. Doesn't matter." Daisy whirled around and was out of the kitchen in a shot, but the damage was done.

Christopher jumped away from her, knocking into the stainless-steel cart behind him, his head hitting the pots hanging overhead and making them clang like tuneless bells. He wiped his hand across his mouth, the son of a bitch, looking horrified.

"I have to go," he said.

Well, if she was his heart's desire, he was doing a damned good job resisting. "Of course you do," she said, scrambling off the counter, pulling a parchment sheet of cookies with her so that they landed on the floor.

He froze, staring at her, and for a moment he looked as if he were going to reach for her again, going to kiss her. . . .

"I can't do this," he said in a strangled voice. And then he grabbed his boxes of cookies and stormed out of the kitchen like the devil was after him.

"Sorry about that," Daisy said, poking her head back in a few moments later. "I thought you guys would come to blows before you . . ." She motioned her hand toward the counter where they'd been. "Although, if you bend your definition of 'blows' . . ."

"These cookies are defective," Abby said. "Either that

or my supposed superpowers are on the blink. I'm not interested in Professor Mackenzie."

"Good thing," Daisy said. "Because Christopher Mackenzie . . . Well. Do you know anything about him? Other than the fact that you want to jump his bones?"

"I do not!"

"He's maybe not the best boyfriend material." Daisy moved in closer, lowering her voice. "You know he's a genius, right?"

"What's wrong with being a genius? I like smart men and smart dogs."

"Smart is fine, but Christopher Mackenzie is a whole new category of smart, and I'm not sure it did him any favors socially. He's like a cross between *Good Will Hunting* and *A Beautiful Mind*. I don't know, Abby. Tell me it's none of my business, because it really isn't, but I'm just not sure he's the one you want devirginizing you."

"I'm really not interested," Abby said, almost believing it. "It was probably you messing around with your stupid pen that brought him back."

Daisy stood up straight. "No passing the buck, babe; the magic clicky pen is in my purse. So if you're done blaming me, maybe now's a good time to think about why you called him to you in the first place."

"I didn't . . ."

"Look, you're the lust goddess—if you eat the cookies, what you want is going to come for you."

"I told you, the cookies are defective. All they produce is ill-advised lust. Maybe you better card people before you sell these." She picked up the undamaged sheets of cookies and slid them onto a serving tray. "Here you go. I'll have more ready in a minute." She took a breath, pulling herself together.

"If you say so," Daisy said, heading back to the front room.

For a long, thoughtful moment Abby looked at the counter where Christopher had planted her. Not just an ordinary math professor, which was bad enough, but a certified genius. And her brain had exploded when she'd tried trigonometry. She turned to Bowser, snoozing on the overstuffed dog bed. "Don't pretend you're asleep," she said sternly. "I know you were awake the entire time."

Bowser didn't move his massive head, but he opened his dark eyes and looked at her.

"Don't deny it," she said.

"Denying nothing," he said in a sleepy voice.

"I've got a treat for you. Come here and eat these cookies off the floor. I can't waste time sweeping."

"No cookies," Bowser said. "They're wasted on me. I've been fixed."

"They're wasted on me as well. If he's my heart's desire, I'm just shit out of luck." She turned and headed out into the main room, pausing at the edge of it. It was jammed with people—the front room must have filled up while she was busy rolling around on the wooden counter with a math wizard. Maybe the cookies were a simple aphrodisiac and they worked on anyone. Which would make her regrettable moments with Christopher more understandable.

Shar was at a table in front of the cash register, in deep conversation with Sam, and Daisy stood behind the register, staring adoringly at the stage while Noah played bluesy guitar riffs. People were animated, smiling, some of them draped on each other, and Abby wanted to call out a warning. *Watch out for the Spanish fly cookies!*

She turned back to the kitchen. If this was her superpower, she could do without it. Though it did have a certain ironic twist to it—a virgin priestess inducing lust in those around her.

She was going to need some answers, and fast. But in the meantime the Anise Stars were ready, the Cinnamon

Daisies were ready to go, and she had people to feed. Answers could wait.

For the first fifteen minutes of their conversation, Shar had tried to get an explanation out of Sam that made sense, but all he knew was that Kammani had called him, as usual, and he'd risen in the room of the sun, as usual, except that now it was Shar's bedroom and the temple was in Ohio. On that part, he was as confused as she was.

"So you just do whatever she tells you?" Shar said, annoyed.

"Everyone does what the gods decree. But I am a god, also, so first I do what is best for my people."

Shar squinted at him, trying to find some clue that he was shining her on, but his face was serious, almost bland in its rough-hewn sincerity. "Your people," Shar said. "Okay, about them. They're not around anymore. I think they were in Turkey. About four thousand years ago."

Sam looked around the coffee shop as Abby opened the doors and said, "The people will come, Sharrat," and sure enough, the place began to fill up.

"For the last time, I am not Sharrat. *My grandmother* was Sharrat; she was probably descended from your Sharrat. . . ." Shar's voice trailed off as a new thought hit.

Grandma Sharrat had known a hell of a lot about Kammani Gula. Without sources.

"So, your Sharrat," Shar said uneasily. "Did she have any scars, any marks, any distinguishing—"

"A scar," Sam said, drawing his finger down the side of his face. "A knife cut from a temple invasion."

Shar felt cold. "She told me that was from a fall." *Okay, maybe it* was *from a fall. One lousy scar—*

Sam nodded, unperturbed. "And marks from lamp sputters on her hands. All the priestesses had those."

Shar thought of the shiny oval marks on the backs of her grandmother's hands, of how there were no pictures of Sharrat before 1925, of how her grandfather had said that Sharrat was the most important treasure he'd found in Turkey—

"Oh my god," Shar said as it all fell together. *"He dug her up."*

EIGHT

"Dug her up?" Sam said as Shar tried to wrap her mind around the enormity of her family history.

"My grandfather went on a dig in Turkey in 1925 and came back with a step temple and my grandmother and her six sisters." Shar put her head in her hands. "He brought everything Kammani needed back here. They weren't sisters; they were Kammani's priestesses. *My grandmother was four thousand years old.*"

"Shar?" Sam said, watching her warily.

Her mother must have known. They'd both known, her grandmother Sharrat and her mother, Sharon, but they hadn't bothered to tell her. "Goddammit," Shar said, thinking about forty-eight years of boring duty and non-stop study, and all the time this huge family secret was heaving under her. . . .

She looked at the god across from her, mad as hell. Her life might have been boring, but it had been her life and now he was screwing it up. Yes, okay, she'd wanted change, but not this, not a god in a bowling shirt. . . .

She looked at him more closely. He was wearing a vintage cream-colored bowling shirt with the name *Dick* embroidered in red over the pocket.

"Where do you get these clothes?" she said, and when he looked confused, she added, "The red flannel shirt yesterday and now this . . . Dick shirt. Where have you been going? What have you been doing?"

He looked down at the expanse of cream polyester. "Kar-en gave me the red shirt. And Lisa gave me this."

"Karen. Who's Karen?" *And who the hell is Lisa?*

"I met Kar-en walking down your road last night after I rose, and she took me to her home. She said it would be better in this world if I were clothed so that the people would recognize me as one of them."

" 'Oh, yeah, you blend,' " Shar said. "She didn't know you; she picked you up in the street; why would she . . ." Shar pulled back a little, remembering the gist of most of the myths that had gods dropping in to chat with humans. "Uh, you didn't . . . have sex with her, did you?"

"Yes," Sam said, with a lot of *of course* in his voice.

Shar closed her eyes. Karen was damn lucky the Mesopotamians didn't go in for bulls and swans. "Tell me she had condoms. No, let me explain condoms to you—"

"Kar-en explained."

"Oh, good. So was the sex her idea or yours? Because this world is different—"

"All women want to have sex with a god." Sam looked at the empty cookie plate. "Fetch me another cookie."

Shar took a deep breath. "Here's something that's different about this world: women don't fetch." He looked at her steadily, and she got up and got a cinnamon cookie out of Abby's glass display case—*not* a butter cookie—dropped it on the plate in front of him, and then sat down again. "Okay, another thing that's different: you can't just assume women will have sex with you just because you want them—"

"Hungry," Wolfie barked at their feet.

"They ask." Sam broke off a piece of cookie and gave it to Wolfie.

She regrouped. "So, this woman you spent the night with—"

"No." Sam bit into his cookie. "I did not pass the night with Kar-en."

"You had sex and left. Nice. And what did you do between earning your new wardrobe and showing up in my kitchen this morning?"

"There was a tavern."

"A bar. You spent the night in a bar?"

"No," Sam said. "There were women who said I should go with them."

"And of course you did." Shar rubbed her forehead. "Did you tell them you were a god?"

"Yes."

"And they said . . ."

" 'Prove it.' " Sam bit into the cookie again.

The Ghostbusters Theory of Dating: if somebody asks you if you're a god, say yes.

Shar considered him in the dim light. As problems went, he was huge. Not only was he planning on helping a wingnut goddess gather followers, he was also sleeping with the general populace, and when women started to look for him again—

"Sam, how many women did you sleep with last night?"

He squinted for a moment as if thinking. Or counting.

"Oh, my god." Shar went back to damage control. "Listen, when you find Kammani, you both have to remember that this is a different world from yours. You can't use people; you can't make them serve you. It's . . . immoral."

"But it's our world now," Sam said, looking perplexed again. "Kammani has been called to rule it, and we are all called to help her."

Wonderful, Shar thought. *Magic tonic and divine sex, that's how they're going to rule the world.* She looked at Sam again and realized that it wasn't a completely bad idea.

"Okay." She kept her eyes on his shirt in case he could

look into her eyes and read her mind, and then realized she was staring at the embroidered name above his pocket. "Dick?"

Sam looked down at the shirt. "Lisa gave me this. She said it was fitting."

"Oh." *Change the subject.* "So explain to me why Abby and Daisy have powers and I don't—"

"Sam!"

Shar looked up to see her grad student Leesa coming toward them, a goofy grin on her pretty face, and the other shoe dropped.

Shar glared at Sam. "*That* Leesa?"

Sam looked at Leesa as she pushed past people to get to the table. "I think so."

"Oh, for the love of god—"

Sam smiled at her.

"Not *you,*" Shar said. "Another god. *Any* other god."

Leesa arrived, beaming. "Sam!" Then she noticed Shar and lost some of her bounce. "And Professor Summer."

Sam nodded to her and then said to Shar, "I must have another cookie. I will bring you one also." He got up and walked into the kitchen, Wolfie on his heels.

Leesa watched him go. "He's not, like, your boyfriend, is he?"

Do I look like somebody who would have a god for a boyfriend?

"Because he was smiling at you," Leesa said. "Like he *knows* you. *Really well.*"

"That was in another life," Shar said. "Now about that thesis you owe me."

"Ohmigod, you were married." There was real sympathy in Leesa's voice. "It must have been terrible when he left you."

"*I left him,*" Shar said, losing her grip on reality, although she certainly would have left him, since he'd have cheated on her right and left. The bastard. "Now about *finishing your thesis . . .*"

Leesa looked past her, and Shar followed her eyes to the doorway where Sam was talking to Wolfie, looking magnificent and sweet as he conversed seriously with her dachshund. Shar turned away, hoping she didn't look as dopey as Leesa did, only to see Ray standing by the table.

"Is that Sam?" he said, staring at the doorway, too.

"What are all you people doing here?" Shar said, and then realized that the coffeehouse was now packed with people who were paying to be there. She looked around and saw Bun and Gen waving to her, Mina scowling alone in a corner, the woman in the gray cardigan with Elbow-Patches Guy—

"Everybody's here," Leesa said. "Well, anybody who's anybody." She looked at Ray, puzzled. "And some other people."

"That's *Sam,*" Ray said. "I don't understand this, Shar. You just met him. What do you even know about him?"

"A lot," Leesa said to Ray. "She was married to him."

"Married?" Ray stared down at Shar, stunned. "When were you married?"

There's a good question, Shar thought. *This is why fantasizing in front of others is a bad idea.* "Uh, when I was on that dig in Ur."

"That dig was only for six months," Ray said, suspicious now.

"Well, it was a damn good six months," Shar said, and then Sam came back and sat down at the table with Wolfie beside him.

"Wolfie wants to go out with me," Sam said, handing her a butter cookie.

"You're going to take him bar-crawling?" Shar said, appalled.

"No," Sam said. "I must find Kammani."

Shar started to say no and then realized that Sam was oing to find Kammani sooner or later anyway, so it might s well be with Wolfie. Wolf's long-term recall probably vasn't great, but he was still eyes in the other camp. And am would never let anyone hurt him.

She looked down at Wolfie. "You want to go, baby?"

"Noisy," Wolfie said, scrambling to one side as someody almost stepped on him.

"Okay, you go with Sam then." She ruffled the fur beind his ears. "Show him the way to the temple."

"Oh, for heaven's sake, Shar, you're acting like you an understand that dog," Ray said.

"She can," Sam said, looking at him as if he were an diot.

Shar sighed. "Thank you for your concern, Ray. You an go now." She turned back to Sam. "Can you bring Volfie home when you're done?"

"We will return to your temple," Sam said.

"Good," Shar said. "Because we need to talk. I still lon't understand . . ." She looked at Leesa and Ray, lisening avidly. "We need to talk."

Sam nodded. He stood and nodded again to Leesa and lay, and then he took Wolfie with him into the kitchen, the ittle dachshund looking small but raffish trotting next to im. She could almost hear Wolfie saying, *Yeah, I'm with he god, how about that?* He was so proud—

Leesa said, "Wow. He loves you."

"Well, I rescued him from a puppy mill—"

"No. *Sam.*" Leesa sighed. "He's never forgotten those ights in Ur."

"Ur?" Shar said, brought back to reality again. "Right. hose nights in Ur. I'm pretty sure he forgot them immeiately. I bet if you mentioned them to him, he'd draw a omplete blank."

"No, he cares," Leesa said. "I think he still wants you. Is he coming back here?"

"*No,*" Shar said, and when Leesa looked back at her surprised, she realized she was angry. As ridiculous as it was, she was jealous. "Go finish your thesis," she said, thinking, *I'm the priestess of finishing. Go finish something. That isn't Sam.*

Leesa blinked at her.

Abby came through the archway again and said, "Shar—," and Shar stood up, powerless as ever. "I have to go, Leesa—"

"I do, too," Leesa said, sounding confused. "I have to finish my thesis."

"Really?" Shar said, and watched her walk straight to the door, past friends who called to her to party, as if she were sleepwalking.

"Good for you," Ray said, watching Leesa go. "She shouldn't—"

"Go home, Ray," Shar said.

"I have to go now." Ray stood up. "I have papers to grade." He shook his head as if trying to clear it, then turned and left.

"I need you to run the cash register," Abby said. "Daisy's so distracted, she's overcharging people." She waited a beat and said, "Shar?"

"Sure," Shar said, staring after two people whose free will she was pretty sure she'd just violated.

Abby went back to the kitchen and Shar thought, *This isn't good,* and followed her.

Abby and Daisy were both there, but so was Sam, polishing off a last cookie.

"Look, all of this has to stop," Shar told him. "It's wrong. We have powers we don't understand and they're making people do things against their wills. So tell Kam mani that she's just going to have to make do with four priestesses, because the three of us aren't coming."

She looked to the others for backup, and Abby said, "You got that right," and Daisy nodded and said, "Damn straight."

Sam looked unimpressed. "Kammani will not relent. She needs the Three."

"Why?" Shar said, exasperated. "She'll have Fertility, Birth, Life, and Death. What does she need us for?"

"You are the most powerful," Sam said.

"Sex is more powerful than life or death?" Shar said. "I don't believe it."

"The others are mortal," Sam said patiently, as if explaining to a small child. "You are goddesses."

Abby stopped mixing batter and Daisy lost her scowl.

Shar looked at them. "We're goddesses." *My head is exploding again.*

Abby nodded. "That would explain a lot."

"I'd like to revisit my con artist theory now," Daisy said, looking a little wild.

Abby looked at her, as exasperated as Sam. "You have *a clicky pen.*"

"*Goddesses don't use clicky pens,*" Daisy said, sounding frantic.

Sam took a step back toward the door. "I must go to Kammani," he said to Shar. "I will return to your temple with Wolfie."

"Oh, good," Shar said, hearing her voice as if it were very far away, and then he was gone and she and Abby and Daisy were alone. "So. We're goddesses."

"What does that entail exactly?" Daisy said, sitting down.

The noise rose from the coffee shop and Abby said, "Right now it entails one of you running the register."

"That would be me," Shar said, and went numbly out into the coffeehouse and began to take money from people buying magic heart's-desire cookies.

I'm a goddess.

She'd wanted a change, but this was ridiculous.

"It's just not plausible," she said to a woman who wanted non-magic cookies to go.

"Cinnamon cookies aren't plausible?" the woman said.

"Ten bucks," Shar said, and took her money.

I'm a goddess, she thought, and rang up the sale.

Daisy sat on a stool by the counter, her body humming with the music as Noah jammed on a bluesy guitar riff. The rhythm ran right through her, from the base of her toes all the way up, making her feel loaded with power and potential, like a . . .

Like a goddess.

She shooed the thought away—*ridiculous*—and watched Noah, his dark hair falling over his forehead as he played, his deft fingers pulling music out of the guitar strings with practiced ease. On an ordinary day, she would have dismissed her little crush with extreme prejudice—no real job, no ambition, no 401(k)—but today was not an ordinary day. She'd skipped out on work, broken into a temple, and been told by a four-thousand-year-old Mesopotamian god-king that she was a goddess. She leaned back against the counter and let herself soak in the loveliness that was Noah; this was not a day to live within her limits.

Abby came by with a fresh tray of lust cookies and Daisy snatched one and bit into it. Damn, they were good.

Abby glanced at Noah playing, then looked back at Daisy and spoke in a low voice. "Are you sure that's what you want? Let's not forget my kitchen counter episode with the math professor."

"Good point." Daisy took two more cookies, feeling almost giddy from the recklessness. She didn't have to be reasonable, or sensible, or even rational. Not tonight. *Tonight,* she thought, watching Noah, *I get a pass.*

"Don't say I didn't warn you," Abby said, and went off, delivering goodies to customers as if she were the Goddess of Hunger. Which was, of course, patently absurd, because goddesses weren't real.

"Cookie!" Bailey hopped at Daisy's feet, the tip of his nose reaching almost to her chin as he leapt for pure joy. "Cookie!"

Daisy took one of the cookies and knelt down to give it to him, then kissed the top of his head, said, "Don't hump anyone's leg," and straightened up as he darted off to hang with Bowser in the kitchen.

The song ended and Daisy bit into another lust cookie. She didn't quite understand how the magic in the cookies worked, but as she watched Noah finish jamming with his buddy, she figured they couldn't possibly make her want him more, so she really had nothing to lose.

Noah settled on a stool by the microphone, adjusting it for his sitting height, then spoke into it: "Is this thing working?" The crowd came back with the affirmative and he nodded and said, "Let's get it going then."

Daisy leaned against the counter to watch him. Despite the overall weirdness of the day, in that moment she felt *right*, comfortable and secure, and she decided to live in that space for a while, to just be a smitten girl in a coffee shop watching a cute guy play guitar.

That she could wrap her mind around.

"Okay," Noah said. "I've got a new song, and you're the first to hear it, so . . . lucky you." The crowd gave an encouraging cheer, and Noah met Daisy's eye and smiled. "Hopefully, you'll like it. But if you don't, don't throw anything, okay? Abby's gotta clean up after you guys."

There was a light laugh from the crowd, and Noah's focus locked onto the guitar as he started to play, picking out a gentle bluesy tune, one foot tapping the floor in time to the rhythm, his fingers working the strings like—

Whoa. Daisy felt a sudden warmth come over her, and a slow breeze tickled at her bare arms. Someone must have come in the front door, but she couldn't pull her eyes off Noah, who leaned into the microphone and sang, his voice somehow soft and rough and worn, all at the same time.

"The winds of summer, they flew out from her
They curled around, pulled me down, but what the hell?
A pretty girl and a whirl of color
She was sauced; I was lost; it was just as well. . . ."

Daisy laughed. Noah's eyes met hers, and she felt a shock wave go through her, killing the laughter. She heard a woman say, "Oh!" somewhere in the coffeehouse, but Daisy had no interest in anything but Noah, his strong arms holding the guitar, his lips looking so soft as they hovered over the microphone, his voice seeming to touch her skin as he sang.

"Give it a try; there's no good reason why
But why not *gets you more, and more is better. . . ."*

"Oh, hey," Daisy said as the breeze picked up the edges of her skirt a little, as if it were Noah's hands shifting her skirt aside, running up the insides of her thighs—

"Frederick!"

Daisy released a breath and glanced over at the door, where Frederick and his elbow patches were dragging a giggling Lucille out of the coffeehouse in a flurry of napkins picked up by the breeze they'd let in. Once outside, he grabbed her and kissed her neck, throwing her up against the glass storefront.

"Yikes," Daisy said under her breath, her heart rate picking up as a feeling of joy and recklessness came over her. She noticed in the back of her mind that some napkins were still flying, even though the door had shut, but her focus was locked on Noah, who looked at her, his eyes smiling as he continued to sing.

I want you, she thought, and he sang, "If you want me, take me; don't make me wait. . . ."

Daisy got off the stool at the counter and started toward Noah, who stopped singing and put down his guitar. The sudden absence of the music was almost jarring, and Daisy caught motion in the coffeehouse out of the corner of her eye, flurries of activity and the sounds of heightened voices, napkins swirling in the air on a breeze that seemed to come out of nowhere. . . .

Oh, who cares? she thought, and moved toward Noah, but Shar grabbed her arm and whispered, "Stop clicking that damn pen!"

Daisy blinked and put her hands up. "I don't have the pen. It's upstairs. I left it up there when I went to go change."

Shar's eyes widened, Daisy turned to see two people tugging at a chair as if it were a case of money; she pulled Shar out of the way just as they lost their grip and the chair flew past them, banging against the counter and falling to the floor.

"Oh." Daisy shook her head. "I swear, Shar, I didn't—"

A girl at one of the front tables said, "Screw the diet, I *have* to have some of those cookies," and got up and rushed Abby, her two friends following her. Abby stood in the middle of it all holding her tray up above her head as the girls mobbed her, grabbing for cookies, and then the door opened again, and a fresh swirl of wind rushed through the place and there were napkins flying everywhere, people grabbing for things. . . .

"Crap," Daisy said, pointing at the melee. "I didn't . . . Did *I* do that?"

"You don't need the pen," Shar said, pulling her toward the kitchen door. "That was just how you focused it. You must have the power within you." She hustled Daisy through the French doors and into the kitchen and then out into the courtyard. "Stay here until we get this under control," she said, and went back inside, leaving Daisy alone in the brick-walled courtyard with its doghouses, stone benches, and tangled weeds.

Daisy leaned against the wall, her heart beating so hard in her chest, she thought it might explode. She breathed deep, taking in the cool night air, staring up at the stars in the sky, wondering what the hell was happening to her. This was insane. All that chaos couldn't be from her. She didn't *do* anything. All she did was get a little hot and bothered over—

Noah.

She closed her eyes and felt it again, a deep want pulsating within her, and then she imagined him there, with her, his hands on her skin and—

A wind blew, throwing the doors open again, and the chaos coming from inside got louder. Daisy pushed them fully shut, then walked over to the stone bench, sitting on its cool, hard surface, gripping her hands around the edge.

Okay. Maybe stop thinking about Noah. She closed her eyes again and took a deep breath. *Ducks. Think about ducks. Ducks aren't sexy.*

Unless they're wading in a lake where Noah and I are having a picnic on a nice, soft blanket and then he reaches over and touches my—

"Daisy?"

Daisy shifted around and there he was, standing in the doorway. His hair was sticking out on one side and his T-shirt was pulled a bit at his neckline, as though he'd had to fight someone to get out there—probably Shar—but he looked amazing, his eyes burning, his skin seeming to give off waves of heat Daisy could feel even through the space between them. They stood motionless, staring at each other, and she felt confused and conflicted and dangerous. She knew she should ask him to go until she figured out what was going on, but the plain fact of it was, she didn't want him to leave.

He closed the doors behind him, lowered his head, and took a deep breath, then looked at her again. Daisy sat where she was, gripping the cool stone, trying to keep her head. She couldn't ask him to go away, and she wouldn't be able to resist him if he touched her, but maybe if they just didn't move, maybe things wouldn't get out of hand, maybe she could control . . .

"Daisy."

His voice had less question in it this time, and she raised her eyes to his. *This doesn't happen to me,* she thought. *I don't understand this.* But she knew what she wanted, and she wanted him, more than anything she'd ever wanted in her life.

Screw understanding. I'm a goddess.

She pushed herself up from the bench. A warm breeze swirled around them, the feel of it on her skin wearing down the last of Daisy's reservations. She rushed toward him, and he met her halfway. He grabbed her, his hands on her hips, pulling her to him, his lips meeting hers with desperate force as she pushed herself against him, throwing her arms around his neck. He lifted her up with so little effort it felt almost like flying, and she wrapped her legs around his hips and let herself go, not caring about how it seemed or what it meant. She knew it was right, knew it in a place so deep inside her she couldn't name it, and it felt so good, *so good,* not to have to think or fight or *control* anything.

He brought her back to the bench, sitting down with her straddling him, his hands moving over her, running under her shirt, over her legs as the breeze picked up around them. He kissed her mouth and worked his lips down the line of her jaw, to her neck, her collarbone. . . .

I am a goddess, she thought, looking up at the stars as one of Noah's hands settled on the small of her back while the other slid over the inside of her thigh. *Oh, yeah.* She looked back down at him, her hands locked at the back of his neck, her eyes on his as he slid one long finger into her, then the next, his thumb working slowly outside, making her feel wild and reckless. She leaned against him, allowing herself to feel everything, to worry about nothing. He moved inside her, his fingers reaching deep, the pressure building. The wind blew around them, picking up pieces of mown grass and random flower petals, the cool of it hitting her hot skin and making her feel like she wasn't tiny anymore, like she had mass, like she didn't have to hold on so tightly . . .

Like she could let go.

She pulled herself up, pressing herself down over his hand as she tasted the skin on his neck. His fingers moved to their own primal rhythm, and the energy pooled within her as the wind whirled around them, smelling of cinnamon and heat and summer.

I am a goddess. She reached down and touched him, and even through his jeans she could feel that he was right where she was. She leaned forward, her entire body pulsing with need for him, and whispered in his ear, "Please tell me you have something."

He reached into his back pocket and held up a condom, and she grabbed it from him and ripped it open. He laughed, then pulled her in for another kiss, and everything else in the world seemed to fade around them. She unbuttoned his jeans and he took in his breath as she took him in her hands and slid the condom over him.

"Oh, god," he whispered, and she slid him inside of her, pushing herself against him, enjoying the low growl that came from him as she moved over him. *I am a goddess.* He pulled her to him and put his lips to her collarbone, his arms tight around her, holding her to him as they moved together, the movements starting small and building up, the heat and need twining tightly in her core as his lips and tongue moved over her skin, his hand teasing her breast until she tightened under him, around him, and the moment was here; it was hers; all she had to do was let it happen, let herself—

I am a goddess!

She opened her eyes as she came, and stars seemed to blow out in the sky, like fireworks exploding and falling down to earth. Noah called out her name, and the feel of him letting go inside of her excited her again. He held her tight as her body shuddered over him, and she allowed herself to release control, trusting him to not let her fall as she gave in. After a moment, she put her hands around his neck and kissed him with everything she had, tasting him again. Finally, she pulled back and looked at him, both of them flushed and smiling.

"Hey there," he said, his breath heavy.

"Hey yourself," she said.

"That was . . . ," he said, his eyes atypically soft as he looked at her. "I can't even think what that was."

He pulled her to him and kissed her, his hands in her hair, cupping her head, making her feel amazing and worshiped and giddy in the moment. When he pulled back, his eyes were sharp again, and the crooked smile graced his face as his eyes focused on her lips.

"Daisy," he said, his voice low as he lifted his gaze to meet hers. "Not to brag, but I think we did that *really* well."

"Yeah," she said, locking her hands at the back of his neck, "I think we did." She leaned in and kissed him. "If you want, we could sneak up the back stairs to my apartment and give it another go, see if we're as good as we think we are."

"I'm game." He reached up and plucked a blade of grass from her hair, his expression growing more serious as he looked at her. "Daisy . . . you are . . ."

A goddess, she thought. Then she got up, took his hand, and led him upstairs to her bed.

Kammani watched as Mina rolled up the last of the posters she'd had printed at something called Kinko's that afternoon, although it didn't sound like a place of printing. "My family will hang these all over town, my goddess," Mina said, putting the poster with the rest on the altar. "The posters will bring the worshipers in, and soon you will be famous, you'll be on TV, and magazines will write about you."

Kammani looked again at the magazine with the celebribaby draped in diamonds on the cover and thought, *It was a hell of a lot easier when they just came to the temple and prayed.* "Very well, we will start with this losing weight and making money," she told Mina. "But then we will bring them to the True Way of the Goddess." *My way or the highway.* That was another phrase from the air, but Kammani liked it. She wasn't sure what the highway was, but she was positive it involved plagues and curses and probably screaming in the streets. At least her highway did.

"Yeah, good luck on that," Mina said, and when Kammani frowned, she added, "O Great One. But I must tell you of the Three."

"Yes?" Kammani said, well aware Mina was changing the subject for self-preservation. That was a good sign. It meant Mina realized now when she was pushing her luck.

"They have become friends since last night at the class," Mina said.

"Good," Kammani said.

"And tonight they opened the coffee shop again. Together."

"Coffee shop?"

Mina came closer. "A place where people come to drink coffee and hear music. A kind of . . . temple."

"Temple?" Kammani said, stiffening, but then the doors to the hallway opened and Samu-la-el came in, tall and strong and beautiful, the greatest sacrifice she'd ever had.

The bastard.

"You're late," she said, and then took in how informal his clothing was, how unsubservient he was before her. *This world,* she thought. "Where have you been? It has been a day since I raised you."

"It's been four thousand years," Samu said, and Kammani straightened at the tone in his voice.

"HAVE YOU FORGOTTEN WHO I AM?"

"No," he said. "The temple is broken. I rose where I always rise. You weren't there."

"So it took you twenty-four hours to find me?" Kammani said, and then thought, *I sound like a jealous wife, not a goddess.* "AN ENTIRE DAY TO FIND ME?"

"It was a long day." Samu nodded to Mina. "Munawirtum."

Mina bowed. "Samu-la-el. I live to serve you."

Someone said, "Terrific," and Kammani frowned at Samu.

Samu pointed to the dog at his feet, and Kammani recognized Sharrat's small long-haired dachshund.

"Wolfie," she said sternly.

Wolfie edged back behind Samu, his tail between his legs, "Sorry."

"It is good you are here," Mina said to Samu, her dark eyes gleaming. "We have plans." She unrolled the poster, and Kammani saw again the portrait of a dark-haired woman who looked vaguely like her, dressed in red, holding some kind of gold snake.

"Who is that?" Samu said, frowning.

"It's a Klimt painting," Mina said. "College kids love Klimt, and they'll be our first worshipers."

Kammani read the bottom of the poster again: *Come join the goddess Kami in THE GODDESS WAY and find the Goddess Within You! Youth! Beauty! Wealth! and HAPPINESS!* And then below that in much smaller letters: *7 P.M. WEDNESDAYS AND FRIDAYS IN THE SUMMERVILLE COLLEGE HISTORY BUILDING AUDITORIUM.*

" 'Kami'?" Samu said to Mina.

"It's catchier," Mina said, rolling the poster up again. "We just need to get them in here. Then we'll go back to the old ways."

Samu frowned at Kammani. "Youth? Beauty?"

"It's a new approach to our divinity," Kammani said, seeing her own distaste reflected in his eyes. "When they come to the temple, they will learn the True Way of the Goddess."

Samu shook his head. "They will come, but they won't stay. I have been among them. It is different here."

"Which you know after one day?" Mina said, scorn in her voice.

"YES," Samu said, and Mina stepped back. "I have spent the time talking with many people," he told Kammani. "They are not like we are."

"Duh," Mina said, and from behind Samu, Wolfie said, "Don't say 'duh' to a god."

Mina glared at him, and Wolfie shrank back again, and Mort panted, *Heh, heh, heh.*

"The people will be as they were," Kammani said. "We will remind them of the way."

Samu stayed silent, but the look in his eyes told her what he thought of that, and Kammani was about to reprimand him when she realized that, even in the ridiculous clothes of this world, Samu looked very good.

"Leave us," she said to Mina.

Mina said, "But—"

"Go," Kammani said, and Mina went, taking Mort with her, the two of them looking stormy and strange as they went into the hall.

"Ha," Wolfie barked after them.

Kammani came down the steps from the altar. "It has been many nights since we were together, Samu-la-el, and my couch is still behind the hidden door." She put her hand on his chest and then noticed the embroidery over the pocket. "Dick?"

"I am very tired." Samu took her hand off his chest. "And in this world, I am Sam. Samu is not a name here." He looked at the poster again. "Kami."

"*You've been here one day,*" she snapped, wanting to obliterate him. "How do you know what—"

"A good king learns the world he will govern. I spent much time with the people of Kamesh before I became king. It made me a good king. It is smart to do the same thing in this world." He looked around the temple. "Have you even left this place? Have you gone out and talked to the people?"

The impatience in his voice made her step back. "Yes. I have talked with Miriam, granddaughter to Munawirtum. And I have drawn my priestesses to me. I need no more."

"No," Samu said with obvious patience. "Have you talked to the *people*?"

"They will come to me," Kammani said, glaring at him. "I do not—"

"And when they come to you, how will you talk to them?" Samu said. "If you don't go out among them, how can you know them?"

"I did not go out among them before," Kammani snapped.

"And you fell," Samu said. "We've been gone four thousand years."

"*That was not my fault,*" Kammani said, wishing him dead. "I tried my best, but Ishtar, *my own sister,* betrayed me and banished me to endless sleep and destroyed my temple—" She stopped, hearing the whine in her voice.

"Then how did your temple come to be here?" Samu said, his dark eyes sharp on her. "How could she vanquish you? Where was your power? *What happened to my people while I was dead?*"

Kammani rubbed her forehead. She was getting a headache. She never whined and she never got headaches; this world was changing her. . . . No. She was a goddess; she was going to change this world.

"What did you do to my people?" Samu said, thunder in his voice.

"It wasn't me. Ishtar seduced the people from me. I tried to stop her; I tried many things . . ." She remembered what some of those things were and talked faster before he could ask. ". . . but she betrayed me and sent me into the desert; she took my robes and my rings; she took my people and my *power*—"

"Here," Samu said, focused as ever. "How did we end up *here*?"

"Munawirtum told Miriam that after Ishtar imprisoned me in the sand, the Three took the priestesses into the secret room and gave them drinks so they would sleep safely until my return. But I could not return without worshipers." She sat down on the altar step. "Without worshipers . . ."

"Gods cease to exist," Samu said, sympathy in his voice now. "So why have you risen again?"

"I was *called*," Kammani said proudly. "Thousands, hundreds of thousands, millions of voices cried out my name."

"And said, 'Come to Ohio'?"

Kammani glared at him. "No, Sharrat did that. She seduced the man who opened the temple and made him bring it and the other priestesses here, to this new world, out of Ishtar's reach. Her granddaughter is the new Sharrat."

"Shar," Samu said. "She is not Sharrat. And this is not our land, and these are not our people. And you are not telling me everything."

"But she has Sharrat's fire within her," Kammani said eagerly. "You can see it in her. It's deeply buried, that passion, but she is the new Sharrat, one of the Three—"

"Yes," Samu said, "but the Three are different now. And they do not remember."

"They will." Kammani stood up. "They will remember as the people remember. The people called me, Samu-la-el, or I could not have risen. A thousand, a hundred thousand, a *million* voices called my name and I rose." She took a step toward him. "And now together, we will rule this world." She put her hand on his arm, sure of him again. "Come. I have waited long for you." She unfastened the pin at her shoulder and gestured toward the secret door as her robe fell open, and she smiled at him, knowing her body was magnificent, irresistible in the light from the torches.

"I must return to Shar's temple," Samu said, his eyes cold on hers. "I swore I would return with Wolfie."

"Don't blame me," Wolfie said from behind Sam.

Kammani grabbed her robe, suddenly feeling naked. "Are you dead to carnal pleasure?"

"I swore," Samu said. "I must go."

"*WHAT*?"

"MAY THE SUN SHINE ON YOU," Sam said, and walked out, Wolfie scrambling for the doors in front of him.

"It is different here," Umma whispered beside her.

"It's not that damn different," Kammani snapped as she pinned her robe together again. *Fucking god-kings, thought they ran the universe.*

Bikka clicked her way across the stone floor. "Cheetos?"

"No!" Kammani said. "We will follow the old ways! THINGS WILL BE AS THEY WERE!"

"Nooooo," Bikka whined as Umma sidled away.

"Professor Summer?"

Kammani looked toward the doors that Samu had left open.

A young man stood there, tall and well-muscled, brown-haired and blue-eyed, looking confused and angry and . . .

Healthy, Kammani thought.

"Professor Summer's office is locked," the man said with ill-concealed impatience. "And I gotta turn this in."

Kammani took a step closer. "You are Sharrat—Shar Summer's?"

"I'm her student," the young man said. "I need to put this paper in her office. . . ." He looked around. "What is this place?"

"Welcome," Kammani said, gliding toward him now. "This is the Temple of Kammani."

"Oh!" The young man's face cleared. "Yeah, right, my sister told me."

Kammani stopped. "Your sister?"

"Bun Essen," the young man said. "She said it was some kind of sorority. Like she needs another sorority."

He snorted and then smiled at Kammani, taking her in with open admiration that was balm to her ego. "Although if you're in the sorority, hey, I'm there."

Samu had been stupid in the beginning, too.

And four thousand years was a long time to sleep alone.

"I'm Doug," he said, frankly staring at her body now.

"Come in, Doug," she said, loosening the pin on her robe. "I have much to show you."

"Like what?" Doug said.

You try to walk out of here, I'll turn you into the dog you are, Kammani thought, and let her robe drop.

"All right," Doug said, and started toward her.

NINE

At eleven, Shar pushed the last of the revelers out the door of the coffee shop, many of them with boxes of cookies in their hands, and surveyed the damage. The place was a mess, but it was nothing they couldn't clean up in the morning, so she went into the kitchen.

"Have you seen Abby?" she said to Bowser, and he growled, "Upstairs," while Bailey mumbled in his sleep, curled next to him.

"Well, tell her I locked up," Shar said, and went out the back door, flipping the lock so it would catch behind her. The night was cool, and she rubbed her hands over her arms and then slung her bag over her shoulder and started down the alley toward home. It was pitch-dark, but it was Summerville, so she was safe—

A huge shadow loomed up in front of her and she screamed.

"It's us," Sam said.

"It's us," Wolfie said.

"Stop *doing* that," she said, and walked past Sam, her heart pounding from more than the fright. *It* lifts, *I can feel my heart lift when I see him, and it must stop doing that.*

"Stop doing what?" Sam said, falling into step beside her, a bulwark in the dark, as Wolfie pattered beside them.

"Rising up in front of me," Shar said. "Coming out of nowhere." *Different verbs, Shar, different verbs.*

He stopped walking and then Wolfie did, too, but she kept going.

"It's just *creepy,*" she said, and he said, "Shhhhh."

She turned around and he had his head up, the way Wolfie lifted his head when he was listening. She listened, too, but there was nothing except faint laughter from the street and the soft sounds of the night. "What?" she said, but he had already turned around and was going back down the alley with Wolfie at his heels, past the courtyard of Abby's coffeehouse, and she followed him until he stopped at a large closed Dumpster.

"That's it," Wolfie said to him, and Sam nodded and lifted the Dumpster lid with one hand to look inside.

"What's it?" she said to Wolfie, and Sam reached into the Dumpster and pulled out a plastic grocery bag, full of something . . . moving. Shar stepped back and Sam let the lid fall as he carefully opened the bag and reached inside.

"Help," something cried faintly, and she went closer as he pulled out a little red-brown dog with floppy ears. "Help," it said again and she reached out without thinking and took it from him, cradling it in her arms.

"It's okay," she whispered, her voice choking as she stroked the little guy. "It's okay. You're okay now."

"WHO DID THIS THING?" Sam said, and she looked up, tears in her eyes even though she was angry, too.

"Some college kid," she said. "They get puppies and kittens and when the year ends, they just leave them, sometimes at the animal shelter, and sometimes they just turn them loose. It's awful, but this . . ." She looked down at the dog in her arms, its dark little eyes imploring her in the dim light of the alley as it wept. "You are going to be just fine, now," she said, stroking him as she cuddled the puppy close. "You're safe. You're coming home with us."

"I WILL FIND WHO DID THIS," Sam said.

"No, you won't," Shar said. "Whoever it is, is gone. We have to get this little guy some food. Come on."

"Food!" the puppy cried, and Shar cooed and cuddled him all the way home while Wolfie trotted at her side, barking up, "You're okay! You're all right now!" until Shar shushed him, while Sam strode at their side, keeping watch.

At home, she put the puppy down in front of Wolfie's food dish and water bottle, and he went to town while she patted him all over, checking him out for injuries. His little ribs stuck out more than they should, but otherwise he was in good shape.

"He's a dachshund," she told Sam as the puppy gobbled so fast he choked and then gobbled again, "probably about a year old. See how his chest hasn't dropped yet? He's still growing."

"Good eater," Wolfie said, watching his food disappear.

"We have more food," Shar told him, but she pulled the puppy back after a couple of minutes, afraid he'd explode. "You can have more later," she said as she brought him back into her arms. "There's always food here. Really." She patted his back and he burped and sighed. "What's your name, little guy?"

"Milton," the puppy said.

"There's your first clue," Shar said to Sam, still patting. "His owner was probably an English major."

"Why would someone do this?" Sam said, and she looked up to see the distress on his face.

Slayer of Demons, Greatest of Kings, she thought. *Savior of Puppies*.

"Dogs aren't sacred to us," she said, holding Milton close to her. "Well, not to all of us." She looked down at Milton, his eyes half-closed now that he was stuffed to the gills. "Some of us still worship them."

Sam reached down and she gave Milton to him automatically, struck by the gentleness in his huge hands as he lifted seven pounds of puppy.

"Are you all right?" he asked, and Milton threw up on the Dick shirt.

"What a shame." Shar stood up.

"He ate too fast," Sam said without anger as he handed Milton back.

And then he took off his shirt.

Goddammit, Shar thought, and turned away, holding Milton close to her. *You start thinking somebody is just an ordinary nice guy who loves dogs, and then he takes off his shirt and you remember he's a god again.* She kept her back to him, but the memory of that broad muscled chest, the dark hair curling thickly there . . . She realized she was breathing deep and her skin felt odd. Prickly. Hot. "You had to throw up on him, didn't you?" she said to Milton.

"I need a shirt," Sam said from behind her.

"I don't have one that would fit you," she said. "Where's your red flannel?" She waited a moment and then steeled herself and turned around.

He was gone.

Maybe he'd gone to get another shirt. From the Big and Tall department at T. J. Skank.

All right, enough, she told herself. *This jealousy is ridiculous and so is all this hyperventilating you're doing. If you're a goddess, act like one. The guy is a promiscuous flunky of Satanella. If he kisses you*—the world went wonky for a minute at the thought—*you'll turn into a Mesopotamian zombie, serving that little freak Kammani. You want him out of here; you want him gone; you don't ever want to see him again—*

Sam came back into the kitchen, buttoning his flannel shirt. "May I spend the night in your temple, Shar?"

"Sure," she said. Well, hell, he'd just saved a puppy. It was the least she could do. "You can have my grandmother's bedroom."

She went to the archway into her grandmother's room, still carrying Milton, and pulled back the heavy curtains that separated it from the kitchen. "I haven't dusted in here for months."

Milton sneezed.

"I'm used to dust," Sam said, and he sounded so modern for a moment that she stared at him, but he was looking around the room as if he'd been there before, and the expression on his face said it wasn't a good memory.

"This isn't where she sacrificed you, is it?" Shar said, horrified.

"No," he said. "That was in the secret room with the altar. Where Kammani is now."

"Oh," Shar said. "What was this?"

"Shall I take Milton from you?" Sam said to her. "Or will he stay with you tonight?"

"This was Sharrat's bedroom here," Shar said. "Did you live here with her?"

"I never lived with Sharrat," he said, sounding surprised.

"She was your lover," Shar said.

"No."

It didn't sound like a lie.

"But you knew her. Well."

He met her eyes. "Yes."

Just hell, Shar thought. Her grandmother had died twenty years before, but Shar still remembered the drive in the old bat, the determination in the silky voice that had said, *You're not what we need, girl, you've got no backbone, but you'll have to do.* Sharrat had probably been hell on wheels back in Mesopotamia. A real match for a god.

Shar swallowed. "I'm sorry, Sam. She lived a long

time; she was in her nineties when she died. My mother said she was waiting for something that never came." She tried a smile. "I guess that was you."

"No," Sam said. "That was Kammani. Sharrat lived to serve her goddess."

"Oh."

The silence stretched out between them as he stared at her, his eyes dark and hooded, looking down on her, and then he smiled and reached out and scratched Milton behind the ears, and she thought, *Touch me.*

"You are very like Sharrat," he said, and she stepped back.

"No, I'm not. I'm not anything like her. You made a mistake on the goddess thing; it's just not me." She smiled as brightly as she could as she held out the drowsy puppy. "I'm going to be up for a while, so why don't you take him?"

Milton yawned as he was passed over. "Food."

"Sleep first, baby," Shar said. "Then you can have more food in the morning."

"Plenty," Wolfie barked from her feet.

"The sheets on the bed are clean, but they haven't been aired out," she told Sam, backing toward the archway and the kitchen. "If you need anything . . ."

"This will be very good," he told her, and she nodded and went out, closing the curtain behind her fast, narrowly missing Wolfie.

"Watch it," he growled, and waddled over to his ravaged food dish.

"So what happened?" she whispered to him.

"He ate all my food," Wolfie said, looking at his dish.

Shar opened up the dog food bin and filled it. "No, I mean with Sam and Kammani," she said when Wolfie was crunching away.

"She wanted him to stay," Wolfie said around a mouthful of nuggets. "He was mad at her. He said no."

"Really?" Shar said, and then felt ridiculous for caring. Grandma Sharrat had had the right idea. No fooling around with playboy gods who owed allegiance to crazy, top-heavy brunettes . . .

He was right through that archway, behind that heavy curtain, in a bed. If she went in there and crawled in next to him, she was pretty sure she could have him. *Everybody else has,* she thought, but it was a knee-jerk reaction, a cheap ploy by her conscious mind to flatten her subconscious that was still back there, crawling into bed with him, sliding against that massive body, feeling the fur of his chest on her skin—

She shivered, and then something started down low, a kind of chill that made her breathe faster, and she leaned against the wall and thought, *I really want him, more than I've ever wanted any man, more than I've ever wanted anything; I* need *him.*

"*Damn* it," she said, loud enough that Wolfie stopped eating for a moment. *I need something to do with my hands,* she thought, and then saw the paint stacked in the corner, eighteen gallons in different colors, with the brushes and rollers and the stir sticks and an opener right there. "I'm going to paint," she told Wolfie, and took off her jacket, ignoring the fact that her hands were shaking.

The colors were luscious when she opened the cans. The first one was a rich honey yellow; the second, a deep cinnamon; the third, the blue of the night sky. "Blue is for my bedroom," she told Wolfie, who said, "They all look the same to me," and went back to his food bowl.

"The yellow in here," she said, and picked up a paintbrush, brand-new, thick, with shiny bristles that gleamed in the light from overhead. She ran them over the palm of her hand, and the stroke and the tickle there made her draw in a sharp breath and shiver. She dipped the brush into the rich paint and then held it above the can, watching the paint run off in ropes, creamy and thick, and the beauty of it as it looped back into the can made her breathe in a deeper rhythm, like music starting in her head, an insistent beat that tripped across her nerves. She imagined something as silky as the paint sliding across her skin, someone's hands sliding across her skin, the beat in her blood solid and strong. The paint was so *there,* in that moment, *real,* and she straightened and slashed the bright brush across the stone gray on the wall, and the amber leapt out at her, making her draw in her breath, and she said, "*Yes,*" and dipped the brush in and slashed again, and then again, splashing the light to obliterate the dark, gasping with the color as the heat rose, the contrast and the slide making her breathe harder as she stroked away the gray, painting faster, watching the room begin to glow, getting dizzier and dizzier as the beat began to coil tight within her, and when she finished the third wall, she stripped off her top and then her pants to paint in her underwear, panting and shivering. The sweat dripped from her as she shook with the beat in her blood, her body splashed with color, sticky with heat, and she looked at the fourth wall and thought, *Red,* and picked up a new brush and dipped it into the brilliant red-orange paint.

The color struck her hard, glowing on the brush, and she splashed it over the gray, dripping and spattering. And when it was done, when the color was huge, glowering at her, overpowering, she picked up the yellow brush again and slashed the amber paint into the red, once, *yes,* twice, *yes,* again and again until she leaned on the table, let her head fall back, breathed in deep, felt all that tension twisting deep inside her, thought, *Yes!* and tried to let go, and then something inside her said, *No, it's dangerous; go back,* and she felt it all slipping away.

She straightened and thought, *No, I want THIS,* and reached for the finish, falling into the color, bringing it all back, the heat and the joy rising so that she lifted her arms above her head, stretching her body as everything spiraled down and hit low, and then she grabbed onto the table as the spasms took her, felt them like bright slashes against the stone inside her, her breath coming "*oh, oh, oh*" as all that heat spattered against her cold logic and she came her brains out for the first time in her life.

When her breath slowed again, she turned and saw Sam in the archway to the bedroom, naked to the waist, beautiful and strong and staring at her, and she walked over to him, grabbed the back of his head, yanked him down to her mouth, and kissed him like she'd never kissed anyone before, her brain shorting out and her body rocking as another orgasm took her and then he put his arms around her and pulled her tight against him, his body hard and hot, and she shuddered again and again, and then he said, "*Sharrat,*" and she froze.

"No." She pushed him away, cold again, the color in her head dulling as the beat in her blood disappeared.

"Shar?" he said, and she said, "I have to go to bed now," and walked away from him as he held out his hand to her, closing her eyes as she went through the dining room and the living room and the archway to the hall, thinking, *He doesn't want you; he wants Sharrat,* her head aching like a hangover. She climbed the stairs to her room and walked straight into her shower and watched as the hard stab of the hot water washed the yellow and red paint in spirals over her body and onto the shower floor to arabesque down the drain, beautiful dancing color, and the water felt like needles on her skin, and the warm peppermint scent of the shampoo tickled her nose, and the music came back into her head, the beat insistent, filling her, heating her, rocking her, making everything go low and twist and . . .

"*Oh. My. God,*" Shar said, and pounded on the tile until the spasms stopped again.

Then she stood trembling under the water and thought, *What's happening to me?*

She toweled herself off, and the rough scrape of the terry put her over the edge again as she held on to the towel bar, and then she put on a nightgown, this time resisting the flutter from the old flannel that was like a lover's touch on her skin. She couldn't keep coming, no matter how good it felt. If she kept this up, every time she saw Sam . . .

She shivered at the thought. He wanted Sharrat, not her, but he was there, and she'd never wanted anybody more, and he was never going to love her anyway, he was a god, so . . .

I could go down there, she thought. *I could go down there and make love with a god.*

She put on her robe and walked into the bedroom and saw Wolfie and Milton sitting on the floor by the bed. She shook her head to clear it and said, "I have to go down to talk to Sam, but you stay here—"

"Sam had to go out," Wolfie said.

"Out," Milton said.

"Oh," Shar said.

"And we're really tired," Wolfie said, scratching at a spot of yellow paint on his fur.

"Food," Milton said.

"Tired," Wolfie said.

"Tired," Milton said.

Shar drew a deep breath. That was good. It was really good. It would have been a huge mistake to go to him. He was promiscuous. And he was working with Kammani. He was the enemy. Boy, she was glad he wasn't there anymore.

"You okay?" Wolfie said.

"Okay?" Milton said.

Dogs were better than gods, anyway. They were faithful and loving and didn't screw up your life.

"I'm okay," Shar said, and put the two of them on the bed, where they scrambled back as she climbed under the covers and then burrowed under the duvet.

"Don't shove," Wolfie growled.

"Shove," Milton said.

"Good night," Shar said, and snuggled down into soft, worn sheets that slid against her body, and told herself that she didn't want a god anyway. She had enough problems without that.

Maybe he'll show up in my dreams.

She turned her face into her pillow and fell asleep, exhausted and confused and unsatisfied.

At two o'clock in the morning, Abby couldn't sleep. It wasn't just the memory of Christopher's hot mouth and cold eyes that was bothering her. It was the cookies. The hunger. The lust that she could supposedly inspire in people. Not to mention the fact that she was a freaking goddess. Maybe goddesses didn't need sleep. Though word had it that Granny B had done more than her share of sleeping, and she must have been a demi-goddess herself.

The air mattress was deflating again. Bowser had a habit of climbing onto the foot of it while she slept, and she wasn't sure whether he'd poked a hole in it or the old thing was just protesting the added weight. She rolled off onto the hard floor and scrambled to her feet. The windows were open to the street, and she could hear voices, music, laughter. And she'd never felt so alone in her life.

She was hungry. She hadn't remembered feeling that way before—like there was something that would fill that emptiness inside her, but she couldn't think what it was. If she ate one more cookie she was going to throw up, and she was out of temple tonic. Maybe it wasn't food she was hungry for. Maybe it was answers.

The summer night was warm. She dressed quickly, draped one of Bea's old shawls around her, and shoved her feet in her sandals. "You coming with me, pal?" she asked Bowser.

He'd already gotten to his feet, albeit with noticeable reluctance. "Can't we just sleep?"

"You can, sweetie. I have some questions I need answered."

"I'm going with you," he growled.

"This is a very safe town."

"Coming with you."

She didn't drive. It was a warm night, the history building wasn't that far away, and the walk might ease her restlessness even if she couldn't track down Kammani.

The heavy doors to the auditorium were locked. Of course. Abby considered pounding on them, but she'd probably get the campus police instead. "Okay, you're right: this was a dumb idea," she was saying to Bowser when suddenly the doors opened and Kammani stood there, barefoot, with her robe gathered loosely around her, leaving her shoulders and her spectacular breasts bare.

Abby blinked. She wasn't particularly modest, but with a half-naked woman, you never could pick a good place for your eyes to go.

"Abi," Kammani said, looking sleepy and satisfied and very glad to see her.

"Er, I just had a couple of questions," Abby said.

Kammani nodded. "Of course. Enter."

Abby followed Kammani into the temple, still feeling uneasy, Bowser by her side. There were torches burning, the smell of sex and sulphur in the air, and Abby shivered.

"Aren't you chilly?" she said as Kammani's robe slipped farther. "I'll lend you my shawl." *Please, take the shawl.*

Kammani smiled at her dreamily, like a benevolent mother. A benevolent, weird, power-crazed, half-naked mother.

Maybe easing into it is a better idea, Abby thought. "Something odd is going on," she said, trying to sound casual. "After the first night of class we started hearing our dogs talk. Really, we could hear them speak, and we could hear the other dogs talking. There's a college professor who's a stuck-up asshole and I can't stand him, but I keep wanting to jump his bones, and he's kissing me when he clearly hates me. And wherever I go, people are hungry or lustful or wanting something, and it's very confusing. Good for business, of course, but disturbing."

"Business?" Kammani said, frowning with her.

"We opened a coffeehouse tonight. Just a small place with cookies and coffee and live music."

Suddenly, Kammani was a lot less warm and a lot more awake. "I have heard of your coffeehouse temple. Why are you doing this?"

"Because Daisy wanted it. And it seemed right. The point is, whenever people are around us they seem to act oddly, and I want to know why."

Kammani pulled her robe up over her shoulders, all business now. "Sharrat was also with you."

"She was helping."

"The Three of you together is a good thing," Kammani said, as if pronouncing a judgment, "but the coffeehouse temple is not. You must not call people there. I forbid it."

"I wasn't exactly asking permission here," Abby pointed out. "I just wanted to know why these things were happening. And then Sam came by. . . . You know Sam, right?"

Kammani grew grimmer. "Yes."

Abby took a breath. "He told us we were goddesses. Brought here to serve you. Which, on the face of it, is ridiculous, and I just ignored him, particularly since he was mainly focusing on Shar, but then these strange things kept happening, and I want this to stop. I don't like it. I won't be coming back to the dog class, and I don't want any more of that tonic, and I really need to get my life together and get out of here. . . ."

"Abi," Kammani said, putting a firm, warm hand on her arm. "You are still learning your path. You will see your way clear when you return on Tuesday. You will return on Tuesday." Then she added in a more down-to-earth voice, "And stay away from the math professor. You are undefiled, as you should be."

Frustration boiled over, and Abby shook her arm free of Kammani's hand. "I don't understand a word you're saying. What kind of path do you think I have? And I am definitely not coming back on Tues—"

Kammani stared into her eyes. "YOU WILL RETURN ON TUESDAY."

The hell I will, Abby thought. "Yes, my goddess," her voice said, and she wanted to slap her hands over her mouth. She sounded like some addled Renfield in a very bad production of *Dracula*.

Kammani nodded, stern. "You will go back to your coffeehouse temple, and you will tell Daisy and Shar that you will never open it again, and you will all return on Tuesday."

I don't think so. "Yes, my goddess."

Abby could feel her free will leaching away. Maybe *Abbott and Costello Meet Frankenstein* was more like it. Except that it wasn't impeding her ability to think. Just the words coming out her mouth, like Kammani was some kind of cosmic ventriloquilist.

"Things have gone very wrong in this world, Abi,"

Kammani said, taking her arm again and turning her toward the doors. "We have much work to do."

Abby wasn't going to say *Yes, my goddess* one more time. She'd rather eat spiders. "I . . ."

"GO HOME," Kammani said, and Abby walked out the doors.

Before she realized it, she was back out on the front step of the old building and Bowser was looking up at her. "Didn't I warn you? Don't trust her."

"You could have said something to her in there," Abby said. "Instead of leaving me there twisting in the wind." She looked back at the temple in the moonlight. "I need to talk with Daisy and Shar, but they're probably too busy having sex. Unlike me," she added, disgruntled and thoroughly creeped out by Kammani.

"Home," Bowser said wearily. "And lay off on the tonic."

Abby looked down and saw that she had a new ceramic bottle under her arm, probably filled with Kammani-hooch. She thought about just tossing it away, but if some unsuspecting student found it, there'd be hell to pay. She put it in her bag. "You're right; I'm not touching the stuff." She squatted down so that her head was level with Bowser's. "Except then I might not hear you talk, sweetie."

"You'd hear me," Bowser said, his deep voice wise and ancient. "Let's go home."

The next morning, Daisy sat curled up in her window seat, luxuriating in her silk camisole pajamas, in love with the world. She had a cup of coffee in her hand, a full day ahead to do with as she pleased, and a beautiful man who had worshiped her well last night sleeping it off in her bed. A bus went by with a movie poster on it, starring the two morons with the new baby, but even

Camisole didn't seem like that bad a name now. Kind of cute.

Life was good.

"Daisy happy!"

Daisy looked down to see Bailey standing next to her, his tail wagging furiously. She smiled and patted his head as his wiry little body vibrated with the force of his intense energy.

"Daisy happy," she said, and thought, *because Daisy had a lot of orgasms last night.* But she figured Bailey didn't need to hear that part.

She sipped her coffee and turned her head to look out over Temple Street below. In the middle of the street, a flower vendor was setting up her cart full of roses and lilies and daisies. Down at the corner, Mr. Casey hosed down the sidewalk in front of his store, washing the Friday night bar urchin detritus away from his little corner of the world. And across the street, on the corner in front of the psychology building, a timid student was trying to hand out brochures to people passing by, but she was so quiet no one noticed her. Daisy watched her and thought, *If you want attention, demand it, sweetie.*

"Morning."

She turned to see Noah standing in her bedroom doorway, wearing just his jeans, his hair shooting off in a million different directions. Damn, he was beautiful.

"Morning," she said, motioning toward the kitchenette off the living room. "I made coffee."

"Mmmm," he said, but instead of heading for the kitchenette, he walked over to her, knelt in front of her, and kissed her on the shoulder. "In a minute." He leaned in and kissed her gently, his mouth cool and minty. "I hope you don't mind. I stole one of your toothbrushes. You had a lot, so I figured . . ."

"Not a lot. Just twelve."

Noah fought a smile, and Daisy flushed.

"You have to replace them every three months, and you save money buying in bulk at the warehouse store and—"

"It's okay," Noah said, squeezing her hand. "I like that you're organized." He looked around the living room, which was a total disaster. Couch pillows on the floor, plants knocked over, television armoire wide open. And yet Daisy didn't have the slightest motivation to neaten up.

Hey. That's growth.

"So, you had a good time last night?" she said.

He looked at her. "If you have to ask, I obviously did something wrong."

She warmed, remembering the events of the night before. "No, you didn't."

He leaned in and kissed her, long and sweet, his arms going around her waist, fitting so perfectly there, as though they'd been made just for her. How had she not noticed them missing all her life? She shifted closer to him, her legs around his torso as he knelt before her. The energy built at her core, her desire so strong it made her breathless. A breeze picked up in the apartment, and Noah broke off, looking out the window.

"What *is* that?" he said.

"What?" Daisy said, trying to sound innocent.

"That. . . ." He looked back at her. "Every time we get going, the wind blows. Have you noticed that?"

Daisy shrugged. "Summer winds. What are you gonna do?"

He looked at her, angling his head and smiling, his eyes narrowing in happy thought. Then he kissed her again, and her body responded; she could feel the energy building. . . .

Control it, she thought, but his hand gripped her butt, shifting her closer as he pressed himself to her, his waist rubbing against her as he picked up a rhythm that—

Oh. God.

"See?" he said, pulling back and looking out the window as the breeze swirled around them. "I swear, it's not even coming from the window."

"Where else is it gonna come from?" Daisy got up and went toward the kitchen, focusing on the coffeemaker as she willed her body to take it down a notch. "Let me get you some coffee."

She grabbed a mug and filled it while Bailey danced in her wake. She turned, facing the little island that served as her kitchen table, and slid the mug to Noah, who sat on the stool across from her.

"Treat!" Bailey barked.

"You bet, baby," Daisy said.

"Hmmm?" Noah asked, looking up from his mug.

"Nothing." Daisy turned around and kicked her kitchen stool over to the refrigerator, then stepped up and reached for the doggie treats she kept on top of the fridge.

"I like your system there," Noah said, grinning at her as she stepped down.

"Alas, the world is not kind to the height-impaired." Daisy looked at Bailey. "Sit."

Bailey sat, his butt shifting from side to side on the floor with the force of his wagging tail. *Good enough.* Daisy leaned over and gave him the treat and he shot back to his feet, downing it in two bites.

"Nice work," Noah said. "He's a quick study."

"You have no idea." Daisy held the other treat up in the air and said, "Leap."

Bailey leapt, and she tossed the treat into the air and he snapped and caught it, landing on all fours like a pro.

"I thought you didn't like that," Noah said.

Daisy smiled. "I think I'm growing."

Noah took a sip of his coffee, then met her eyes. "So . . . what happened here last night?"

She grinned. "You don't remember?"

"No, I remember but . . ." He glanced around. "I don't remember doing this kind of damage." He pointed to the hallway, where a framed print was lying sideways against the wall. "When did we knock your picture down?"

I'm a goddess, and when I come, so does everything else, she thought, but then just said, "Like I said, summer winds. We left the window open and it got . . . windy."

He watched her for a moment, then nodded, but she could tell something was going on behind his eyes that he wasn't sharing. "Right."

Daisy worked to keep her expression carefree; if this kept up, she was going to have to come up with something better than wind. But she had noticed that by the third time last night, things had calmed down considerably. So maybe it was just a matter of not letting herself get that pent up again.

Or bolting everything down first.

Maybe both.

"Yeah, the winds were pretty wild last night." She picked up the overturned pen cup on the end of the kitchen island and set it upright, putting the pens back in. "Abby's coffeehouse was a mess, too."

Noah didn't seem to hear her, just stared down into his coffee mug for a moment before saying, "You know, I have an appointment that I need to get to soon."

"An appointment?" Daisy said. "On a Saturday?"

"Life of a freelancer." He looked around. "Want me to help you put this place back together before I go?"

Daisy looked at the living room and shook her head. "That's okay."

He got up, walked around the island to her, and kissed

her, slow and deep, then pulled away as if checking for more wind. This time, it was barely a breeze.

You want wind, Daisy thought, *you're gonna have to put some shoulder into it.*

Noah looked back at her and kissed her on the forehead. "I'm gonna go find my shirt. Should be in the bedroom somewhere."

"Okay." She stepped back and watched him go back into her bedroom, the sleek muscles of his back working under his skin, and she remembered her hands on that skin the night before, her lips tasting him as his hands—

A gentle breeze shifted through the apartment, fluttering the reminder notes tacked up on the corkboard by her front door.

She looked down at Bailey. "Well, this is ridiculous. This can't happen *every time;* it's not . . . ," and she trailed off as her eye caught her magic clicky pen sticking out of the pen cup. Inspiration struck, and she grabbed it.

"Let's test a theory," she said to Bailey as he followed her to the open window. She looked out of the window and saw the timid girl still trying to hand out those brochures. Daisy closed her eyes and concentrated on the energy she had pooling at her base. She almost felt like she could see it, glowing bright orange, the fire within to act, to do, to—

She opened her eyes, focused on the girl, and clicked her pen, directing all her energy at her. A wind blew around the girl, tousling her hair, and she looked around, seeming confused.

"Huh," Daisy said, looking down at the pen, which felt kind of hot in her hand, but that could have been her imagination.

"Hey!" the girl yelled.

Daisy's heart banged in her chest, thinking she'd been caught—*messing with magic, bad idea, should have thought this through*—but then she looked out to see the girl climb up on the squat stone retaining wall that held up the lawn around the psych building, looking intently at the people passing by.

"Hey!" the girl yelled again, and people around her stopped and stared. She held up her brochures, waving them over her head. Daisy could see her chest rising with every breath from all the way across the street. "This is important!"

"Oh, that's so cool," Daisy whispered, shifting to make room for Bailey as he poked his head out to watch, too. She put her hand on his back to keep him safe, petting him as they watched the girl demand the attention she needed.

"This is information about women's safety on campus!" she yelled, handing out brochures as people came up to her. "Make sure you give one to every woman you know! You could be the difference!"

The flower vendor woman walked over, got one, and headed back, reading it as she did.

Daisy looked at Bailey and smiled. "Dig us," she said, and Bailey licked her face. "We're good doers."

"What's going on?"

Daisy turned her head around to see Noah watching her, looking concerned.

"Nothing." She tucked the pen into the window seat cushion and stood up. "You found your shirt."

Noah glanced down at his rumpled T-shirt. "Yeah. It was hanging on the shower rod." He looked back at her. "We were in the bathroom?"

"Guess so." Daisy walked over to him, Bailey close on her heels. "So, you really have to go?"

He pulled her to him. "Yeah, I really think I do." He kissed the top of her head. "I'd like to take you out for dinner tonight, though, if you're free."

Daisy wrapped her arms around his waist, let her head

rest on his chest for two heartbeats, then pulled back and smiled up at him. "Sounds like a plan."

"Then, maybe we can come back up here and talk a bit," he said.

She pressed herself tighter against him. "Or, we can come back here and *not* talk."

"Lady's choice." He kissed her slowly, the heat building between them until finally he broke it off with a breathless, "Appointment."

"Appointment," Daisy said, taking a step back. "Right."

He hesitated for a moment, then left, and Daisy leaned back against the wall, her entire body full of energy, and the breezes started to swirl in her apartment. . . .

She ran to the window seat, grabbed the clicky pen out of the cushion, and closed her eyes, concentrating the energy, but unable to focus on where she needed it to go, her thoughts on Noah and how his touch made her feel, and the winds started picking up. If she didn't send the energy *somewhere*—

She opened her eyes, saw a man looking at the flowers in the cart, and clicked her pen. The wind swirled around the man, and he glanced around, then started picking bundles of flowers off the cart while the flower vendor smiled.

Daisy looked behind her at Bailey, who jumped in the air. "It's not saving the world from a fiery apocalypse, but small things matter, too, right?"

"Right!" Bailey barked. "Treat!"

"Yes," Daisy said. "In a second."

She turned back around to look out the window at the man buying flowers, but when she did, she saw Noah standing in the middle of the street, staring up at her.

"Uh-oh," she said to Bailey. "You don't think he saw, do you?"

"Uh-oh!" Bailey barked.

Then a horn honked and she jumped; a guy in a pickup truck had almost hit Noah.

Noah stepped out of the way, but the guy rolled down his window and yelled, "Watch where you're going, asshole!" as he moved on toward the intersection.

"*Excuse* me?" A red-hot anger ran through Daisy, and this time the wind was warm and sharp. Without thinking, she looked at Mr. Casey and his hose and clicked her pen. Mr. Casey's arms jolted to the left, dousing the guy through his open window.

"Jesus!" the guy yelled, and Mr. Casey said, "Sorry!" and the light changed and the guy drove through, cursing.

"Serves you right, dickhead," she muttered as the guy laid on his horn; then she turned around and sat down on the window seat, her heart beating furiously in her chest, excitement and exhilaration running through her.

"I never thought I'd say this, Bail," Daisy said, leaning forward and patting him on the head as a giggle erupted from within her, "but I think I'm gonna like being a goddess."

TEN

Kammani stood before her altar and considered her underlings.

Mina, clicking on her computer on the steps below, was a Wortham, and the Worthams' belief was passionate and strong, and therefore essential. Bun's and Gen's belief was not passionate, but they were young and easily controlled, and two of her original seven, and therefore essential.

But Doug . . . A long and energetic night with him had convinced Kammani that while he was a fine example of this new world's manhood, he was going to make a lousy sacrifice. For one thing, he had no tolerance for pain. Which meant she was going to have to get Samu back. And the Three. And find the missing Vera and—

The doors opened and Kammani turned, her head high.

Noah strode toward her, frowning. "What the hell are you doing?"

"How dare you question the goddess?" Mina said, outraged.

Noah stopped at the foot of the altar. "Something's going on here, and you're going to tell me what it is."

"I am the goddess," Kammani said coldly. "I am here to rule this world."

"I don't want to hear that crap," Noah said. "What was in that drink you served the class?"

"The tonic?" Kammani laughed. "Honey. Cinnamon.

Anise. And a very old wine from my country." She fixed him with her eyes. "But you presume. Your tone—"

"Wine." Noah took a step closer. "You told me there was nothing alcoholic in it. *I* told *her* there was nothing in it. Have you seen her size? What if she had been driving?"

Ah, Kammani thought. *Daisy.*

Mina stood. "You go too far. The goddess is not here to answer your questions; you are here to serve her."

Noah looked at her as if she were insane. "I don't serve her; I work for her. And that's over if she's hurting these women." He looked at Kammani again. "You deliberately chose those seven. I saw the list. Why—?"

"They're the youngest women of age from the Seven Families," Kammani said. "They were chosen long before they were born."

Noah narrowed his eyes. "Tell me what you're doing with them or I'm out."

"You overreach." Kammani frowned down on him. "You have been a good servant and worked hard, and I have been lenient, but you go too far. Go."

Noah took a step back, seeming almost surprised as he did. Then he lifted his insolent eyes to Kammani's. "I don't know what you think you're doing, and I don't really care. But if you hurt her, I swear to God—"

Kammani shook her head at him, impatient. "Noah, of all my people, I love best the Seven, and of the Seven, I love best the Three." Mina whimpered as Kammani added, "No harm will come to Daisy."

Noah hesitated, then seemed to relax a bit. "Fine. I'm telling Daisy what I know, though."

Kammani looked at him, exasperated. She could just blast him where he stood or turn him into a dog, which would at least make him faithful and obedient, but she needed him. And he loved Daisy. He would follow Daisy when she came again, and he would serve his goddess with her.

Mina stepped forward. "You can't tell her; you'll spoil the surprise. Look." She took a poster from the stack at her feet and let it unroll in front of her so he could see it.

" 'Youth, Health, and Wealth'?" Noah said, looking skeptical.

"It's Kammani's self-help group," Mina said. "We're going to meet twice a week to improve ourselves—"

The secret door in the back wall opened, and Doug came out, yawning.

"Hey, Noah," he said, still bleary-eyed, and then he caught sight of Kammani. "Hey, babe, gotta run." He walked up the altar steps, kissed her on the mouth, swatted her on the rear end, and then headed for the door.

It took everything Kammani had not to obliterate him on the spot, and she only managed it because it would be disastrous to do it in front of Noah. Besides, from the look on Mina's face, something bad would happen to Doug shortly. With luck, not fatally bad, but at the moment Kammani didn't really care as long as he paid.

"Wow," Noah said, amusement pushing the anger out of his eyes. "You're really serious about this Seven Families thing, huh?"

I don't need you that much, Kammani thought, and then realized that Doug had done her a favor: Noah no longer saw her as a threat.

"It's just a women's group," Mina said to Noah. "We're going to talk about diets and investing and skin care. You know. Women's stuff."

Noah looked at her for a moment and then relaxed. "Okay." He looked up at Kammani. "I'm sorry I busted in here like that. I didn't get much sleep. I think I saw something that wasn't there." He shook his head, handed the poster back to her. "I'm not going to lie to her, but I won't spoil your party, either. Just . . . don't give her anything to drink without telling her what's in it, okay?"

Mina nodded.

"I'll see you Tuesday," Noah said, and left.

When he was gone, Kammani looked at Mina. "That was very well done. Good, Mina."

Mina flushed with pleasure. "He is easy to fool. He does not believe."

"And you restrained yourself well with Doug," Kammani went on. "You are showing much wisdom, Mina."

Mina lifted her chin, smiling as if the sun were shining on her. "My mother was wrong; I am good enough to serve you, O my goddess. Which reminds me, I have seen the robes of ceremony."

"They are very beautiful still," Kammani said, waiting for Mina's praise.

"But maybe not for the Goddess Way," Mina said carefully. "We don't want to scare people off."

"Scare people?" Kammani said, annoyed.

"You should wear a business suit. I saw a black Jones of New York on clearance at T.J. Maxx that—"

"I don't understand," Kammani said.

"The robes and the headdress thing will freak people out," Mina said. "You need to be less Joan Crawford, more Oprah Winfrey."

"I will wear my robes," Kammani said, and Mina nodded obediently, so Kammani took pity on her. "You are a good and loyal priestess, Mina. You may punish Doug as you see fit. Short of death."

"Thank you!" Mina's face lit up. "I will punish him with the death of others, my goddess. He will live but wish to die."

"Just things," Kammani said hastily. "No dead dogs. Or people. Kill things, not people."

"Yes, my goddess," Mina said, looking up at her with delight in her eyes. "Only as you command."

"Good girl, Mina," Kammani said, refraining from patting her on the head.

"As good as the Three?" Mina said, more pleading than insubordinate.

"Of course," Kammani lied, and returned to her room behind the secret door.

This world was indeed different, she thought as she looked at her ceremonial robes. But not so different that it wouldn't recognize a goddess dressed in gold. *This world will be mine,* she thought, *and things will be as they once were.*

But for the moment, she was hungry. She went to get a strawberry yogurt from the minifridge Mina's mother had brought her.

When the revolution came, they'd be keeping refrigeration.

Abby wasn't sure whether she should blame her rotten night of sleep on her unsettling conversation with Kammani or the fact that her air bed had decided to give up the ghost. She didn't fall asleep until four in the morning and when she woke up, with just a thin layer of rubber between her and the hardwood floor, every bone in her body ached.

Hell, if she was going to be a demi-goddess she was at least going to be comfortable. Especially if she was going to spend the day baking fresh goodies, which she had every intention of doing.

Amanda Richmond, the Real Estate Goddess of Escondido, was easy enough to reach—she slept with her cell phone on her pillow—and it took less than five minutes to get a decent amount of money deposited in Abby's bank account. Her life would have been a lot simpler if she'd given in and simply written Professor Christopher Mackenzie a check for what Granny B had owed him, but that would have involved going to her mother, something Abby hated to do.

But here she was, doing it anyway. Maybe it was meant to be.

For some reason her mother's all-too-practical suggestions didn't bother her that morning, any more than the questions about her weight and her love life and when she was going back to school. After all, she was the demigoddess in the family—she no longer had to worry about pleasing her impossible-to-please mother. Even her refusal to discuss Bea was par for the course.

Besides, Amanda Richmond was a master at denial. All Abby had to do was say, "A funny thing happened to me in the ancient history building on campus," and Amanda had another call. Which came as no surprise—Amanda had never wanted to talk about the tiny Ohio town she'd come from any more than she wanted to discuss her colorful mother. Amanda's aversion seemed normal—now Abby was wondering exactly how much her mother knew about the family tradition.

Abby was back at the coffeehouse before noon. No sign of Daisy to give her a hand, which was probably just as well considering what kinds of things happened when Daisy set her mind to it. Besides, the bed wasn't that heavy; it was just bulky. She'd hauled bigger things by herself.

She'd chosen a full-size, pillow-topped piece of luxury that was guaranteed to cradle her like a bed of clouds. Fortunately, the box spring was lightweight, and she somehow managed to get it up the narrow stairs in the kitchen without knocking over anything but the new bottle of Kammanipunch. Unfortunately, it didn't break, but it rolled under the counter, where Abby intended to forget about it.

"Hey, watch it," Bowser growled when she sideswiped his head.

"Sorry!" By the time she got the foundation seated on the bed frame she was exhausted. Bowser plopped himself in the corner of her bedroom, well out of her way, and stayed put while Abby hauled the big, heavy mattress off the roof of her station wagon and partway up the stairs.

Where she immediately got stuck. Mattresses were supposed to be flexible, but this one was proving to be incredibly stubborn. It wedged itself in the opening at the top of the narrow stairs, and Abby was trapped halfway down, her exit shut off by the rest of it. She was standing there, unable to move, when she heard a noise in the kitchen and she breathed a sigh of relief.

"Daisy!" she called out. "Come and give me a hand with this thing. I'm trapped on the staircase."

A moment later the mattress moved, shoved forward, pushing past the doorway so quickly that Abby fell forward on the staircase, sprawling awkwardly.

"Thanks," she said, rolling over on her back. "I didn't know you were that strong."

"Strong enough," Christopher Mackenzie said, and Abby wasn't able to bite back her groan. "What in the world possessed you to try to move something like that on your own?"

Damned punch. Or damned cookies, or damned demigoddess/semi-goddess. Whatever it was that was affecting her was making her life completely miserable. He was too damned good-looking, and today he was dressed in old jeans and a T-shirt. Even better.

He was also socially retarded, according to Daisy.

"I'm used to taking care of myself," Abby said. "Why are you here?"

"I came to apologize for yesterday."

"For what? For kissing me or for being an asshole?
Shit, why had she even brought that up?

"I believe we were both involved in the kissing,
Christopher said politely. "As a matter of fact, you wer
the one—"

"Apology accepted," she said hastily. She knew per
fectly well she'd been flirting and she'd only gotten wha
she deserved. The best kiss she'd ever had in her entire life

"Since I'm here, why don't I give you a hand gettin
that mattress in place?" he said.

She would have liked to refuse the offer, but the mat
tress was now resting in the upstairs hallway and her delu
sions of being superwoman were rapidly vanishing. "Tha
would be very kind of you," she said, trying to sound dis
tant and failing miserably. Especially since he came up th
narrow, enclosed staircase so that he was very, very close

"Where's it going?"

She edged backward, away from him. *No cookies Abby. No punch, no cookies, no superpowers.* "In my
room. If I can get past it, I can pull it while you push."

"Sounds logical." He was his usual practical self, al
math brain and no heart. So why was she caring? She man
aged to squeeze past the thick mattress, into her bedroom
and then grabbed onto the pillowed end of it. "Ready," sh
said, prepared to use all her strength to haul the damne
thing into the room.

A second later she jumped out of the way as the mat
tress flew into the room, landing crosswise on the box
spring, followed by an unruffled Christopher. "Why didn'
you let the furniture store deliver this instead of trying to
drag it up here by yourself?

She really didn't want to be talking about beds with
him. "That would have taken a week. I've been sleeping
on an air mattress and it sprang a leak. I decided if I was

going to stay around here for a while, I might at least be comfortable, and I didn't want to spend another night on the floor." She started to yank the mattress onto the foundation, and he pushed it into place with seemingly no effort.

It went right up under the window, and it looked so wonderful that she immediately sat down on it, bouncing lightly. "Good God, this is heavenly," she said in a voice that came out almost sexual in its pleasure. *Damnation,* she thought, jumping up quickly.

"I'm sure it is," he said, his voice cool and even. "You never let me tell you what I came to apologize for."

God, they weren't going to talk about the kiss again, were they? She sat back on the bed, bouncing lightly. "No need," she said.

"I'm not usually rude."

"Really? You could have fooled me."

He grimaced. "My life is . . . complicated. Not that it's any concern of yours. I just wouldn't want you to get the wrong idea."

"You mean you're not really a stiff-rumped bastard who cares more about numbers than people?" she said, her voice syrupy sweet. There was no way she was going to soften around him again.

She saw a flash of amusement in his eyes, but he still didn't smile. "No, I'm definitely a stiff-rumped bastard who cares more about numbers than people. I've never wasted much time on social skills."

"Could have fooled me. Maybe you've just been having trouble sleeping. I gather your house is haunted."

The amusement fled, leaving his eyes cool. "Who told you that? I don't happen to believe in ghosts. There's a rational explanation for everything."

"And what's your rational explanation? Who's haunting you? The old math professor who used to live there?"

"Someone has been far too busy talking about my personal life. And I'd like to know what business is this of yours?" His voice was frosty.

"Just curious. I've never known anyone who's actually seen a ghost."

"And you still don't," he snapped. "There are no ghosts. There are just . . ." His voice trailed off.

"Just what?"

"Voices.

Abby froze. "You hear dogs talking?"

He looked at her like she'd lost her mind. "Of course not. Why in the world would dogs be talking? That's totally ridiculous."

"Totally," she said as Bowser grumbled in the corner. "So who is that you hear?"

For a moment she thought he wasn't going to say anything, just turn and leave. "A four-thousand-year-old mage."

Abby hooted with laughter. "Been playing too many computer games recently, Professor?"

"As a matter of fact, I do play," he said stiffly. "But this has nothing to do with it. The wizard I'm talking about is from Mesopotamia."

Suddenly things were no longer so amusing. "Mesopotamia?" she echoed, uneasy. She shook her head, as if shaking off the shadows. "That's easily explained. The college is a major center for Mesopotamian studies. Even the ancient history building has been moved from the Middle East. It just sank into your subconscious and . . ."

"And whispers math equations in my ears? The kind of thing no one else could possibly think of?" He sounded as removed and logical as one of his math equations.

"Well, Shar said you were some kind of child prodigy. You're brilliant. Maybe that's just the way your twisted brain works," she suggested, trying to be helpful.

"My brain isn't twisted, thank you very much. And I

know exactly who's talking to me. The man who invented modern mathematics. Milki-la-el."

"I hate to tell you this, Professor, but if he lived four thousand years ago, it's not modern mathematics."

He just looked at her. "You're fairly pedantic for a flower child. Are you sure you're not a closet mathematician?"

"Perish the thought." She shuddered. "So you're being haunted by the ghost of an ancient math professor. What's that got to do with me?"

"Hearing voices isn't normal."

"You're telling me," she muttered.

"And this isn't the first time I've heard them."

She was momentarily at a loss for a snappy comeback. "When did you first hear them?"

"When I was a child I had an imaginary friend named Uncle Milki who told me stories about the beauty of numbers. It annoyed my foster parents no end, so I eventually stopped telling them about him and eventually he stopped talking. But once I moved here, he started up again." He pushed away from the dresser. "Ever heard of John Nash?"

"*A Beautiful Mind,*" she said promptly. "And you think you're crazy as a loon like he was?"

"Such a delicate way to put it," he said. "It appears to be that way. So I have no business getting involved with anyone, kissing anyone, moving beds with anyone. . . ." He gestured toward the bed angrily. "I have no business being around you."

"So why are you here again?" she said, climbing off the bed. He was still leaning against the dresser, and on impulse she moved closer. Something was moving in the air between them, mystery and desire and irrational longing, and she had no idea whether he felt it as strongly as she did. . . .

"Oh, hell," he said, and pulled her into his arms.

"Oh, hell—" The word was cut off as his mouth silenced hers, and she flung her arms around his neck, pressing her body up against his, trying to get closer, for one brief moment not giving a damn about anything but kissing a crazy mathematician.

And then Christopher tore himself away with a muttered curse. "Hell, no," he said.

"Hell, no?" she echoed. "What do you mean by that?"

"I mean there's no room in my very complicated life for an irresponsible flower child. There's no room in my life for anything but numbers."

"Numbers are pretty cold comfort in bed."

His eyes narrowed. "Are you suggesting we sleep together?"

"Of course not," she said. *Oh my god, yes*, she thought. For a moment she didn't move, as everything suddenly became clear. She knew what she wanted. He was standing right in front of her. He heard voices, but then, so did she. A crazy, annoying, gorgeous math genius with the social skills of a kumquat.

She was out of her mind. Maybe the temple tonic had a long-lasting effect; maybe the cookies were hallucinogenic. Whatever it was, she wasn't about to give in to it. "That's all right, Christopher," she said in a calm voice. "I agree. You go home and play with your prime numbers."

He stared down at her, obviously struggling to find something cool and dismissive to say. Nothing came. He left without another word, his feet clattering down the wooden stairs, and she heard a brief, polite exchange with Daisy before the door slammed.

"Are you okay, Abby?" Daisy said from the doorway.

Abby stood up. "I'm not sure. He's not my type, is he?"

Daisy grinned. "Not at all, but when has that ever had anything to do with it?"

"With what?"

Daisy didn't answer. "What do the cookies tell you?"

"I'm not going to eat any more. I'm not going to drink temple tonic, and I'm going to put this all down to temporary insanity," she said, determined. "There's absolutely no reason for me to see him again."

"Of course not, honey," Daisy said in a soothing voice.

Abby didn't want to think about it. Think about what it felt like when he put his hands on her, what his mouth tasted like, the crazy feelings that started between her legs and spread through her body. She'd never been interested in sex before, and she could easily go back to that nice safe state again.

As long as she kept out of the way of a certain gorgeous, neurotic math genius, all would be well.

At least she could hope.

When Shar got up the next morning, Milton was gone, but when she and Wolfie went downstairs, they found him on the back of the chair by the window, barking, "CatCatCatCatCat!"

Wolfie jumped up beside him, looked out the window, and said, "That's a squirrel."

Milton sighed and then barked, "SquirrelSquirrelSquirrelSquirrel!" and Wolfie waited a moment and barked, "SquirrelSquirrelSquirrelSquirrel!" too, until Sam yelled, "ENOUGH!" from the kitchen and both dogs shut up.

And Shar thought, *He's back,* and tried not to be glad.

She went in and saw him sitting at the kitchen table, eating the anise star cookies she'd brought home the night before. She had to work on her book, she wanted to paint her bedroom, the kitchen needed cleaned from her paint orgy, but there he was, and she thought, *Now what?*

What did you say to somebody you'd come in front of the night before, with no participation from him? Somebody you'd kissed hard enough to rearrange his tonsils? Somebody—

"Good morning, Shar," Sam said, and she said, "Good morning," and made eggs because he needed some protein with his sugar and because he hadn't mentioned the orgasm. Instead he asked questions about the world, so after breakfast she sat him down on the couch and the dogs climbed on top of him and she turned on CNN. "This isn't the whole truth," she said, "but it's some of it." He nodded and began to watch, and she went to clean up the kitchen, and since Sam wasn't there, distracting her this time she really saw the kitchen.

It glowed with color, and she stood there and soaked it in, feeling it beat in her blood again as she stared at the eight amber wedge shapes she'd slashed into the red-orange paint, like a sunburst or a daisy or a star. The symbol looked familiar and then she realized what it was, the ancient cuneiform symbol for "goddess." The colors vibrated and she felt herself begin to tense again and thought, *This is going to be really inconvenient,* and then she gave herself up to the sensations, little ones this time more like a series of pops instead of the cataclysm that had shaken her the night before, no pounding and very little moaning.

She was developing an understanding of why Grandma Sharrat had painted everything beige and gray.

She cleaned everything up and went into the living room and found Sam looking bleak, which made her want to go to him, enfold him, make him smile again. . . .

Don't even think about it.

"These are terrible stories," he said, and she said, "I know, I know," and to make him feel better, put in a DVD—*Big Trouble in Little China,* because she figured Sam could relate to Jack Burton better than he could to, say, Elizabeth Bennet—and then watched as he and the dogs stared at the TV fascinated, occasionally talking back to it. Wolfie's contribution mostly consisted of, "Bite him!" with Milton chiming in, "Bite!" (which made Shar say, "Wolfie!" and Wolfie nudge Milton with his nose and say, "We're not allowed to bite") while Sam just shook his head during the fight scenes. He stayed intent, focused, absorbed enough that Shar could look at him without drawing his attention, which was good, because it was hard to look away from him. By the end of the movie, Shar realized she'd found the perfect god-and-dog-sitter, and for the rest of the weekend Sam and the dogs watched adventure—*Ghostbusters*, *Romancing the Stone*, all three *Indiana Jones*es, *The Mummy*, and *Big Trouble in Little China* two more times—while she worked on finishing up the citations for her mother's book and painted the rest of the house, doing one wall at a time because the color made her come. So did the pizza with sausage and olives they ordered for dinner Saturday night, and the smell of the daylilies in the front yard when she opened the door Sunday morning, and the feel of her worn Egyptian cotton sheets when she slid into bed each night, and about forty other things. And through every paroxysm, she heard gunshots and squealing tires from the TV, Milton toddling around the living room saying, "Slimed!" and, "Sonofabitch," and, "Toast!" while Sam talked back to the TV in adventure-hero-speak.

"You know these movies aren't real, right?" she said to Sam after *The Bourne Identity*. "They're just stories. This isn't the way life is here."

"They're your myths," Sam said. "They tell me much . . . a lot about this world."

"Not really," Shar said. "They're not like Gilgamesh or—"

"Gilgamesh," Sam snorted, "that loser."

"Your English is getting better," Shar said. "Nobody would know you weren't from this century."

In between writing and coming and watching DVDs with Sam and the dogs, Shar walked to the coffeehouse, stopping along the way to buy bright-colored gauze skirts and cotton sundresses from the boutique that she'd never gone into before, and then opening the door to the coffeehouse and inhaling the scent of whatever marvelous thing Abby was baking before joining her and Daisy at the big kitchen table to talk and laugh and then grow sober as they tried to figure out the goddess thing. She also stripped off Bea's old wallpaper and primed the walls white, mostly managing not to come by super-vigilance and helped by the fact that stripping wallpaper was not an orgasmic experience. Abby seemed distracted, but Daisy was ecstatically happy, so Shar didn't point out something that worried her: Noah, the source of Daisy's happiness, worked for Kammani.

Like Sam.

Actually, there were so many things that worried her—what Kammani was doing, what Sam was doing with her, what Sam was doing with other women, what it meant to be a goddess, what their powers meant, whether there was a price to pay for using them, whether she could keep from coming in the middle of the coffeehouse—that it was hard to pick one to focus on, although the fact that Sam was not expansive when she asked him about Kammani pretty much moved that one to the top of her list.

On Tuesday morning, she had to go into the college to teach, so she put on a deep blue sundress shot with turquoise, kissed the dogs good-bye, and waved to Sam as he concentrated on *Gladiator.* She walked down Temple Street to the history building, passing the coffeehouse on the way and thinking that they really had to paint the outside and give it a new name. A bright red car seared across her eyes and blared its horn at her just as the scent of Abby's baking wafted out, and her brain shorted out again and she had to hold on to a lamppost until she stopped shuddering and gasping, smiling at a guy who'd stopped to watch and saying, "Asthma!" to get rid of him. Everywhere she went, everything was sharper, sweeter, richer, brighter, more *exciting*. . . .

Stop that, she told herself.

The history department definitely wasn't orgasmic. Her mailbox was stuffed full of meeting notices, messages from students, and the miscellaneous flyers that people put into faculty mailboxes under the misapprehension that they'd be read; her department head remarked that she was late for her office hours and then stopped to compliment her on her dress and her hair; and one of the student aides told her that her class handouts weren't finished.

"They will be," Shar said to her. "I need them in half an hour."

"Well, that's just impossible," the student began, and then Shar stared at her and she faltered.

"You will finish them," Shar said.

"Half an hour," the student said, and Shar turned and walked down the hall to her office, not sure that what she'd done was right but completely sure she needed the damn handouts.

The door to Ray's office, next to hers, was open, and he called to her as she went past, so she stopped.

"I'm sorry about the TV," he began, and then he stopped and looked more closely at her. "Are you wearing a dress?"

"Yes, Ray," Shar said, obviously swathed in about six yards of gauze skirt. "I'm wearing a dress."

She shook her head and started to move on to her office and Ray said, "Wait, listen, what do you know about this guy Sam? You were only married six months—"

"I know a lot," Shar lied, and then remembered what

Ray knew a lot about. "Ray, what do you know about Kammani Gula? I know she had seven priestesses but after that, I can't find anything."

"I can find out," Ray said, stepping closer. "I should have offered before. Listen, Shar—"

"Thanks," Shar said, stepping back.

"So." Ray stepped back, too. "Uh, do you have an era? Assyrian? Babylonian?"

"Not Babylonian," Shar said, thinking back to the relief. "Northern, near the site my grandfather excavated. I'm betting it's early. Three thousand B.C.? Two thousand? Give or take a millennium? I can't find anything on her except for this bas-relief at the back of the auditorium, but I know she existed. And if anybody can find her, you can."

"Thanks," Ray said, ducking his head a little, and she knew he'd do his damnedest, which was pretty darn good. "I like your hair."

"Thank you," she said, and went into her office, ignoring him when he called after her, "Wait a minute, what bas-relief?" She'd drag him down there later when she had time.

Three students were waiting in her office, two asking for extensions and one complaining of writer's block, but when they left, they were planning on getting things done, and two of them said they liked her hair.

What's with my hair? she thought, and went down to the faculty restroom to look in the mirror. Her hair seemed longer now, curling around her ears instead of close-cropped, and the gray was shot with white. She looked closer at the streaks. Almost blue-white. It would have been disturbing if it hadn't looked so much better than it usually did. Maybe being a goddess meant you got good hair. With any luck, it would work on her skin, too.

She went back to the office and picked up the finished handouts and walked up the flight of stone steps to her classroom, where her students seemed dumbfounded to find her focused and summing up on time, not caught by the hour bell. She taught her second class with equal efficiency, and then she went to the coffeehouse to paint.

And during all of it, while people finished things when she told them to, helpless to resist, she wondered, *What's the price going to be for all of this? What the hell is Kammani up to?*

And what is Sam doing with her?

ELEVEN

When Shar got to the coffeehouse, she stopped to consider the big blank white wall she'd painted to the left of the door. They'd talked about what they were going to do with it, but now as she stared at it, she could see figures there, three of them, and a sky, and . . .

"I'm going to do a mural on that wall," she told Abby, who was filling the cookie case.

"Cool." Abby closed the sliding glass door just as Daisy came out with her laptop.

"You know, we could make this place hugely successful," Daisy said, sitting down at a table next to where Shar was working. "I accidentally charged some people two bucks for a cookie on Friday and they paid it. And they've been lining up every morning since then."

Abby took the other seat, brushing powdered sugar off her hands. "I'm out of cookies by eight every morning. If this keeps up, I'm going to need help."

Shar picked up the thick cylinder of charcoal she'd bought on her second trip to Mr. Casey's. *I want those three goddesses on here,* she thought, seeing them float on the wall before her still. *And the outside of the coffeehouse behind them. And behind that I want an amber sunrise that starts on the left and then turns into the heat of day with a cinnamon sky and then ends in a blue night sky. I want suns and flowers and stars.*

And a frieze with dogs. Lots of dogs.

And I want Sam.

No, not Sam.

Daisy frowned at the figures on her laptop. "It's a shame we can't hire more bakers, but you know, not many goddesses are looking for work."

"There's Gen and Bun," Abby said. "I don't know that fertility and birth cookies are a good idea, but maybe they'd be . . . inspirational. . . ."

"Shar?" Daisy said.

"I'm listening," Shar lied, and began to draw, big sweeps of the charcoal on the white primer, tracing the goddesses that floated there, clear as day, the contrast between the charcoal and white startling, the lines rough and crumbly as they curved and scraped and made her breathe faster, and her spirit lifted as she drew because it was the right thing to do, this picture, this wall, *this coffeehouse, these people. . . .*

She leaned against the wall until the spasm passed, while behind her, Daisy outlined the plan for the coffeehouse: a website, a logo, a signature drink, souvenir mugs, T-shirts, the works.

"Sounds good to me," Abby said. "Maybe I can figure out Kammani's tonic recipe, too."

Shar kept drawing. "That might be good. If we could figure out what was in it that kicks up our powers without having to get it from Kammani . . ."

Abby nodded. "I've found Granny B's notebooks, and it was clear she was trying to figure it out herself. I'm not sure how she even knew about temple tonic, but I'm guessing there must be some sort of racial memory going on. Anyway, the stuff would sell like crazy, so I'm all for making this place a real business. There's only one problem. Who's going to pay for the logo design, that stuff?"

Shar waved that away. "I have money. If you design the website, I know an art prof I can pay to get the logo done. But those butter cookies, as good as they are, aren't just cookies, and neither is that tonic. We're messing with forces we don't understand and—"

"And there's a line from every bad horror movie ever made," Daisy said. "What's to understand?"

"Kammani," Shar said. "She did a mind meld on Abby, remember? And there's Sam, working with her." *And Noah.* She stopped drawing and looked at them both. "I don't think we should go to the class tonight."

"You don't trust Sam?" Abby said. "He seems really nice."

"He is really nice," Shar said, trying not to think of him holding Milton as they watched movies, or of the earnestness with which he asked questions about *The Big Lebowski,* or of the surprising sweetness he could exhibit in everyday things. He wasn't a complicated man, but he was a good man. Except . . ." But he's working with Kammani. That does not inspire confidence."

"So is Noah," Daisy pointed out. "We trust him."

Shar put her eyes back on the wall. "I think I'm ready to paint now."

"We trust Noah," Daisy said firmly. "Don't we, Shar?"

"Where's Sam?" Abby said.

"Home with the dogs." *Or out hooking up. The bastard.*

"Shar?" Daisy said.

"I mean on the wall," Abby said, coming to stand beside Shar.

Shar blinked. "He doesn't belong on the wall. This is our wall."

"I'm not so sure about that," Abby said. "But it's your mural. I have to make more cookies. It's okay with me if we don't go to class tonight. I'll work on the tonic recipe." And she went back into the kitchen while Daisy looked at Shar speculatively.

"It's your wall, but you don't want your guy on there."

"He's not my guy," Shar said, trying to keep her voice light. She drew a line on the wall and the charcoal snapped under the pressure.

"Shar Summer, you've got some springs inside that are wound way too tight," Daisy said. "When they pop, you're gonna take somebody's eye out."

"I'm not as trusting as you," Shar said miserably. She'd been so happy, dazzled by the paint and the punch and Sam. And then reality had returned. "I don't know about Noah because I don't know Noah, but Sam . . . Sam is Kammani's right-hand man. Besides, Sam's slept with at least a dozen women since he got here. He has a hard time remembering their names, but he has no trouble getting their phone numbers. I'd just get lost in the crowd."

"Your god is a manwhore?" Daisy speculated for a moment. "Well. That's some chewy delicious irony for you."

Shar dropped the charcoal and picked up her paintbrush. "Other than that, he's a good guy. Who's working for a goddess who may want to eat our brains."

"That's Mina," Daisy said. "Kammani probably just wants our fresh, beating hearts. Another good reason not to go to the class tonight."

Shar thought about Sam's heart in the wall of her bedroom and shuddered. Then she thought about Sam in her bedroom and shuddered again, imagining him reaching for her.

Deep slow breaths.

"Shar?" Daisy said, and Shar said, "It's okay, I'm on top of it," and began the underpainting, laying in the shadows and the contouring in browns and creams until the mural looked ominous, brooding.

"You *really* need to lighten up," Daisy said over her laptop.

An hour later, all the underpainting was in and Shar was ready to do the hard part.

Sky first, she thought, and painted in an amber sunrise streaked with creamy clouds tinged with cinnamon, and a big sun, like a huge butter cookie, coming up over the horizon. She breathed deeper and then moved to the middle, where she painted the heat of day in cinnamon streaked with cool blue clouds, the colors practically bouncing off the wall and setting up that low hum inside her as she added yellow daisies, flying over the sky. And then she sank into the deep indigo of the night, her blood pounding to its beat, picking out pale blue stars faintly blushed with cinnamon that prickled on her skin, set around a crescent moon of palest amber. Then she thought, *Not yet,* and picked up the blue again to dash small blue birds in the yellow sunrise, that went on like little gasps. *Now,* she thought, and stepped back.

The sky was exactly what she wanted. Primitive but still modern, bright but comforting, cheerful but strong . . .

"It's us," Daisy said from behind her. "I forgive you for starting with brown."

"It's going to take me days," Shar said, keeping a lid on the bubble in her blood, "but it'll be great when it's done." She heard the confidence in her own voice and was amazed. "And we need a new name for this place, too." She looked over at Abby, who'd come out of the kitchen to see, dusting flour off her hands. "If that's okay with you."

"Yeah, I don't see us as Granny B," Abby said, staring at the wall. "It's gorgeous. Are those scribbles under the sky us? How about Three Goddesses and a Lust Cookie?"

Shar laughed, and then the door to the coffeehouse opened and she turned, and Sam came in with Wolfie and Milton, dressed like any other guy in the jeans and the chambray shirt she'd bought him, looking like the god he was—*a veritable lust cookie*—and her smile widened in spite of herself because it was so good to see him, especially with the dogs looking up at him adoringly. Bowser and Bailey came out and barked their hellos, and the place seemed filled with dogs and goddesses and one amazing god.

"Hey," Sam said to her, with his open smile that made her bite her lip. "We watched *Big China* again. Milton insisted."

"I'm feeling kinda invincible," Wolfie barked.

"Sonofabitch," Milton barked, and Shar met Sam's eyes and laughed with him, feeling the lightness in her bones, the lift in her heart again.

"Three Goddesses and Their Four Dogs," Abby said, and shook her head. "That's not it, either. We'll get it."

"Three goddesses and their four dogs?" Sam said.

"A name for this place." Shar turned back to the mural and started to paint in the flat planes of the coffeehouse in Bea's happy lavender that popped beautifully against the sky. The color made her skin prickle, and Sam was standing so close, if she reached out she could touch him. She wasn't going to touch him; she drew a deep breath as the pressure built inside her and began to twist, and she thought, *Not here, not with Sam here,* and forced the feeling down. "It doesn't have to be Three Goddesses."

"Three is the perfect number," Sam said.

"Perfect for what?" Daisy asked.

"Three goddesses began the world," Sam said. "In the beginning, before time began, there were the Three. The First saw glimmers of light and caught them in her bowl, beautiful and strong. She threw them to the Next, who gathered them on her spindle and spun them to make the sky bloom with the heat of the day. Then the Last took the light and shattered it into stars with her sword to give the world night and peace and rest."

"Triple goddess," Shar said, pausing with the paintbrush in her hand. "Why is three the perfect number?"

"My uncle Milki told me that."

"Uncle Milki?" Shar said, startled, and Abby came out of the kitchen, looking interested.

"He was big on numbers. 'Without three, there would be no dimension,' " Sam said. " 'Two lines cannot enclose a space.' There was more, but I always tuned out about then."

"Milki-la-el?" Shar said.

"Yes."

"Milki-la-el who invented mathematics," Shar said. "He was really your uncle?"

"Of course not," Sam said. "He was mortal. He was a priest to my aunt Nisaba."

"Who was a goddess." Shar went back to her mural. Every time she got to thinking he was a guy, he said something that reminded her he was a god.

Abby spoke from behind the counter. "Milki is real? Because Christopher has somebody talking in his head and he says it's someone named Milki."

"Talking in his head?" Sam said, and looked at Shar.

"No, that is not usual for this world," Shar said, and went back to painting.

"But if Milki really existed—," Abby went on.

"He existed," Sam said.

"—then Christopher isn't crazy at all."

"No crazier than the rest of us," Daisy said, watching Shar. "We bring down the curve."

"Go talk to Christopher about Milki, Sam," Shar said, painting thick strokes of lavender for the frame around the coffeehouse windows, not adding, *It would be so nice if you had some* male *friends.*

"Are you angry with me, Shar?" Sam said, sounding puzzled.

"No," Shar said, and the silence stretched out.

"It would help if you'd quit having sex with every woman in town," Abby offered, and when Shar turned and glared at her, she said virtuously, "If nobody tells him, he'll never know."

Sam looked at her. "This bothers you, Shar?"

"I think you sleep with too many women." Shar lined the side of the building in the mural with a purple shadow, concentrating to steady her hand so she wouldn't turn around and run him through with the end of her brush, screaming, *Yes, it bothers me!*

That would be hard to explain.

"How can there be too many?" Sam said.

"And that confirms my manwhore diagnosis," Daisy said.

"Manwhore?" Sam said.

Shar kept her eyes on her mural. "Okay, I'll try to explain this to you." *Stay calm. He's a god. He doesn't think like you do.* "Men who constantly sleep with many different women for short periods of time are not attractive. They are immature and callous and incapable of establishing human bonds, and while they often feel that they are in some way superior by doing this, they are in fact compensating from deep inferiority or a lack of basic human decency. They are pathetic loser sleazeballs, and by behaving like this, you are joining their ranks." So much for calm.

"Loser sleazeballs," Sam said.

"That's the technical term," Daisy said. "The popular term is 'manwhore.' " She pushed the plate closer to him. "Have a cookie."

"Never mind," Shar said. "Four thousand years ago as a god, you were probably perfectly in sync with prevailing values. It's just that it's the twenty-first century, you've been here four days, and you've probably slept with a dozen women—"

Sam opened his mouth, and Wolfie wagged his tail and whined, "Don't say it; don't say it; don't say it."

"More than a dozen," Shar said, clamping down on her temper.

"Has anyone complained?" Sam said, looking honestly concerned. "Has anyone called me a sleazeball?"

"Just me," Shar said. "No one is complaining; they're probably all singing your praises. They're probably forming clubs."

"Temples," Sam said.

"I was *kidding,*" Shar said, turning around to glare.

"So was I," Sam said.

Shar looked at him, amazed. "Where did you learn to kid people?"

"I've been here five days," Sam said. "You are not a complex people."

"Oh, yeah?" Shar thought about it. "No, I guess we're not. Never mind." She went back to her mural.

Sam got up and came to stand behind her, surveying the mural over her head, and he was so close—even with her eyes closed, she'd have known it was him—that it took everything she had to keep from turning around.

"Dogs and Goddesses," Sam said.

"What?"

"Dogs and Goddesses," he said. "That's what this place is about. That's a good name."

"I like it," Abby said.

Shar turned and looked up at him and found him gazing down at her, those hot, dark eyes locked on hers.

"Dogs and Goddesses," he said. "Best things in the world. My world."

Mine, too, she thought, and didn't kiss him because Abby and Daisy were watching, and because it was a really bad idea, but she wanted to, the memory of that first kiss came back at the worst moments, and then he nodded and turned away and went out, and she knew he was going to Kammani because the dog class was in three hours.

It doesn't matter, she thought, although it did, tremendously, but there was nothing she could do, so she went back to painting the coffeehouse on the wall, and when it was finished, with a new striped awning in yellow and coral, she carefully lettered *Dogs and Goddesses* on the windows and it looked exactly right.

Abby came out and said, "I like it."

"Good," Shar said, staring at it. The wall was so much better than her life.

"Uh, I'm going out," Abby said.

"Okay."

"I have to see a man about a voice."

"Okay."

Shar stared at the mural as Abby left and Daisy came out to look at it, too. "I see your problem," she said quietly.

"Did I misspell something?" Shar said, squinting at the painted windows. There were an awful lot of *s*'s in "goddesses."

"No," Daisy said. "About Sam. He's a manwhore, yes, but you can trust him, like I trust Noah. You have to believe in something sometime, Shar. You can't footnote your way through life, double-checking everything."

"Yeah," Shar said, looking at the three figures she'd sketched on the wall. "I think I'll believe in goddesses. I'll believe in the three of us."

Then she went back to painting and thought treacherously, *And Sam.*

At the last minute Abby decided to walk. She only had the vaguest idea of where Christopher's haunted house was, and it would be easier finding it on foot than driving around in circles like a stalker. Plus there was always the possibility he was at the math building.

She walked past Bun and Gen sunbathing on the green, dressed in matching bikinis, and for the first time,

Abby had no doubts at all that she was looking at the incarnations of Fertility and Pregnancy, cheerful and fecund.

"Hey, Abs!" Bun said, feeding a Cheeto to her tiaraed dog. "Where are you going?"

"You guys have any idea where Christopher Mackenzie lives?" Abby asked, while Bowser held a muted conversation with the elderly Baby, making polite inquiries about her health and digestive system.

"Of course I do," Gen said, peering up from behind her oversized sunglasses. "He's my cousin."

Bun rolled her eyes and giggled. "Professor Mackenzie is scary as shit, and he's wrong. You and I are just alike and I suck at math."

"Yeah, you do," Gen said, giggling, too. "But Christopher isn't scary—he's just, you know, reserved. And he's a great teacher."

"Now that surprises me," Abby said. "I would have thought his students would bore him."

"He loves math," Gen said. "I mean, he really *loves* math, and he loves it when other people get it. Anyway, Cousin Christopher isn't nearly as whacked as some people"—she cast a pointed look at Bun—"think."

But Bun was oblivious, shoving another Cheeto at Baby.

"Damned things give me gas, but I love 'em," Baby muttered to Bowser, who made sympathetic noises.

"You going to see him, Abs?" Gen asked.

"I needed to tell him something," she said dismissively. "Uh, how long has your family lived here?"

"Forever. Just like Bun's. Our families were here when the town was founded."

"The first families," Bun said. "Seven of them. You're one, too. My mother says you should come to dinner." She smiled up, cheerful. "Don't. My family is nuts."

"Hmmm. So that makes Christopher a descendent from one of those families?"

"I guess so," Gen said, pushing her sunglasses up onto her forehead to look at Abby. "Why?"

"Just putting pieces together."

Gen grinned at her. "You like him, don't you?"

Abby could feel the color rise in her face. "Certainly not. Bun's right—he's cold and unfriendly."

"Oh, I'm never right," Bun said genially.

Gen nodded. "You do like him. Good. He needs someone."

"He doesn't need me!" Abby protested. "I just want to tell him something."

"O-kay." Gen drew the word out with appropriate skepticism. "He's in the old house at the edge of the quad." She pointed, her flower-stenciled fingernails sparkling in the sunlight. "Say hi for me."

Abby and Bowser started across the green. "I bet you think I shouldn't be doing this," she said to him. "But he needs to know he's not crazy."

"Very noble," Bowser growled.

"You know, nobody likes a sarcastic dog," Abby said.

"Know you too well," Bowser said.

It was a muggy day, and Abby was wearing nothing but a thin sundress. Maybe she should have put on something a little less revealing, she thought as they crossed the street, moving toward the old house. Christopher had already said she wasn't what he wanted, and he certainly was a far cry from her heart's desire, no matter what the fucking cookies tried to tell her, but something a little more demure might have been a good idea.

She started up the cracked sidewalk. Professor Mackenzie's house was straight out of a Gothic nightmare. It looked about a hundred years old, with leaded windows, dark shingles, a slate roof missing several pieces, and wildly overgrown landscaping. It looked about as welcoming as a funeral home, and Abby and Bowser both faltered on the front steps.

"Maybe I should have called first?" she said. "Maybe I should have stayed home?"

For once Bowser wasn't talking. He padded up the front steps beside her, his huge presence at least some source of comfort, and waited beside her while she knocked on the door.

She was half-hoping he wouldn't be there, but the door opened with suspicious speed, and Christopher Mackenzie stood there, looking none too pleased to see her. He was wearing jeans and a shirt with the sleeves rolled up. His glasses were pushed to the top of his head, and he looked dusty, sweaty, and bad tempered. He should be the last thing she wanted. She hadn't even eaten cookies in a couple of days. So why was she feeling this sudden ache inside her, which only he could fill?

"Well?" he said, after a minute. "Are you just going to stand there staring at me? Or did you come for a reason?"

"Such a lovely welcome," she said. "I was momentarily dazzled by your charm and beauty." Unfortunately, that was only half a lie. "I came to talk to you."

"All right," he said, opening the door wider.

"We could talk on the porch," she said, suddenly nervous.

"And have half the student population of Summerville College watch and conjecture? I don't think so. If you want to talk to me, you can come in. Otherwise go home."

So much for errands of mercy. She was half-tempted to turn on her heel and stomp away, except you couldn't stomp very well in sandals, and she could see the troubled darkness in his eyes, and that treacherous softening inside her pushed her forward. "Okay," she said, stepping inside the cool, dark house.

Bowser hadn't moved, sitting down on the peeling front porch. "Aren't you coming?" she said.

"Your dog is welcome," Christopher said.

"Staying here," Bowser growled. "Waiting."

"I thought you didn't like dogs," Abby said to Christopher, hesitating in the open doorway.

"I like dogs," Christopher said, and the admission seemed almost painful. "I've never had one, but I like them."

That was enough to shock her. "Never had a dog? Even as a child?"

"My foster parents were allergic. And we didn't have the time to care for a dog."

Bowser had collapsed onto the porch with a peaceful sigh, clearly determined, and she gave up trying and followed Christopher into the darkened hallway. He closed the door behind her, and for a moment it felt like they were floating in the shadows. A stained-glass window let shards of colored light splintering the darkness, and the house smelled of dust, old books, and fresh coffee.

"That's ridiculous," she said, forcing herself to stay on task. "Even if they worked full-time you could have taken care of a dog."

"I worked full-time, too."

"Child labor?" she said, disbelieving.

"Child prodigy," he replied. "We had government grants, research. I spent my childhood in a laboratory."

"What about school?" she asked, appalled.

"I didn't need conventional schooling. My foster mother took care of the basics. By the time I got my second Ph.D., it really didn't matter."

"And how old were you at that point?" No dog, no

school, no real family. It was little wonder that he seemed like an antisocial pain in the ass, when in truth he was nothing more than a sad little boy, and she wanted to put her arms around him.

He'd probably run screaming if she tried it.

"I was seventeen. Did you come to talk to me about my peculiar childhood or did you have some other pressing reason?" he said, clearly impatient.

"Why did you have foster parents? What happened to your real ones?"

He let out a long-suffering sigh, sounding bored. "My mother died young, and my father wasn't equipped to raise a child with my . . . talents. He put me in the care of people who could properly train me. Unfortunately, I never learned the gift for small talk. Why are you here?"

"It's never too late to learn," she said, at least some of her nerves vanishing. "When someone comes to visit, you invite them into the house; you offer them a place to sit and something to drink. And you don't bully them."

He said nothing for a long moment. "This way," he finally muttered, heading into one of the adjoining rooms, leaving her to follow him.

She immediately wished she'd kept her mouth shut. The room was dark, as shadowy as the hallway, with heavy velvet curtains blocking the windows. There were piles of books everywhere, a couple of chairs covered with more books and papers, and a brass bed pushed up against the marble fireplace. The bed was rumpled, unmade, pulling her.

"This is the only room that has furniture," he said. "I haven't gotten around to buying more. Have a seat." He gestured toward the bed, daring her.

"I think a chair will be fine." She scooped up the books and papers and set them carefully on the floor before sitting in the old chair. The springs were long gone, and she sank down with a definite lack of grace.

"Suit yourself," he said, taking the bed. "I'm afraid I can't offer you anything to drink, or eat for that matter. I just finished the last of the coffee and I usually go out to eat."

"Somehow that doesn't surprise me." He was too thin. He needed more than cookies and punch. He needed something to make him whole as well. "I wanted to talk to you about the voices."

He froze. "I'm really not interested in discussing that with you. I can't imagine why I even told you in the first place. It was a moment of weakness."

"Maybe I'm easy to talk to?" she said, getting impatient.

"You're annoying."

Abby gritted her teeth. "Did you ever stop to think there might be a reason why you're here?"

"I know why I'm here. I dropped out of my foster parents' research program and came here to teach math."

"But why Summerville College?"

"My mother's family lived here. There aren't many people left—"

"Only Gen."

He looked at her. "You've been busy," he said, his voice cool.

"I saw her on the way over. She told me where you lived."

"She's the one I get to thank," he said, not sounding particularly grateful.

"So you left your parents' research program and moved back here. . . ."

"My foster parents," he said in a stiff voice.

"How old were you when you went to live with them?"

"What the hell business is it of yours?" He stared at her, stony-faced. "I was four."

"You lived with them for more than twenty years and you never thought of them as anything but your foster parents?" she said, appalled.

"The Hedleys were not particularly parental. Which was fine; I wasn't particularly childlike. Are you going to get to the point or are we going to continue with group therapy here?"

"I think there's a reason you hear Miltie's voice."

"Milki's," he corrected her, glowering. "And I'm not particularly interested in your theories. If that's all you came to talk about, you can leave."

She was tempted. If it weren't for the shadow in the back of his eyes . . ."I don't think you're imagining it. You're not channeling Einstein or Stephen Hawking; you're hearing someone who is specific to this time and place."

"Specific to 4000 B.C. Mesopotamia, you mean."

She bit her lip, not sure what to tell him, what he might believe. She kept thinking of the Wicked Witch of the West—"these things must be done delicately"—and pushed up from the sagging springs, crossing the shadowy room with the dust motes dancing in the air.

"There's something about the original Seven Families," she said. "Things that have been passed down." She took a deep breath. "I don't hear a Mesopotamian mathematician talking to me. But I hear dogs talking."

He didn't look impressed, so she persevered. "It turns out I'm descended from an ancient Mesopotamian priestess. There are seven of us, and we meet at a dog-training class in the history building. . . ." Her voice trailed off at the expression on his face.

"You think this is funny?" he snarled.

"I'm telling you the truth. And it's not just me; it's Daisy and your cousin Gen and Shar Summer and—"

"You're all descended from Mesopotamian priestesses?"

"And Sam . . . he came from the bas-relief, and he's related to your friend Milki, and you know, I even have powers. . . ." She was standing in front of him, and he was staring up at her like she was out of her mind. "I can prove it. Those cookies I gave you. They make you hungry for your heart's desire. That's why you came back to the coffeehouse."

"I wanted more cookies?"

She took a deep breath. "You wanted me. At least, maybe not consciously, but why do you think you kissed me when you don't even like me?"

"I like you," he said. "You're a little strange, but I like you." He leaned back a little, looking at her, and the defenses and the sarcasm dropped away. "So if the cookies made me come and jump you in the kitchen, what did they do to you? Assuming you were eating these magic cookies, too?"

"I was."

"And?"

Oh, shit. She was standing too close to him, and she started to back away, but he reached up and caught her hand, and the darkness was gone from his eyes. He was looking at her with none of the defensiveness and anger that had danced around them, looking at her with a sudden, heated intent. "And that's why I kissed you back," she said nervously, wondering if she should pull away.

But his thumb was moving back and forth over her skin, bringing forth a frisson of reaction, and she wasn't going anywhere. Not when he was finally ready to open up.

"I'm no longer worried about being insane," he said, his voice wry. "Compared to you I'm a paragon of mental health."

"You don't have to believe me," she said, flustered.

"No, I don't," he said. "As a matter of fact, there's only one interesting piece of information in your entire long-winded fantasy."

"What's that?"

"That I'm your heart's desire." He was tugging her toward him gently, and she knew she ought to pull free, get the hell out of there. Because she'd tried, he didn't believe her, and by now he was even more convinced she was a nutcase, and . . .

He pulled, and she stumbled out of her sandals, and his body was hard and warm and strong as she tumbled onto the unmade bed. She found herself flat on her back in the middle of the mattress, and he was leaning over her, his eyes dark, searching, though she didn't know what he was looking for.

And then it didn't matter. He brought his hand up and carefully pushed her tumbled hair off her face. He let his fingertips touch her skin, her nose and her cheeks, her lips, her jaw. "You actually think you're the descendent of a Mesopotamian priestess?" His voice was soft and low.

"Actually I'm a demi-goddess." Her voice shook just the tiniest bit as his fingertips danced across her lips.

"Even better," he said. "I've never been to bed with a demi-goddess before."

She didn't move. "Who says I'm going to bed with you?"

"Where do you think we are? You aren't getting up, are you?" He began unbuttoning his shirt slowly, waiting for her protest.

"No," she said. "I'm not." She reached up and pushed his hands away, unfastening the buttons with shaking hands, pulling the shirt away from him. He had smooth, hard skin, sleek and perfect, and he was hot; everything was hot in this shadowy room. She touched him, put his hand on his chest to feel his heart beating, fast.

"Are you checking to see whether I have a heart or not?"

"You have a heart."

His faint smile was unexpected, and for the first time she could see what his habitual glower had hidden. He had dimples. The most gorgeous dimples bracketing the sides of his mouth. "So are you going to finish undressing me?"

Shit. Now was the time to tell him she'd never done this before. She opened her mouth to say something, but he covered it with his own, a fierce kiss of such hunger that all hesitation vanished, and she kissed him back, rising to meet him, sliding her arms around his neck, and pulling him down to her.

He had her naked in under a minute. She was so busy kissing him, being kissed, that she barely noticed that he'd managed to slide off her sundress with far too much practice.

Somewhere in the back of her mind she thought, *I ought to be nervous. Wary.* But the way his long fingers slid over her skin, touching her, the way his mouth moved slowly, so slowly down the side of her neck to her breasts, kissing her, and she let out a little squeak—she wasn't sure if it was surprise or arousal or both—but Christopher was too busy.

Not that she had anything to compare it to, but damn, he was good. He knew just how and where to touch her, and when he slid his fingers inside her, she arched, feeling a little explosion of pleasure, and she gasped, throwing her head back in shock as the ripples ran through her body, and he rubbed her harder, and a stronger climax rocked her body, and she tried to say something, but no words came out, just a soft, keening kind of sound, as her body went rigid and the spasms shook her.

He took his hand away, and she wanted to cry, but he simply kissed her again, a slow, deliberate kiss that had her sweating and shaking and ready to come again, just from his mouth on hers, his hands on her breasts, and she wanted so much more, she was going crazy.

She tried to pull him over her body, between her legs "Now," she said in a rushed little voice.

"Why are you in such a hurry? Afraid the dogs will tell on you?" His voice was slightly strained, as if he was trying to sound cool and failing.

"Now," she said, desperate. She needed him inside her she needed to be filled, deep and hard, and it was him only him, she had to have.

"Whatever you say," he said, pulling her legs apart. He handed her something, and she realized with shock that he'd given her a condom. He must expect her to put it on him. She tried to tear open the package, but her hands were shaking too much, and she was going to try to tear it with her teeth when he took it back from her, ripping it open and sheathing himself. She could feel his erection against her hard, waiting, and she realized she hadn't touched him hadn't even looked at him. She'd seen enough porn in her life to know what to expect, read enough romance novels to know it would be somewhere in between, and she really didn't want to think anymore; she just wanted to feel.

But a last moment of honesty stopped her, and she put her hands on his narrow hips, running her fingers across the silken skin. "I've never done this before," she managed to say.

She wasn't sure what she expected. Sweetness. Tenderness. "Everyone gives in to irrational lust at least once in their life," he said. And he pushed inside her with a muffled groan of pleasure.

She was expecting pain, blood, but there was nothing but a sharp twinge. She couldn't keep back the small cry of pain as he pushed deep inside her, but then it was suddenly wonderful, and for the first time in her life she felt complete.

He was frozen, not moving, and she couldn't see his expression in the shadows. She didn't need to. He was looking down at her, but she kept her eyes closed, and he must have guessed what she'd tried to tell him.

It didn't matter. He'd eaten the cookies and he'd come to her. Whether he knew it or not, they belonged together, and this would only make it clearer to him. But she needed more, not this sudden, almost unearthly stillness.

"No." The protest was low in his throat, and she felt him start to pull away from her.

"Yes," she said, her fingers digging in, pulling him back, desperate not to lose him. They weren't finished; he wasn't finished.

And then his last reserve vanished, and he reached down, pulling her legs around him, so that he was deeper still, and he closed his eyes, the thick slide of his cock inside her sending sparks through her body, and she realized she wasn't finished, either.

She was covered with sweat and so was he, their bodies slapping against each other, and each deep thrust shook her, shook the bed, shook her soul. He put his hand between their bodies to touch her, hard, and she looked into his eyes for a frozen moment, into eyes dark with passion and pain and need, and she wanted to tell him something, anything to drive the pain away, but it was too late; he touched her and she splintered, her body dissolving, and she heard his muffled groan as he went rigid in her arms.

She expected him to collapse against her, to draw her into his arms. She wanted to hold him until the tremors passed, but instead he pulled away, rolling off her, beside her, and she heard him trying to catch his breath as the last stray shudders danced through her body.

"This is wrong," he said in a flat voice. "This is all wrong."

She said nothing, unmoving.

"We need to talk," he said. She waited for him to touch her, to hold her, but a moment later he was out of the bed, leaving her alone there as he vanished into the shadows. "Stay there. I'll be right back."

She curled up for a long moment, wrapping the discarded sheet around her, hugging herself. It was hardly hearts and flowers. Irrational lust, he'd said, misunderstanding her tentative confession. She'd been an idiot, and he'd treated her like one. And the best thing she could do was slink away and try to forget it ever happened. She wasn't going to wait for him; she wasn't going to talk to him. She was going to run like hell.

Goddamned cookies. Goddamned Mesopotamia and demi-goddesses. She should never have come here in the first place—someone could have sold the coffeehouse for her. Her mother had connections all over the world, but no, she had to drive to southern goddamned Ohio and fall in love with a goddamned math professor and make a fool of herself.

She scrambled out of the bed, looking for her scattered clothes, pulling them on as quickly as she could. There was a bloodstain on the sheet, and she was half-tempted to drag it off the bed so he wouldn't notice, but she couldn't afford to take the time. She could only find one sandal, and she heard him coming back, through the dark, musty hallways, and she ran.

Bowser was already on his feet, waiting for her, and he looked concerned. "Abby okay?"

"Fine," she said. "Let's go home." She took off at something close to a sprint, her one sandal tucked beneath her arm. She thought she heard the front door open behind her, but she was far enough away that he couldn't come after her, couldn't call her. Not that he would.

Goddamn it. She brushed the tears from her face, determined that no one see them.

"Are you sad?" Bowser said.

"I'm a freaking idiot," she said, moving back across the green. Bun and Gen were just packing up, a new layer of toasted skin covering their ripe bodies.

"Hey, Abs!" Gen called out to her, but Abby ducked her head down. She couldn't let them see her crying. She couldn't let anyone see her crying.

"See you tonight!" she called back briskly, determined not to slow down.

The moment they were out of sight, she sped up, Bowser keeping pace with her as she turned onto Temple Street. The coffeehouse lay ahead, and there was just a small ounce of comfort to fight the chill that had taken over her body. Daisy would be there. Shar would be there. She wasn't alone.

And she broke into a run.

TWELVE

At five-thirty Shar stopped painting, turned the lights off in the front of the coffeehouse, and went into the kitchen to wash her hands. Abby had come back earlier, silent and subdued, and even Daisy's general joy in the world seemed tempered by something, probably that Kammani was holding court in half an hour with Noah by her side.

"We can't go," Shar said. "Kammani—"

"I think you're overreacting," Daisy said. "Hell, so far the worst she's done is make Abby call her Goddess—"

"Hey, it was a moment of weakness," Abby said.

"—but I don't see her doing any serious damage. Noah wouldn't work for her if she was dangerous."

Bad assumption, Shar thought.

"And if she tries anything, we have powers, too, now. We'll just kick her ass."

"Powers we don't know anything about." Shar leaned against the sink, drying her hands on one of Abby's towels. "I've been thinking about this since Sam left this afternoon. I ask him about her, about what she wants, and he says he doesn't know, he doesn't know what the tonic does, he doesn't know what she's doing here. I think—"

A movement in the doorway caught her eye, and she saw a man in a ski mask, a gun in his hand.

"Oh, *shit,*" he said.

"What the hell?" Abby said, and he pointed the gun at her.

"Everybody does what I say, nobody gets hurt," the guy said, sounding tough. "I know you're here alone, so—"

"Not alone," Bowser growled, standing up.

"Not alone," Wolfie growled, moving closer.

"Not alone," Bailey growled, moving in, too, and putting his head low.

"Son of a bitch must *pay*," Milton yipped, and Shar grabbed him before he could launch himself at the gunman.

The guy pointed his gun at Milton, and Bowser barked, "No!" and the guy swung the gun at Bowser, and Abby stepped forward, intent and angry, and while Shar watched, the gun began to stretch toward Abby, as if she were gathering it to her, as if it *wanted* to go to her, and as it began to melt from the effort, the guy yelled and flung it from him.

Then Daisy caught it somehow, steadied it in space, and it began to revolve, spinning, faster and faster until it had flattened out like a Frisbee, and then Daisy flung it toward Shar, and Shar knew it was her turn and smashed it, the pieces of it spinning into the guy's forehead as he screamed and fell backward, going down like a sack of potatoes.

Bowser lumbered over and sat on the guy's chest, and Wolfie grabbed one sleeve and Bailey got the other and dragged his arms out flat on the floor. Milton chewed on his shoe. Wolfie dropped his arm long enough to growl, "The mask, Milton!" and Milton scampered over the man's body to grab the top of the ski mask in his needle-sharp teeth and tug until the mask came off and he toppled back with it in his mouth.

"Hello, Doug," Shar said.

Doug was in no position to argue, but he did anyway.

"Get these dogs off me!" he yelled. "This is assault!"

"You come in here with a gun and you're screaming *assault*?" Daisy said, standing above him on the other side. "You must have balls the size of Manhattan."

"You weren't supposed to be here," Doug said. "You're supposed to be at the temple. And anyway, that gun was a fake. And it melted. . . . How did it melt?" He let his head drop back to the floor, overcome.

"He's not one of our major minds," Shar said.

"You're my professor," Doug said, breathless from yelling and from a hundred and fifty pounds of dog on his chest. "I can make a lot of trouble for you at the school."

"Yeah, that's a threat," Shar said. "Listen, I'm annoyed with you. You scared the hell out of all of us, and now thanks to you, my baby's first sentence was a line from a B movie."

"Yes, but it was *Big Trouble in Little China*," Abby said. "As B movies go . . ."

Doug tried to get up and Bowser wiggled his butt. All the air went out of Doug's lungs.

"So who sent you?" Daisy said.

"I came on my own," Doug said. "I just needed the money."

"You're from one of the wealthiest families in Summerville," Shar said. "You're from one of the seven original families, which makes me even more suspicious. Tell me who sent you or we turn Bowser loose."

Bowser growled, "I don't bite," and Doug's eyes got wider.

"He's growling! He's gonna bite me!"

"Not if you come clean," Abby said.

"Just spit it out," Daisy said. "Or Bowser levels Manhattan."

"Okay, okay," Doug said. "It was Mina."

"*Mina?*" Shar said. "Kammani told her to order you to do this?"

"No," Doug said. "Just Mina. She said you were getting too powerful, that we needed to shut you down before the place got too popular. She said it would help Kammani, that she'd be grateful. And Kammani's been mad at me since I slapped her on the butt."

Daisy laughed, and Doug looked surly as he began to whine.

"You wouldn't believe the stuff that's been happening to me. My car won't start and my credit got zapped. And I can't get . . ." He stopped. "Nothing works anymore."

"In other words," Daisy said, "everything died on you. Finally, Mina's powers are useful."

"Explain this to me," Shar said. "You thought stealing money would stop the coffeehouse?"

"Mina did. She thought if I took all the money and trashed the place, you'd have to close down." Doug tried to move under Bowser, but it was hopeless. "Could I get up? I can't breathe under here."

"What a shame," Abby said, and the Three faced one another over Bowser's back.

"What do we do with him?" Shar said. "I vote we call the police."

"Oh, let him go," Abby said. "He's a clueless minion of an evil minion."

Daisy looked down at him. "Or we could ask him some questions."

"He's not going to have any answers," Shar said. "We're going to have to go straight to the source for that."

"So we're going to class?" Daisy said. "Good. How about we tie him up and stick him in cold storage, keep him fresh for later?"

"Hey!" Doug said.

Bowser shifted his weight and Doug shut up to breathe.

"I think that's kidnapping," Shar said.

"I see it as more of a citizen's arrest," Daisy said. "Potato, po-tah-to."

"Okay, we're going to let you get up," Abby told him. "But if you try anything, the dogs will get you before you take a step."

"I'm not allowed to bite people," Wolfie growled. "I could go for a pant leg, though."

"Pant leg!" Bailey yelped, sounding like he was calling dibs.

"Pant leg!" Milton yelped.

"He won't try anything," Bowser growled. "I've been sitting on him."

Doug listened to the dogs growling around him and said, "Get them off me!"

"Should I get up now?" Bowser growled.

Doug looked at Bowser in terror.

Abby said, "Up, Bowser," and Bowser pushed himself off Doug, shoving the last of the air from Doug's lungs as he did.

"Okay, you can go," Daisy told Doug. "I'm pretty sure we know everything now anyway."

Like what? Shar thought. *That Mina is out to get us? And she can kill cars and cause erectile dysfunction? That's not a* help.

"I agree; let him go," Abby said. "We have bigger fish to fry."

Doug got up and looked around. "I should sue."

"Good idea," Shar said. "You can talk to your lawyer about it when he visits you in the Big House for your conviction on breaking and entering and assault. Plus cruelty to animals."

Doug flushed. "I wasn't cruel to animals."

"You scared Milton," Shar said.

"Let me bite him," Milton yipped.

"No, you may not," Shar said to Milton.

"You're all nuts," Doug said. "I'm not having anything else to do with any of you."

"Good plan," Daisy said, and he left, trying to look defiant and just looking thick as a plank.

"Great," Shar said when he was gone. "So Mina has gone from glaring at people to sending minions. What do we do now?"

"Let's go to obedience class," Abby said. "And be disobedient. I'll bring cookies. Maybe Kammani will eat one and then Daisy can click her pen and we'll see what she really wants."

"Be careful," Bowser growled.

Abby picked up a box of cookies, and Daisy said, "I've got my pen."

Shar thought about saying, *You don't need the cookies and the pen, it's all within you, but even so, this is a really dangerous idea.* But since Kammani and Co. had decided to go aggressive, anything that helped them figure out what was going on was probably worth the risk.

"Let's go," Daisy said.

"Let's go!" Bailey yipped.

"Bad idea," Wolfie whined.

"Bite him!" Milton barked.

"No biting," Shar said to Milton, and opened the back door.

As Daisy and Bailey walked into the temple behind Abby and Bowser, Daisy turned to Shar and said out of the corner of her mouth, "I don't think this is a dog obedience class anymore, Toto."

The first tip-off was that the lighting was now actual

flaming torches. Wolfie eyed them uneasily and hid behind Shar, and Bailey and Bowser weren't happy about them, either.

The second clue was Umma and Bikka dressed in what looked like mini–horse blankets of white linen, embroidered in gold.

"Cute," Daisy said.

"Uh-huh," Shar said.

"I brought cookies," Abby said loudly, and headed into the room, laden with sugar, flour, butter, and purpose. Daisy followed Shar to their seats at the center of the half circle of chairs at the bottom of the altar and then stopped, startled to see Vera sitting in the last chair in the row. Vera put her cup of tonic down, took a cookie from Abby, shared a piece with Squash, and then noticed them and said, "Oh, hi, Daisy!"

Daisy waved back as Mina appeared, dressed in a severe black business suit. Abby handed her a cookie on her way to Bun and Gen, and Mina bit into it cautiously. *Thatta girl,* Daisy thought, and then Mina looked up and caught Daisy watching and frowned, straightening to stare at her, and Daisy felt a chill as Mina's eyes bored into her.

What the hell? It was bad enough the wench had sent Doug to rob the coffeehouse, now she was using her powers on them? Daisy drew up her anger from her center and shot back, sending the chill away as her breeze blew Mina's hair into her bug eyes.

On the wall, a torch started to slip out of its brace, and Mina ran to right it again.

Good. Daisy smiled down at Bailey, who quivered at her feet. "And that, m'love, is how it's done."

Abby sat down next to Daisy and picked up one of the cups of tonic that had been set on a tray behind the chairs. "I need to get this back to the coffee shop so I can figure out what's in it. Anybody bring a bottle with you?"

Shar took a water bottle out of her purse, poured the last bit of water on the stone floor behind her chair, and handed the bottle to Abby. Then she said to Daisy, "I saw that."

"What?" Daisy said.

"You used your power just to annoy Mina."

Daisy held up her hands. "Do you see a clicky pen?"

Shar met her eyes. "Daisy."

Daisy sighed. "Okay, *fine*. So I blew a little chaos wind at Mina. Big deal."

"Look," Shar said, her voice low as the three of them leaned together in their seats. "We have to be careful. Everybody's had Abby's cookies. Be careful who you activate. God knows what Mina wants; we don't need her acting on it. It's Kammani we're here for, remember?"

"It's no big deal—," Daisy began, but then Mina said, "You! Move!" and Daisy looked up to see her glaring down at Vera.

"I'm sorry?" Vera said, sounding surprised.

"I need to be seated at my goddess's left hand," Mina said.

Squash raised her head and said, "Tell her to bug off."

"Oh, well," Vera said, "Squash is so comfortable, do you think you could . . . ?" and she motioned genially to the empty seat between her and Shar.

"No," Mina said, her voice laced with a deep contempt that went surprisingly well with her business suit. "You are weak." She shot a look directly at Daisy. "Those who are weak do not deserve to be at my goddess's hand."

There was a silence while the sane people in the room watched Mina to see what her next move would be, and then Vera said, "Um. Okay. I'll just move over then," and fumbled with her bag and leash and cup of tonic as she shifted into the seat next to Shar.

Mina watched, showing teeth but definitely not smiling. *Little bitch,* Daisy thought as Mina settled into the last chair, Mort *heh-heh-heh*ing on her lap.

Daisy smiled and turned to Vera. "These seats are better, anyway, Vera. It's warmer over here."

"What are those little dogs?" Vera said. "Are those sweaters *gold*?"

Daisy squinted at Bikka and Umma. The fur around Bikka's mouth looked orange, and Umma was gazing steadily at Wolfie, who was looking at the ceiling, and they were both wearing something glittery. "I wouldn't be surprised," Daisy told Vera, but Vera's attention had already wandered.

"Hi," she was saying, holding her hand out to Shar. "I'm Vera Dale; I work with Daisy." Her eyes widened as she looked at Shar. "Oh! Professor Summer! I didn't even recognize you. Your hair is practically glowing. Have you been using that herbal tea rinse I recommended?" Before Shar could say anything, Vera leaned over her to see Abby. "And it is so nice to meet you; you are such a lovely, lovely girl."

"She *is* lovely," Daisy said. "Her name is Abby."

"So let me ask you, Abby," Vera said. "Do you take vitamins?" She took a sip from her cup, and Daisy waited for her reaction.

"This is so *yummy*." Vera drained her cup.

If you think it's good now, wait till your dog starts talking to you.

"Mina gave me a bottle as I came in," Vera whispered, pulling a ceramic bottle out of her bag. "Is it the same stuff?"

"Yep," Daisy said.

Vera uncorked her bottle and poured more into her cup. Daisy bent down to pet Squash, who opened one eye.

"Be kind," Daisy whispered. "Don't mention the Snausages."

Squash barked, "Nice shoes!"

"Oh my god!" Vera gasped, and looked at Daisy, tears of amazement in her eyes. "Squash just told me she likes my *shoes*."

"Sweet dog," Abby said, but Shar was staring at the table behind them.

"What's wrong?" she whispered to Shar.

"We drank the tonic and got our powers," Shar whispered back, nodding her head to the cups on the table. "I'm torn. I think it's a bad idea to drink anything that Kammani makes, but . . ."

"We can use all the power we can get," Daisy finished. She picked up two of the glasses and gave one to Shar and one to Abby and then got one for herself. "I vote we drink."

Shar looked into the glass, nodded, and knocked some of it back, coughing a little as she swallowed. "This is *not* what we drank Thursday."

Daisy tasted it and the impact hit her hard. It was at least twice as potent as it had been on Thursday, and where it had been delicious before, now it was irresistible. *Power,* Daisy thought, and drank it down, almost choking at the end when Kammani appeared to stand before the altar. She wore white linen heavily embroidered in gold and beads, draped and twisted over her perfect body, tied with a golden jeweled belt with a wicked-looking knife stuck in it, and she looked taller than she had last week, more exotic, probably because of her headdress, a wreath of gold leaves with stars just above that and then—*overkill, party of one*—a gold sun at the back of her head with seven flower shapes, fanning out on top, ending in gold ribbons that fell over her ears. It looked to Daisy like a hat you'd wear at a New Year's Eve party, and then only after you'd had at least six drinks.

Abby leaned over Daisy and said to Shar, "Thin. Pretty.

Big tits. Your basic nightmare," and Daisy said, "Huh?" and Shar said, "*When Harry Met Sally*," and laughed, but then Sam followed Kammani out to the altar, and Shar's smile faded fast. He was dressed in jeans and a chambray shirt, and looked as close to ordinary as a god following a goddess in a gold party hat could, except that there was a faint glow to him.

"Look at Sam," Daisy whispered to Shar, staring at him. "Does he look—" She broke off as she saw Shar, tipping back the last of her drink.

Shar had a blue outline. Very faint, but it was there.

"Uh," Daisy said, and looked to her other side, at Abby, who had an amber glow as she put her empty cup on the floor.

Kammani walked up to the altar as Daisy looked at Gen and Bun. No glow there but a wispy haze as they moved, like a very faint trail of smoke, Gen's yellow and Bun's orange. *Poor Bun. Nobody looks good in orange,* Daisy thought, and looked at Vera, who lifted her cup to drink and left a green trail, like a special effect in a movie.

Beyond her sat Mina in a purplish smoky shadow, a definite shadow that moved with her. *Permanent darkness,* Daisy thought.

"IT BEGINS," Kammani said, and Daisy felt a sudden urge to lean forward.

Kammani said something in a language Daisy couldn't understand, but she could see color as Kammani moved, too, a pale, glittery aura, and she could feel Kammani's words floating out and folding around her like a blanket, warm and comforting and familiar.

She forced her eyes open and thought, *This isn't right,* and the comfort left her, replaced by cold suspicion.

The torches flickered, and Kammani looked at Gen. "COME."

Gen got up and crossed over to the center of the steps

and went up to meet Kammani, who raised her hands over Gen's head, holding something that glittered. Gen seemed to expand, her shoulders going back and her chin lifting, and then Kammani fastened a necklace around her neck—more of a collar, Daisy thought—and then cupped her hands over Gen's head. Daisy saw a flash of yellow light, and Gen said, "Oh!" and stumbled back, and Daisy said, "What the hell was *that*?"

Kammani's eyes flashed at Daisy, and Daisy could feel her rage as their eyes locked. For a moment, Daisy wanted to lower her head in submission, but she fought it as Gen shuddered and then came down the steps, putting her hand up to feel her new jewelry, which looked like a beaded dog collar to Daisy, gold with blue and red-orange beads.

"This is what they did four thousand years ago here," Shar whispered. "This is an investiture." She was watching Sam, who was watching her. He looked troubled, but Daisy couldn't tell if it was because of what was happening or because Shar was so tense.

She's right to be tense, Daisy thought, and looked at Abby, pale beside her. *This is bad news.*

She cast a glance at the door, suddenly feeling Noah's absence, and looked down at her watch; it was only eight past seven. He was probably just running late.

Shar put her cup on the floor as Kammani summoned Bun, and Bun approached as Gen had. As Kammani put a beaded collar around Bun's neck, Shar said, "Look."

"What?" Daisy said.

"There's an orange glow—"

Kammani had placed her hands above Bun's head, and now there was a flash of orange light and Bun squeaked. Daisy drew in her breath: that orange light had come from Bun rather than Kammani, and that wasn't right. The shocks or whatever that was had to be coming from Kammani. It didn't make any sense otherwise.

Bun felt her collar and squealed, "This is so cool!" and walked down the steps to Gen to show her the new bling.

Kammani looked at Abby, the glittery glow around her stronger now, shifting with small streaks of red and orange, and said, "COME," and Daisy felt the pull just sitting beside Abby as Shar drew in her breath.

For one moment they were motionless, and then, as if they were one person, they all leaned back.

Kammani looked startled, her eyes moving from Abby to Daisy to Shar in growing awareness, and then after a beat she set her jaw and moved on to nod at Vera, who stood immediately and walked to the altar, trailing faint green light, a little unsteady on her feet. Daisy reached over Shar and picked up the ceramic bottle on Vera's seat.

It was empty.

Kammani gave Vera her collar and put her hands over Vera's head. The light flashed, green this time, and Vera cried out and stumbled down the steps, staggering into the middle of the circle, her hand over her heart, struggling for her breath.

"Oh . . . *oh* . . ." She blinked twice, and then the faint greenish glow around her flickered and died and she collapsed.

Time stopped, and then, like the moment of impact in a car crash, everything rushed together. Sam strode forward and leaned over Vera, Kammani rushed down the steps, Mina was holding one hand behind her back, the dogs barked, Bun and Gen covered their dogs' eyes, and Daisy and Shar and Abby went to Vera as Kammani put her hand over Vera's heart.

Daisy moved forward to kneel at Vera's side and saw her eyes staring lifelessly up at the stone ceiling.

"RISE," Kammani whispered, bending low, light pulsing under her hands. "RISE!"

"Vera," Daisy said, her voice breaking, and Shar said quietly from behind her, "I called 911."

Sam straightened, looking calm but serious. "She has gone to Ereshkigal," he told Daisy, his voice kind. "She is in the Netherworld now."

"CPR!" Daisy cried out. "Does anyone know how to do CPR?"

"Clear out!"

Daisy turned as Noah pushed between Bun and Gen to get to Vera. He put his ear to her mouth for a second and then started doing chest compressions.

Daisy looked around, helpless. Gen and Bun stood hugging their dogs, their eyes wide, but Mina stared down, a slight smile on her face, and Daisy felt fury sweep over her. She wanted to rush Mina, overpower her, knock her down. Around her, wind started to blow, she could see it now, a reddish-orange wind, a fiery trail that swirled around them, but then there was warmth on either side of her as Shar and Abby drew close. Daisy looked away from Mina—*not worth it, not worth it*—and the wind calmed and the air cleared as she focused on Kammani, who stood beside Noah, her face ashen.

"What did you do?" Daisy said, breaking away from Shar and Abby to advance on her.

Kammani looked up at Daisy. "I did nothing."

"Come on," Noah urged Vera. He leaned down and put his ear to Vera's mouth, then cursed and continued chest compressions.

Daisy grabbed Kammani's hand. "Shock her. Whatever you used to make the light come from her, give it back to her. Shock her."

Kammani jerked her hand away. "I have done all I can. She is with Ereshkigal now."

"No," Daisy said. *"Do something!"*

The doors slammed open and the paramedics came in fast, competent, and—Daisy knew—useless. Noah pulled her out of the way, and all she could do was stare as the dogs barked and the paramedics worked over Vera. Finally, they shared a grim look, and one of them reached down and closed Vera's eyes. Noah stayed close to Daisy as the paramedics lifted Vera's body to the stretcher. One of them wheeled Vera out and the other spoke to Kammani, but all Daisy could do was stare at the space where Vera had been and lean against Noah.

"Hey," he said, running his hand over her shoulder, down her arm. "You okay?"

"No," she said.

The paramedic stepped away from Kammani, who stood there, looking confused and ridiculous in her costume linens and her stupid gold party hat.

A useless fucking goddess.

Daisy stalked over to her, and Sam stepped between them. Daisy scooted around him and faced Kammani, going almost nose to nose with her.

"What have you done?" Daisy yelled, her fury and panic and dread feeling like they were shooting out from her. Harsh breezes started to blow all around them, but Kammani lifted her hand and they stopped. She looked at Daisy and said, "Go."

"You killed her," Daisy said. "Whatever you put in that tonic, this is your fault. You killed her. You knew there were consequences, but you just did whatever the hell you wanted to anyway, and *now she's dead*."

"It was her time, Humusi," Kammani said. "She has left us, but you are still with me and must show respect—"

"Humusi's dead," Daisy said, her voice brittle in her throat. "I'm Daisy, and I want no part of you."

Kammani stared at her, ice in her eyes. Daisy felt herself weakening under Kammani's gaze, but then she heard a howl, "Vera!" and she turned to look.

Squash scrambled behind the paramedics as they wheeled the stretcher out, and then one of them dragged Squash back in and closed the door as she howled Vera's name again. She scratched desperately at the door, trying to dig her way back to Vera, and Bailey stood next to her, not wagging his tail or jumping, just standing quietly, like the rock he was.

"Go," Kammani said, and Daisy stepped back from her, her mind reeling, her stomach sick.

"You don't belong here," she said to Kammani. She felt Noah's hand on her shoulder and turned to look at him, his face hard and unsmiling in the flickering torchlight.

"Let's go," he said. She nodded, then headed toward the door to take Squash and Bailey home, away from this place of power and death, promising herself that she would never, ever come back.

When they were back in the coffeehouse kitchen, Shar dropped her bag on the counter and said, "I need a drink," feeling guilty that she hadn't tried to stop the investiture, and furious with Kammani for putting Vera at risk, but mostly concerned for Daisy, who looked like hell.

Abby said, "I'll see if there's anything in the pantry."

Daisy sat down heavily at the table, and Noah watched her, not hovering but ready to be there if she needed anything.

Like Vera alive again, Shar thought, and went over to sit beside her. Daisy still had that warm reddish-orange glow to her, and Shar wasn't sure if it was anger or power or—

"It was the tonic," Daisy said, her eyes glued to the table. "I knew it was powerful and I didn't stop her, I didn't warn her, and then she went up there and Kammani did her light-suck thing and . . ." She released a long breath, looking sick.

"It wasn't the tonic," Shar said. "We drank it, too. It didn't make your heart race; it made you see colors."

Daisy looked at her and said, "I could have stopped her."

Shar reached out to pat her shoulder and then drew her hand back. She was just not a patting person. "I think the tonic made her happy," she said instead. "She heard Squash talk before she died."

Wolfie barked, "Go along now," and Shar looked back at the dogs where Bowser was curled up on his huge pillow and Wolfie was nudging Squash toward him with his nose. Squash went over to the pillow and lay down in the curve of Bowser's big body, and Wolfie and a quiet Bailey followed, curling against Squash so that she was completely surrounded.

"You're in our pack now," Bowser growled, and Squash sighed, and Milton climbed on top of all of them and went to sleep.

"Do you think Vera would mind if I kept Squash?" Daisy asked.

"I think she'd love it," Shar said.

"I have Vera's address," Noah said quietly, and when Daisy looked up, he said, "From the class list. I know the super in the building. I can go pick up Squash's things, if . . ."

"Yes," Shar said when Daisy just looked at him, and then Daisy nodded and he went.

Abby came out of the pantry with a basket. "Where did Noah go?"

"To get Squash's things," Shar said, turning away from Daisy because she didn't know what to do for her. If only Daisy had flunked her history final—*that* Shar could fix.

Abby put the basket on the table. "This was all I could find."

Shar pulled it toward her. It was full of miniature bottles of booze. Bacardi, Grey Goose, Jack Daniel's, Absolut, amaretto, Drambuie: the breadth of choice was amazing.

Daisy craned her neck to see. "Looks like Grandma had a little drinking problem." Abby and Shar both looked at her, and she smiled weakly and said, "Little bottles, little drinking. Ha."

"Oh," Abby said. "I think she was using them in recipes. There's a notebook in there that has a bunch of them. I think she was trying to make the tonic. It makes sense. Your grandmother kept the history, Shar. My grandmother was trying to keep the tonic." She pulled out a tiny bottle of Amaretto. "What's your mother trying to keep, Daisy?"

"Her skin tone." Daisy took a bottle of Bacardi from the basket. "Little bottles of booze. Boozles."

Her voice was strained, but she was making jokes, so Shar took a bottle of Grey Goose because it was so pretty and said to Abby, "Do you have orange juice?"

Abby put a cup of milk in the microwave and then brought juice and Diet Coke and two glasses, and Daisy and Shar poured and stirred and looked at the two little empties as the silence stretched out. *Alice in Wonderland goes on a bender,* Shar thought, and knocked back some of her screwdriver. It wasn't as good as the tonic, but it still gave her a glow, probably because she never drank.

She looked down at her hands. The faint blue was gone, which was reassuring. Kind of.

"I saw goddamned colors," Daisy said.

"It was the tonic," Abby said. "I drank it and saw them, too." She sounded listless. "I don't know how I'm going to get that in our tonic. I'll look at Bea's notes again. She has some fairly strange ingredients in the pantry."

"Did your mom ever say anything about your great-grandmother?" Shar asked Daisy, trying to distract her from her misery. "Your mom's third generation; she's probably too far from Humusi—"

"Mina's far from Munawirtum and she has the Wortham tradition down pat," Daisy said bitterly as she stared into her glass. "She *enjoyed* Vera's death. Did you notice that?"

"The Worthams are weird as hell and always have been," Shar said, and then remembered Noah was a Wortham. "The Wortham women always have been. The men have been *wonderful.*" She took another sip. She was having two drinks tonight. It would be a first for her, but this was a two-drink night if there ever was one.

"My mother never said a word about it," Abby said, and then the microwave dinged, and she ripped open an envelope of hot chocolate mix, stirred it into the hot milk, and poured in some amaretto. It smelled like heaven.

Maybe after my second vodka, Shar thought, and said to her, "You have a mother?"

"She's out in California," Abby said. "Amanda Richmond, the Real Estate Goddess." She stopped. "Oh, hell. I always thought that was just a business thing, that she called herself that. It's on her *business cards,* and I never got it."

"So you think she knows?" Shar said.

"They all know," Daisy said. "Right when Kammani showed up, my mother dumped Bailey on me and went to New York for allergy treatments. She's not allergic to Bailey; she's allergic to responsibility." She lifted her drink, took a generous gulp, and set it back on the table. "My money says they all knew."

"Did your mom know?" Abby asked Shar.

"Oh, yes," Shar said. "I remember her arguing with my grandmother, saying, 'She's never coming.' I think . . ."

She tried to remember her mother, what she'd been like aside from the default "my mother," and all she could remember was Sharon bent over her research. "I think my grandmother kept her under her thumb, kept her trained as a priestess because she thought Kammani was coming back at any minute."

"And your grandmother learned that from her mother," Abby said.

"No," Shar said. "My grandmother was Sharrat. She was one of the original seven."

"Whoa." Daisy put her glass down, empty, and reached for another little bottle. "So you actually knew the real deal."

"Yes," Shar said, thinking of her flintlike grandmother. She'd had a kind of terrible beauty, even into her nineties, all cheekbones and dark eyes, driven by impatience and fury. "Be glad you missed out on knowing your ancestor."

"I think Granny liked her mother." Abby looked around the kitchen. "Her mom started this coffeehouse back in 1925 when the college was built and then gave it to Granny. I think Abi-simti was okay."

"Who cares?" Daisy put her empty glass on the table again. "That's history and this is now." She poked her finger into the basket. "Where the hell did all the rum boozles go?"

Shar pulled the basket over and found her another Bacardi. "We care," she told Daisy as she handed it to her. "We have to know what they were doing then, because it'll help us figure out what Kammani is doing now. Especially if Abby can make the tonic. I have a feeling being able to see those power colors is going to be helpful, but not helpful enough for me to drink anything else Kammani brews."

"Well, Humusi must have been a real go-getter," Daisy said. "All I know about her is that she married a pal of John

Summer's, made sure he made a fortune in construction, and then swanked around in that big yellow house down the street. My grandmother inherited all their money and lost it somehow, and let me tell you, Peg is not happy about that."

"Peg?" Shar said.

"My mother of the sudden allergies," Daisy said, and knocked back another hit of Bacardi and aspartame.

"What does she do for a living?" Shar said, trying to put the pieces together.

"She outlived my father." Daisy picked up one of the empty little bottles. "You think Bea was trying to make tonic, Abby, and your grandmother was trying to keep the history, Shar, and the Worthams have obviously stayed big on death. Vera sold vitamins, and I bet she inherited that from her mom. It's like—what do they call those agents who live normally for years until they're activated? Sleepers?"

"I think that's right," Shar said. "I think they were supposed to wait for Kammani and she never came."

Daisy sat back, and Shar could see she was more relaxed now. Actually, she was loose as all hell now.

Or maybe that's me, she thought, and finished her second drink.

Daisy put her empty little bottle down on the table. "Well, she's here now and we have to do something about it, because I am not going to watch you guys die, and nobody's touching Gen and Bun, either." Daisy held out her hand for the basket. "Mina I can spare. Give me another boozle."

Abby looked through the basket and tossed Daisy another Bacardi, which she almost missed, and then handed Shar another vodka. "More orange juice?"

"Oh, yeah," Shar said, feeling a little echoey. Abby brought back the juice and Shar squinted up at her. "Are you okay? You're really quiet."

"I'm all right," Abby said, not meeting her eyes. "So I'll keep looking for anything from Abi-simti here, especially the tonic recipe."

"What's wrong?" Shar said, the booze slowing her down enough that she was noticing things now. "Did something happen?"

"You know who you could ask?" Abby said. "Sam."

"Talk about an easy nut to crack," Daisy said. "It's up to you now, Shar. Drag that boy's ass to bed and screw the information out of him."

"Daisy!" Shar said.

"It's not a bad idea," Daisy said. "We need inside information, and you want him so bad, you vibrate with it. Plus, he's totally into you. Three birds, one bone."

"He's into everybody," Shar snapped. "Manwhore, remember?"

"Yes, but you'd be doing it for *us*," Daisy said, leaning forward.

"Like a sacrifice," Abby said. "Just go throw yourself on his horned altar. . . ."

Daisy giggled, a real little-girl giggle, and Shar bit her lip so she wouldn't giggle, too.

"Very funny," she said, picking up her glass again. "Unfortunately, Sam's altar is a little crowded—"

"Not after he sleeps with you." Daisy sat back, smug with her drink. "You have a Glittery HooHa."

THIRTEEN

Shar choked on her screwdriver, and Abby put her cup down and said, "She has what?"

"You never heard of the Glittery HooHa?" Daisy straightened. "Oh, this is gonna be good. You guys know movies, but I . . ." She thumped herself on the chest. ". . . I know soap operas."

"Uh-huh," Shar said, reaching for another boozle. She didn't care about soap operas, but since Sam wasn't on one and Daisy was no longer near tears over Vera, it was a damn good topic.

"There is a certain kind of heroine on soap operas," Daisy said. "She is always blond, always beautiful, and always stupid beyond the telling of it."

Abby snorted over her hot chocolate and Shar relaxed. Daisy was okay. Abby was getting better. And Sam was still with Kammani. *Two for three,* she thought. *Not bad.*

"And yet," Daisy said, "there is a man. We'll call him . . . Hero. Hero is handsome, he is strong . . ."—Daisy cocked a drunken eyebrow at Shar—". . . he is godlike . . ."

"Watch it," Shar said, and knocked back more juice and booze.

". . . and he stays by her side and loves her through thick and thin. He opens the door to the microwave she's trapped herself in; he disentangles her hair from the curling iron; he saves a puppy from a Dumpster for her—"

"That kinda sounds like Sam," Abby said, her voice wistful, and Shar looked at her and thought, *Something bad happened to Abby,* and felt angry. Abby should have only good things. They all should have only good things, not that damn temple and death and—

Daisy talked on, oblivious in her rum haze. "And why does Hero not care how breathtakingly stupid his girl is? It's the power of the Glittery HooHa." Daisy slammed her glass on the table. "A woman with a hooha as glittery as this girl merely needs to walk around as glitter falls from her netherparts, leaving a trail for Our Hero to follow. And once he finds her, it only takes one dip in the Glittery HooHa to snare him forever." Daisy raised her glass. "For yea, no matter how many hoohas he might see, never will there be one as glittery as hers. . . ."

"What are you *talking about*?" Shar said.

"Your hooha," Daisy said, lowering her glass. "It glitters. For Sam."

"Oh," Abby said wisely. "Of course."

Shar looked at her. "Of course? *Of course?*"

"That's why Sam won't look at other women after he sleeps with you," Abby said. "You have glitter. Blue glitter, probably."

"Yep," Daisy said, raising her glass to Abby. "Abby gets it. And Sam's gonna get it, too. One dip and he's done." She waggled her fingers in the general direction of the door. "Now go jump that puppy."

Shar looked at the ceiling. "The puppy's a god working for a goddess who plans to take over the world using us as her minions. And you want me to get naked with him."

Daisy leaned forward and tried to put her chin in her hand as her elbow slipped on the tabletop. "That's the whole point. Once he dips, he'll be yours. He'll switch sides. He can't help it."

"'Cause your hooha glitters," Abby said, and Shar realized she was drunk, too.

"My hooha does not glitter," Shar said, and giggled. *Oh, hell, I'm drunk, too.*

"It totally glitters," Daisy said. "As mine glitters for Noah, who is also working for that Barbie Doll from Hell—"

"Mesopotamia," Shar said in the interests of accuracy.

"—but he's totally trustworthy. I'm sure of it." And she downed the last of her drink, looking miserable.

"Mine doesn't," Abby said, a catch in her throat, and Daisy and Shar both swung to face her.

"Doesn't what, baby?" Shar said, and reached out and patted her arm. "What's wrong?"

"My hooha," Abby said. "It's not glittery."

"Of course it is," Daisy said, her voice hearty. "Christopher follows the trail back here twice a day."

"Not anymore," Abby said.

"Did you have a fight?" Shar said, patting faster.

"We had *sex,*" Abby said, her voice breaking, and Shar stopped patting and Daisy leaned forward.

"You devirginated?" Daisy gaped at her. "And you didn't *tell us*?"

"I wanted to, but I was going to wait until after the temple thing, and then Vera died, and this is nothing compared to that—"

"Was it bad?" Shar said, sympathetic from much experience.

"It was *wonderful,*" Abby said.

Shar blinked. "Then what—"

"If it was good during, then it was bad after," Daisy said, her voice suddenly grim. "What did the asshole do?"

"He walked away," Abby said, and burst into tears.

"Oh, baby," Shar said, and got up to put her arms around

Abby and met Daisy, moving in on Abby's other side, and they held her and each other, the three of them tightly bound together, and Daisy said, "You're in our pack now," and something clicked through the booze and the sympathy and the grief for Vera, and they looked at one another, and Shar felt tears in her eyes.

"Here's my plan," Daisy said. "We kill Christopher and bury Kammani in her little temple."

"Yes," Shar said, blinking her gaze clear again. "We're going to have to find a way."

"Don't kill Christopher," Abby said. "I think I love him."

"Okay," Daisy said. "Kneecaps only, then." She stepped out of the group hug to face Shar and Abby. "New plan. When Peg comes back home, I'm going to grill her on what she knows. And I'll snoop around to see if Great-Gramma Humusi left a clue."

"That's good," Shar said, patting Abby.

"And Abby will find out how to make the power tonic and see what she can find in Bea's stuff."

"That's good," Shar said again, and Abby nodded, sniffing once.

Daisy looked at Shar. "And you look through your book and everything in that temple of yours and see what Sharrat was up to."

"I love this plan," Shar said. "I'm excited it could work! Let's do it!" They both looked at her and she said, "Sorry. *Ghostbusters*. I had to watch it last this weekend. Milton loves it."

Daisy nodded. "Okay then. Next, we'll crack Christopher's kneecaps—"

"No!" Abby said.

"Okay. We'll put the kneecapping on hold." Daisy's smile faded. "And I'll see if Noah knows anything about Miss Mesopotamia," she said, looking grim.

"That's good," Shar said.

Daisy perked up. "And Shar will sleep with Sam."

"Okay, now on that one," Shar began.

"Trust me on this, it's gonna happen sooner or later anyway, and sooner will help," Daisy said. "Fuck a god, save the world. It's really a win-win."

Abby nodded. "When she puts it like that, how can you refuse?"

Shar thought of Sam, not Sam the God, but Sam who'd picked up Milton and treated Wolfie like a pal and protected her wherever they were and loved *Big Trouble in Little China* and cookies. Sam the Guy, not Sam the God.

"You sure I have a glittery hooha?" she asked Daisy.

"I'm blinded," Daisy said.

"Maybe," Shar said, and thought, *Yes.*

"And then we'll send that bitch Kammani back where she came from," Daisy said.

"Now that's a plan," Shar said, and prayed it would sound just as good once they sobered up.

When the temple was quiet again, Kammani stood at the altar and thought, *How could this happen?* She had not decreed that Vera should die. Vera was under her protection. This was *wrong.*

Someone is against me, she thought, sinking down to sit on the altar steps. *Someone is working against me.*

Did Ishtar come into this new world, too?

The thought of it made her sad. No, it was deeper than sadness. It was that strange feeling again. . . .

Umma and Bikka came to stand beside her, and she bent to stroke their backs, comforted by their familiarity, but the weight stayed on her: doubt, uncertainty, pain . . .

I hate this world.

Sam came to the bottom of the steps. "Is there anything you require?"

Yes, Kammani thought. *I require my priestesses; I require worshipers; I require a temple with a top on it; I require my old world back. . . .*

He stood there, strong and silent, the only thing from her old world left to her.

I require you.

"You can go," Mina said to him, moving to stand between them. "I will serve the goddess."

Sam ignored her.

Kammani came down the steps to him. "What happened here?" she demanded. It was probably his fault somehow. What kind of king put his people first, anyway?

"She died," Sam said.

"Did you see—"

"She put her hand over her heart and she died," Sam said. "You've done this many times before, and no one has ever died. It wasn't you."

"I know it wasn't me," Kammani snapped, and then doubt rose up again, another gift from this lousy world, and she said miserably, "They're usually younger when I take them. Maybe . . ."

"These people are strong." Sam looked at her kindly. "You didn't kill her."

Kammani nodded. "Daisy was angry."

"She lost a friend."

"But she'll come back," Kammani said, as much to herself as to him. "They'll come to me."

Sam took a step back. "I have to go."

"Go?" Kammani felt anger swamp grief. "You would leave me now?"

The doors scraped open again, and Noah strode across the floor to her, his face dark. "What the hell happened here?" he said as Sam watched.

He didn't step in front of Kammani to protect her.

He knows Noah will not hurt me, Kammani thought,

but still, he had not stepped in front of her. This was all wrong.

"What the hell did you do?" Noah said to Kammani, ignoring Sam.

"Nothing." Kammani lifted her chin. "She had a weak heart, it was her time. I did nothing."

"You did something," Noah said. "You told me no one would get hurt—"

"I did not hurt anyone," Kammani said coldly. "I will not hurt any of them. Daisy—"

"You can forget Daisy," Noah said. "She's never coming back here."

"Daisy will come to me," Kammani said coldly. "As will you. You are my servant—"

"Bullshit," Noah said. "I quit, and you're going to stay away from Daisy, do you understand me?"

"You overreach, son of a cockroach," Mina said, stepping between him and Kammani.

Where Sam should have been, Kammani thought.

"You stay away from her, too," Noah said to Mina. "Whatever you two are up to here, Daisy's out of it." He turned and walked out, and Kammani felt real fear. If Noah kept Daisy from returning—

Mina drew close. "I stay by your side, my goddess."

But I need Daisy. I need the Three. Kammani opened her mouth to send Mina away and realized that Mina was all she had. Noah was gone; the Three had withdrawn; Bun and Gen had very little faith, and that was commanded, not freely given. Only Mina was strong. Mina and and Miriam and the Worthams . . .

But there should have been more. Millions called her name; they were why she was here; they had called her to save them—

"I hate this world," she said. "Nothing is right."

"You're in the wrong place," Sam said gently. "You're in the wrong time."

She looked at him, startled.

"I've learned a lot in five days," Sam said. "We're not gods here. If we want to stay, we have to join their world, follow their ways. We can't bring our world back, Kammani. It's gone. It was buried a long time ago."

"My goddess will rule again," Mina snapped, coming forward. "We will bring her word to the people of this world tomorrow at the Goddess Way meeting and they will love her." She stuck her chin out. "And she has an audition at Channel Four on Thursday. They will love her and put her on the air, and she will reach thousands and they will come to her."

The words were balm to Kammani—*they will come to me*—but Sam ignored Mina and said to her, "There was a time and a place where the people came to you, and you had no need of posters or auditions. That you have to do all of this to reach the people shows you they are not yours."

Kammani put her hand on her forehead. Headache again, maybe a migraine, she'd seen those on TV. *Mortals get aches, not goddesses,* she thought, and tried to ignore it.

"Don't try to be what you were, not here," Sam said. "Go back to sleep or go back to Kamesh, but do not try to be a goddess here. You'll fail. And you'll hurt this world doing it."

"*Traitor!*" Mina spat, and Sam turned to go.

"STAY!" Kammani said, but he kept walking. "*Where are you going*?" she said, and then he was gone and she knew where. *Sharrat.*

If she could bring the Three back to the temple, Sam would follow Sharrat, and she could sacrifice the bastard again, and the people would follow her, saved by his blood—

"Do not grieve, my goddess," Mina said, drawing closer. "For I am faithful, and the Worthams are strong, and we will stay by you until the others learn—"

Kammani lifted her head, a new focus for her anger in front of her. "Why must the others learn, Mina?"

Mina stopped, confused.

"Samu asked why we needed posters and auditions. If millions of people called my name, why are they not here, worshiping me?"

Mina's eyes slid left, and Kammani thought, *You stupid little bitch.*

"COME TO ME," Kammani said, and Mina came to her and stood before her. "WHERE ARE THOSE WHO CALLED ME?"

"Well." Mina drew a deep breath. "I looked into that because I thought they just couldn't find the temple. And when I couldn't find any of them, I Googled for your name."

Kammani frowned, her rage momentarily sidetracked. "Googled?"

"It's . . ." Mina frowned. "Well, one thing it is, is a way of finding out what people are looking for. So I Googled for 'Kammani.' And there's a place in India, and a song on YouTube, and some stuff in foreign alphabets that I couldn't read, but there wasn't anything about . . . you." She stopped again, and Kammani felt her heart beat faster.

"So no one is looking for me," she said. "Then where are all the people who called my name?"

Mina shifted.

"MINA."

"Well . . ." Mina swallowed. "Since I couldn't find anything under 'Kammani,' I tried 'Kami.' My mother said that was also your name, one that your worshipers of old used, and I really think it's much better than Kammani; that's why I put it on the posters—"

"Mina."

Mina smiled weakly. "Did you know it's Japanese for 'Divinity'?"

"No one was looking for Kami, either?" Kammani said, feeling hollow, as if a desert were trying to open inside her.

"No, they were," Mina said. "Kind of. The first search on the page was for Kami. But it wasn't you." She closed her eyes and spoke very fast. "Two famous Hollywood stars had a baby and named it Camisole, but they call her Cami and over a million people misspelled it and typed it into the search engine as 'Kami. . . .' " She looked helpless for the first time since Kammani had met her.

"I don't understand," Kammani said.

"They didn't call your name," Mina said. "You were Googled here by accident."

"Accident?" Kammani said, still trying to understand.

"Nobody knows who you are," Mina said. "You're a . . . typo."

The desert opened, a bleak emptiness that filled her entire being, even though she didn't know what a typo was.

Mina caught her arm. "It doesn't matter," she said, holding Kammani up as she sagged. "This world needs you; you can save it. We can save it. *It doesn't matter.*"

I wasn't called. Without belief, I do not belong here.

Four thousand years of sleeping beneath the sand, forgotten forever, not remembered now. *I'm dead,* Kammani thought, and sank to the steps before her altar, dragging Mina down with her. *I will die forever this time.*

Mina shook her arm. "We will bring them back. You will be Kami, their new guru."

"I feel . . . strange," Kammani said as the weight settled over her again.

"The people need you," Mina said, her voice urgent. "You must lead them. You will see, they will come tomorrow, some of them, and you'll wear the suit I got you and talk to them as if they're people, not slaves, and then more will come, and they will see your beauty and your wisdom and you will rule them."

"I feel . . . heavy," Kammani said, and put her face in her hands. "There is no hope, Mina. Everything is so dark. I have never felt like this before."

"You're just depressed," Mina said. "And who wouldn't be after the day you've had?"

"Depressed?" Kammani said.

"Depression is a real problem in this world," Mina said. "But don't worry, there are pills for that. My mother has a medicine chest full of them. I'll bring you some later. The thing to remember now is that this world needs you."

Depression, Kammani thought. That's this horrible feeling. *This world is full of plagues and darkness. I'm supposed to cause those, not be afflicted by them. I hate this fucking world.*

"Did you hear me?" Mina said. "This world needs you."

Kammani turned to look at her. The girl was crazy, but there was the light of truth in her eyes.

This world needs me.

"You will rule us."

I will rule them.

"You are the goddess," Mina whispered, closer than she'd ever been before.

"I am the goddess," Kammani said.

"I'll get you some anti-depressants in the morning," Mina said.

"All right," Kammani said.

"Now *rise,*" Mina said, and Kammani stood.

"Will they come to the meeting tomorrow?" she asked Mina, unsure and hating it.

"Some," Mina said. "Not many. We'll start small. But

your reputation will spread. What you will do for them will make many come. You will rule again."

"Yes," Kammani said, knowing that she was closing her eyes to the truth, that she had not been called, that she had no place in this world—

But they need me to rule them.

And I will not die.

"And I will be at your side," Mina said, and Kammani looked at the girl, at the slyness and the ambition and the death in her buglike eyes.

Whatever it took, even if she had to keep Mina at her right hand, she would not die.

She straightened, trying to banish doubt and fear. There were ways of making sure that people followed her. She had Bun's and Gen's power now. Tomorrow more people would come. Enough to begin. She fought her way past the darkness of depression to the old world she knew. The ways she knew.

"I will rule them," Kammani said to Mina, who relaxed and nodded. "But we will not do this with money and weight loss. We will do this the old way. They will come to me, and I will warn them of the danger in the air, and tell them that if they are faithful to me, the swarm will not touch them."

"Swarm?" Mina said, tense again. "What swarm?"

"I will send a swarm," Kammani said, remembering how it had been.

"Okay, that could be a PR disaster," Mina said.

"The faithful will be unscathed, but those who do not believe will be laid low."

Mina sighed. "Everybody in my family is faithful, right?"

"Yes," Kammani said.

"Well, if you need a swarm, you need a swarm." Mina

frowned, thinking. "We'll start with you in the business suit and you tell them how following your ways will make them thin and young and keep them protected from evil, and *then* you bring up the swarm. First the carrot, then the stick."

Kammani frowned at her. "Carrot?"

"Never mind," Mina said. "Trust me, it's better that way." She straightened and looked at Kammani directly, no longer subservient. "It's my turn to be invested. Make me your priestess now. And then I'll need more of the tonic. A lot more." She climbed the steps to the altar and then returned to hand Kammani a collar of lapis, carnelian, and gold, the symbol of her priestesshood. There had been seven on the altar. Bun and Gen wore two, Vera's had spilled on the steps, three more were waiting for the Three, and this one . . .

Kammani took the collar. If she invested Mina, she'd draw on her power. She looked into Mina's crazy black eyes and hesitated, but the power there was strong, much stronger than Gen and Bun together, almost as strong as the Three, and her need for it was great.

"COME," she said, and led Mina up the steps.

Tomorrow she would warn of the swarm, and on Thursday it would descend.

That'll show them who the goddess is around here, she thought, and felt much better.

Shar made sure Abby got safely into bed while Noah got Daisy settled and then almost killed herself lurching back down the stairs. She thought about making coffee and realized she'd probably set the place on fire. Better to just go home. She looked at Wolfie and Milton dozing with Squash, and thought, *They need to be here together tonight,* and went out the front door, pulling it locked behind her.

The night air was cool and that helped clear her head a little, but the bottom line was, she was drunk.

I'll probably get mugged on the way home, she thought. It would be Summerville's first mugging, so it was appropriate that it should be her. She was the granddaughter of the bitch who'd brought Kammani to Ohio, so her family had it coming.

She went past Lionel's Bar next to Casey's Hardware as Elvis's "One Night" wafted out, glancing through the big plate-glass window.

Sam was in there, three women looking up at him in admiration. Well, that made sense. "One Night" was practically his theme song.

He looked up and caught Shar's eyes, and she stared back, feeling the same way she had the first time she'd seen him carved in stone: He was beautiful, and she wanted him.

That was the problem when you had too much to drink. Everything got too damn simple.

He came out into the street. "Are you all right?"

"Fine," she said, waving her hand at him. "I'm going home. You stay here."

He took her arm to steady her. "Where are the dogs?"

"Sleeping with Squash." Her eyes filled with tears again. "They're taking such good care of her."

"They'll take her into the pack," Sam said, and tugged on her arm, guiding her into the bar. "How about some coffee?"

"Actually, I could use another screwdriver," Shar said, looking at all the faces looking back at them. "It's been a rough night."

"Coffee," Sam said to the bartender as one of the women came up and asked him to dance.

"No," another woman whispered loudly, and Shar squinted and saw that it was Leesa. "That's his *ex-wife,*" Leesa said, a little unsteady on her feet.

Sam looked at Shar.

"I have no idea how that rumor got started," Shar said, and then smiled at the bartender, who put a cup of coffee in front of her.

"We'll always have Ur?" Sam said.

"Boy, you just talk to everybody, don't you?" Shar said, and sipped her coffee. "I'll tell them your ex-wife is over at the temple. Killing people."

"She's not my ex-wife," Sam said. "My father was consort to her."

"She's your stepmother and you slept with her?" Shar said, and several people turned to look.

"It was more of a ceremonial position," Sam said, unfazed. "Drink your coffee and we'll go home."

"Ceremonial position," Shar said. "Is that like the missionary position?"

Sam looked at her over the tops of his glasses. "Why are you so angry?"

Shar drew back. Glasses? "When did you get glasses?"

"There was a place on the street behind the college. I was squinting at the window and this woman came out—"

"Of course she did," Shar said, and drank more coffee.

"And told me I need to have my eyes examined and it turns out I'm farsighted."

"Depends on how you define the term," Shar said into her coffee cup.

"It means I can see well at a distance but not well up close. It's good for battle." Sam looked around the bar. "But for this life, the glasses help."

"I bet they do," Shar said to her cup.

Sam sighed. "You're the worst kind. You think you're low maintenance, but you're really high maintenance."

Shar looked up. "No fair quoting my movies back to me. And I am very low maintenance. All you have to do to keep me happy is not give me a Taser."

"And not sleep with other women," Sam said.

Shar waved her hand. "Hey, no business of mine. I know you have ceremonial duties to perform." *You bastard.*

The nice thing about being drunk was that she no longer felt the need to be fair. So what if it was none of her business? Screw him anyway. Everybody else did.

". . . Doug," Sam finished.

"What?"

"Kammani's taken your student Doug as her new consort," Sam repeated. He didn't seem too upset about it.

"Doug," Shar said, and then it registered. "She's going to sacrifice Doug?" She frowned. "That's not good. I mean, I don't like him, but I don't think the price of arrogance and stupidity should be death. We'd lose half the student body and three-quarters of the faculty."

"She won't sacrifice him; he's not a king," Sam said.

"So, she's just sleeping with him." Shar nodded. "I'm sorry your stepmother's a nympho."

"*The Big Lebowski,*" Sam said. "I'm taking bowling lessons because of that movie."

"Bowling lessons?" Shar said. "How did you . . . never mind." He'd walked into a bowling alley and some woman had said, *You need free bowling lessons,* and given him free shoes and lunch, too.

"I've learned a lot from those movies," Sam said.

"That's not actually how the world works." Shar drank the rest of her coffee and turned to him, still rocky on her feet.

"Sure it is." Sam smiled at her and made her head reel. " 'Rescue the damsel in distress, kill the bad guy, save the world.' "

"I don't know that one," Shar said.

"*The Mummy.*" Sam took her arm. "Let's go home and watch it again."

Let's go home. That was dangerous, thinking they had a home to go to. And liking having his hand under her arm. And being glad he wasn't sleeping with Kammani anymore. That was all really dangerous.

"No." Shar tried to shake off his hand, but his grip was firm and he was a lot more stable than she was. "You were partying. You stay here with the girls, and I'll go home."

"I was waiting for you."

He moved toward the door and she moved with him. Didn't have much choice really. It was like being dragged along by a force of nature.

"You were waiting for me?"

"I saw the three of you talking when I came to the back door, so I went to the tavern to wait. I knew you'd go by."

"I could have taken the back way," Shar said, annoyed that she was so predictable.

He opened the door to the bar and steered her out into the dark street. "Not drunk. You're careful."

Shar yanked her arm out of his hand. "You think you know me, but you don't. I'm not Sharrat."

"I know," Sam said, and caught her when she tripped on the sidewalk.

"You didn't know I was drunk when you saw me," Shar pointed out when they were walking again. *Damn,* it was dark. "We were just *sitting* there."

"There were a lot of bottles on the table. And you don't drink."

"This god thing you do." Shar thought about jerking her arm away again and decided she liked the stability. "It's annoying. Like you know everything."

"Sorry," Sam said.

She couldn't see his face, but he didn't sound sorry.

"But you *don't* know everything," Shar said. "You

don't know that I'm supposed to seduce you to find out what Kammani's doing."

"I do now," Sam said.

"And you don't know that I have a glittery hooha," Shar said, and Sam slowed on that one. "See? You don't. Which is why we can never sleep together. It would be unfair to you."

"No, it wouldn't."

"You don't even know what a glittery hooha is," Shar said, plowing on so that he had to catch up. "You have no idea of the dangers you'd be running."

"I'm used to danger," Sam said, and even though it was dark, Shar could have sworn he was grinning.

"There's nothing funny about this. One dip and you're done."

"It's fatal?" Sam said. "It's okay; I'm a god."

"No, no, you'd be my slave for life," Shar said, slowing now in front of her house.

"I'm that anyway," Sam said. "Don't trip on the steps."

"I'm not that drunk," she said, and tripped.

He caught her again, and she looked up into his dark eyes and thought, *I really want you.*

"You can't be my slave for life; you don't even know me," she said, swallowing hard.

"I know you," he said. "You have Sharrat's brains and Sharrat's drive and Sharrat's concern for people, and just like her, you'll always do the right thing. . . ."

"I am not—"

"But you have joy and kindness and laughter, too," Sam said. "You kiss Milton on the top of his head and watch movies like a little girl, and when you're happy, your entire face glows. I know you. And you know me."

Oh, Shar thought, and tried to find something that was wrong with that.

Sam waited a minute and when she didn't say anything, he said, "We should go in."

"That was a really great thing to say," Shar said.

"Let's go in," Sam said quietly.

Shar hesitated, and then she thought, *Who am I kidding?* She'd wanted him since she'd seen him on the damn wall. This was a once-in-four-thousand-years opportunity. *Don't screw up, Shar.*

Shar swallowed. "If we go in there, are you going to be a gentleman and not take advantage of me because I'm drunk?"

"No," Sam said.

"Good," Shar said, and walked up to her front door with her head exploding again. "You know, it probably would have been better if I hadn't said that, because then you could have just jumped me when we got in the house and I wouldn't be feeling so self-conscious now."

"Key," Sam said with godlike calm.

She fumbled in her bag and handed over her key, and he unlocked the door and pushed it open for her. She went into the cool stone hall and dropped her bag on the table and turned to face him as he pulled the door shut and real darkness enveloped them, and she waited, so aware of him standing inches from her that she could feel him breathe. When he didn't move, she took a step closer and put her hand on his chest, let her fingers slip to trace the line of his side, down the flat of his belly, the curve of his hip, and he sucked in his breath. She lifted her face and pulled him down to her, her lips touching his, tasting him, and then kissed him the way she had the first time, with everything she had, rising up on her toes as he pulled her to him, frowning as she kissed him again and again, trying to consume him, drink him in.

He sighed against her mouth and pulled her tight against him, kissing her back with an expertise that was almost annoying, so she stepped away, took back control, and pulled her sundress off over her head. *It's just sex,* she told herself. *I'm doing this to save the world.* Then she stripped off her underpants, dropped her bra, and stood naked in the dark, thinking, *This is just like Joan of Arc. Or something.*

"So," she said, turning toward the stairs, and he caught her around the waist and pulled her through the archway into his bedroom and toppled her onto the bed—her head swam as she fell—and as she struggled to sit up, she heard him strip his own clothes off. The room swung around and she didn't know if it was from drink or lust, but then he was beside her, huge in the darkness, his body hot on hers as he pulled her to him and rolled so that she was on top. She pushed herself up to straddle him and almost fell off (he was broad and she was dizzy) and he caught her again—*he's always there to catch me*—and guided her down to the bed beside him.

"I'm a little clumsy," she said.

"You're beautiful," he said as he ran his hand up to her breast.

"I bet you tell all the girls that," she said, closing her eyes at his touch.

"I do," he said. "They're all beautiful."

She caught his hand. "So not the right answer."

"What difference does it make?" he said, bending over her. "They're not you."

She opened her mouth to protest the lousy line, and he kissed her, slipping his tongue into her mouth as his hand tightened on her breast, and then she lost her place in the conversation as he explored her, touching her everywhere she wanted to be touched—"a little higher, nope, not there, oh, *oh*"—making her breath quicken and her body glow, and she forgot to be careful not to come and shuddered against him over and over again as he stroked and licked and invaded her with fingers and tongue. Finally, she pushed him away, not too far, and heard the ragged rasp of his breath, knew he needed her, and felt the thrill of that power through her. She pulled his mouth to hers again, feeling as savage as the death goddess she'd descended from, no, more savage, because she was going to take him forever and make him hers. She raked her fingers through the thick hair on his chest, making him flinch, and then went lower, making him suck in his breath as his hand slid over her hip, caressing the curve there, and she slid her knee up to his waist, curving against him, feeling him hard against her as she wrapped her legs around him, rolled to straddle him, and said, "*Now.*"

He shifted under her, lifting her until she felt him push against her, and then she sank down over him and jerked at the shock of him impaling her, filling her, at one with her as he rocked under her and she tightened everywhere, shaking with heat, trying not to slip into another mindless orgasm because this time was different, this was Sam and he was her finish, he'd end her, and there would never be anyone after him, anyone but him.

He pulled her down and kissed her, solid and sure and right, becoming part of her, slowing his breathing as she slowed hers, time suspended, and then he brought her hard against him, rocked up into her, and she blurred into him, felt him everywhere as she clenched around him, heard the gasp and the choke in his throat as she felt everything twist and clench, and she said, "*Finish me,*" and bore down on him. He surged against her, breathing against her skin, tight around her, hard inside her, and she became part of him, muscle and sweat and blood and something that made them glow as everything in them twisted and turned until they broke, all the colors in her head exploding as their bodies tightened and jerked together, again and again, until she was left sobbing in his arms and he buried his face in her hair.

Then he began again, touching her everywhere, and she lost herself in him again in the blur of heat and passion and wildness as a god surged below her, above her, inside her. They made love through the night, their bodies sliding and shuddering until they finally slept, tangled in the sheets and each other, waking again to fall together, kissing and biting, twisting and crying out, rising and falling to each other's rhythm, finishing each other and beginning again, making love like gods. And as exhaustion turned to dreams and visions, Shar expanded into the universe, saw light gathering, spinning, arcing, shattering, and then fell again into his arms, half dream, half real, rising and breaking and gasping, "*Again,*" as the night rocked by.

I'm changed, she thought as the sun rose, and then curled herself against him in the shelter of his arms and fell asleep again.

FOURTEEN

Thursday morning dawned bright and clear, which Abby knew, as she'd been baking cookies since four in the morning. For two days she'd left the kitchen only to catch a few hours' sleep on the big, comfortable bed that she now hated. She looked around her and realized that the old kitchen had become her sanctuary, her temple, the great copper-clad island her altar, flour and sugar and honey her communion, and that damn tonic recipe her Holy Grail. But it wasn't enough. She couldn't stop thinking about Christopher's long, deft hands touching her, his unsmiling mouth on hers, his bleak eyes softening, looking into hers with something like love

Oh, hell no. It was probably gas. Or annoyance. Or a facial tic. Or—

Whatever. She needed to Get Over It. She needed to get dressed for Vera's funeral, be ready when Shar came by to pick them up; she needed to concentrate on the tonic; she needed . . .

The front door to the coffeehouse slammed, and a moment later Gen ran into the kitchen, Ziggy at her side, both of them dressed for a funeral, which depressed Abby even more. She reached out for a cookie. Then pulled her hand away. *Step away from the cookies, Abby.*

"There are bees," Gen said, looking anxious, Ziggy pressed against her leg. His usual camo kerchief was now a subdued black. Camo.

"Yes," Abby said. "Did you doubt their existence?"

"No, I mean there are bees everywhere. Swarms of them. I got dive-bombed on my way over here. Bun called me to tell me they're putting off Vera's funeral till tomorrow, to give them time to get the bee population under control."

"Shit," Abby said. "Did you get stung? I've got baking powder. . . ."

"I'm fine. I just . . . wanted to talk to you."

Abby moved to the French doors, looking out over the back courtyard. There were bees all right, dark clouds of them, swarming the deep red flowers that had sprouted everywhere. "Sure. What about?"

For a moment Gen didn't move. "I'm scared," she said, her voice flat.

"Scared?" Abby pulled out the counter stool for her. "I'm sure the local beekeepers will get the situation under control."

Gen hesitated. "Not the bees. Mina." She sat down as Ziggy edged over to say hi to Bowser. Gen looked pale and serious, no giggles left. "I think Mina killed Vera and I think she's coming after us next. All of us. You, too." She put her hand on the countertop and Abby saw it was shaking.

"How about some tea?" Abby said, and put the kettle on.

"I'm not crazy," Gen said. "She has this thing she does with her hand. She reaches out and makes a fist . . ."—Gen made a fist and held it out, her arm shaking—". . . and things . . . die. She killed Baby that way, but Kammani brought her back."

"Kammani couldn't bring Vera back," Abby said, but it was a hollow argument. She knew Gen was probably right.

"Mina didn't let go of her fist," Gen said. "I saw her. She didn't straighten out her hand. I didn't get it at the time, but I've been thinking about it, and I think Kammani couldn't raise her because Vera's heart couldn't beat. Mina was squeezing it."

"Oh, god," Abby said, horrified.

"So I was thinking, maybe I could stay here," Gen said, carefully not looking at her.

"Here," Abby said, startled.

Gen gave up on being cool and tried for pleading. "Bun has her family to look out for her. I can go there if I want to, but they make me crazy, and since you're practically family—"

"Whoa," Abby said.

"—what with my cousin Christopher and everything—"

"I don't know where you got that idea," Abby said firmly, "but there isn't anything going on with us, and if there had been anything, it would be over. But there wasn't. So it's not."

Gen blinked. "He doesn't think so. When I told him you were in danger, he freaked. Well, it was Christopher, so he didn't scream or anything, but I know Christopher and he freaked. He said you should *call* him."

"Right." Abby popped a sugar cookie in her mouth. She'd been trying to cut back, but even going cold turkey wasn't keeping Christopher out of her daydreams, and they were just so damned good. "I'm not going to call your cousin and I'm not going to answer if he calls me. And tell him not to call me."

"I don't think he's going to listen. He's very stubborn. He said he's there if you need him. Actually, he said to call him anyway."

Well, I'm not going to, Abby thought, and put a cup in front of Gen, got out a peppermint tea bag, and picked up the kettle just as it whistled. She poured the hot water over the mint and the smell wafted out, gentle and soothing. Maybe she should call him just to say she wasn't in danger so he didn't need to call again. Just to tell him not to call—

"Tea in the summer?" Gen said.

"I'll tell you what." Abby put a plate of cookies in front of her. "You can move into the vacant apartment upstairs if you help me down here. I need an extra pair of hands to bake while I work on this damn tonic recipe."

Gen nodded, her mouth full of cookie, and said a crumb-muffled, "Sure," and Abby reached for the basket of boozles and pulled the Grand Marnier out while she definitely did not think about Christopher, who was irrelevant and absolutely not part of her life.

The bittersweet orange might just be the source of the faint citrusy taste of Kammani's tonic, she thought, and she poured three drops into the current batch, which so far consisted of Hawaiian Punch, Earl Grey tea, and rosewater. She sniffed it, but it wasn't quite right. Much like the rest of her life. She shoved back from the counter in frustration.

"Have a cookie," Gen said. "They're making me feel better. More purposeful."

"I'm trying to cut down," Abby said, reaching for the plate of butter cookies. Each bite was like taking a bite of Christopher, and if she had any sense, she'd be on bread and water.

She had no sense.

"So when are you going to talk to Christopher?" Gen said, reaching for another butter cookie.

"When hell freezes over," Abby said genially.

Gen looked past her. "I think Satan's gonna need mittens."

Abby turned around.

Christopher was standing in the doorway to the courtyard.

Her reaction was instant. She didn't stop to think; she

was halfway up the stairs, moving so fast, Bowser sat up and barked, "What's up?" She tried to keep going, but Christopher was too fast for her, and his arm clamped around her waist as she tried to scramble out of the way, so that she had no choice but to give up or they'd both fall down the stairs.

He released her, stepping back, but she didn't make the mistake of thinking there was any way she could escape. She sat down on the stairs, yanked her skirts down over her knees, and managed to keep her expression stony. "What are you doing here? Besides manhandling me?"

"I think I'll go get my stuff," Gen said, sidling out of the kitchen before Abby could voice a protest.

"I've been trying to talk to you for days now and I'm not manhandling you," he said in a mild voice. "I just didn't want you running away, which you appeared to be trying to do."

"I don't want to talk to you."

He shoved a hand through his already rumpled hair, looking distracted. "You can't just ignore what happened."

"I certainly can. You called it. Irrational lust. You should be grateful I don't intend to make a fuss about it, or show up at your door, or expect any kind of—"

"You were a virgin." His voice was flat, interrupting her.

Color flamed her face. "Could you keep your voice down? You don't have to announce it to the world."

"Then talk to me. Stop playing games."

"I'm not playing games. We had sex. I simply hadn't gotten around to having it before, but it's no big deal. You got up and disappeared, which I figured was my signal to leave as well."

"So fast that you pulled a Cinderella?" He held up her abandoned sandal. "I told you to stay."

"I'm no Cinderella and you sure as hell aren't Prince Charming, and I'm not very good at obeying orders," she said, and snatched the sandal away from him. "Thank you. And now you can go."

"I'm not going anywhere until you talk to me. We can talk here and Gen can eavesdrop, or we can go somewhere quiet like your apartment."

"That's not going to happen." She pushed up from the stairs, and he took a step back. Bowser was sitting up, looking at them both worriedly. "We can talk in the courtyard."

"Haven't you heard? We have a bee infestation."

Abby growled, "The coffeehouse then." There was a tray of sugar cookies cooling on the counter, and he reached a hand out for one.

"Don't touch those!" she snapped. The last thing she needed was for Christopher to get back in touch with his appetites.

The coffeehouse was dark and cool, the shades still drawn, and Abby took one of the bentwood oak chairs and sat. "Okay, say what you have to say and then go away. I'm really not into rehashing ancient history."

"Ancient history is Mesopotamia, not five days ago," he pointed out, ever logical. "I need to know what the hell is going on. If you don't want to talk about the sex, tell me about Mesopotamian goddesses and what they have to do with my cousin. She's scared to death of something and she's not talking."

"Someone in your family is showing some sense then. You could take a lesson from her."

He was being annoyingly patient in the face of her hostility. "So explain this to me again. You and Gen and the others are the reincarnation of Mesopotamian goddesses and you're here to do what?"

Abby closed her eyes for a moment. He almost sounded like he believed her. She was half-tempted to try to convince him, to explain exactly what was going on, but better to keep her distance; otherwise she might throw her flour-dusted body all over him. "Don't worry about it," she said. "It's none of your business."

"I disagree. You came to my house to tell me about it in the first place and I want to know why. I'm worried about Gen. And I'm worried about you."

Crap. That was the last thing she needed to hear. "Is Milki-la-el still talking to you?"

"Loud and clear. Which makes me think that maybe you're not delusional."

"It doesn't matter," she said, feeling desperate.

He was looking at her, puzzled. "It matters to me. Why did you come to my house? Why did you let me—"

"We're not going there!" she said. "We're not talking about it; we're not referring to it ever again."

"I can't promise." There was clear concern in his blue eyes, concern and something a little more elemental. Like he wanted her.

"Go away, Christopher," she said wearily. She was too tired of fighting, and she was reduced to begging. "I have work to do."

"So tell me this. Are you going to let Gen move in? I could let her stay with me, but I don't have any furniture, and I think having an undergraduate underfoot would drive me crazy. But I don't want her alone right now. She's scared of something, even if she won't tell me what it is, and she seems to think being around you will make things better."

"I've already told her she can. She'll be perfectly fine."

"I'm sure she will. There's safety in numbers. In the meantime, Sam will help me move her stuff in, probably this afternoon if they've got the bee problem taken care of."

"How do you know Sam?" Abby said, confused, and then the other shoe dropped. "*You're* going to move her?" It was nothing more than a horrified squeak.

"Unless you've got goddess powers that can transport things."

"Very funny," she muttered. Maybe she could tell him to just let Sam do it. Sam was strong enough that he could probably move her on his own. But then, Christopher was strong, too, deliciously so, and . . .

Goddamn cookies.

"And I'm very fond of my cousin," Christopher went on. "I intend to keep an eye on her, just to make sure she's all right."

"We'll keep an eye on her," Abby said. "You don't need to worry."

"I'll be checking in anyway," he said. "You're just going to have to get used to seeing me. Talking to me. And besides, I've developed a taste for your sugar cookies."

How a stuffy math professor could make such a simple sentence sound sexual was beyond Abby's comprehension, but she'd about reached her limit. "All right," she said. "I'm sure Gen appreciates it."

"Even if you don't."

"I don't care one way or another," she said airily.

"Liar."

She wasn't sure what would have happened next, but thankfully Gen pushed open the front door, with Sam looming behind her. "I'm ready, Christopher," Gen said. "That is, if you're finished—"

"He's finished," Abby said, rising. "Believe me, he's finished."

Christopher looked down at her, unimpressed. "We'll have to see about that."

And she stood alone in the deserted coffeehouse, watching them go, telling herself that that odd feeling in the pit of her stomach was dread and not joy; indifference, not desire.

And she knew she lied.

Friday morning, Daisy stood next to Vera's grave, Noah at her side and Squash and Bailey at their feet. The last of the funeral attendees were leaving, and with no eulogy to distract them while she waited for alone time with Squash, Daisy decided to pry a little.

"So, kind of strange about the bees, huh?"

"Yeah," Noah said, eyes scanning the cemetery. "Strange."

"I mean, what are the chances, right? All those bees descending on one town?" She looked up at him. "How do you think that might have happened?"

He shrugged. "Good thing the beekeepers needed them. They got them all wrangled pretty fast."

See? He doesn't know anything, she thought, but then wondered what she expected him to say. *Kammani loosed a swarm on the town and I helped her*? He wouldn't.

Because he was innocent and he didn't know anything about Kammani. She was sure of it. Mostly. But the last of the mourners were finally out of sight, and she had other things to focus on.

She handed Bailey's leash to Noah. "Do you want to take Bailey back to your car and wait for us?" She glanced down at Squash. "There's just a little thing that Squash and I need to do."

Noah shook his head. "I'm fine right here."

Okay. Daisy walked Squash over to the grave, knelt down, and scratched the dog behind her ears. She glanced back at Noah, then huddled next to Squash and whispered, "How ya doing, girl?"

Squash looked at her, her eyes baleful. "She was mine."

"I know." Daisy pulled the small green quilted sachet she had put together the night before out of her pocket and held it up in front of Squash, who gave it a light sniff.

"Lavender," Squash said.

"Good nose," Daisy whispered.

"Dog," Squash explained simply.

"Vera liked herbs, and lavender helps you rest." She held the sachet up and turned it in her hands. "It's also got a little bit of vitamin powder, for strength. And I put in a fiber supplement—inside joke. Laughter's important. And that paw print I got from you yesterday? It's in there, too." Daisy scratched Squash behind one ear. "I thought maybe you could . . . if you want to, you don't have to . . . I thought you could bury it with her. You know." She met Squash's eye. "To say good-bye."

Squash stared at her for a long moment, and Daisy thought that maybe she'd screwed up. "You don't have to. It was just that a funeral is closure for people, but for a dog, I didn't know if it would have any meaning. I thought maybe—"

Squash took the sachet between her teeth. Daisy straightened, stepping back to give Squash privacy as she dug a small hole in the fresh dirt, directly over Vera's heart. Squash dropped the sachet in and buried it, whining a little as she did, but Daisy tried not to listen to what she said. When Squash was done, she returned to Daisy, and Daisy took her leash.

"I'm yours now," Daisy said.

"I don't fetch," Squash barked.

"Good," Daisy said. "Me neither. You like *The Office*?"

She looked up to find Noah still watching her, a curious expression on his face. Daisy tucked her hand in the crook of his arm and they made the trip back to the coffeehouse in silence.

"Squash!" Bailey barked as they all entered the kitchen together. "Squeaky toys in the courtyard! Let's go!"

"All right," Squash sighed, and followed Bailey out to the back while everyone else went into the front where the tables were.

"Where's Gen?" Daisy asked.

"Lunch with Bun and Christopher," Abby said, an edge in her voice as she said Christopher's name.

Daisy sat down next to Sam, who took up two places on his own.

"Jesus, you're big," she said.

"Different god," Abby whispered as she placed a platter of cinnamon cookies in the center of the table.

"But still a god." Shar took a cookie, looked at Sam, and bit into it deliberately and with intent, and Sam grinned at her.

Noah took that in stride, Daisy noticed. *He takes everything in stride,* she thought, but still her shoulders tensed.

"Hey, Noah," she said, "would you grab my sweater for me, please? It's in the kitchen."

"If you're cold, I can turn down the—," Abby began, but Daisy cut her off with a look, and Abby regrouped. "The AC's stuck."

"I'll be right back." Noah got up and headed for the kitchen. Daisy waited until he was gone, then leaned in and looked at Sam.

"So, Sam, we haven't really had a chance to chat. What the hell did Kammani do to Vera?"

Sam lost his smile. "It wasn't Kammani."

"Could it be the tonic? What's in that stuff anyway?"

Shar shook her head. "It wasn't the tonic."

"It was just her time," Sam said to Daisy.

"I don't think so," Abby said, but then Noah came through the kitchen door, Daisy's sweater in his hand.

"No goddess stuff in front of Noah," Daisy whispered, and Abby said, "You haven't told—?" and Daisy said, "I *will,*" in a harsh whisper that shut the conversation down.

Noah gave Daisy her sweater and sat down, and everyone went stiff and quiet around the table. Noah glanced around from face to face, and Shar nudged the platter of cookies toward Noah. "Have a cookie."

"Thanks." Noah reached out and took a cookie, and there was another long, awkward silence as he bit into it. He chewed slowly as he realized everyone was staring at him, then swallowed and looked at Daisy.

"Oh, hell," Daisy said. "Kammani's a goddess. Sam's a god. Abby and Shar and I are some kind of kick-ass ancient goddess sisterhood of three. We have powers, and we can hear dogs talk."

Noah stared at her. Just stared. No shock, no surprise, no choking on his cookie. Ice shot down Daisy's spine as she came face-to-face with the reality she'd been secretly dreading all along: *He already knows.*

"Maybe you two should . . . ?" Abby said, motioning toward the kitchen.

"Yeah. Maybe we should." Daisy stood up and led the way through the kitchen and out to the courtyard, where the dogs met them at the door, tails wagging.

"Treats!" Milton barked.

"I got nothing," Daisy said, holding up empty hands. "Scoot."

Bowser and Wolfie headed to the far corner with Milton, but Bailey stayed, his tail wagging slow and low as he watched Daisy and Noah with concern in his eyes. Squash, who was curled up in a sunny patch by the wall, simply lifted her head.

"It's okay, Bail," Daisy said. "Go."

"Ball!" Bowser barked, and Bailey turned and ran over to them. Daisy watched them for a moment, not wanting to start the conversation, because once it started, there'd be no turning back.

"Daisy?"

She turned to see Noah looking at her, his expression wary.

"You were saying?" he prodded.

"Right. To recap. I'm a goddess."

Noah nodded. "Okay."

"Oh my *god,*" Daisy said. " 'Okay'? Are you kidding? Don't you have questions? Don't you want proof?" *Please want proof. Please don't already know everything.*

"Do I want proof?" Noah said, staring at her like she was nuts, but then he just shrugged. "Sure. Okay. Prove you're a goddess."

"Okay." Daisy glanced around at the menagerie in the corner. "Come here, Bowser."

Bowser lumbered over and barked, "What?"

"Noah's going to whisper a word in your ear; then you tell me what it is."

Bowser did the dog version of a shrug, then looked at Noah. Noah glanced at Daisy, tentative, and Daisy motioned encouragement.

"Go ahead."

Noah took Bowser aside and said something to him; then they both walked back.

"What'd he say?" Daisy asked Bowser, and Bowser barked, "Buttgig!" and Daisy turned to Noah and said, "What the hell is buttgig?"

Noah stared at Bowser for a moment, then looked back at Daisy. "I made it up. How . . . ?"

"I can understand him. I can understand all of them," Daisy said, comforted that Noah seemed at least a little thrown. But still, the gnawing in her gut remained.

"And talking to dogs makes you a goddess?" he asked.

"Well, that and . . . you know. Other things. It's complicated."

"Other things. Right." Noah walked over to the stone bench and sat down.

Daisy hesitated a moment, then sat next to him. "I know it's a lot to—"

"So, it's real, then?" he asked, looking at her.

Her stomach sank. "Wha—what's real?"

"The goddess thing." Noah shook his head, looking slightly stunned. "The women in my family—Mina, Aunt Miriam—they're part of this . . . religion, I guess. A long-lost goddess, powers over death, all the women have a dog. Usually they're creepy and black." He looked at the dogs playing in the corner. "Guess that's just *my* family."

Daisy felt a cold chill go down her back. "You . . . you *knew*?"

He let out a short, stuttered laugh and shook his head. "But it can't be real. They're all insane." He looked at her. "It's real?"

Daisy stood up, her knees wobbling under her. "Oh, god, I'm gonna be sick."

Noah stood up, too, moving closer to her. "Why? What's the matter?"

"What's the—?" she sputtered, backing away from him. "You knew and you didn't tell me that you knew and we had sex, *a lot*, that's what's the matter. You helped her and you gave us the temple tonic and—" Daisy put her hand over her stomach. "Oh, god."

Noah's voice was tight and quiet. "What are you saying? You think I drugged you?"

"No," she said. "God, no. No." *A little. Maybe. NO.* "No."

He went deathly still. "So, working for Kammani makes me a rapist, then?"

"No." Daisy put her hand to her head. "*No*. I mean . . . I wanted what happened between us; you know that."

"Yeah, but only because I drugged you, right?" He stared at her, his eyes hard. "That's your working theory, isn't it?"

"What do you want from me?" Daisy said, desperation and frustration winding her stomach in knots. "I drank the stuff and my whole life went haywire, and there you were. I'm not saying it was you, I'm saying I'm confused, and you lied to me—"

"I didn't tell you about my family's crazy goddess thing because I liked you. That's different from lying, and you know it."

"Well . . . why were you even working for her in the first place?"

"Because crazy money is as good as sane money," he said. "Because my aunt asked me to. Because I'm good with dogs. Not to . . . drug innocent women and lure them into my trap, or whatever you're cooking up in your head."

"I'm not—" Daisy took a breath, felt the emotion welling within her, heating up behind her eyes. Around her, the wind started to build, out of her control. "I didn't mean— But you— *Damn it!*" She closed her eyes and breathed deep, calming the air around her, pulling it back in.

Control.

She opened her eyes and looked up to see Noah staring at her, the anger on his face replaced by a blank expression. He motioned vaguely around them.

"So, that . . . with the wind," he said. "That's you?"

"It's tied to my emotions. I'm the Goddess of Chaos." She shrugged and rolled her eyes. "I have a clicky pen."

They stared at each other for a moment, and then Noah's face cracked into a smile and Daisy's entire body relaxed in the warmth of it.

"You have a clicky pen?" he said.

"It's a . . . like a tool," Daisy said. "It helps me focus the chaos."

"The clicky pen?"

"Shut up," she said. "Don't make me laugh. I'm still very upset." And then she laughed, and he laughed, and Daisy knew it was going to be okay.

Maybe.

"Look," he said. "I don't know what the hell's going on here. You probably don't, either. I get that. But I need you to know that I would never hurt you, or your friends. If you're not sure, then say the word and I'll walk away. No hard feelings."

She looked at him, still confused about so much, but deep inside, she felt sure of him. She wasn't sure of herself, her world, her life, but she was sure of him.

"I know you'd never hurt us," she said, putting her hand on his arm.

Kammani might.

"Yeah?" he said, and when he looked at her, she could see in his eyes how much this mattered to him. For the first time, it occurred to her that he might be as deeply affected by her as she was by him.

Maybe Kammani drugged both of us.

"Yeah," she said.

"Good." He pulled her into his arms, and Daisy's whole body relaxed at his touch, and she wondered how he did it, made her feel so safe just by holding her in his arms.

It can't be real. It's too fast. If I can do magic that makes people take action, Kammani can—

"I don't want you to worry about anything," he said, then pulled back and looked into her eyes. "I won't let her get near you again."

His face was earnest, his eyes steely and committed. She could see how strongly he cared for her, feel it in his touch. And she cared for him, too. If Kammani hurt him, she'd kill her, without even thinking twice.

It's not real. It can't be real. It's magic, and it'll wear off.

Daisy shuddered and Noah ran his hands over her arms. "You cold?"

"No." She leaned in to kiss him until the dark thoughts went away, replaced by the warm comfort of his touch. He kissed her back, then leaned his forehead against hers and whispered, "We're okay?"

I don't know, she thought, but just said, "Yes," and kissed him again.

Kammani was staring at the Summerville newspaper when Mina came into the temple that night, dressed in a black suit, Mort tucked under her arm.

"They *loved* you at the TV station, KG," she said, taking off her sunglasses. "They—"

"The swarm was conquered," Kammani said, staring at the headline. Somewhere, buried deep within her, was rage and fear, but Mina's pills held all that at bay. Which was a damn good thing, because otherwise she'd have been depressed as all hell.

"I know; it's terrible." Mina reached her side, her face sympathetic, and pulled a small orange bottle out of her bag. "Here, have another Paxil."

Kammani popped the pill and took the bottle of water Mina handed her to wash it down, as Mina went on.

"It turns out we got hit really hard by something called Collapsed Hive Syndrome a few years ago and we really needed the bees. But it did the job anyway; none of the faithful were stung. Now, the TV people . . ."

Collapsed Hive Syndrome, Kammani thought, tuning Mina out. *These people label disasters like TV shows. I need something more, something that will shake them to their cores. . . .*

She drank from the bottle of water again, trying to remember back to the old world, to something that had worked before. Before, that was a good time. Anything was better than now. She sighed and went back to thinking, as Mina droned on about not wearing stripes on TV.

She never wore stripes anyway. Back to the problem, she needed something big, something this hateful world couldn't control. Something like . . .

"—and then the station manager said—"

"Plague," Kammani said, smiling.

"What?" Mina said, thrown off stride.

"Tonight at the Goddess Way, I will announce a plague. The faithful will be spared—"

"Wait a minute," Mina said, looking alarmed. "You don't understand how this world works. You're going to get us busted." Kammani glared at her and she flinched, but she went on. "You send a plague, we'll have the Center for Disease Control here in twenty-four hours. They'll look around to see where it came from. We could get in big—"

"A plague," Kammani said, feeling a goddesslike calm descend as the meds kicked in. "The sickness will sweep across the land."

Mina rubbed her forehead. "I know that worked in the old days, but things have changed." She looked at Kammani, woman to woman. "A plague will just get us—"

"A plague," Kammani said, smiling, full of peace.

Mina sighed. "Okay, KG, a plague it is. Can I pick who dies?"

"No," Kammani said, and went back to the newspaper. *Miracle of the Bees,* the headline said, and showed some fool in a beekeeper's hat looking delighted.

I'll give them miracles, Kammani thought dreamily. *I'll give them a miracle to remember.*

"Now we need to decide what you're going to talk about," Mina said, "because you only have twenty minutes, and I don't think you should mention the plague, because then they'd have evidence it was our fault."

Kammani sighed and put the newspaper down to concentrate on Mina's plan.

Plague and television.

That should bring them in, Kammani thought, and listened to Mina tell her how she was going to be the next Summerville cable star.

At midnight, Shar sat naked and cross-legged at the foot of her bed, with a plate of blue-iced star cookies in her lap, trying to find her bearings. She was supposed to find out things from Sam. And in the past three days she had, many things, not one of which was going to help them bring Kammani down.

I sure liked them, though, she thought, and took another bite of cookie while she surveyed the guy stretched out beside her who was watching her eat with a half smile on his face.

"I have to get back to work," she told him. "I'm this close to finishing the citations on that damn book. I'm deleting Kammani for the good of the universe, so that simpled everything up." She licked some anise icing off her lip. "You know, I'm looking at that book in a whole new light, now that I'm a goddess, too. Although technically, I'm not."

"You're a goddess," Sam said.

"Technically, I'm a *demi-goddess,*" Shar said. "Goddess mother, human father." She chewed slower. "That's not right, either. If my grandmother Sharrat was a goddess, then my mother was a demi-goddess and I must be a hemi-demi-semi-goddess or something. I'll have to ask Christopher. He knows fractions."

"My father was mortal," Sam said. "I'm a god."

She looked at him, naked and magnificent, tangled in her sheets. "Yes, you are, baby."

He grinned at her, and she wondered how it was possible that any woman had ever said no to him.

Sharrat had.

"What?" Sam said. "Your smile went away."

Sharrat was stupid. Thank god. "So tell me what it was like back in the day. With Kammani."

"Kammani," he said, losing his own smile.

"Or you," she added hastily. "Tell me about you. You were a king."

"Only for the last four years." He leaned forward and snagged a cookie off her plate. "I was raised to be a soldier and that's what I did. I liked it. Fighting, drinking, fu—" He stopped. "Women."

"Good times," Shar said, annoyed. "So, I'm confused. How did you end up king?"

"My father got bored," Sam said. "He'd taken over Kamesh when the old king stopped paying attention to Kammani."

"I'm assuming she helped him take over," Shar said. "And he was . . ."

"The great king Lugal," Sam said. "The king is always consort to the goddess. He got tired of her demands, especially when she began asking for a sacrifice, and he gave it all to me."

"What a great guy," Shar said, thinking, *Do not get Lugal the "World's Greatest Dad" mug, the bastard.*

"The last I heard, he was invading the Assyrians." Sam took another bite of cookie. "That's like kicking a cobra. I figure he's dead by now." He stopped, a strange look on his face. "Of course he's dead by now. They're all dead. I keep forgetting."

"Right," Shar said. "He must have been a real prize." Unbidden, a memory came back of her sharp-faced grandmother, swearing because something had not gone her way. "Son of that pig of a king Lugal."

Sam laughed. "Sharrat."

Shar nodded, trying to ignore the affection in his voice. "She used to say that whenever she was really angry."

"She was angry a lot."

"You should have seen her once she started to age."

"Taking mortal form is dangerous for a god," Sam said around his cookie. "It can become more real than the divine. And then you are trapped, as she was here. She wouldn't have liked being trapped."

"You knew her really well," Shar said, hating that.

"No," Sam said, meeting her eyes. "Not like this."

Shar stuck her chin out. "Because you didn't sleep with her."

"No," Sam said. "I told you. Because she wasn't you."

Tell me again. Shar picked up another cookie, trying not to be pathetic and vulnerable. He was still taking off after dinner in the evenings and not coming back until midnight, so really, how special could she be to him? *Get back to work.* "So, is Kammani trapped?" *Can we untrap her and send her someplace else?*

"I don't know. She has remained in that body whenever I have been with her, in the old world and this one."

Define "with." "How did she get here? I mean, we know that the Seven were in some kind of deep sleep until my grandfather woke up Sharrat by knocking over her sarcophagus"—there was a movie meet for you—"but there were only seven coffins in the temple. Sharrat must have woken the other six, but where was Kammani?"

"Within them, probably," Sam said, not sounding interested. "Or in the ether, waiting to be called. Gods live on belief. If no one believes, they can't be called back."

"But there were seven who believed." Shar saw him frown and said, "Look, if you don't want to talk about this—"

"Why do you want to know?" Sam said. "For your book?"

Shar started to say, *Yes,* and then thought, *If you love*

him, you trust him. "No. I want to know how she got here so we can reverse it and send her back."

Sam nodded. "She was called. I don't think the Seven had enough power to call her back from wherever Ishtar sent her, but something happened here, and many people called out her name, and she came back."

"Many people." Shar hesitated, but he hadn't seemed upset when she'd said "send her back." "If we could get many people to yell, 'Go home, Kammani,' would that do it?"

"No, she's here now." Sam shifted on the bed, looking uncomfortable.

"Is this bad?" Shar asked. "Does it upset you to talk about sending her back?"

"No." Sam looked tired. "I think she has to go back. She doesn't understand this world at all. I've tried to tell her, but she only listens to Mina now."

"You've tried to tell her?" Shar put down her cookie, stunned. "You're trying to get her out of here?"

"She doesn't belong," Sam said. "But I was with Ereshkigal in the Underworld when Ishtar banished her, so I don't know how Ishtar did it."

"Thank you for trying to get rid of her," Shar said, trying not to lunge for him in gratitude. "You are just the best god ever."

"If you knew the gods, you'd know that wasn't much of a compliment."

"So, you know Ereshkigal?" Shar said, diverted in spite of herself.

"I was stuck with her four months of every year for three years," Sam said gloomily. "Talk about a buzzkill."

Shar laughed and he smiled, too, and she thought, *I don't ever want to leave this bedroom.*

Except they had to save the world.

"You said Sharrat was trapped here." Shar swallowed. "Are you trapped?" *Do you want to leave?*

"I've always had mortal form." Sam looked content with that. "I was born to my mother when she was in mortal form. The divine is within me."

It was within me an hour ago, and it was divine then, too, Shar thought, knowing she should get back to vanquishing Kammani, but just wanting to look at him in her bed.

Sam crooked a finger at her. "Come here."

"Uh-uh," Shar said. "I bow to no god's command. Tell me about the family."

"Family?" Sam frowned.

"So Mom was . . ."

"Nanshe." Sam pushed himself up to lean back against the headboard.

"Whoa," Shar said, in part for Nanshe and in part because he looked great flexing. "Uh, Nanshe. Lady of Dreams. Major goddess there."

Sam nodded. "She saw my father in battle and went to his tent that night."

"Smarter than Ishtar with Gilgamesh," Shar said, and took another bite of cookie. Cookies and Sam telling Kami to beat it. *Life is good.*

"Ishtar takes what she wants," Sam said in the same kind of voice most people use to talk about Aunt Gladys who steals the silverware. "And Gilgamesh was a fool. Why do you want to know about my family?"

"Oh," Shar said, and realized she'd been thinking about marrying in. *Yeah, that's going to happen. This is Sam the God, not Sam the Guy Next Door.* "Just curious. I don't have any family, so I like hearing about others."

"Hey," Wolfie said from under the bed.

"Just me and Wolfie," Shar said hastily.

"Hey," Milton said from under the bed.

"And Milton."

"Hey," Sam said, and she smiled and said, "And you,"

and felt herself expand a little inside because he wanted to be with them.

"And maybe there's a clue in your history," she said, trying to be honest. "We really need to get her out of here. I think she sent the bees that swarmed yesterday."

"That sounds like her," Sam said. "She tried to send locusts to Kamesh once, but I stopped her."

"How?" Shar said.

"I said, 'No.' She needed me, so she didn't do it." Sam's forehead creased. "But I think she did something while I was dead this last time. I saw Ray yesterday at the college—"

"You talked to Ray?" Shar said, astonished.

"—and asked him to find out what happened to Kamesh." He met her eyes. "There's no history of it. At all. It's not in any books in your library; there's nothing on the Internet; it's as if it never existed."

"You think Kammani did something?"

Sam nodded. "Something went so wrong that the people turned from her and let Ishtar take her. And then they all disappeared from history." His face was dark now. "And I wasn't there to save them."

"I doubt they died from swarms of bees," Shar said. "Maybe their records just got lost. I'm always amazed that we have what we do have from then. The clay is so fragile and there's so much destruction . . ."

"If they were conquered, the victors would have kept a record," Sam said. "But everything is just . . . gone."

His voice was so bleak that Shar stopped in mid-bite. "We have to stop her."

Sam nodded. "I don't know how to send her back, but if we find out why she fell the first time, that might help you do it. The three of you."

"It will take all three of us, won't it?" Shar said. "Three demi-goddesses against one goddess."

"Three is a very powerful number. The ancient goddess my uncle told me of was a triple goddess, three in one." He stopped and smiled and was Sam the Guy again. "You can take her."

"We have to." Shar thought about Her, not a goddess with a bas-relief, but a force in the universe so great She was Three. "Three with no name."

"My uncle called her Al-Lat," Sam said.

"That just means 'the goddess.' "

"One goddess," Sam said. "One divine spark with three mortal forms."

"Who disappeared," Shar said. "Like your people. Did her mortality overtake her? If we knew how she became lost, maybe we could shove Kammani in that direction."

"Nobody knows," Sam said, settling back against the covers again. "So this book you're working on. It's only about goddesses?"

"Yes," Shar said, thinking of Al-Lat. Maybe Kammani had destroyed her, too. Kammani didn't seem like the kind of goddess who invited other goddesses in to share the wealth.

"Maybe you should study a god," Sam said.

"I have enough troubles with the goddesses, thank y—," Shar began, and then caught his grin. "Oh."

"Let's go chew up something they like," Wolfie said to Milton under the bed.

"Chew!" Milton said, and followed him out the door.

Shar crawled off the bed and closed the door behind them.

"So," she said, standing naked with her hands on her hips. "You think you've got something good enough for me to write about?"

Sam grinned.

"Yes, you do," she said, and went to him.

FIFTEEN

For Abby, things had been mercifully quiet since Vera's funeral. The swarm of bees had been successfully corralled into beehives and they were now busy making honey, the coffeehouse was booming, and Gen was a genius in the kitchen, creating new and wonderful desserts. Dough seemed to rise faster around Gen, pastries were lighter, and when Bun starting coming by daily to help, things came out of the oven faster, too.

Unfortunately, Christopher Mackenzie had been stopping by just as often, on some made-up excuse or another, but since Thursday he hadn't tried to talk to Abby alone, and she could almost think she was beginning to relax around him. Unless he showed up when she wasn't on her guard or she happened to brush against him, and then she was an emotional mess all over again, her stomach aching, her skin prickling.

But she'd get over it. Granny B had probably lost track of all the lovers she'd gone through, and Abby had every intention of following in her colorful, free-spirited footsteps. As soon as she found someone even half as appealing as Christopher Mackenzie, she was going for it.

Assuming that was even a possibility.

At this point every time he appeared, she chose that moment to duck into Granny B's storeroom and go through the boxes of papers, looking for even the most remote mention of Kammani, tonic, or Mesopotamia.

On Sunday she found the mother lode.

It was one of those marbled composition books that no one used anymore, filled with Granny B's familiar hen-scratch handwriting that Abby had learned to decipher days ago, full of notes and drawing and cryptic references to "sacred geometry" and "hot spots" and "ley lines." She found a map she recognized as Summerville in an earlier incarnation—no strip mall off the highway, only half the college buildings present, even before Temple Street had been populated with small businesses—but some things were constant. The history building–slash–temple, Shar's house, the wide swath of green, and Christopher's house. Which told her exactly nothing, except that his house had been in the town as long as the ancient history building.

She thumbed through the pages, catching a phrase here, a note there, until she came to another drawing, of someone like Kammani standing over a crowned man, a knife raised, with seven women surrounding them who looked very familiar, including poor dead Vera. It looked eerily like a sketch from an ancient temple but done with modern sensibilities. As if someone had looked four thousand years into the past and drawn it in lifelike detail.

A shiver ran across Abby's skin. There was no reason it should make her uncomfortable—it was from a time long ago, and most likely it had simply come from Granny B's overfertile imagination. But there was no denying that the scene could fit inside the auditorium of the history building.

She shoved the book away from her, shuddering, and a slip of paper fell on the floor. She was half-tempted to leave it there—she'd always had a thing about human sacrifice and public execution—but she opened it anyway. It was a diagram, again in Granny B's handwriting with her usual peacock blue ink, a series of numbers set in a box that made absolutely no sense.

And there was only one person who really understood numbers, and she was hiding from him.

She was a grown-up, wasn't she? She was over him, or at least well on her way. She was her grandmother's descendent, not a sniveling romantic coward hiding in a storeroom.

He was sitting at the wide wooden counter, laughing at something Gen had said, and emotion hit Abby so hard she couldn't breathe for a moment. And then he turned to look at her, the laughter dying, and she still wanted to storm across the room and kiss him.

"I found something," she said.

Gen and Christopher just looked at her.

"Anything good?" Bun asked as she pulled a tray of pastries from the massive oven.

"I'm not sure." She should go back into the storeroom, wait until he left, wait until her heart started beating normally.

Hell, no! She was Granny B's offspring—she could face down math professors with one hand tied behind her back. "Numbers," she said before she could chicken out.

Shit, it was like handing a sandwich to a starving man. He practically sailed across the room, whisked the paper out of her hand, and a moment later he was in a completely different world.

Good thing she wasn't in love with him. Marrying a man who could lose himself that completely in whatever interested him would make for a very frustrating life. Unless, of course, he applied that much intensity and concentration to making love as he did to numbers. Which, at least by Abby's brief experience, was unfortunately true.

And if he was as good at numbers as he was at sex, it was no wonder he was *Good Will Hunting* and *A Beautiful Mind* all rolled into one.

He looked up from the paper, and she realized he hadn't

moved that far away from her. In fact, he was dangerously close, at least to her frame of mind.

She took a step back, coming up against a countertop. "Do the numbers mean anything to you?" She cleared her throat nervously.

"Coordinates, maybe. Was there anything else?"

"There's a notebook. . . ." She gestured back toward the storeroom, and Christopher took her hand and pulled her into it, slamming the door behind them.

She had the fleeting hope he might pull her into his arms, but he had more important things on his mind, which was a good thing, she reminded herself. Or she might have had to push him away, and that would complicate things. Or even worse, she might not have pushed him away, and . . .

But he'd forgotten about her in his hunger for math. "Where's the notebook?"

She handed it to him, watching as he sank down into the chair she'd abandoned, and silence reigned for an endless two minutes. Minutes she could stand and watch him without him being even remotely aware of her.

He wasn't that gorgeous—hell, Brad Pitt had him beat by a mile. His tousled dark blond hair was pushed back, his wire-rimmed glasses set firmly on his strong nose, and even with his mouth thinned in concentration, it was still distractably luscious. And he had the kind of body she'd always liked: tall and lean and strong. It was just an unfortunate combination of genetics that she'd find him so irresistibly attractive. She could get over it; she would get over it. Particularly since he seemed to be having no trouble getting over her.

"What are you looking at?" He lifted his head to look at her. "I don't have measles, if that's what you're thinking."

The non sequitur startled her. "Why would you have measles?"

"There's an outbreak in town. Most everyone's been vaccinated, but some people's immunization has worn off. I wanted to make sure Gen and Bun were all right."

Of course he did. She was simply imagining he was making excuses to see her. "And they're okay?"

"Yes." He looked at her. "What about you?"

"I had measles when I was six."

"You could get them again, you know. I can check."

"Check how?"

"See if you have any spots. They usually start on the stomach or the back." He started to rise.

"Get away from me!" she snapped.

"Just offering in the interests of science," he said in an even tone.

"I'm fine," she said, ignoring the thought of those intense eyes sweeping over her naked body. It was too hot in the storeroom with the door closed. "What about the notebook? Does it make any sense to you?"

"It might. Do you mind if I borrow it? I'd like to make a few calculations."

"I'm not letting it out of my sight."

His half smile was devastating. Way too hot in the room. "Did you think I was going to run off with it?"

"It belonged to Granny B. I don't want to risk losing anything of hers now that I'm learning about her."

"Then you can come with me."

"Come where?" She didn't bother to keep the suspicious tone out of her voice.

"Apparently this is a diagram of the center of the ancient history building. It appears to be in the auditorium."

"That's what it looked like to me, too," Abby said, resigned.

"And you were there . . . why?"

"You wouldn't believe me if I told you."

"Try me."

"I already did." The moment the words were spoken she clapped her hands over her mouth.

"I wasn't talking about that—"

She interrupted him. "Neither was I. I meant I tried to tell you—"

"Not that I'm unwilling to talk about it."

"Well, I am," she said.

"Are you sure you don't have measles? You're looking flushed."

"I don't have measles," she said in a tight voice. "And yes, the auditorium in the history building is a temple, and we've been going to dog-training classes there, which actually aren't dog-training classes but goddess-training classes. But you don't believe in goddesses from ancient Mesopotamia." She was running on and on and she couldn't help it.

"You'd be surprised what I believe in," he said in a steady voice. "Let's go."

"You think I'm going with you?"

"I'm thinking you don't have any choice. Gen and Bun can finish the baking, and you may have fewer customers because of the measles."

"It would take more than a few spots to keep the hordes away from my cookies," Abby said in a lofty tone.

"Understandable," he said gravely, and there was no hidden meaning as far as she could tell. "You want to drive or should we walk?"

She stared at him. There was really no way out of this, was there? She wasn't going to let him go off with Granny B's notebook, and they needed to find out anything they could about Kammani's haunt. And even if she was secretly pining for him, he seemed to have taken his dismissal in stride.

The thought of being in a car with him was just a little too distracting. "It's a nice day," she said. "We'll walk."

Which kept her in his company even longer, but for some reason, with the bright June sun beating down and the soft breeze blowing and the smell of summer in the air, she couldn't quite object. He said nothing as he followed her into the building and she stopped before the doors to the auditorium.

"I'm pretty sure Kammani's not here," she said, suddenly nervous. "There was an article in the paper about her filming the Goddess Way for cable, so I'm assuming she's doing that, but there's no telling when she'll be back. We should hurry."

"And exactly who is Kammani?"

She stared at him, surprised. Kammani had become such an overarching shadow in their lives that she assumed everyone knew who she was. "She's the goddess," she said flatly. "The one our ancestors, including yours, worshiped. She's the one who's brought us together to make us goddesses again. And I think she's batshit insane."

"Good to know," he said evenly. "Lead the way."

The auditorium was pitch-dark, and Abby froze. Christopher bumped into her, and she jumped away so she wouldn't be tempted to lean back against him, and an electric flashlight speared the darkness.

"Oh." Her voice was shaky. "You brought a flashlight. I didn't think of that."

"I always carry it."

"You have a habit of walking into dark places?"

"I like to be prepared." He flashed the light over the walls, and she could see his face in the reflected glow of the powerful little beam. He had that math look in his eyes, as if he were mentally calculating equations.

"I think there are some electric lights somewhere," she said nervously.

"We don't need them. Just light the torches."

"Electricity would work better."

"Torches will give us a more accurate estimate of the area. Are you going to argue with a mathematician?"

"I wouldn't think of it. Does the mathematician come with matches?"

"Always prepared," he said, tossing the small box to her.

He was damned lucky she caught them, she thought, cranky, as she crossed the darkened room to light the torches. Slowly the light filled the room, and by the time she finished with the last one and turned, he was off in some kind of numerical trance, stalking around the room, muttering beneath his breath, his forehead knotted in concentration.

"Don't you want to make notes?" she said.

The look he gave her was one of withering disdain. "I don't need notes. I have the kind of brain that holds on to these things. Your grandmother's notes are good enough." He still had Granny B's marbled notebook in his hand, his eyes sweeping down to check it, then darting up to the high ceiling. "There are power points in this room. The building wasn't just dumped here—the placement is critical, at the juncture of the ley lines, with power surges going from east to west and north to south."

"Great," Abby said, half-mesmerized by the sound of his voice, half-irritated that he seemed to have forgotten all about her. "And what do these power points do?"

"Beats me," he said, switching off the flashlight and taking out something white. "But we're going to mark them so we can find them again. They're here for a reason; I just don't know what that reason is yet."

"How are we going to see the marks?"

"Chalk." He took a few steps and drew a mark on the floor.

"You come equipped with that, too."

"I'm a teacher. Of course I have chalk. Though in fact,

you'd be surprised what I'm capable of, spur-of-the-moment."

She could feel the color rise in her face again and she turned away from him, surveying the torches. If he noticed, he'd probably ask her if she had measles again, and insist on doing a proper inspection, and if he put his hands on her she'd have a hard time remembering that she was completely over him, and . . .

"I'm done," he said. "While you've been standing there daydreaming I've finished marking the power spots, and I've got the dimensions in my head. Sacred geometry is really quite fascinating, you know."

"I'm sure it is," she said hastily. "But I think we need to get out of here before Kammani comes back. You can explain it to me some other time."

"Can I? You run away whenever I walk in a room."

"Your imagination," she said stiffly.

He didn't argue. "I'll douse the torches on the right side, you do the ones on the left, and we'll head back to the coffeehouse."

"You're coming back?"

"Unless you've changed your mind and decided to let me take the notebook home."

"I'll get the torches."

One by one the torches went out, and the cavernous room grew darker, and darker still. The torches were placed at various intervals, various levels, and the final one was too high for Abby to reach. She considered jumping up like Bailey in a futile attempt to reach it, but she couldn't bring herself to be that ridiculous in front of Christopher.

And then he was there, directly behind her, his body almost touching hers. He was taller, he could reach, and she would have moved out of the way except that he put his hands on her arms, gently.

"I'll get it," he said, his voice low in the velvety darkness.

And then there was no light at all except for the faint pool coming from the faculty room, and he turned her in his arms and kissed her.

She should have shoved him away, but there in the darkness, no one could see, and it was the sweetest kiss in the world, his lips soft, gentle against her, faintly nudging, and all she could do was sink against him, flow into him, and kiss him back, wanting to put her arms around his neck, wanting more.

But she wasn't going to make that mistake again. She stepped back, moving away from him. "We need to leave before Kammani gets back." There was only the faintest waver in her voice.

"Yes." His voice was huskier, and in the darkness she found she could smile. So maybe he did have a reason for haunting the coffeehouse that had nothing to do with his cousin and everything to do with her.

It was later than she'd realized when they left the building. A wind had begun to pick up, messing up Christopher's hair even more. She wanted to reach up, push it away from his troubled forehead, but she kept her hands by her sides.

They stood there for a moment, saying nothing, and she knew that if she didn't get away from him she'd either jump on him or burst into tears, and neither was an option.

"You can take Granny B's notebook home with you," she said abruptly. "We've got to get busy opening the coffeehouse, and I won't have any time to look at it. Just be careful not to lose it."

"Do I strike you as the kind of man who loses important things?"

You lost me. The thought popped into her head and there was nothing she could do to get rid of it.

"I've decided to trust you," she said stiffly.

His smile was slow, deliberate, and heartbreakingly beautiful. "Well, that's a start," he said.

And without another word he turned and walked away.

"So," Daisy said as she cut tomatoes for the salad, "you don't think it's anything to worry about? The bees, the measles outbreak . . . you don't think that's weird?"

"Ah-ah-ah, *stay*." Noah held one hand out to Bailey as he reached for a treat from the bag next to him on the couch. Meanwhile, Squash indulged in a constant state of *stay* in the corner on her bed. "*Stay*." Bailey stayed, if you didn't count the almost involuntary swish-swish of his back end on the floor, and Noah gave him a treat, then turned to look at Daisy. "Sorry. Did you say something?"

"What? Who? Me? No." Daisy put down the knife and reached for her wine. It was Monday night, almost a week since they'd all sworn to get information on Kammani, and she'd come up with bupkes. Her search of Peg's apartment had yielded a big, fat zero, and Noah . . . well, he just didn't know anything.

She hoped.

There was a small—*very* small—part of her that wondered if maybe he was under some kind of spell, and that as soon as she shared their intent to get rid of Kammani, the whammy would wear off, he'd realize he had never really been that into Daisy, and he'd run off to tell Kammani everything. Which was ridiculous, she knew.

Mostly.

She downed a larger gulp of her wine and picked up the knife again, just as two quick knocks sounded on the door and her mother entered, saying, "Daisy, I'm telling you, you absolutely *must* move into a building with an elevator."

Bailey saw Peg, barked, "Peggy!" and dashed up over Noah and the couch to launch himself across the room and come skidding at her feet. Squash, for her part, lifted her head and barked, "Hello."

Peg giggled and knelt down, ladylike in her powder blue dress and—of course—matching pillbox hat, and made smoochy noises at Bailey as he danced around her, his tail wagging furiously. Noah got up off the couch and walked over to stand next to Daisy by the kitchen island and mouthed the word, *Mom?* to which Daisy just lifted her glass and drank again.

Peg straightened up, her face flush with glee, and turned her attention to the humans in the room.

"Daisy!" she said, throwing her arms open and pulling Daisy into a hug. They tipped side to side three times in one of her mother's trademark metronome hugs, and then Peg tucked her arm through Daisy's and looked up at Noah.

"And you must be the reason my daughter hasn't called me in two weeks," Peg said, leaning her head against Daisy's.

"I called you," Daisy said, wriggling out of her mother's grasp. "Twelve times. You didn't answer your cell phone."

"I didn't?" Peg laughed, then held her hand out to Noah. "I'm Peg, Daisy's mother. Don't even try the you-must-be-sisters line; it'll only embarrass us both."

"I'm Noah." He shot an amused look at Daisy, then said to Peg, "Great hat."

Peg patted the powder blue pillbox, thrilled beyond measure. "Isn't it? I just got it. There was this wonderful little store in Manhattan—"

"That's great," Daisy interrupted. "When did you get back?"

"Why, yes, I would love a glass of wine while we catch up, thank you." She put her hand on Daisy's cheek, giving it a gentle, corrective pat. "I've missed you, too, sweetheart."

Peg walked over to the couch, making smooching noises at Bailey, who followed her happily. Noah looked at Daisy, and Daisy waved him on to go sit. She poured another glass of wine, and in her imagination heard the *ding* of the boxing ring. *Round One, to Peg. Round Two, starting now . . .*

Daisy put her mother's wine on the coffee table and settled in the window seat. Noah sat in the chair opposite the couch, legs outstretched in a relaxed pose, and Daisy envied him his ease.

"So," Daisy said, turning to her mother, "let's revisit the rule about knocking *before* you walk in—"

"I was excited to see you. My plane just got in an hour ago, and I rushed right over." Peg leaned down and smooched at Bailey. "Didn't I, darling?"

Bailey barked, "I don't know!" and danced around Peg's powder blue leather pumps. Peg straightened up and looked at Daisy.

"You look different," Peg said. "Anything . . . *new* . . . going on?"

You know damn well what's going on, Daisy thought, but smiled even wider. "I take it your treatments went well. I notice you haven't sneezed once since you got here."

"Isn't it a miracle? But you must tell me what's going on with you." She smiled with practiced casualness. "How was that dog class? Did you ever go?"

"Oh my god." Daisy threw her arms up in the air. "You are shameless, you know that?"

"Well," Noah said, pushing up from his seat. "I'm going to let you girls catch up. Peg, it was nice to meet you."

"The pleasure was all mine," Peg said, eyeing him with girlish glee.

Vomit, Daisy thought. Noah left, and Bailey hopped up on the couch next to Peg, his tail wagging. She smooched at him and said, "Get your ball," and Bailey shot off the couch.

"Back to the subject," Daisy said. "How could you not tell me?"

"Tell you what?" Peg said, taking the ball from Bailey and bouncing it down the hallway toward the bedroom. As Bailey raced after it, Daisy concentrated all her anger at her mother, drawing it up in bits and pieces from a lifetime's worth of little offenses, but instead of directing it this time, she let it run wild through the room, fluttering up papers and almost displacing her hat.

"Oh . . . my . . . What the . . . ?" Peg said, putting her hand on her hat as her eyes widened.

Daisy lifted her hands and clenched her fists, drawing it back in.

"Is that how it works?" Peg muttered. "Amazing."

Bailey ran back into the room, hopped up on the couch, dropped the ball next to Peg, and barked, "Again!" Peg picked up the ball and tossed it, and Bailey went flying over the back of the couch, his little nails skittering across the hardwood, a testimony to his joy. Daisy leaned forward.

"All right," she said. "I've got ground to cover and Noah's going to be back soon, so let's cut to the chase. How do we stop her?"

Peg picked up her wine and sat back on the couch. "Stop who, darling?"

"You know who." Daisy leaned forward. "Kammani. She sent a swarm of bees over the town, and hit us with a plague of measles, and . . ." Daisy took a breath, feeling the stab in her chest as she remembered Vera. "She's just dangerous."

"Is she, really?" Peg said as Bailey came back and dropped the ball at her feet.

"Yeah, she is, really." Daisy huffed and sat back. "Jesus, Peg. You run off and leave me to get blindsided with all this, and now you're acting like it's no big deal. What the hell?"

"Peggy!" Bailey barked. "Ball!"

"Oh, come on," Peg said, waving her hand in the air dismissively. "How bad can it be? You're young, beautiful, and now . . . supernatural. That's gotta be a high. What's it like?"

"Doesn't matter," Daisy said. "Did Great-grandma Humusi ever tell you anything about maybe . . . how to get rid of her or something?"

"Ball!" Bailey barked.

Peg waved one manicured hand in the air. "Oh, she rattled on sometimes about serving the goddess, the honor of family duty, which you know I'd be no good at. I spent twenty-two years married to your father, God rest his soul, and I am past my service days, honey. To a goddess or a man, it's the same damn thing."

"I'm not in service to her." Daisy walked over, picked up the ball, and tossed it down the hallway, and Bailey skittered after it.

"You're not?" Peg said, seeming startled. "You can *refuse*?"

"Apparently, because I have." Daisy sat back down in the window seat. "Now, focus. Did Humusi ever say anything about how to banish Kammani?"

Peg sighed. "She said a lot. Blah blah blah, the goddess. Blah blah blah, service. To be honest, honey, I didn't listen too closely. When she and Mama died in that car crash, it was my chance to raise you normal, and I took it. The Worthams were still off the deep end, but the rest of the Seven had gone pretty quiet about it. I figured we'd never have to deal with it." She caught Daisy's look and shrugged. "Whoops."

"Yeah, whoops is right," Daisy said, playing her last card to get her mother to understand the seriousness of the situation. "Someone died."

Peg leaned forward. "Oh, please tell me it was a Wortham."

"No." Daisy realized she was clenching her teeth and loosened her jaw. "It was Vera Dale who died. Kammani tried to call her to service, and it killed her." Daisy nodded to Squash, who snored quietly in the corner. "That's her dog. *Was* her dog."

"Vera," Peg said, her voice soft. "She was the last of Iltani's line. I wonder what happens—" Her face went white. "You don't think they'll call me, do you?"

Daisy released a slow breath. "No, Peg, I really don't. One per bloodline, far as I can tell."

"Oh." Peg relaxed and then, finally, her face morphed into an expression of sympathy for Vera. Bailey came back, this time with a dusty tennis ball in his mouth. He dropped it at Daisy's feet and sneezed.

"Bless you," Daisy said, and picked up the ball. "Jeez, Bail, where did you find this?"

"Under the bed!" Bailey barked. "Throw!"

"Ugh," Daisy said. "I've got this kind of dust under my bed?"

"Yes!" Bailey barked. "Throw!"

Daisy threw the ball and sat back, her mom staring at her, eyes wide in childlike fascination.

"Did he just . . . talk to you?"

"Yeah," Daisy said. "They all do."

"All dogs?" Peg said. "They can talk now?"

"No," Daisy said. "We can understand them now."

"Who? You and Noah?"

"No. Me and Abby and Shar. And the rest of the Seven." *Six now.*

Peg nodded, seemingly fascinated for a moment; then

a mischievous glint sparked in her eye. "So, what *do* you and Noah do?"

"Oh, for the love of—" Daisy picked up her wine and went to the kitchenette, Peg close behind.

"Honey," Peg said, "just tell me the sex is good. If the sex is good, you can fix everything else. Except drugs and other women." She sipped her wine thoughtfully. "And other men." She waved her hand in the air, then grinned at Daisy. "So tell me. How is it?"

"Now, this is fascinating. You, who lied to me, expect me to just open up to you, is that it?"

"I didn't *lie*. . . ."

"Yes, you did," Daisy said, her hands clenching at her sides. "Not telling is lying. You should have told me what was happening, and you didn't, and someone died. How can you expect me to trust you now?"

Peg stared at her. "Where is this coming from, Daisy?"

Daisy lowered her eyes. "Let's just drop it, okay?"

Peg hesitated for a moment, then shrugged. "Okay. As lovely as this little visit has been, I have unpacking to do." She went to the hall table and picked up her purse, then said, "Come on, Bailey."

The air around Daisy went suddenly still. "Wait, *what*?"

Peg blinked at her. "I'm taking Bailey. I thought you couldn't wait until . . ." She trailed off, realization hitting her. "Oh."

Between them, Bailey dropped the ball on the ground, his tail slowing down and lowering. "Peggy's going?" he barked.

"Yeah, Bail." Daisy's chest hurt as her mind reeled. How had she not seen this coming? The instinct overcame her to send some chaos her mother's way, to make her back off, force her to give up Bailey, but she looked at Bailey and thought, *No*. Instead she stepped out from behind the island and knelt by Bailey, petting his head.

"Bail," she said, "if you want to go with Peg, that's okay. I'll understand."

"If he *wants* to . . . ?" Peg said, stepping forward. "He's been my dog for three years, Daisy, of course he *wants*—"

Daisy stood up and shot a look at her mother. Peg's mouth stayed open, but she went quiet. She looked from Daisy to Bailey and nodded. "It's okay, Bailey. You can come with me, but you don't have to." Then she shifted her eyes to Daisy and said, "He can understand me?"

Bailey lowered his head, and Daisy said, "He understands."

There was a long moment of silence, and then Bailey lifted his head and trotted over to Peg, who said, "That's my boy!" and knelt down to pet him.

Daisy leaned against the island and looked at the ceiling for a second while her heart sent stabs of sadness through her on each beat. *Not gonna cry, not gonna cry . . .* She blinked hard, got it under control, and looked at Bailey. He was wagging his tail, putting his front paws on Peg's knees, licking her face. He would be happy with her, and that was what mattered.

"Love you!" Bailey barked, and licked Peg one last time before Daisy's mother straightened up and looked at Daisy, her face uncharacteristically conflicted. "Honey . . ."

"It's okay," Daisy said, but it was not okay, and the sooner her mother and Bailey left, the better.

"Okay." Peg walked to the door and opened it, then turned to Bailey and said, "Let's go, Bailey."

But Bailey turned and trotted back to Daisy's feet, then barked, "Love you!" at Peg again, and relief flooded through Daisy.

Peg stared for a moment, then looked up at Daisy. "What did he say?"

"He said he loves you," Daisy said.

"What does that mean?" Peg looked at Bailey. "Bailey, do you want to stay here with Daisy?"

"Daisy's mine!" he barked.

Daisy could tell by the look on Peg's face that she didn't need to translate.

"Okay." Peg nodded and put on a strong smile for Bailey. "Love you, too, baby."

Then the door opened, and Noah stepped into the apartment. Peg looked at Daisy, said, "Good-bye," and left.

Noah watched her go, and when the door closed behind her, he turned to Daisy. "Everything okay?"

"As okay as it ever is." Daisy knelt down to Bailey and scratched behind his ears, and he jumped up and licked Daisy's face, then ran over to Noah and hopped up, scrambling his front paws over Noah's knees.

"Noah!" he barked, glancing back at the tennis ball. "Ball!"

Noah picked up the ball and threw it, then looked at Daisy. "So, what happened?"

Daisy watched him for a moment, then said, "Nothing. I asked her for help banishing"—*no, no, no*—"I mean, doing something, and she wouldn't help me because she's Peg and that's just who she is."

Noah walked over to her, looking into her eyes, his own dark and thoughtful. "Is it something I can help you with?"

She looked into his eyes and he looked back at her, and she wondered what she was so worried about. He would never betray her; he would never lie to her. This was no whammy, it was real, and she knew it.

Almost all the time, she knew it.

"No," she said finally. "I don't think you can." Then she kissed him, picked up her knife, and sliced into the last tomato.

Wednesday dawned cloudy and dim. Abby dragged her sorry ass out of bed and into the shower later than usual. So late that the coffeehouse was deserted. Daisy was gone—off with Noah, no doubt—and Gen was missing as well. Friday was the one day the place was closed—Abby usually spent the time baking in preparation for their now-regular open-mike night, but last night she and Gen had stayed up till the middle of the night, coming up with new and startling combinations, like anise-poppyseed muffins and cinnamon-pomegranate pressed cookies.

When she went into the kitchen, the room was spotless; having Gen move in had been a godsend, even taking into consideration that Christopher Mackenzie seemed to consider it his responsibility to check on his cousin at least once a day. At least he'd kept his distance since the day they'd gone to investigate the temple hot spots. The next day he'd returned the notebook and a seven-page paper, with illustrations and footnotes, for heaven's sake, listing the possible use of the power spots. And then nothing. He still came by every day but assiduously ignored her. As if that kiss in the dark had never happened.

She pulled the apron over her head and began setting out Granny B's mason jars and her own pathetic attempts. Thank heavens for her grandmother's colorful clothes. The jeans she'd brought with her were getting tight, but her grandmother's gypsy clothes swirled around her like they were made for her. Normally she would have worried—she could just imagine her mother's voice in her head, criticizing her—but in her new life of demi-goddesshood she just dismissed it. She was feeling strong, ripe, healthy, and her skinny, boyish figure had bloomed. Her A-cup bras were useless, her hips wouldn't fit in her jeans, but at least her waist was still small enough for the skirts to button around it. She was becoming a goddess in body as well as in spirit, and instead of worrying she felt as if she were glowing.

She still intended to avoid cookies as long as Christopher was around. Self-preservation could only carry her so far, and she couldn't look at him without something inside of her melting. But at least she could cover it up.

She grabbed one of the soft brioches Gen had baked at the crack of dawn, letting the flavor dance on her tongue. Gen's baking didn't start all sorts of longings—she could look Christopher in the eye while she ate one of Gen's raspberry muffins and not betray a thing.

She pulled Granny B's notebook toward her, reading over the notes she'd added yesterday. She'd come to at least one conclusion last night—despite the euphoric effect of the tonic, there was no alcohol involved. She'd placed the depleted basket of tiny liquor bottles on the back table for anyone to grab and focused on the base.

"Any luck with the tonic?" Gen said, coming in from the front room.

"I'm getting closer. Cider. Barley malt syrup. Turbinado sugar. Even some Irish moss Granny had, but something is still missing. I've tried everything I can think of, repeated Granny B's experiments, but each time I end up with nothing but a brown, unappetizing mess."

"Tough." Gen reached for one of the raspberry muffins. "I still think you can do it."

"The answer is here—it's got to be. It's just maddeningly out of reach." She put her head down on the butcher-block counter, resisting the impulse to pound it a few times, and closed her eyes. Desire, chaos, completion. She had the desire, and the results so far had been chaotic. Where was the completion she needed?

Which immediately made her think of sex, and of Christopher, and she sat up, shaking her head. "You know, I think we'd all be better off without sex. I spent most of my life not knowing what I was missing, and now I can't stop thinking about it."

"That's the way of it," Gen said, sounding wise beyond her years. "The longer you do without, the less you miss it. But I'm not quite sure why you're missing it."

"It . . . complicates things. And I need to concentrate on this freaking tonic." She poured the base liquid into the ceramic urn she'd found back in Granny's storeroom. It was round, almost bowl-like, and decorated with female figures, each carrying an offering over her head. They were graceful, powerful, and Abby liked to think they were the five of them, the five who were left. Well, actually six, but Mina didn't count. Abby stared down into the graceful urn, stirring the muddy mixture, and then on impulse she closed her eyes again.

"What are you thinking?" Gen moved closer.

"Hunger. Desire. The sweetness of delight at the heart of all this." On instinct alone she picked up the honey pot, swirled the wooden spoon into it, and then stirred the honey into the mixture.

It immediately turned a rich, golden color, like honeyed amber, and the scent drifted up, warm and inviting. She took a taste, letting it dance on her tongue, but nothing happened. A beginning, a hunger, and nothing more.

"God, look at that!" Gen said.

Abby closed her eyes again, listening to the voices in her head. Hunger. Chaos. She could picture Daisy, her blonde hair now a deep red, the passion that drove her, the chaos that followed her, the piquant spice of her. Cinnamon. She reached for the cinnamon sticks, dropping one, two, three of them into the mixture.

There was a flash of light, and the tonic turned a deep red, the color of carnelian, the color of the flowers that had begun to grow wild in the courtyard. The scent from the urn was different now, a little wilder, almost like a song that changed tempo.

"Holy shit! How did you do that?" Gen said.

Abby dipped a silver spoon in and took a sip, then offered one to Gen.

"It's close," Gen said, awed. "But not quite right."

"Not yet. But I know where I'm going now." She needed Shar. She needed completion. Something to finish it. She closed her eyes, and the taste of anise came to her, black licorice, strong and distinctive, and it felt right. It didn't matter that Kammani's tonic had never tasted of anise—she knew that was what she needed.

"Hand me the anise seed, would you?"

Gen put the little vial in her hand, and she opened it and dropped three tiny seeds into the rich red mixture, then two more for Bun and Gen. Another pop, and the color turned the color of lapis, clear blue and shimmering, and the scent was amazing, a rich combination of all the glorious tastes and smells that seemed to blend rather than clash. Almond and mint, honey and cinnamon, anise and rosewater. She dipped the silver spoon in it again and took a small sip, then waited for the bliss to wash over her.

It didn't. It tempted, teased, played with her senses, but there was something wrong, something held back, and she wanted to cry with frustration. She was so certain she'd finally understood what was needed. Not the actual flavors, but the essences of their powers.

She shook her head, turning to Gen. "It's still not right. And I was so sure. All we've got here is a deep blue liquid that tastes divine but does nothing." She wanted to cry. "What am I missing?"

"Well, I'd add yeast," Gen said. "Yeast is all about growth and health and . . . You know what? You're amazing—you'll get it. I have classes, but when I come back I'll do all the baking for tomorrow and you can concentrate on the tonic. I need to work on my croissants."

Abby managed a smile. "You're a saint," she said.

And then she was alone in the kitchen, staring down into the beautiful blue liquid. What the hell was missing? She'd been so sure she'd finally figured it out.

After a moment, she realized she wasn't alone anymore. Someone was watching her, without the malevolence she always felt in Mina's presence, without the dark power she felt from Kammani, but with power nonetheless. She turned, slowly, to see Christopher Mackenzie standing in the doorway, watching her.

She drew in her breath and felt a storm rumble in the distance. "How did you get in here?" She cleared her throat, nervous.

"Gen gave me a key."

"Well, Gen's not here." *Businesslike,* she reminded herself. *Unemotional.* There was a crackle of thunder outside, getting closer, and she jumped.

The room grew darker, and she could see through the windows that the trees were beginning to sway in the wind. A storm was coming, a powerful one, and the ozone practically crackled in the air. A bolt of lightning snaked through the sky, followed by a distant rumble, and she stared, mesmerized.

"I came to talk to you." Christopher moved into the room, and the impending violence of the weather seemed to glide through his lean body, like threads of electricity, and they danced back to her, tying them together, as the thunder cracked louder.

Oh, shit, she thought as the low hum of desire began to heat her belly. And she hadn't even touched a cookie.

He'd given up his jacket and tie sometime in the past two weeks, and he no longer looked like the cold, uptight math professor. He looked rumpled, distracted, troubled, delicious.

Now the trees were dancing in the wind beyond the glass door. "What do you want to talk about?"

He looked uncomfortable. "Do you have any cookies?"

"You can do this without cookies. What do you want to talk about?"

He ran a hand through his tousled hair. "I think we should date."

SIXTEEN

She stared at him as the storm grew stronger. "I beg your pardon?"

"You heard me. I think we should date. I think I should ask you out to dinner, bring you flowers, kiss you good night at the door, and then do it all over again."

"Until when?"

"I hadn't thought that far ahead."

"Think about it now. Why in the world do you want to date me? You don't seem the type to waste your time with anything as superficial as dating."

"You were the virgin, not me," he said with a distinct lack of tact. "And I don't want to go on dates. I just figured it was the only way you'd let me near you."

"And why do you want to be near me?" Her heart was beating a little too loudly, and there was nothing she could do to quiet it.

"Because you're all I think about, day and night. I don't know what the hell is going on with us; I only know I can't get rid of it. I don't care if you're batshit insane and think you're the reincarnation of Cleopatra. I hear voices; you hear dogs. We'll work it out. Maybe get a discount on therapy."

The branches outside slapped against the window as the wind grew fierce. "Cleopatra was Egyptian, not Mesopotamian. And I'm not the reincarnation I'm the descendent. And Cleopatra was a queen, not a goddess."

"And you insist you're a goddess?" He wasn't looking happy about it.

Neither was she. "A demi-goddess. And you still hear voices from ancient Mesopotamia?"

"Yes."

"Then I think we're past the point of dating," she said, sliding off the stool. She needed to get closer to him. Now. She couldn't fight it anymore.

"I can't keep away from you," he said, making it sound like the plague.

She couldn't blame the cookies. It had been more than a week since she'd eaten one. She couldn't blame the tonic—she was getting close, but it still wasn't right, and she'd finished the stuff Kammani gave her long ago.

"I can't keep away from you, either," she said, needing him. Wanting him. Craving him. "I think we're doomed."

"Good," he said, and pulled her into his arms.

Another crack of thunder, so loud that it shook the building, and she kissed him, letting the hunger out, roaming free, taking from him. His body was hard, strong, shaking just a little bit, and she ran her hands up his chest, then ripped the buttons open, so that some went flying across the room. He picked her up, wrapping her legs around his hips, and she could feel how hard he was, how empty she was, and she needed him more than she needed air to breathe, and she wanted to tell him that, but she couldn't stop kissing him, taking his mouth, his lips, his tongue, squirming closer.

He pushed her against the wall, supporting her, and tore his mouth away. "Where can we go?"

"Right here. Right now," she said.

He carried her over to the waist-high counter, shoving the cookies and mason jars out of the way. She lay back, spreading her arms over her head as he pulled her underwear off her. "Hello Kitty?" he muttered, tossing it to one side.

"So I like anime," she said, waiting for the rasp of his zipper, waiting for him to push inside her, fill the emptiness that had been tormenting her for weeks. For all her life.

She felt his hands on her hips, and a moment later his mouth between her legs, and she let out a little shriek of surprise, reaching down to push at him.

He caught her hands in his, holding them, as he tasted her, his tongue wicked and wonderful, and in a moment she climaxed, hips arching, straining, needing more. He touched her, one finger sliding inside her, and the feelings multiplied until she could think of nothing at all but the waves of pleasure rippling through her body.

She came down, slowly, and he pulled away, wiping his mouth on his open shirt, and his eyes were glittering in the stormy darkness. Abby was panting, her heart banging against her chest, trying to find her voice.

"I didn't think math professors did that," she gasped.

"Only when we're particularly inspired," he said, pushing her back on the counter so that she lay across it, her skirts up to her waist, and he climbed up after her, between her legs, and he cradled her head in his arms, kissing her, and she could taste her own desire on his mouth, and it only made her hotter.

She reached down and fumbled with his jeans, undoing them with shaking hands, shoving them down his hips, reaching for him, putting her hands on him, the hard, smooth length of him, and another ripple hit her, without him touching her.

She heard the rip of paper. "You brought a condom?"

"Condoms, plural. Always prepared, remember?" He slid his hands under her butt, cupping her, and she could feel him against her, hot and hard, and she was so wet that when he sank into her, there was no pain, just a glorious fullness that made her body begin to shiver and clench once more.

He froze, as she shattered around him, keeping very still until the last stray shudder left her, and then he began to move, so slowly that each thrust shook her, pumping into her, and she wanted even more, wrapping her legs around his hips to pull him in deeper, wrapping her arms around his neck, closing her eyes and meeting him, thrust and push and a shattering delight that was so powerful she let out a low, keening wail as she felt him climax inside her.

And somewhere in the distance she thought she heard the dogs howling in unison.

He collapsed on top of her, gasping, and she cradled him, shivering as the last tiny orgasms drained away, and she felt limp, exhausted, and complete. Totally and forever, and all she wanted to do was hold him.

The thunder had died away, the wind had slowed, and in the distance she could hear the soft, soothing sound of rain as it fell outside, a gentle benediction after the anger of the approaching storm. All was as it should be, calm, peaceful. Right.

It was quite a while later when she heard his voice, soft and wry. "Did your dog howl at the same time you did?"

She laughed. "I think so. I don't know where he is—he must have decided to give us some privacy."

"Great," he grumbled, lifting his head to look down at her. "Let's hope the voice in my head is just that, and doesn't come equipped with eyes as well. I'd rather not be on display for dogs or gods."

"I don't think Milki-la-el is a god. Just a mathematician."

"Hey," Christopher protested. "That's close enough.

You ready to go upstairs? Not that this counter isn't delightful, but the butcher block is hurting my knees."

"And my butt," she said. She reached up a hand to push his tumbled hair out of his face. "You realize this doesn't make sense, don't you?"

"Love isn't supposed to make sense."

She froze, looking up at him. "Love?"

"What do you think this is? Recreational therapy? I'm a logical man, and I can draw logical conclusions. I've never been at the mercy of my biological needs or, even worse, my emotions. And I am now. Totally. And if that isn't love, then I don't know what is."

"What makes you think I'm in love with you?"

He grinned then, his dimples deep and adorable. "You can spend the next sixty years trying to convince me you're not," he said simply. He pulled away from her, climbing off the high wooden counter, and yanked up his jeans before he reached out a hand to help her down. "That sound acceptable to you?"

She looked up at him, feeling the warmth and joy flood through her, and she put her hand in his. "It sounds perfectly logical," she said.

And she led him upstairs to her nice, soft bed.

Kammani was waiting at the altar with Umma at her side, preparing for that night's Goddess Way meeting—there'd been a hundred people there on Saturday when she'd announced the plague, and there'd be more tonight, and that knowledge, mixed with the strange and alien contentment that Mina's pills brought her, was making her sure and steady again—but for some reason her black jacket didn't feel right. The cloth strained and the buttons turned sideways as if they were about ready to pop—

The doors opened and Sam came into the temple, wet with rain.

"It is good!" she called to him, leaving her jacket unbuttoned as Umma and Bikka danced out to meet him. "The worshipers are flocking to us. We will soon reign again—"

"No." Sam stopped at the foot of the steps.

Kammani lost her smile as she felt the desert stir inside her again, muffled by that chemical contentment. "We have called many to our side for the Goddess Way. Our worship meetings now fill the auditorium."

"Cheetos?" Bikka whined to Sam.

"Not here, Shar has some at home," Sam said to the little dog. Then he looked back at Kammani. "You don't have worshipers; you have groupies."

"Groupies?" Kammani said, confused.

"And you sent a sickness—"

"Cheetos?" Bikka whined to Sam again.

"Shhhh," Umma said to Bikka.

"I sent a plague," Kammani said, thinking, *What's the big deal?* "It has been four days and my worship swells as hundreds die—"

Sam shook his head, looking equal parts tired and angry. "Mina didn't tell you, did she?"

Kammani frowned at him. In another life, a life without meds, she might even have been alarmed.

"You sent a plague this world has conquered," Sam said. "Most of these people have been vaccinated; they've taken medication that keeps them from getting sick. The others are healthy enough to survive. No one is dying. They're just angry and they're looking for where the sickness came from."

"It's a deadly plague," Kammani snapped, her contentment falling away. "The last time I sent it—" She stopped, seeing the pit before her.

"Nobody is dying here." Sam took a step closer and she could see the winter in his eyes. "But the last time you sent it, people died, didn't they?"

Kammani took a step back.

"You sent the measles to Kamesh and killed them," Sam said, his voice like a knife. "That's why they stopped worshiping you, because you were greedy and sent the plague to command obedience, and too many of them died and the rest left the plague city. Ishtar didn't overthrow you, the people left you, and when you were weak and alone, Ishtar took you."

"They were not *devout,*" Kammani said, and heard the whine in her own voice.

"They were not yours to kill," Sam said.

"The world is mine to kill." Kammani drew herself up. "As you are mine to sacrifice. The solstice is Saturday—"

"I will come to the sacrifice only if you take us back to Kamesh," Sam said. "Back to the time *before* the plague. I'll be your sacrifice there, and only there, but you must swear an oath that you won't send the plague to this world or that one, that you'll return us to our time before you betrayed my people so that we can save them."

"Do you order me, Samu?" Kammani said, trying to find her outrage somewhere in the calm fog in her brain.

"I'm telling you. Your time in this world is finished. I will not help you here."

Mina came in, slamming the door behind her, shaking out an umbrella, Mort tucked into her coat pocket. She stopped as she saw Sam. "Did you come to gloat?"

"I came to stop you," he said, looking at her as if she were a bug.

"Well, you can't." Mina went up the steps and put her briefcase on the altar. "Our first telecast is Saturday. With KG's beauty and wisdom, it's only a matter of weeks before we go national." She looked at him with the same contempt he was showing her. "You are no longer needed."

"Watch it," Umma said.

Mort whispered, "Heh, heh, heh," from his coat

pocket, and Umma looked up at him and said, "You, too, you little freak."

"Cheetos!" Bikka barked at Sam.

"I told you, there are some at home," Sam said to her. "Go see Wolfie if you want Cheetos." He looked at Mina and said, "Tell her about the measles. She doesn't believe me."

Mina turned to Kammani, almost rolling her eyes with her insolence. "I tried to tell you the plague was a bad idea. You have to stop that stuff, swarms and plagues. It just makes you look foolish. Next you'll be wanting to ransom somebody for *one million dollars.*"

Sam laughed, and Kammani looked between the two of them, knowing they knew something she didn't, that even though they loathed each other, there was a bond of knowledge, of culture, that she had missed completely.

"Enough," she said to both of them, trying to draw her jacket around her again. "I am the goddess. And we will do this the Goddess Way."

"Don't start believing your PR," Mina said briskly. "That's how all the big ones fall." She looked at the jacket critically. "That doesn't fit you anymore. You're putting on weight. It's probably the Paxil. My mother put on twenty pounds in a month on it."

Putting on weight? Kammani looked down at her once flat stomach and saw paunch. "The pills make me . . . fat?"

"You just have to lay off the frozen Snickers," Mina said, dismissing her. "Nobody wants to follow a porko."

The room crackled with rage as Kammani froze her with a glance, literally, Mina's eyes bugging out as she realized she couldn't move.

"Do not forget," Kammani whispered to her, "that I am a *real goddess*. Do you remember, Mina?"

The fear in the girl's eyes was evident but not as strong as it had been before.

She knows I will not harm her, Kammani thought as Sam said, "You can kill her, but you can't take her free will; she will think what she wants to think. This time is different. You can't rule here."

"I can rule anywhere," Kammani snapped. "On Saturday, *on the solstice,* you will come to me for the sacrifice—"

"No," Sam said, his voice final. "If you take us back to Kamesh and leave this world alone, I'll bleed and die for you there one last time, to save that world and this. If you won't go back, I'm living out my years here with Shar."

I don't know how to go back to Kamesh, Kammani thought, and then realized that even if she could, she wouldn't. Kamesh had no lemonade, no refrigerators, no flush toilets, no television that would bring her the worship of millions—

"No," she said to him. "You can't accept mortality. You'll become human on the solstice. Without me to intervene, you'll die *forever* if you stay here."

He shook his head. "Even if we go back to Kamesh for the sacrifice, when I rise again, I'll rise here. I belong here now."

He turned and walked away from her, and she yelled, "Don't be a fool. *I won't raise you again.*"

He turned at the door and smiled at her in the dim light of the temple, sure and confident like the damn god he was. "I'll rise."

"*Not without me,*" Kammani shrieked at him. "*You can't come back without me.*"

"I'll come back for her," Sam said, and left, and Kammani sat down on the edge of the altar platform, panting with frustration and exertion, and thought, *Bloody hell.*

Umma padded up. "Mina."

"What?" Kammani said, staring at the little dog. "Oh." She released Mina from her rigor.

Mina relaxed, stretching a little, wary but by no means cowed. "He deserves to die."

"Yes, and he's going to on Saturday," Kammani snarled.

"I don't think he's coming back for the sacrifice," Mina said, sounding exasperated with her. "He's part of this world now. Most men who look like him are gods here anyway, so he fits right in." She leaned closer. "You could, too. You're beautiful; people would follow you for that alone, if you'd just stop with the swarms and the plagues. . . ."

Mina talked on and Kammani thought about freezing her again, this time permanently, but she was already short one priestess, and she still needed the Worthams. Plus Mina probably knew how she could take the damn weight off. Hell.

Back to the problem at hand: what would make Sam come to the temple to be sacrificed?

Sharrat.

And what would bring Shar and the others?

"I need the Three," she said to Mina.

"They're pretty mad about that plague," Mina said. "One of Gen's little cousins is really sick."

Kammani brightened. "Fatally?"

"No," Mina said, "It's the *measles.* We have that one licked."

Kammani scowled at her and then looked closer. "You're wet."

"It's raining." Mina brushed at her damn jacket. "We weren't even supposed to have rain, but everything's screwy lately." She stopped and looked at Kammani. "You didn't bring the rain, did you?"

Rain. Lots of rain. In a town close to a big river. She tried to stand in one graceful motion and had to push herself off the steps with one hand instead. "Tonight at the meeting, we will announce a Flood."

Mina stopped brushing. "Flood? No."

"This rain will not stop; I will see to it," Kammani said. "And then I will raise the river. I will flood Summerville—"

"No," Mina said. "Look, KG, I know you like the big gestures, but we're on high ground. If you flood us, you'll take out half the state—"

"—but the faithful will be spared—"

"You can't build an ark big enough!" Mina said, exasperated. "If you kill everybody, there'll be nobody left to worship you. Isn't that what happened to you in Kamesh? Will you just do this my way?"

"—and the Three will come to us," Kammani finished.

"The Three," Mina spat. "Always the Three. *I'm* the one who serves you absolutely; *I'm the one you need.* And it won't work anyway. They've got their own temple in the coffeehouse; they won't come here."

There was a ring of truth in her voice. That coffeehouse . . .

"Fine," Kammani said. "Go there. Tell me what they have there that draws people to them."

Mina sighed. "Whatever." She picked up her umbrella, said, "Don't forget to take your pill," and went out the door, taking her little nightmare of a dog with her.

"Mistake," Umma said.

"What?" Kammani said, staring down at the little dog.

"Sam's right."

"Who the hell do you think you are?" Kammani snarled to her dog. She looked around. "And where's your sister?"

"She followed Sam," Umma said, not cowering. "He has Cheetos. She wishes to live in the other temple."

"There is no other temple," Kammani snapped.

"And I think I am your companion and solace," Umma said. "As you are my human."

"I am not your *human*," Kammani said, seething. "I am your *goddess*. And you are just my *damn dog*."

Umma stared at her unblinking, and Kammani turned and walked away.

Even the *dogs* were talking back to her. And the biggest dog of all was Sam. *I'll come back for her.* Who the hell did he think—"

The door scraped open again and a man she'd never seen before—tall, dark, rangy, and befuddled—came in, blinking at the light from the electric torches. He caught sight of Kammani and looked . . . annoyed. "Hello. Are you working on the relief, too?"

"Working?" Kammani said, caught off guard.

"The relief." He gestured to the back wall as he came closer. "I'm studying it."

"You've been here before," Kammani said.

"With Professor Summer. We're researching the relief together." He looked at her cautiously. "If you're researching it, too . . ."

"I already know about the relief," Kammani said.

"So you're not going to publish on it," the man said.

"No." Kammani came down the steps. "I am Kammani," she said, holding out her hand.

"Uh." The man shifted his notebooks and laptop to one arm, dropping the notebooks in the process, and took her hand. "I'm Ray Reiser, Professor Reiser, very pleased to meet you. So if you're not—"

"What is it that Sharrat wants to know about the relief?" Kammani said.

"We think there's something wrong with it." Ray looked around the temple. "See, usually the first layers of a step temple were just filled with rubble, as a platform for the two-storied temple on top. So this room is wrong."

"No," Kammani said. "This room has always been here, in the center. The rest was filled as you say, but there was always a passage to this room." She stepped closer. "A secret room."

"Oh." Ray stepped back. "You really know your step temples."

"Just this one," Kammani said. "You must tell Sharrat there is nothing wrong with it."

"Well, there is," Ray said. "That relief was added later."

Kammani went very still. "Yes, it was carved into the wall, much later."

"No," Ray said. "That wall was added later. It's a false wall."

"Yes," Kammani said, measuring her words. "The chamber for the priestesses is behind it."

"No," Ray said stubbornly. "That wall is a new wall covering an old wall."

Kammani smiled. "Have you told Sharrat this?"

"Who?"

"Shar," Kammani said, keeping her temper until she knew if she'd have to kill him. "Have you told Shar?"

"No," Ray said. "I was going to meet her here today." He looked around. "She's not here, right?"

"Good." Kammani took a step closer. "So you know Shar well?"

"Uh." Ray looked down at her and began to perspire. "Well, we used to, uh . . ."

"I see," Kammani said. "You were lovers."

"Well, yeah," Ray said.

"Until Sam came," Kammani said.

Ray scowled. "You know Sam?"

"He is my . . . ex-husband."

Ray made an exasperated sound. "*Man,* that guy gets in everywhere."

Kammani let that one pass and took another step closer to Ray. "He broke my heart."

Ray looked down at her, so close, and swallowed. "Bastard." He frowned. "So he's no good for Shar."

I'm right here, Kammani thought, but she smiled and said, "I will show you the secret room behind the wall and we will talk." She slipped her hand through his arm and pulled him gently toward the door to her chamber. "I've been very lonely without Sam."

"Uh . . ."

"Have you been lonely without Shar?" she said, looking up at him with all the intent she could put in her eyes.

"Well, I have my work. . . ." Ray met her eyes. "*Oh.* Oh, well, yeah."

"We have much to learn from each other, Ray," Kammani said, guiding him toward her door.

"Okay," Ray said. "Say, didn't I see your picture in the paper?" He snapped his fingers. "You're that new self-help guru with the cable show. I bet you can teach me a lot."

Yes, and while you're learning it, you're going to forget about that wall. Kammani looked down at Umma. "Stay."

Umma looked back, silent and unflinching.

Damn dog, Kammani thought, and then sent some extra energy to the rainstorm, seeing it in her mind as it swelled the rivers and lakes.

Let them vaccinate against that, she thought, and led Ray into her chamber.

Daisy hurried through the rain, holding her hand over her head, shielding herself as best she could from the downpour. She ducked under the tiny awning in front of Noah's apartment building, hit Noah's buzzer, and waited; there was no answer. *Crap.* She hit the buzzer once more, and was met with silence.

He wasn't home. Where the hell was he?

Off with Kammani, plotting to take over the world, she thought, then sighed. Since her mother's visit the day before, things hadn't been right. She'd been distant, he'd been wary, and the sex had been good but tentative, as if all the things she hadn't been saying had somehow wedged between them.

She hit the buzzer twice more, but there was still no answer. *Oh, come on. I skipped out early on work to deal with this; the least he can do is be here.*

But he wasn't. She turned around into the rain, running down the empty sidewalk with her head down, hoping to find him waiting for her at the coffeehouse, and she barreled right into someone who caught her before she bounced off his chest and fell to the ground. She looked up and her entire existence lightened at the sight of him.

Noah.

"Hey, you," he said, smiling as the rain pattered down on him, not seeming to care that he was getting soaked. What kind of guy just didn't care if he got all wet?

A minion. Minions never care if they get wet.

Stop that.

"Hi," she said, swiping at her face. "I left work early. . . . I mean, I thought I'd come over and . . ." A big, fat raindrop hit her in the eye, and she sputtered. "What is up with this rain?"

"Come on," he said, taking her arm. "Let's get you out of those wet clothes."

She went two steps with him and the anxiety hit in her gut as she thought, *No.* Then there was a crack, and the thunder rolled, and she pulled her arm back. He stopped to look at her, his smile fading as the lightning flashed again.

"Daisy?"

She raised her eyes to his. This had to stop. She had to come clean, tell him everything, beg his forgiveness for all her suspicions, and get over it. If she didn't do it now, they didn't stand a chance, and she wasn't willing to risk that.

"I need answers," she said, then swallowed hard. That wasn't what she'd meant to say, but as the relief rushed through her, she knew it was what she needed to say.

Noah took a step closer as the rain started to beat down harder and said, "What?"

"I need you to tell me what you know!" she shouted over the rain.

He watched her for a moment; then his smile disappeared. "About what?"

"About Kammani." She looked at him, forced herself to say the words. "I need you to tell me."

"Tell you what? Daisy . . ." He shook his head, ran his hand through his wet hair. "Look, come on inside where it's dry and we can—"

"Are you working with her? Do you worship her and she needs us and so you're making me fall in love with you to get me for her?" She sounded crazy, and from the way Noah was looking at her, he'd picked up on it. People rushed into the building past them and the rain started coming down in earnest.

"What the hell are you talking about?"

"How long has your family known Kammani was coming? Did Mina bring her back? How? Why did you really teach that class? Did you know about the bees, and the measles? And where were you just now? Were you with her?"

He stared at her, then shook his head. He pulled a piece of paper out from the inside of his jacket and held it out to her. She took it and glanced at it but couldn't read the handwriting in the rain. She tucked it in her jacket to keep it out of the rain and looked up at him.

"What's this?" she asked.

"I went to see one of my saner cousins, and she gave

me that. I thought it might help you, or whatever." He shook his head. "You know what? It doesn't matter. I'll talk to you later."

He turned around and headed toward his building. Daisy watched him for a moment, shock and fear running hot and cold through her. How dare he walk away? Wasn't she important to him at all?

And the answer she'd been afraid of since that day in the courtyard hit her.

No.

She stood in the rain, staring after him, trying to process it all. She'd been right; he'd been lying. He was in league with Kammani. He'd never cared about her. He'd never—

Before she realized it, she was rushing after him. She caught the door before it closed, and slid into the lobby behind him just as two flashes of lightning cracked hard outside, followed almost instantly by sharp blasts of thunder.

"Look," she said, grabbing his arm. "I'm sorry if I've offended you or whatever, but what did you expect? You lied to me."

"When did I . . . ?" he started, then shook his head. "What, because I didn't tell you that my family believed a goddess was going to rise? Seriously?"

"Yes, seriously," she said. "Noah, you just expect me to accept everything when my whole life is turning upside down and—"

"I never expected anything. I tried to get you to talk to me, and you said everything was fine, even though it obviously wasn't, so don't dump all that on me."

"Well . . . but . . . you . . . ," she sputtered, trying to get ahold of her righteousness, which was getting damned slippery. "I mean . . . I don't know. Maybe it's Kammani. Maybe she put the whammy on you. She made Abby go all

Renfield, and she's releasing swarms and sending plagues—"

"What?" Noah said. "The measles thing? That was Kammani?"

"It wasn't Dick Clark."

His expression tightened. "And you think I was part of that?"

Daisy shifted uncomfortably. "I don't know. But that's why I need answers from you, and it bothers me that you won't tell me."

"No, it's not that I won't tell you," Noah said. "It's that there's nothing to tell and you won't believe me. And you know what? That's your problem."

He slammed his thumb on the call button for the elevator and Daisy stood behind him, feeling cold and wretched as doubt started to seep in through her wet skin. Outside, the clouds gathered in tighter as the rain pelted down, darkening the lobby.

"So that's it, then?" she said. "You're just going to go on upstairs and leave me here?"

"That's the plan," he said stiffly.

"Good plan," Daisy said. "Makes a lot more sense than staying here and talking this out with me."

He turned and looked at her, his eyes hot with anger. "Hey, I've been bugging you to talk about this, and you shut me down, every time. Then you come to me and accuse me of . . . god only knows what. I can't even follow your logic anymore. So what is there to talk about?"

"A lot," Daisy said, her throat tightening in her desperation to find some solid ground she could stand on. "With everything that's gone on, what do you expect from me?"

"I expect you to think about someone besides yourself for a minute."

Daisy felt struck in the chest, and her breath left her. Outside, the rain seemed to silence, or became such a steady white noise that she didn't hear it anymore. All she could hear was the sound of her own heart beating cold in her chest as Noah stared at her, looking like a man who'd finally said exactly what he meant.

"What the hell?" Daisy said when her breath came back. "I *have* been thinking about other people. That's *all* I think about. Abby, Shar, Bun, Gen. The people in this town." She felt her throat start to close with the emotion. "And Vera. I told her to drink that punch, I told her everything would be fine, and now . . . How can you say I haven't been thinking of anyone else?"

"Exactly," he said. "You told her to drink the punch, so even her death is about you."

"What is that supposed—?" she started, but the elevator door opened. Two people got out, walking around them as they each held their ground. The elevator doors closed, and Noah waited until the people were gone before speaking again.

"Vera died," he said, his voice low and even, "and that sucked. But maybe it was her time and if she hadn't been in the temple, she would have choked on a chicken bone or gotten hit by a bus. And if she had died from something that had nothing to do with you, would you even care this much?"

"How can you say . . . ?" She blinked heavily, her stomach knotting. "Of course I would care."

He nodded but didn't seem to believe her. "Look, I get that things are confusing for you. You got power and you don't know what to do with it. Fine. But I've been right here, all along, and you've been keeping all this stuff in, concocting scenarios in your head and slamming me with accusations when you can't take it anymore." He shook his head and released a breath. "I'm just a bit player in your show, Daisy, and it's getting a little old."

Oh my god, she thought, horror cutting through her in a fiery swath. *I'm Peg.*

"I'm sorry. I didn't mean to—"

He held up his hand. "Forget it, okay?"

"Noah—"

The elevator dinged and the doors opened; this time, it was empty. Noah stepped inside and Daisy stood where she was, waiting for him to motion her in, but he just kept his eyes on the floor and let it close between them. Daisy stood in the lobby, her thoughts whirling around her so fast she almost forgot where she was until another crack of thunder sounded outside and suddenly the chill in the air and the sound of the thudding rain became overwhelming.

"Goddamn it," she muttered, and reached inside her jacket, pulling out the paper Noah had given her. In the light, out of the rain, it was easier to read.

Banishment Chant—Ereshkigal was scribbled across the top in a woman's handwriting. Daisy read the rest of it, twice, not really sure what it was, but pretty sure Shar would have a good guess.

"Hey," a voice said, "are you going up?"

Daisy looked up to see a man and a woman, drenched but happy, holding the elevator door open for her. She knew she needed to go up and see Noah, to thank him and beg his forgiveness and tell him that she was the stupidest human being on the planet, but she was too close to tears and she didn't want to see him like that. It wouldn't be fair to him, and the least she could do after all this was be fair.

"No," she said. "Not yet."

"Oh." The woman smiled. "Okay. Be careful if you go out. It's damn near apocalyptic out there."

The man laughed and took her hand, and the two of them grinned at each other as the elevator doors closed on them. She and Noah had been happy like that, for the nanosecond before she'd screwed everything—

Apocalyptic.

Daisy blinked and looked outside; the rain was coming down in sheets now, the puddles running down the street so large that they almost joined together.

Swarm. Plague.

"Flood," Daisy said, then shook her head. *No.* Storms like this happened all the time in the summer. But still . . . She folded the banishment chant and carefully tucked it in her back pocket, then pulled out her cell phone and dialed Shar.

"You've reached Professor Summer—" the voice mail said, and Daisy shut her phone and took a breath. Being crazy and paranoid had caused enough problems; she needed to go home, take a bath, and gain some perspective. If, in the morning, things still looked bad apocalypse-wise, she'd get Abby and they'd find Shar together. And then, if Kammani didn't kill them all, she could work things out with Noah.

One thing at a time.

She pushed out of the lobby and walked out into the rain, trying to convince herself that it wasn't the end of the world.

She was only marginally successful.

Kammani heard the doors to the temple scrape again, wrapped herself in her robe, and left Ray sleeping as she went to see who it was, some of her rage spent on him in sexual fury.

But not all of it.

"I did what you asked," Mina said, coming to stand before Kammani, her chin up and her dog under her arm.

Mort said, "*Heh heh heh,*" and Kammani waited for Umma to snarl at him, but the little dog was silent.

"You went to the coffeehouse," Kammani said.

"It's not a coffeehouse; it's a temple," Mina said, sounding fed up. "They even have a painting on the wall for worshipers. I took a picture with my cell phone. Look."

Kammani took the phone and looked at the tiny screen. The picture was small, but it didn't have to be big; she could see the three figures in the mural, see how they were posed, Three-as-One with bowl, spindle, and sword, and her blood ran colder than it had while she was sleeping under the sand.

"Destroy it," Kammani said, looking out into the distance. *They must not find out. "Destroy that place."*

Mina blinked. "Did you take your pill?"

"Do not do this," Umma said.

"There will be no more pills," Kammani said, thinking of her waistline. "Destroy that temple before the sacrifice at dawn tomorrow."

"Okay," Mina said. "Look, it's a bad idea to quit those pills cold turkey. They—"

"Destroy that temple."

Mina nodded. "Sure, you bet. Uh, they've got an open mike night tonight, so it'll have to be after midnight, and it's a storefront, so there are, like, stores on each side of it—"

"This is wrong," Umma said.

"Level it," Kammani said. "Make it dust and ashes."

"No," Umma said.

"You got it," Mina said. "Now seriously, about this flood—"

"Go," Kammani said, and Mort *heh*ed as they left, leaving the door open behind them.

It was not wrong; it was good. A people could not stand with competing temples; it led them to destruction and war and desolation—she felt the desert within her stir again—it had led to her downfall the last time, and the world had gone to hell. She had to destroy the temple to save herself; she had no choice.

"It is good," she said to Umma, still staring at the door. "This will bring the Three to the temple for the sacrifice tomorrow. They'll be angry, but they'll come, and it will all be as it was."

When Umma didn't answer, she looked down and realized the little dog was gone.

Bikka and Umma. Both gone.

"It doesn't matter," she whispered. "I don't need *dogs.*"

And then, for the first time in four thousand years, she walked up the steps to the altar. Alone.

SEVENTEEN

Shar came out of the history building after her last class and found that the gentle drizzle had changed to a downpour. She thought, *Oh, hell,* and then walked through the rain, letting it hit her skin and make her blue sundress heavy, breathing the heavy wet smell, her feet pattering on in the gleaming, wet stone as she went down the steps. It was lovely, warm, real, it set the beat in her brain moving again, and her blood pounded in her ears as the pressure built and twisted inside her, and even though she'd learned to control herself in the past three weeks, now she looked around and thought, *Nobody's looking. I could have this one.* Then she thought about Sam, maybe waiting for her in her stone bedroom, and banked up all that good stuff to keep her tingling on the way home.

A good long walk home in the pounding rain. Maybe she wouldn't wait.

She held on as she went down the last flight of steps—coming on stone steps could be fatal—and then she saw Sam at the bottom, leaning against a blue Toyota Highlander as relaxed as if it weren't pouring.

"Nice," she said, raising her voice to be heard over the rain when she reached him. "That's a hybrid that's propping you up. If you knock it over, its owner is going to be annoyed."

"It's ours," Sam said, reaching to open the door for her.

"Ours." Shar blinked at him. "Where did you get the money to buy an SUV?"

"They gave it to me," Sam said, his hand on the door handle.

"They did."

"Christopher took his car into the shop to get an oil change and we looked at the showroom." He looked at her through the rain, puzzled by her reaction, oblivious to the storm.

Well, he was a god. With an SUV.

That made no sense.

"Okay, tell me this again. You and Christopher went to get his oil changed." That was even less believable than somebody giving Sam a car. "How do you know Christopher?"

"I met him on campus."

"On campus." Shar frowned. "You went to the math building?"

"I've been everywhere. It's good to meet people. I was talking to his cousin, Gen, and he came up and asked for an introduction."

"I bet he did," Shar said. "He's very protective of her."

"When he found out I was living with you, he asked me to help him move her to Abby's."

"Quite a coincidence," Shar said.

Sam shrugged. "It's a very small town."

"And you know everybody in it."

"I'm working on it."

"Right." The rain beat down on them while she processed it all, Sam fitting into her hometown, not just because of natural god-charm, but because he worked at it. Well, he was born to be a leader, so that made sense. She looked up at him, the warmth and the rhythm of the storm making her skin hum, and he seemed so . . . real.

"What?" he said.

You look like you belong here. Maybe they could go home and make love in the rain.

In his SUV.

"Okay, so Christopher needed an oil change . . . ," she said, prompting him.

"And I went with him. Do you want to get out of the rain?"

"I like the rain." *A lot. Boy, you look good wet.* "And then they gave you a car. See, that's the part I'm having trouble with."

"The man at the showroom said that if he could take a picture of me with the car and I drove it around town, he would give it to me."

"A whole car." Shar went around to the front to check the plates. They were temporary tags, not showroom plates, from the only Toyota dealer in town.

Sam came to stand beside her in the rain. "People give things to the gods."

"Uh-huh."

"Christopher said it was all right. He showed me how to drive."

"Christopher did."

"I told the man it had to be blue. Because you like blue."

"I do. Thank you. Why were you with Christopher again?"

"We were working on our game."

"Your game." Shar had a sudden bizarre vision of Sam and Christopher playing tennis. Very badly.

"Christopher is designing a video game. It's a war game. Based on the Assyrians."

"You're *kidding* me." Christopher Mackenzie was a video game nerd? Then the other shoe dropped. "The Assyrians. It's based on Mesopotamian battles?"

"Yes," Sam said. "That's my part. I tell him what it was

like. We've been working on it for a while. We're calling it Slayer of Demons."

"For a while," Shar said, her breath going. "That's where you've been going in the evenings?"

"Yes." Sam looked at her, confused. "Christopher says it'll take months, but it—"

"Every night you've left, you've gone to Christopher's house?" Shar said, eyes on the prize.

"Yes." Sam cast his eyes up. "This storm is getting worse."

"For two weeks, you've been going to Christopher's?" Shar said.

"Yes. What are you upset about?"

"I thought you were with other women," Shar said.

Sam looked down at her.

"Well, you were sure with a lot of them before that," Shar said, defensive now.

"Before you," Sam said, patiently.

"Oh." Shar blinked up at him through the rain. "My god. The Glittery HooHa."

"What?" Sam said.

"You were faithful."

"Well, you'd sacrifice me in my sleep if I touched another woman." He looked as stunned as she felt. "You thought I was with others all this time? And you still came to me?"

"I love you," she said, her heart in her throat. "I didn't like it, I hated it, but I love you. . . ."

They stared at each other, dumbfounded while the rain beat down around them, and then Sam said, "I love you, too."

Shar grabbed his shirt and pulled him down to her and kissed him, crying against his mouth, so obliterated by happiness and relief and the rain and the heat and *him,* steady and strong and *he loved her*—

"I need you." She pushed him back against the hood of the car.

"Here?" he said as she stripped off her underpants and threw them over his shoulder onto the grass.

She stepped up on the bumper and pinned him to the hood, crazy with lust and relief and love.

"*Now,*" she said, and he said, "People are watching," and she really didn't care, she was a fucking goddess, but she arched back and spread her arms out and pulled the storm to them—*finish HERE*—and the rain gushed down everywhere like a silvery curtain as she shoved down his jeans, and then his hands were sliding up her sopping wet skirt to pull her on top of him, and he kissed her the way he always did, but more this time.

"On the hood of our new car," he said, and laughed as the rain obliterated everything around them, everything but them.

"Think of it as an altar," she said against his mouth, and kissed him, sliding her tongue into him as he pushed into her, and they found their rhythm, moving together as the rain pulsed around them, and Shar threw back her head and laughed, too, exuberant in ecstasy, safe in his arms, on top of their new SUV. Sam laced his fingers in her hair and brought her mouth to his and Shar gathered every iota of emotion she'd stored up and let it go, coming against him, convulsing and crying out and taking him with her, exploding together, along with three streetlights, a car window, and a small sapling near the math building.

The rain slowed to a drizzle, and Sam stood up and dropped her to her feet, using her as a shield to zip his jeans. Then he looked up and said, "The sun's out. Why is it still raining?"

Shar stretched her arms over her head as her wet dress clung to her, her body loose and satisfied. "My life just became perfect."

"You're easy," Sam said. "Sex on the hood of an SUV and your—"

"And a lover who's faithful," Shar said, and kissed him again, loving him so much she was dizzy with him.

"I didn't think I had a choice," Sam said, coming up for air but still holding her close.

"Do you want a choice?" Shar said, clutching him.

"I made a choice." He kissed her again, and somebody in a car going past honked at them.

"Come on," she said. "Take me for a ride in your new wheels, and then we'll go home and I'll take you for a ride."

He walked her to the passenger door with his arm around her and opened it for her, and Shar slid into the front seat and heard a bark. She turned and saw Wolfie, lying down on the backseat, sitting on top of Milton, who was taking it pretty philosophically, and ignoring Bikka, who, unbelievably, was sitting on the seat beside them.

"What are you doing?" she said, and then realized they'd been in the car the whole time.

"That could have scarred me for life," Wolfie said. "And Milton. For god's sake."

"For god's sake," Milton whined from under him.

"Where did you get Bikka?" Shar said.

"She came to the house looking for Cheetos."

Shar looked at Bikka, who looked back at her hungrily.

"It was traumatic," Wolfie said.

"Yeah," Milton said.

"You were in the backseat," Shar said to Wolfie.

"I have *eyes*." Wolfie sat up so that Milton could breathe, and then put his feet on the door to look out the window. "I like this car."

"So do I," Shar said as Sam got in. "We'll take many rides. But now, we're going home." She looked over at Sam and smiled. "All of us, together."

The rain came down hard again, as hard now as it had

been before she'd told it to finish, and she thought, *So I can't control the weather, big deal; a god loves me.*

Sam put the car in gear and pulled into Temple Street, only to slow as somebody ran a stop sign.

"Hey!" he yelled over the steering wheel. "Watch where you're going, jerk!"

No, a guy *loves me,* she thought, and sat back, for once in her life sure of her future.

Abby slipped out of bed, and Christopher held her for a moment, reluctant to let her go. "We've got to open the coffeehouse," she whispered. "I think Gen is already down there working."

He groaned in protest, rolling over on his back. If he'd looked delicious when she couldn't have him, he looked absolutely irresistible rumpled in her rumpled bed. "How long will you be gone?"

"We're open from six to midnight on Fridays. I'll be back at one minute past midnight. If you'll wait." There was just a trace of uncertainty in her voice, banished at his lazy laugh.

"I'm not going anywhere. Except a shower. I think I have sugar on my knees."

"I have sugar on my butt," she said, pulling on her clothes with more haste than care.

"You do have a very sweet butt," he murmured, looking at her with appreciation.

"How can you tell? You aren't even wearing your glasses."

"I only need them for reading. I can see you just fine. And you look absolutely . . . luscious. You want me to come down and help?"

She couldn't help it; she grinned back at him. "No, I'd rather have you well-rested. Take a cold shower. I'll be back as soon as I can."

"I'll be waiting," he said. "Bring honey."

She was still laughing by the time she reached the kitchen. Bowser was back on his cushion, his head down, Ziggy curled up beside him, and Gen was busy filling up trays with muffins and cookies. She looked up at Abby and grinned. "So where's Christopher?"

She considered playing innocent, but she was just feeling too joyful to hide it. "Upstairs in bed," she said. "Or maybe in the shower by now."

"I told you," Gen said genially, heading toward the front room. "We've got a full house tonight in spite of the rain. Do you think we could talk him into running the espresso machine?"

"I'd rather have him save his energy for me."

Gen hooted with laughter. "Very cool!" She paused, tilting her head sideways to look at her. "You like babies? Because I think you're going to have a lot of them."

"Oh, god, not yet!" Abby said, not sure if she was horrified or thrilled.

"Not yet," Gen, high priestess of fertility, said. "But whenever you're ready."

"I don't have time for this right now," Abby said, trying to ignore the sudden tenderness in her breasts, the heat in her womb. "One thing at a time."

"Just let me know." Gen's grin was saucy. "Make up a tray of honey-sugar cookies, will you? They've been clamoring."

Abby shook her head, trying to concentrate. She took one look at the wooden countertop, the spilled sugar that had somehow gotten ground in into the wood. Glittery amber-colored sugar crystals, the kind she used to dust on the butter cookies. No wonder her butt felt like she'd been lying in sand. The health inspector wouldn't have been too happy if he'd walked in on that, she thought, laughing softly as she pulled out a tray and began loading it. She popped one in her mouth. She was in over her head—cookies couldn't make her any more besotted. Adoring. Fuck it. In love. Who would have thought it?

"You made a lot of noise," Bowser growled from his cushion. "I had to go lie down in the front room."

"Sorry, baby," she said. She ate a second cookie, then tossed another to Bowser, who caught it expertly, bit it in half, and dropped the second half in front of Ziggy. "I'm in love. Would you believe it?"

"Could have told you that weeks ago," Bowser grumbled. "Humans make things so complicated sometimes."

"I should have listened to you." She reached over the refrigerator and pulled down the dog biscuits she'd made the day before. "These are better for you."

By that time Ziggy was sitting up, his tail wagging desperately. "Biscuit," he barked. "Gotta have a biscuit, dude. Abby biscuit."

She knelt down beside them, rubbing Ziggy's head as she gave him his biscuit. "Abby's in love, Ziggy," she said.

"Biscuit," Ziggy said, single-minded. "Love biscuits, fer shur. Abby biscuits."

"Don't humor him," Bowser said. "He doesn't get enough exercise." He took his own biscuit with delicacy, then wolfed it down with one bite.

She could hear the noise from the front room. It was still pouring—if anything, it had gotten even heavier. The occasional rumble of thunder could be heard above the sound of the crowd, and someone was singing, but it wasn't Noah, and Abby sighed. Things weren't right with Daisy and Noah, and they hadn't been since Vera died. For some reason the happier Abby was, the more concerned she felt for Daisy.

She sat down at the far end of the counter, trying to distract herself from exactly what she'd been doing on it a few hours ago, and she pulled the urn toward her. It was still that shimmering blue—sitting hadn't changed it. Maybe she should try Gen's yeast. On impulse she took the wooden honey spoon and stirred. . . .

The mixture began to swirl and glow. Tiny sparkles, like the amber-colored sugar, danced along the top of it, and she watched as it turned back to muddy brown, then rich amber, carnelian, and lapis once more. It bubbled, fizzed, and she half-expected fireworks. When it finally calmed down she brought the wooden spoon to her lips and took a sip.

Oh my god! It wasn't temple tonic; it wasn't even close. It was better. The power surged through her body, a rush of joy and well-being that seemed to touch every inch of her. She closed her eyes, savoring it, and set the wooden spoon down. It was too powerful to mess with—God knows what would happen if she drank an entire glass of it. She wasn't going to find the love of her life, her heart's desire, and then pop off from an overdose of temple tonic.

And she wasn't going to let such powerful stuff sit around. She pulled out the industrial-size carafe and a funnel and proceeded to pour the tonic into it, watching in amazement as the liquid shifted colors, from blue to carnelian to amber, the sparkles dancing through it.

She screwed the lid on tight and tucked it in the corner, then carried the ancient jar to the sink. Later, when the others were there and she wasn't thinking about Christopher lying naked in her bed or, even more tempting, naked in her shower, then they could test the tonic and their own reactions to it. Though right now she couldn't imagine not having Christopher foremost in her mind.

The hours dragged so slowly she wanted to scream. At one point she gave in to temptation and crept upstairs, but Christopher was sound asleep in her bed, his hair still damp from the shower, and the rain outside provided a stormy curtain of sound.

By one minute of eleven she had Gen lock the door as

the last customer disappeared in a blanket of rain, sending the lingerers off with extra cookies on the house. By one minute past midnight she'd finished cleaning the kitchen, said good night to Bun and Gen, and run up the stairs, taking a quick peek at the still-sleeping Christopher. By three minutes past midnight she'd finished her shower and was slipping naked into bed with Christopher, who reached out for her, pulling her body against his. "You're late," he said sleepily.

"I know," she whispered. "But I brought the honey."

And he laughed, low in his throat, as she began to move her mouth down his lean, gorgeous body.

Long, busy, tasty hours later, Abby didn't want to wake up. She was lying sideways across the bed, half on top of Christopher, half beneath him, and she was sticky, sugary, and utterly blissful. She could smell the comforting scent of wood smoke, and it made her think of Christmas and log cabins and all sorts of lovely things, and then she heard Bowser's voice, barking as loudly as he possibly could.

"Fire!" he roared, and she heard the clamor of other dog voices, barking, "Fire, fire," and claws scrabbled at the door leading to the stairway.

Her eyes flew open. People didn't have wood fires in the summer, and she could hear the crackle of flames, the acrid scent of burning paint. The rain had stopped, and she scrambled out of bed, landing on her butt on the floor, and Christopher was halfway into his clothes before she managed to get to her feet.

"The dogs say there's a fire," she said, grabbing the old silk kimono that she wore for a bathrobe.

"We don't need the dogs to tell us," Christopher said. "The door's not hot—I don't think it's spread upstairs yet." He opened the door, and the smell was stronger, smoke rising in tendrils from the staircase.

Daisy was already in the hallway, fully dressed, and

Gen was behind her, wearing baby doll pajamas. "The dogs!" Daisy said, panicked. "I left them all downstairs!"

"Fire!" Bailey barked, excited. "Daisy come now!" Squash chimed in, sounding equally distressed, and even managed a faint cough.

Abby tried to push past Christopher, but he blocked her, going first down the narrow flight of stairs, and she followed close behind. "Get the dogs out first," she said. The dogs were huddled by the courtyard door, and as far as she could see, the flames were contained to the front room, the heat crackling in the night air, as life crashed down around her and her world went up in smoke.

Abby tumbled into the kitchen after Christopher. The dogs were dancing around, barking in distress. "Fire!" Bailey yelped, jumping up and down. "Fire! Fire! Go!"

Daisy ran to open the back door and the dogs scrambled out into the courtyard, into the pounding rain, barking at them to come, too, but Abby glanced back into the coffeehouse and caught a black shadow moving toward the front door. She yelled, "Hey!" and then the shadow escaped into the street and Abby could see her face in the light from the street lamp.

"Mina!" Abby shrieked.

"Come on!" Christopher wrapped his arm around her waist and pulled her toward the courtyard door, and she grabbed Granny's earthenware bowl off the counter as they passed.

Daisy was soaked in the downpour, trying to calm the dogs as the lightning cracked, but she looked up when they ran out. "I called 911. What took you so long?"

"Mina," Abby said.

Daisy looked confused for a second; then her eyes narrowed. "Should have known."

Something crashed inside and Abby's mind whirled. Her world, her life, was in that coffeehouse. She started toward the French doors. "I have to see what I can—"

"You can't go in there," Daisy said, blocking her, and Abby shoved open the back gate and ran down the alley in her bare feet, splashing through puddles as she raced around the corner to the storefront of the coffeehouse, Christopher and Daisy following behind. When she got to the sidewalk entrance, she saw that one interior wall was engulfed in flames, the smoke billowing out, thick and black and evil, impervious to the heavy rain.

A blue SUV skidded to a halt in the deserted street, and Shar, her beautiful white hair wet from the storm, wrenched open the door and ran to her. Sam wasn't far behind but much calmer, and behind him, in the windows of the SUV, Abby saw what she thought were four small dogs, all barking their heads off.

"Is everyone all right?" Shar yelled over the barking and the crackle from the fire and the roar of the thunder above. "Did you get your dogs out?"

"They're safe." Abby stared at the building as smoke began to curl against the windows inside, filling the place. "How did you know . . . ?"

"Umma," Shar said. "She'd been searching for one of us all night—"

Ziggy's keening wail cut through the cacophony: "Gen!"

"Where's Gen?" Daisy said, looking around frantically.

"Gen!" Abby lunged for the front door, but Sam was there first, breaking the glass in the door and striding into the blaze like the god he was.

Abby tried to follow him, shielding her face from the heat as she looked at the blaze, but Shar pulled her back. "It's all on the mural wall, all in one place," Shar said, but all Abby could think of was Gen; how could they not have noticed that Gen—

Sam was back a moment later with Gen in his arms. She was covered with soot, her head was bleeding, and she was trying hard not to cry.

"I'm okay," she choked. "Mina . . ."

"She was knocked out, on the floor," Sam said, and Gen coughed.

Christopher touched Gen on the arm, looking furious. "Are you okay?"

"I'm sorry." Gen coughed, looking at Abby. "I tried to stop her—"

"Sweetie, no," Abby said, trying not to cry. "I'm just glad you're okay."

"Where the *fuck* is the fire department?" Christopher said.

Abby looked at Daisy and Shar, despairing. Mina had hurt Gen. Her coffeehouse was burning. She had to *do* something—

And then she remembered. She was the beginning.

The rain pounded down on them, splashing into deep puddles in the street. She closed her eyes, held out Granny B's bowl, and gathered the water to her, dark and dirty and swirling, filling the bowl, making it glow with golden light, overflowing. . . .

"Okay," Daisy said.

Abby opened her eyes and watched Daisy pull the water from the bowl, wrapping it around a red glowing stick that appeared in her hand—*a clicky pen?* Abby thought—and she spun it out into the night air, arcing it in a stream high into the sky, faster and faster as Abby filled the bowl behind her.

Then Shar stepped forward, and a sword of blue light sprang from between her hands, and she slashed it into the water and cast it into the coffeehouse, into the flames where it spattered and ran down onto the floor, and Abby gathered it again and Daisy spun and Shar slashed, the

Three moving closer to the fire, a circle of Three that hummed with power, and by the third time the water returned to Abby, there was nothing but the hiss and smell of wet, cooling wood and the crash of the thunder above them as the rain kept falling.

They stood panting in shocked silence and stared at the blackened wall.

"The mural's still there," Daisy said, and Abby went to stand next to her and saw the faces of the Three shining out from the soot and scorch marks that had crawled up the wall beneath them, and something seemed to snap within her; the tension was broken.

"Way fucking cool," Abby said in awed disbelief. "I mean, not the coffeehouse almost burning down, but that power! The sword and the spindle and the bowl! I'm still going to kill Mina, but still . . . Just amazing."

From a distance they could hear the fire sirens. "That's fine, guys; we got it," Daisy said, looking at her empty, dirty hands.

Sam stood there, still cradling Gen in his arms, while Ziggy jumped up and down at his feet, trying to reach his mistress. "Gen!" he barked. "Gen hurt?"

"I'm fine, sweetie," Gen said. "You can put me down, Sam."

"No, he can't; there's broken glass all over the street." Shar moved toward them, her hands empty now, too. "You're going to the emergency room and we're going with you. Let Sam hold you until the EMTs get here."

"You're not going with me," Gen said firmly. "You can't let Kammani get away with this. Just call Bun and tell her to meet me there. And take care of Ziggy for me. He's worried."

"Gen!" Ziggy barked, a little frantic.

"I'm fine, baby. Help Bowser take care of the others for me."

They watched in silence as the paramedics surrounded her, and then Daisy spoke. "Okay, Mina's crazy, but what the hell? Why would she try to burn down a coffeehouse?" She walked over to the doorway and peered through the broken window, and Shar and Abby joined her as the fire trucks pulled up in front.

"Not a coffeehouse, a temple," Shar said, staring at the burned mural. "That's what Kammani sees. A threat to her power. All the damage is to the wall, to our version of the bas-relief." She set her jaw. "I'm repainting that in the morning."

Abby looked around her as Sam went over to meet the firefighters, to tell them god knew what. "You know, it isn't so bad. If the dogs hadn't called the alarm, it might have been far worse. We can fix this." She looked at Christopher, standing a little apart from them, with the look of disbelief on his face, and for a moment she panicked. He'd seen her use her power; it was too much; he was going to leave; he was going to turn his back . . .

He had a blank look on his face, the kind he had when he was working on an equation. And then he blinked, shook his head, and managed a crooked smile, and all she wanted to do was lean against him, letting the fear and anger wash away.

"Let's get out of the way," Shar said, pulling them back as the firefighters swarmed past them. "They need to make sure the fire is out."

"Where can we go?" Daisy said, sounding lost for the first time since Abby had known her. She looked like a drowned rat—the rain had soaked her hair, flattening it against her skull, and she looked miserable.

"Out of the rain," Shar said. "Into the kitchen. Because we need to talk."

"Talk?" Abby said. "We need to take that bitch down. And her little arsonist with her."

"We need a plan," Daisy said, a spark of her old life coming back.

Shar shoved her sopping hair away from her wet face. "Good. A short plan. And then we go get her."

"Sonofabitch must pay," Milton growled.

And they headed in out of the rain.

Daisy held back a little, letting everyone else head on down the street to the alley while she stood in the rain and looked at the smoking wreckage that was the front of Dogs and Goddesses. She wanted to burn the image into her brain, so that when they banished Kammani's ass she wouldn't waste any time feeling bad about it.

That wench was going down.

"Daisy?"

She turned around and there was Noah, drenched to the skin in his T-shirt and jeans, stomping toward her through the rain. Her spirits lifted, just at the sight of him.

Not the time, she thought, and stole another glance at the coffeehouse.

"Are you okay?" Noah asked when he reached her. "I heard sirens and I thought . . ." He glanced at the smoking coffeehouse, then looked at her. "You're okay?"

"I'm fine," Daisy said. "Come on."

She led him down the street to the alley, then through the courtyard and finally to the kitchen, where Sam, Shar, Christopher, and Abby stood huddled by the counter as firemen kicked through the wreckage in the dining room. The dogs milled about, too wired to stand still.

"All right," Daisy said, walking over to them. "It's time we ended this."

"Past time," Shar said. "Umma says Kammani has a new plan. A flood. If she brings the river up enough to flood Summerville, a lot of people are going to die." She

glanced at Sam, who looked equally grim. "We have t
stop her tonight."

"We can." Daisy looked at Noah, then reached into th pocket of her robe, where she'd stuffed the paper with th chant when she smelled the smoke. "Thanks to Noah."

She handed it to Shar, who took it and read it, the looked up at Noah. "Where'd you get this?"

"One of my cousins," Noah said. "I asked her if sh knew of anything that could banish Kammani, and sh gave me this."

"A Wortham wanted to banish Kammani?" Abby' eyes widened and then she said, "Sorry."

"It's okay," Noah said, not seeming offended in th least. "She's a little bitter that Mina was called and sh wasn't. I played that up to get what we needed."

Daisy looked at him, but he didn't look back.

"So, I say we memorize this thing, go to the temple and banish her ass," she said, squelching the ache Noah' presence was causing in her gut. *Bigger fish to fry.* "Let' get cracking."

"How is that going to work, though?" Abby said. " mean, we just . . . chant? And that sends her away? I seems a little easy."

"Stand on the hot spots we marked," Christopher said

"Hot spots?" Shar said; then Abby said, "Places o power in the temple. Christopher figured them out. If w stand on them when we chant, it might help."

"Can't make things worse." Daisy turned to Noah, fo cusing on the problem at hand. "Did your cousin tell yo anything else about how we do this?"

Noah shook his head, and Sam said, "Do it the wa you put out the fire."

Daisy looked up at him. "What, throw water on her' Then what? She melts, like the Wicked Witch of the West?'

"No," Sam said. "The Three did what you did, with th

bowl and the spindle and the sword. Ishtar's priests sent men, but only that once and not again. The Three fought back and they got hurt, but they cast Ishtar's men out of the temple, working together. Maybe you can cast Kammani out of this world the same way you put the fire out."

Daisy looked at Abby and Shar, then back at Sam. "Yeah, I'm not sure how we did that."

"We just kind of . . . did it," Abby said.

Sam frowned, as if trying to remember. "They stood in the temple, in a triangle—"

Abby and Christopher shared a glance, and Abby said, "The hotspots."

"—and raised their arms above their heads and their symbols appeared," Sam went on. "They spoke together, and a great wind came up, and the men disappeared from the temple." He looked at Shar. "I asked Sharrat where they went, and she said, 'Where they belonged.' "

"Great," Daisy said. "Christopher, you said you marked the spots?"

"Yes," Christopher said. "They're on the wrong side of the altar, behind the altar instead of in front of it, but Abby and I marked them with chalk. You should be able to see them pretty easily."

"Okay," Daisy said. "So we storm the temple, stand on the hot spots, and chant the . . . chant." She looked up at Noah and gave him a small smile, and he nodded and looked away.

"Okay then," Shar said. "I love this plan."

"I'm excited," Abby said, getting up from the table. "It could work. Let's do it!" She grinned at Shar and then said, "I was a little worried we'd be running off to our certain deaths, but this is encouraging."

"Yeah, I'd say our odds of not coming to a brutal and untimely end are a solid fifty-fifty now," Daisy said. "So should we rehearse? Or something?"

Shar and Abby looked at each other and nodded, and Daisy picked up the paper and read out loud:

" 'You must descend
To the darkness beyond
Into the sands
Of the place without souls
Depart from us
Go where you belong
To the place of despair
We now cast you out.
" 'We abjure you by
The Great Goddess Who is Three
Now you are bound
Now you are sealed
Now you are nightmare
Now we awake.' "

Somewhere deep inside, in a part of her experience so primal she couldn't name it, she recognized the words, knew their power. She could see in Abby's and Shar's faces that they felt it, too, and the knowledge heartened her.

"Can I see that?" Shar said, and Daisy handed it to her, then turned to Noah.

"Thank you," she said.

"No problem. I'm glad it helped."

"It did." Daisy sighed. "Well. Okay. I guess I'll see you around? I mean, if we don't get killed?"

Noah didn't move. "You say that like I'm not going with you."

Panic raced through her at the thought of Noah being in Kammani's line of fire, and she sputtered, "You're not."

"The hell I'm not," he said, and went to stand by the back door with Sam and Christopher, his posture stiff and angry. Daisy wanted to run after him, to explain and apologize and make it all better, but she had to stay focused. Getting into it with Noah was not going to rid their world of Kammani, and that was the priority.

She pulled her eyes away from Noah and turned to see Shar reading the chant. "What do you think?"

"It's good," Shar said. "It reads like it's in three parts, with a chorus after the second part. Based on what happened this morning, I think we should chant it in parts and read the chorus part together. That'll make it easier and faster to learn. And then we pray that the bowl, the spindle, and the sword show up again."

"Works for me," Daisy said.

"One more thing," Abby said, and both Shar and Daisy looked up.

"What?" Shar asked.

Abby motioned for them to follow her and led them to the far counter where a big urn sat. She grabbed three cups and filled them, then handed one each to Shar and Daisy.

"You figured out a tonic?" Daisy said, looking at the swirling colors. "Uh, this is different."

"I realized I didn't need to match flavors so much as the essence of things, and I went with what felt right. What felt like us. At first I didn't think it worked, but when I came back to it and tried it again, it was suddenly magic."

Daisy put the cup to her nose; the scent was heavenly, and goosebumps broke out on her skin.

"Oh my god," Shar said, sniffing her own cup.

"I don't think that phrase is usable for you anymore," Daisy said.

"If I'm right, if this is our version of that tonic, then it should boost our powers," Abby said. "And if it doesn't, it's not like it can make things worse."

"Good point," Daisy said, lifting her cup. "Here's to positive thinking."

Shar raised hers in the air, too. "Here's to Dogs and Goddesses."

Abby raised her glass and smiled at both of them.

"Here's to us," she said, and they all clinked and drank it down.

Daisy swallowed, the flavors crashing in her mouth, a mystical warmth rushing through her as the liquid found its way to her core, but it was more than warmth that she felt. It was strength. Confidence.

It was power.

And Abby and Shar glowed with it—bright amber around Abby and deep blue around Shar—they almost vibrated with it, and Daisy looked down and saw bright carnelian glowing around her hands. Then it faded, for all of them, but the power was still there. Daisy knew that whatever the tonic had awakened, it was there, within them, it was—

"One."

She heard the whisper and, not sure if it was Shar or Abby, raised her head to look at them. "Did you—?"

"*One,*" the whisper echoed in her head.

They watched one another for a moment, frozen as they listened, and Daisy heard: *"One,"* a third time and saw in their eyes that they heard it, too.

Shar set her empty glass down. "If that's the weirdest thing that happens to us today, I'll be happy."

"Me, too." Daisy shot one last look at Noah before turning her attention to Abby and Shar, her best friends, her goddesses. Whatever happened next, they would get her through it, and together they'd save the world.

If nothing else, she was sure of that.

EIGHTEEN

An hour before sunrise, Abby stood behind Sam as he pushed the room doors open and walked into the cavernous temple. She followed him in with Daisy and Shar, Noah and Christopher right behind them with the dogs. There'd been no leaving anyone behind, and there was a worried kind of relief that they were all together. It put everyone in danger, coming to Kammani's temple to do battle, but it had its own power, in the unity and core of their family.

The room had no chairs now, no happy half circle; even the curtain was gone. Kammani was standing beside the altar in the middle of the room, facing the back wall, toward the bas-relief that was now illuminated by the torches, and Abby could see them all, their ancestors, carved into the ancient stone. Kammani turned, and Abby saw that she was in full regalia again—heavy linen robes with jeweled collar and headpiece, a belt of golden links around her waist with a jewel-encrusted knife stuck into it—kind of like Cher dressed as a nun—but she'd changed from the first time they'd seen her in full goddess drag. There was a wildness in her eyes now, an instability in her stance. And her robes didn't fit anymore; the bands of embroidery now didn't meet where they were supposed to and the ceremonial knife sat cocked on her hip instead of hanging by her side. She looked like somebody dressed up like Kammani, not the goddess herself. Mina stood beside her, in a business suit, which oddly made her more threatening, except that she had no eyebrows or eyelashes and the dank hair that usually half-covered her face was now singed and slightly curly.

"Arsonist bitch," Abby snarled at Mina. "You're going down."

Mina ignored her to watch Kammani, not slavishly but the way a girl might watch a mother who was about to humiliate her. She had Mort in her arms, and he watched them all, breathing hard, his scratchy little "heh heh heh" underscoring their tension.

"Vanquish Kammani now; pull Mina's hair later," Daisy said from the corner of her mouth, then spoke louder. "Hey, Kammani. We need to talk."

Kammani regarded them with regal grace, unfazed. "I am the goddess. You are my servants. And my great plan is begun."

"About that," Daisy said. "The Flood. You need to stop it. Right now."

"This is what happens when a people are unfaithful," Kammani said, looking pointedly from Abby to Daisy to Shar. "The Flood will cleanse the earth of non-believers. Only those who respect my power will survive."

"*How?*" Abby said. "Do they float longer? You're not making sense."

Mina shook her head at them. "She went off her meds and now she's impossible."

"You were medicating her?" Shar said, appalled.

"Enough." Sam went up to the foot of the altar, and Shar put out a hand as if to stop him and then pulled it back. He climbed the steps to Kammani. "Stop the Flood."

Kammani turned to Sam, her eyes glittering. "You think to command me, Samu? This world is mine now. I have taken it. And all will be as it was before."

"No," Sam said, and she turned from him to face the back wall, pushing past him to the other side of the altar.

Abby looked from Shar to Daisy, and they both nodded.

"It's showtime," Abby said in a soft voice. She crossed the floor to the back of the altar to face Kammani in front of the bas-relief and found the first hot spot marked with chalk. Kammani frowned at her, but Abby ignored her, waiting until Daisy and Shar found their spots. Then Abby raised her hands over her head, praying like hell the mystical bowl would reappear.

"What—," Kammani began, and then it must have registered, the marks on the tiles and Abby's hands upraised. She turned to Sam. "You told them!"

"Enough," Sam said. "Take us back to Kamesh—"

"Us?" Shar said, but even as she took a step, Kammani snarled, "Traitor!" and grabbed the knife from her belt and plunged it into Sam's stomach.

"*NO!*" Daisy yelled as Shar screamed and Sam went down on his knees. Daisy looked at Abby, who was staring at Kammani, concentrating hard, her arms over her head.

A bowl of amber light appeared between her hands.

"Is it working?" Abby stage-whispered.

"Yes," Daisy said, staring at the bowl as a bright amber glow washed down from it, shimmering around Abby's body like waves of heat over asphalt. Daisy raised her hands as well, and said, "*Chant!*" to Abby.

"*You must descend,*" Abby began, her words slow and sure, "*To the darkness . . .* "

Behind her, Daisy heard a crack, as if stone was breaking, but her attention was on Shar now, staring in horror at Sam trying to raise himself on the platform as blood seeped from around the knife. She took a step to go to him, but Daisy whispered, "Shar!" and Shar looked at her, her eyes hot with tears and rage, and then nodded and stepped back onto her spot, raising her hands over her head, the blue glow around her growing stronger as she focused.

Daisy looked back and saw that Kammani was floating now, suspended above the altar in a spiral of amber light, looking oddly calm, while Mina jumped up to grab her foot and missed. *What the hell?*

". . . *Of the place without souls,*" Abby finished, her voice strong and firm, and Daisy felt the spindle form in her hands over her head. She clamped onto it, warm and ancient and powerful in her grasp.

"*Depart from us / Go where you belong,*" Daisy said, and Kammani began to spin in the air, trailing carnelian light, and Daisy could feel the heat of shimmering power radiating out from her like firelight, a wind rising within the room. Behind them, she heard another crack and something heavy smashed on the stone floor. She thought, *Not good,* but she kept chanting. "*To the place of despair . . .*"

Kammani began to spin faster, her robes whipping around her, and Daisy shouted, "*We now cast you out!*"

Then in unison, they chanted, "*We abjure you by / The Great Goddess Who is Three,*" and Kammani spread her arms out wide, threw her head back, and laughed.

"Wait a minute," Daisy said, but Shar had already begun.

"*Now you are bound,*" she said, the sword materializing blue-white overhead, her body electric with color as her eyes glittered, and Kammani held out her arms.

"*Now you are sealed,*" Shar chanted, and Daisy said, "*Shar, stop!*" as Kammani seemed to inhale the blue light that surrounded her.

Shar stopped, and Kammani stopped revolving and looked down at them, larger than before, multicolored light pulsing from her, and then she reached out toward Abby, taking all the amber light around her, absorbing it into herself, Kammani glowing brighter and Abby dimmer.

"Abby!" Christopher shouted. He grabbed a torch off the wall and swung it as he charged Kammani.

Kammani turned to him, and Abby stumbled back, dropping her bowl, as Kammani flung her hand in Christopher's direction, sending him and the torch flying back, crashing into the sidewall with a horrible crack. Then she settled back onto the platform, glowing with amber light, and stared into Daisy's eyes.

"*Daisy!*" Shar screamed as Daisy's ears filled with a deafening whoosh and her breath was pulled out of her. She went dizzy and weak, her vision dimmed. It didn't feel like falling, more like the ground coming up to meet her, pounding into her hands and knees, and she tried to pull air into her lungs, but she couldn't.

This is how I'm going to die, she thought distantly. *Huh.*

Then the whoosh died down, and vaguely, somewhere behind her, she heard the dogs barking and Kammani snarling in fury.

Daisy raised her head. In the torchlight, everything seemed to move in slow motion, Noah behind Kammani, pulling her away, and then Kammani, her body awash in stolen amber and red-orange power, lifting him by the throat. He struggled, feet flailing, and clawed at her hand. Daisy drew breath, wanting to rush Kammani, to pull her hair, scratch her eyes out, but her muscles felt weak and heavy, and Noah was dying . . . but then Sam was there, heaving himself up from the altar to grab Kammani's robes.

Save him, Daisy thought. *Please—*

Kammani threw Noah against the wall and then turned, ripped the knife from Sam's stomach, and plunged it into his heart.

Sam fell back, toppling down the stairs to land at the bottom, his blood splashing everywhere as Shar screamed.

They're all dead, Daisy thought with an eerie calm. *And we're next.*

Power, Kammani thought, and reveled in the richness she had sucked in, amber and carnelian, swirling inside her. They had no idea what they'd just given her—

Then Shar was before her, her face hard with rage, her white hair glowing blue. "*You're finished,*" she said, but she was powerless without Daisy and Abby, stumbling to their feet behind her, shells of the goddesses they'd been.

Good, finish me, Sharrat, Kammani thought, smiling at her. *Chant your chant and give me your rage at losing your lover in all that beautiful blue power.*

But Shar stood there, suddenly immobilized as if she was listening, her face strange and intent. . . .

Act, Kammani thought, losing her smile. *Lift up your arms and take your sword, dammit,* and then Shar shook her head, as if shaking off a voice, and began again.

"*Now you are bound / Now you are sealed—,*" Shar said, the blue of her power glowing around her, and Kammani began to suck it in.

But then, the glow stopped, and Shar choked and grabbed her heart, staring, pointing beyond Kammani—

Like Vera. Kammani turned and saw Mina, her hand outstretched in a fist, gloating as Shar fell to her knees, dying.

"*I need that power, you idiot,*" Kammani said, and Mina released her fist, startled. "*You took Vera's power from me!*"

"You didn't need her," Mina said, backing away. "All you need is *me; I* am your daughter!" and Kammani said, "*Be what you are to me!*" and threw all her fury at Mina, hitting her squarely in the chest, and then forgot her to turn back to all that ancient blue power.

Shar staggered to her feet, supported by Abby and Daisy, the three of them close together now, standing by Samu's body, far from the sacred symbols Kammani had made for them.

"*You are all fools,*" she said to her three rebel priestesses. "You think you're goddesses, but I'll show you the real power in the room. . . ."

She stopped because they weren't paying attention. It was as if they'd forgotten she was there, as if they were listening to something else, far away, words in the air. . . .

"We are one," Abby said, putting her arm around Daisy, her voice barely a whisper now that her power was drained, and yet steady and sure.

"You are nothing," Kammani said, and raised her hands before her to take Shar's power, but Shar put her arms around the others and smiled at her, a smile colder than darkness, and then they looked at her, their arms around one another, just *looked* at her, and Kammani felt power flow out of her, shimmering, tangled, gold and red. "No!" she said, and tried to draw it back to her, but it stopped just out of her reach, shimmering in the air between them.

"*We are One,*" Daisy said, and pulled Shar closer, and Kammani's power flowed out to theirs, amber, carnelian, and blue twining together in the air in front of them.

"You are *mine,*" Kammani said, reaching for it greedily.

"WE ARE ONE," Shar said.

Kammani rolled her eyes. *Enough of this. Banish me again, and make me invincible!*

Abby lifted her arms and the bowl appeared and Kammani closed her eyes in ecstasy and began to draw on her—

"No," Abby said, and threw the bowl to the ground, and it shattered and Kammani shuddered from the blow.

Daisy lifted her arms and caught her spindle and said, "No," and broke it over her knee, and Kammani screamed, cracking and breaking, too, as she fell to the altar, panting with pain and rage.

Shar lifted her sword and smiled at Kammani, and for the first time Kammani was afraid. "No," Shar said, and smashed the sword on the floor, and the shards splintered and pierced Kammani and she screamed again.

"*WE ARE ONE*," the Three said, and the wall behind them cracked like thunder and fell.

No, Kammani thought, seeing the old wall revealed, pulsing with the old power, the crude figure, scratched there by savages, now alive and fixed on her. "*NOT YOU, I DEFEATED YOU*." She rose tottering to her knees and lifted her arms and a great wind swirled in the temple as she said, "*You are gone!*" and threw all the force she had at the Three and at the wall, her power a dirty stolen mixture of red and orange, green and purple, screaming pieces of light and energy and rage—

And Abby stepped forward as if in a dream, and caught the pieces in her arms and gathered them to her heart and warmed them until they were clear and amber like the sun. Then she threw the pieces to Daisy, who caught them, graceful in her exuberance, and spun them out to bloom in one wide swath in the air as the temple glowed carnelian. Then she threw it all to Shar, like red petals in a sunset, and Shar caught it, her face pale with rage and vengeance, gathered the energy with hands as cold as death, and shattered it into stars that spun around her, blue-white. Kammani screamed, "*No, you will not!*" and Shar said, "THE HELL WE WON'T," and slung the stars at her, saying, "*NOW YOU ARE NIGHTMARE / NOW WE* AWAKE*!*" and Kammani felt cold beyond knowledge of god or mortal slice into her heart.

And the world went dark.

The wind stopped, the humming in Shar's ears went away, the light evaporated, and the temple was normal again, except that Sam was dead at her feet. She dropped to her knees, forgetting everything but him, crying out at his sightless eyes as Daisy said, "*Where did that bitch go?*"

Shar touched his body, still warm, and yet she knew he was gone because of the bleakness inside her. He was dead, and she couldn't breathe without him. She leaned over him, cold and desperate and terrified, and said, "Rise!" her voice shaking, and there was nothing.

She kissed him, trying to breathe life back into him, and said, "Rise!" and there was nothing.

"*I love you,*" she cried to him. "*I love you; I'm a goddess; you must come back to me; RISE!*"

And there was nothing.

She felt Daisy's hand on her shoulder, and then Wolfie moved in beside her and nudged Sam's body with his nose.

He looked up at her, his beady little eyes full of pain. "He's not there."

"I know," Shar said to him, choking through her tears. "I know. I know; I'm so sorry, baby."

Milton crept up beside him. "Sam?"

Wolfie climbed into her lap, and Milton followed, and she held them close, weeping helplessly as she looked down at the body of the man she was going to love for eternity, the best man she'd ever known.

"I'm sorry," she said to Sam, putting her hand on his heart. "I'm sorry; I should have done better; I should have been here faster; *I should have been stronger; I—*"

"Honey," Daisy said, tightening her hand on Shar's shoulder. "Sam will rise again, right? You can—"

"*How?*" Shar said, jerking her head up to meet Daisy's tear-filled eyes. "*How* is he going to rise? *She's not here to bring him back.*" She looked back at Sam's body, and the enormity of his death hit her all over again. "*I don't know how to save him,*" she raged, hysterical. "*I'm not a goddess; I don't know how—*"

"THIS PLACE IS A MESS," Abby said, and Shar looked up at her through her tears.

Abby's face was smooth and calm as she gestured to the temple—overturned chairs, Sam's blood splashed down the steps, the bas-relief behind them in big chunks on the floor—but her gesture was odd. Slow. As if her arm were moving through water, as if there was something in the air . . .

And an amber glow trailed her as she moved.

"POWER ALL OVER THE PLACE," she said, and stooped to pick up a piece of something that glowed in her hand. "LOOKS LIKE THE INSIDE OF A GOAT'S STOMACH."

"Abby?" Christopher said, limping toward her, his face creased with worry.

Abby brushed at the lump of glow in her hands. "DOG HAIR. DUST. DOESN'T ANYBODY EVER SWEEP IN HERE?" She bent to pick up another clump of glow, and Shar blinked back tears and saw that the floor was littered with pieces of the stuff, pale, watery, weak but there. "HONESTLY," Abby said, and moved serenely through the temple, gathering it all into one dirty gray, glowing ball. Then she smiled at Shar, and Shar realized Abby was missing the pupils of her eyes; her entire eye glowed white.

"Abby?" Shar said, wiping her cheek with the back of her hand, suddenly afraid. "Abby, honey? You're not feeling . . . possessed or anything, are you? *That's not Kammani in there, is it?*" She felt Daisy move away to stand up, and she looked up at her. "Daisy, she's—"

Daisy's eyes were glowing white, too.

"Daisy!"

Abby spun the ball between her hands, and dog hair and dust went flying, and the glow became amber, beautiful and strong. Then she tossed it into the air in slow motion, graceful and laughing, and Daisy caught it, and said, "YES," in a dreamy voice and spun it out so that it arced red across the temple, filling the dark room with warm, carnelian light as she moved.

Then she turned to look down at Shar with an unearthly smile, the smile of a goddess, and Shar knew it was her turn, but there was nothing in her except loss.

She shook her head. "I . . . I can't . . . I'm not—"

And Daisy slung the red toward her and Shar surged to her feet and caught it, and the world went blue and quiet, and she felt the peace of completion flow through her as an ancient voice whispered inside her and told her that she was the last. She stood with all that blue power in her hands and looked within it and saw the spark that was Sam. "SEND HIM TO HIS REST," the voice whispered, and she looked down at Sam and knew the voice was right, that he was at peace after thousands of years, that his time had come, and that death was natural and good—

Something cold touched her ankle and she looked down through the glow to see Wolfie, staring up at her, worried and loving.

"IT'S ALL RIGHT, WOLFIE," she told him. "ALL THINGS END."

"Why?" he said.

"SO THEY CAN BEGIN AGAIN," Shar said.

"Then begin them *now*," Wolfie said, and Shar stopped, Sam's life between her hands.

"Please," Wolfie said. "It's bad. Fix it." He licked her ankle. "Sweet baby. Love you forever."

Love you forever.

Shar looked at Daisy and Abby, the circle of Three, no beginning and no ending, and an ancestral voice rose deep within her and them, and said:

WHAT ARE YOU DOING? END HIM.

Shar lifted her head. "HIS TIME IS NOT YET."

HOW DO YOU KNOW?

"MY DOG TOLD ME."

Abby smiled and Daisy nodded, and Shar knew, as the voice within her knew, that tomorrow the power that was in Abby now would be out in the universe, gathering the stars into the sunrise, the power that was in Daisy now would go out and spin it into the heat of the day, and at night the power that was in Shar would go out and shatter it into stars again. It wasn't theirs; it was part of everything. They were only drawing on it now.

But they had descended from it and it was their birthright.

EVERYTHING IS A CIRCLE, the voice within them said.

"THEN WHAT LIVES, DIES, AND LIVES AGAIN," Shar said, and as Abby and Daisy came to stand with her over Sam, Shar looked down at him, inside the glow of their circle, and Abby said, "RISE!" and Daisy said, "RISE!" and Shar said, "RISE, DAMN IT," and released their power.

And the glow snapped, and it was just them in the temple again.

Shar held her breath for a long minute, and then Sam stirred.

She fell to her knees as Christopher limped over to Abby and said, "I believe you."

"Sam?" Shar said, her voice high as Noah moved in the corner and Daisy ran to his side, helping him up.

Sam opened his eyes, his face creased with effort.

"Oh, *god.*" Shar pulled the knife out of his heart and threw it from them and then wrapped her arms around him, holding him as close as she could.

"Ouch," he said, and she kissed him, dying in the warm taste of his mouth, breathing again, while Wolfie pawed at them and Milton yipped and shook all over. "Usually they take the knife out before they raise me," he said, trying to sit up. "Not that I'm complaining, but—"

"I thought I'd lost you forever," she sobbed as she helped him upright. "I thought—"

"I'll always come back to you." Sam held her tight as he looked around. "How many months was I gone?"

"Fifteen minutes, tops," Abby said. "Things move fast these days. Although it was long enough to scare us."

Daisy led Noah over to the group, smiling her gratitude as she said in a choked voice, "Yeah, don't pull that shit again, Sam."

"*Love you,*" Wolfie said, trying to worm his way between Sam and Shar. "*LOVE YOU FOREVER!*"

"Love you forever," Milton said, scrabbling at his side.

"Hey." Sam scooped up Milton and rubbed Wolfie's head as Shar moved back a little to let them in. "How you doin', boys?" He looked around the temple again and said, "Kammani?"

"Gone," Shar said. "To wherever she belongs. If we did it right, she's explaining things to Ereshkigal."

Sam nodded. "Who's the new kid?"

"New kid?" Shar turned around and saw a black Mesopotamian Temple Dog standing by the altar. "Oh."

"*Traitors,*" the dog said, and pawed at the ground while Mort stood off to one side, a speculative look in his eye.

"What's it doing?" Daisy said, frowning at it.

"It's trying to make a fist," Abby said grimly.

"*Mina?*" Shar said.

Abby looked at Mina sternly. "Bad dog."

Daisy nodded. "Yeah. Bitch."

"You will die screaming!" Mina said, and then stopped to scratch behind her ear.

Shar looked at Abby and Daisy.

Abby shrugged.

Daisy said, "It's official. The universe has a sense of humor."

"Is that what that voice was?" Abby said.

Sam stood up, wincing, and pulled Shar to her feet. "I'm hungry. I need a steak. It was fast, but I think I still lost some . . ." He looked at all the blood splashed down the steps onto the floor. "Two steaks."

"That's it?" Shar said, holding on to him like a vise. "You died, we blew Kammani into nothingness, you rose, Mina's a dog, and now you're hungry?"

"Man's gotta eat." Sam slung his arm around her shoulders. "And I really fucking hate this temple." He kissed her on the forehead and she loosened her grip.

He was alive. Miracles.

Or not miracles. That voice . . .

Sam bent to pick up Milton as Wolfie pressed close to his leg. Squash came up and nudged him, and he patted her, and then Bowser came by and butted him gently to get a head scratch and Bailey leapt in front of him, saying, "Welcome back! Welcome back!" as Bikka and Umma danced around him.

"Out of here," Wolfie whined, and Sam moved toward the door, careful not to step on anybody.

"I could use a steak," Christopher said, limping beside him. "And a primer on exactly what Abby is when her eyes go like that."

Noah clapped Sam on the shoulder as they went to the door. "Thanks for saving me, man. Sorry you got killed."

"You get used to it," Sam said, and the three men went toward the door surrounded by the dogs.

Shar looked around one more time, at the altar, the bas-relief—"Oh my god."

The relief was gone, smashed on the floor in front of a very old, roughly hewn wall. Painted on it in dark reddish brown were three women joined into one at the hip, the first stretching her arms to catch something round that might be the sun, the second spreading her arms out across the sky to encompass flower shapes, and the third pulling her arms down, scratches like stars around her. At their feet, dogs leapt and played—

"That's our mural," Abby said, coming to stand beside her. "That's what our mural at the coffeehouse looked like. Except ours was, you know, pretty."

"That's Al-Lat, right?" Daisy said. "The One who began it all?"

"I think so," Shar said.

"She was in our heads at the end," Daisy said.

"And She was pissed at Kammani," Abby said. "Did we wake Her up?"

"This was Her temple first," Shar said, staring at a mural she must have seen ten thousand years ago in another life. No, as another goddess. "Kammani must have taken the temple from her. Sam said Al-Lat walked among mortals as three sisters and lost her power. She's been walled up here, and then—oh, hell, we *called on her*. The Great Goddess Who is Three. Kammani took her power and walled up her symbol, but we played with our powers and stirred her dreams and then we called her awake and the wall fell." She looked around the temple, straining to find Al-Lat.

"She's gone now," Abby said, sounding a little sad. "I can't hear Her anymore, and you guys aren't using god-speak. Does that mean our powers are gone?"

Shar looked at Daisy, who shrugged and said, "I can't hear Her, either."

"Maybe we burned the powers out," Shar said. "Maybe She took them back. It's better that way. We're not really goddess material, anyway. We want mortal lives . . ." She looked toward the door where Sam was waiting for her. "Mortal men."

The little black Temple Dog stared at them malevolently.

"My goddess will return," Mina growled. "And she will have her vengeance!"

"Huh," Daisy said. "You have Snausage breath."

"I do not fear you," Mina said. "I am *Death!*"

"Death in a flea collar," Abby said. "We're not impressed."

"I will regain my form," Mina said, "and then I will *end you!*"

She turned and walked away toward the door where the other dogs barked at her, her tiny butt swaying insolently.

The Three stepped closer, side by side, and Shar felt the click inside her and smiled.

"STAY," Abby said, and Mina stopped.

"COME," Daisy said, and Mina turned and came toward them, malevolence in her beady little eyes as Daisy held up her hand to stop the pack from coming, too.

"SIT," Shar said when Mina reached them, and Mina sat, and the pack sat, and the guys looked like they were considering it.

"YOU WILL NOT KILL AGAIN," Abby said to Mina.

"NOT IN ANY WAY WILL YOU HARM ANOTHER LIVING THING," Daisy said.

"OR WE WILL *END YOU*," Shar said.

Mina sat for a moment, her eyes glittering with hate, and then she put her paws out and her head down, bowing in submission.

"So," Shar said, feeling much better about everything.

"That was fun," Daisy said.

"Now what do we do with her?" Abby said. "We can't let her run wild. She might get hit by a car." She looked down at Mina. "I *think* that would be bad."

"I'll take her," Shar said, knowing she had to. "Wolfie and Umma will kick her ass if she gets out of line."

"So we're . . . done here?" Abby said, eyeing the room again nervously.

Daisy looked around. "Granny Al-Lat?"

"Do *not* call her again," Shar said, and headed for the door and Sam.

In the light of dawn, the burned-out coffeehouse didn't look so bad to Abby. "We can get some plywood to cover the window as soon as the stores open," Christopher said to Sam. "The damage isn't that bad. We can get this place up and running in less than a week." He looked at Abby. "Unless there's a goddess HGTV we don't know about."

We. It had a wonderful sound, but Abby wasn't quite sure she could believe it. She stood in the street outside the broken window, staring at it, and Christopher came over to stand beside her. She was covered with mud and soot, and she could barely keep herself upright. She turned to him, and he was looking at her like she was the most beautiful thing in the world, and she went straight into his arms.

He smelled like soot, too, and she burrowed her face

against his shoulder, breathing in the safety and wonder that was her pedantic math genius. "You believe me now?" she said as his arms came around her, holding her.

"I believe you," he said. "It's impossible and illogical, but that's one thing you learn in math. Impossible things happen all the time. You just have to figure out the logic."

"Let me know when that happens, would you?" she said sleepily.

"Bed," Bowser barked.

"Yes, we're going to bed," she said. She pulled back a little, looking up into Christopher's clear blue eyes. "Are we?"

"I need a shower and clean clothes. We both do."

She didn't protest. "Okay."

"I don't have any clean clothes here," he continued.

"Very logical," she said, starting to pull away from him, determined not to cry.

"So I think we should go back to my house and take a shower together, and then we'll come back to the coffee-house and come up with a plan. I don't think it's going to take that much—the damage wasn't that bad. And . . . what?" he asked, puzzled. "Why are you crying?"

"Because I thought you changed your mind," she said, snuffling against his damp, sooty shirt. "I thought you wanted to leave me and go back home alone. And it's been a tough night and I need you!" she wailed.

He cupped her face with his hands, his thumbs gently brushing her lips. "I'm not going anywhere without you. I told you, I love you. You couldn't get rid of me if you tried. You get me, my bad temper, my house, and if you're really lucky, you might get my voice-in-my-head as well. Unless banishing Kammani got rid of him."

She smiled up at him, as a sense of well-being, more powerful than any goddess hooch, filled her. "Milki's probably gone."

"The hell I am!" an ancient, cranky voice said.

And Bowser began to howl.

Daisy stepped into the courtyard, Bailey darted out to mark all the foliage, and Squash went into one of the doghouses to lie down. She watched them both for a moment, amazed at how different her life had become in so short a time. She'd always had relatives, but she'd never had family, and the thought of her dogs and her goddesses gave her a sense of peace like she'd never felt before. Her limbs were still buzzing from the power she'd wielded with Abby and Shar, and as she walked out to the middle of the courtyard and stared up at the bright morning sky, she felt as though anything was possible. When the doors opened and shut behind her and she turned to see Noah standing there, watching her, she hoped she was right.

"Hey," he said after a moment.

"Hey," she said.

"Noah!" Bailey barked, then went back to peeing on some weeds that looked like they'd been peed on enough. Squash raised her head from the doghouse, yawned in greeting, and lowered her head again.

Noah nodded at the dogs, hesitated a moment, and walked over to stand next to Daisy, his face lifted to the sky. "Anything interesting up there?"

"Not really." The idea of small talk exhausted her, so she turned to face him. "I'm sorry."

He looked surprised. "What for?"

"For not believing in you," she said. "For accusing you of . . . oh, hell, everything."

"Forget it," he said. "You just saved the world. You get a pass."

"I don't," she said. "I was suspicious and self-centered, and you helped me save the world, so no, I don't get a pass."

"Ah." He touched his neck, still marked with Kammani's handprint. "So my getting my ass kicked helped you? Glad to hear it."

"Stop it," she said. "You gave me that chant, even when I was being a total ass, and you came here when you thought I was in trouble and you believed in me and—"

"All right," he said, raising his hand. "Enough, okay? I did what anyone would do. Don't make a big deal out of it."

Daisy's stomach tightened. "Oh. Right." She wrapped her arms around herself and tried to keep the tears from coming, but it had been a hell of a night, turning into a hell of a day, and Noah would have done what he did for anybody. It wasn't about her. She wasn't special.

He didn't love her, and the sooner she accepted that, the better.

"Hey," he said, moving closer, angling his head to look at her. "Are you okay?"

She sniffed. "Who? Me? Great." She swiped at her eyes.

"Daisy," he said. "Look at me."

"No," she squeaked.

"Daisy," he said again, and she stomped her foot and raised her head, unable to hide her tears from him.

"There," she said. "Happy?"

He looked down at her, his eyes full of something she couldn't read—neighborly concern, probably—and he pulled her into his arms, which only made the pain in her chest more intense.

"Hey," he said, smoothing his hand down over her hair. "It's okay. It's over. You won."

"Agh!" she said, pushing away from him. "This isn't about Kammani."

"What's it about, then?" he asked.

"I love you," she said. "That's what it's about."

Noah stared at her, frozen where he was, and Daisy sighed.

"Look, it's fine," Daisy said, swiping at her face, trying to regain her dignity. "I blew it. I get it. I was horrible and selfish and I didn't know what I had when I had it. And I don't want you to feel bad for not loving me back, you know, because that's okay. But I think, maybe you should go, because I just can't . . ." Her voice went high and tight and warbly ". . . I can't be around you right now."

But he didn't go. He stayed right where he was.

"You love me?" he asked.

"Yes." *Yeesh, pour salt on the wound, why don't you?* "Bye."

"No," he said. "Christ, Daisy, you don't just tell me you love me and then ask me to leave. Give me a minute to—"

"I can't," Daisy said, sniffling. "I'm tired and I just banished a bitch goddess and my apartment smells like smoke and as much as I'd like to make you feel better for not loving me back, I'm a little beat right now. I need to go upstairs and run a bubble bath and listen to Joni Mitchell, and I can't do that unless you—"

"Oh, god, shut up," Noah said, and pulled her into his arms and kissed her, long and full, then released her. "Can I talk now?"

"Uh-huh," Daisy said, nodding.

"Good," he said. "I love you, too. Idiot."

Daisy sniffled. "You do?"

"Yes. You're this frustrating little bundle of crazy, and you think too much without talking, and you talk too much without listening, but mostly you . . ." He shook his head and released a breath, his eyes softening as he smiled at her. "Mostly, you amaze me. And that was before you got all glowy with your girlfriends and saved the world."

Happiness spread tingly warmth through her entire body, and Daisy smiled. "Yeah?"

"Yeah," he said, then leaned down and kissed her again, making her feel happy and complete and suddenly not exhausted at all.

"Happy Daisy!"

Daisy pulled back from Noah and looked down to see Bailey dancing around them, barking like mad while Squash merely lifted her head from her resting space in the sunny corner of the courtyard.

"Happy Daisy! Happy Daisy!"

"What's he saying?" Noah asked.

"He's saying that we should go upstairs and run that bath," Daisy said.

Noah broke out in a grin. "Really? He's saying all that?"

"He's a really smart dog," Daisy said, and took Noah's hand to lead him to the stairs to her apartment, where she showed him just how good being loved by a goddess could be.

Shar and Sam put Wolfie, Milton, Umma, Bikka, Mina, and Mort in the backseat of Sam's SUV and got into the front. Then Shar grabbed Sam's arm and said, "Don't you *ever* do that again."

Sam looked at her as if she were an idiot. "What are the chances?"

Shar swallowed. "I know. But I just want you to know that if you try to die to save the world again, I'm coming to the underworld to get you. *And it's not going to be pretty when I find you.*" She looked at him, trying not to cry now that everything was over but crying anyway. "You were going to go back there with her to save us. I'd never have seen you again. I can't . . ." She swallowed back tears.

"You'd have seen me again," Sam said. "I'd have found you. Don't cry."

"Can we go now?" Wolfie barked.

"Go now?" Milton barked.

"Somebody's going to pay for this," Mina snarled.

"Silence, fiend of hell," Umma growled.

"Cheetos," Bikka yipped.

"Heh heh heh," Mort breathed.

"Quiet," Sam said to the backseat, and then put his hand on Shar's shoulder. "I will not do that again. If Kammani comes back, if Ishtar rises, if *my mother* comes back and asks me to die, I swear to you, I'll say, 'No, my wife won't let me.' "

"Wife?" Shar said, sniffing back a sob.

"Really, can we go now?" Wolfie said.

"I'm going to have hysterics right here unless somebody changes me back," Mina barked.

"Nobody cares, you murderous bitch," Umma growled.

"This chick is toast," Milton said.

"Heh heh heh," Mort said.

"Don't make me come back there," Sam said to the backseat, and turned to Shar. "I don't think I can refuse to die for this world because of my girlfriend."

"It lacks weight," Shar said, blinking away the last of her tears. "But you're mortal now. You marry me, that's it. I'm the last woman you're going to see naked."

"Not as long as we have cable."

Shar swallowed. "Plus . . . I still have powers. Al-Lat . . . I think it's big stuff. Is that going to bother you? You used to be a god and now you're mortal and—"

"Shar," Sam said. "I love you. I loved you from the moment I saw you."

"Oh, I loved you, too," Shar said, leaning toward him.

"No, you didn't," Sam said. "You Tasered me."

"Well, I sensed what was coming." Shar looked up into his beautiful, mortal face. "You're really going to give it all up for me?"

"Give up what?" Sam settled back against the seat. "I'm tired of being sacrificed and I never did like being a king. Too damn much paperwork. I'm going to retire and make video games with Christopher and sit on the couch and eat Cheetos with Bikka while you go out and support me."

"Cheetos!" Bikka yipped.

"Damn straight," Sam said over the seat. He smiled at Shar. "My family's big on ritual. Let's get married."

Shar felt goofy inside. She didn't want to get married, she'd never wanted to get married, but it was Sam and she was never going to leave him, so—

"You're just trying to get your hands on my temple," she said, smiling at him as she leaned forward again.

"I'm gonna get my hands on your temple anyway," Sam said, and kissed her, and she fell into him again, divinely happy.

Mina yapped, "Stop it; stop it; *stop it!*" and the rest of the dogs chimed in, barking at her in a cacophony of "*freak-bitch-toast-die-heh-heh-heh-Cheeto!*" and Sam turned and said, "ENOUGH!"

The car went instantly silent.

He turned back to Shar and said, "I love you," and kissed her again, and she sighed against his mouth, and kissed him back, and knew she'd have him forever.

She looked up into those dark hooded eyes and said, "Can we go home now?"

"That's what I said," Wolfie barked.

"You're sitting on my tail," Milton said.

"Get off of my leg," Mina snapped.

"Heh heh heh," Mort breathed.

And Sam put the car in gear and they went home.

It was dark and she was walking on sand and her head hurt and she finally could not walk any farther and fell on her knees, crying out in pain. She was lost forever, forever; she was lost—

"Who's out there?"

She lifted her head and saw a light, flashing on the sand, and then on her, and she shielded her eyes.

"Holy shit, you're naked," a man said, and the light went away and she felt something soft go around her. "That's my bathrobe, sorry about the damp."

She pulled the robe around her and felt his strong hand under her arm, helping her stand.

"What happened? I was out on the deck when I heard you scream. Did you fall off a boat?"

She blinked. "I don't know."

"What's your name, honey?" The hand on her arm tugged her up the sand, and as they went around a dune, she saw lights blazing and large houses, made mostly of glass.

"I don't know."

He stopped. "You have amnesia? My house is right up there; we'll call nine-one-one."

She leaned on him and they made their way across the sand to wooden steps and a wood-planked walkway.

"You're an actress, right? That face and that body, you're an actress."

"I don't know."

He stopped again. "A beautiful woman with a killer body and amnesia washes up in front of the beach house of an agent. You telling me that's for real?"

She blinked at him. "I don't know."

"Right. Well, you washed up to the right place, honey. I can make anybody a star. You know who my latest client is? A month-old baby. Camisole. Cami. The kid's gonna be huge. And you're gonna be just as a big. Of course, you'll have to lose a little weight."

Something stirred inside her. "No."

The man snorted in the darkness. "A diva already."

"No," she said, seizing the only glimmer of a memory she had. "I'm a goddess."

"That's good," he said, "a goddess. I can work with that."

And then he led her up the beach to her new life.